dangerous LIES

LYING TO YOURSELF WAS THE MOST DANGEROUS GAME OF ALL.

KRIS BUTLER

Dark Confessions Series

Book Two

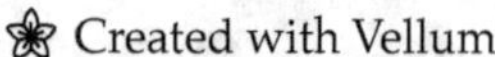 Created with Vellum

dangerous LIES

KRIS BUTLER

CONTENTS

BLURB

Lying to yourself was the most dangerous game of all

I'd once thought the only thing that mattered was the truth. But perhaps I'd been naive.

Learning to navigate life with my eyes open, I'd found things weren't as they seemed. The good guy didn't always get the girl, the right thing wasn't always easy to spot, and the bad guy wasn't always the villain. Life was more about perception than truth. Maybe... that was the biggest lie of all.

My mother and ex-husband hid behind their mansions and club memberships, making everyone believe they were better and had it all together. Deep down they were twisted and cruel, covering it up with pretty lies.

The mask I'd worn for so long no longer protected me, the facade cracking as I began to emerge into my own person. Heartache, deceit, and treachery kept knocking at my door, but they had no place here. I could see through their betrayals and I was no longer alone to carry the pain.

I used to think my biggest confession was having it all and losing it so epically, laying splattered on the floor in a million pieces. Yet, piece by piece, I was being put back together. Which led me to wonder if I'd ever been whole to begin with?

When your whole life was a lie, did you ever know the truth?

FOREWORD

This is a why-choose novel, meaning the main female character doesn't have to choose between love interests. This is a dark contemporary mafia romance with dark themes including grief, depression, child loss, divorce, past history of sexual assault, and violence. This is a medium burn with a slow-burn MM relationship. This is an adult romance and is intended for readers 18+ due to language and content. Cuss words are used throughout, and sexual scenes are explicit. This book ends on a hook, though some will argue it is a cliffhanger. While this book might not destroy you emotionally, you still might want to shout at me, and that's okay. I actually enjoy it.

To fighting against the lies we're told to believe and finding our own truths.

One lie has the power to tarnish a thousand truths.
– Al David

PROLOGUE

MONROE

Never in my adult life had I imagined finding myself in this situation, facing down a judge, fighting for my reputation. Brittni had always been a heinous bitch, but I never thought she was capable of *this*. I wanted to pretend I'd hallucinated the Judge's words, but unfortunately, it was very real.

"It's come to the court's attention that there have been several incidents of child endangerment and neglect while the minor, Levi Miller, was in your care. That you've placed him in danger by the company you keep and broken the custody agreement by having him supervised by an unapproved adult. Nor did you verify with the child's mother before leaving him in their care. There is significant cause for concern of neglect, and possible undiagnosed mental health issues."

The claims slapped me across the face as he read them out. Everything had been twisted in such a way, it sounded as if Brittni was the better parent in this scenario.

"There's been a misunderstanding, Your Honor. The man in question is a lifelong friend, and the woman who watched Levi is my neighbor. It was an emergency, and I didn't have time to reach out to Brittni."

He glared at me, not impressed with my argument. To be fair, I wasn't either, but I'd been flabbergasted by the case in the first place that nothing was making sense.

"Did you or did you not have one, Wells Young, in your place of residence, Mr. Miller?"

"Yes," I admitted, fear crawling up my throat.

"And would you say this man is a good example to your son?"

"I think the concept is debatable, honestly. He's good with Levi. I'm not going to say Wells hasn't made some poor choices in his life, but he's not a bad— "

"Hmph, it says here he was responsible for embezzling millions from the clients of D&D Trade corp?" He cut me off, not allowing me to finish my statement. I didn't miss the tic in his jaw, nor the gleam in Brittni's eye at his revelation. If I had to guess, *he* had been one of them.

"Allegedly," I headed, attempting to find some foothold. The Judge scoffed, not agreeing with my statement. "How is this related, Your Honor?" but again, I went ignored as he continued to lay out the crimes *I'd* supposedly committed.

"Did you or did you not allow a woman, Mrs. Kimpton had never met, to watch Levi?"

"Yes." I gave up on trying to explain, the verdict clearly written on his face.

"And what does it say in the custody agreement in terms of care? Emergencies, specifically?" The Judge raised an eyebrow at me, my denial a clear annoyance to him.

"It states that the other parent is to be notified first and in cases when this is not possible, told immediately after."

Hanging my head, I knew I was sunk. Brittni had found her loophole. One toe found out of line, and she'd nailed me to the wall. It was utterly ludicrous and uncalled for, but Brittni was the type of woman who needed to win in order to feel good about herself.

"Your Honor, due to the circumstances, we'd like to request full custody to Mrs. Kimpton in lieu of these events," her slimy lawyer proclaimed.

"*Granted*. You are hereby ordered to attend mandated parenting classes, Mr. Miller. You'll be granted supervised visits with the minor in question. A court date will be set out for six months. At that time, the court will determine if you've met your requirements and are fit to be a parent. It is recommended, but not required, for you to attend court-appointed therapy to deal with your reckless and impulsive choices. Perhaps, taking a look at your friend list as well is in order if the company you keep is a washed-up crook who can't seem to stay out of fights."

Tensing my jaw, I had to physically keep myself from retaliating. Being found in contempt of court wouldn't help my case and only play into Brittni's. It was one of the hardest moments of my life as I clenched the edge of the table to keep me grounded.

"My personal life has nothing to do with this, sir. It's not your job to comment on my friends."

"That might be the case, Mr. Miller, but don't fool yourself. While I can't deny you custody for your bedroom preferences, I can run you through so much red tape your son will be eighteen before you see him again. I'd remind you not to forget where you are. Good day."

He slammed the gavel down, and I tensed, the sound echoing around my head. Everything he'd done and said, outside the last comment, had been by the book. On paper, there was nothing for me to use to appeal his decision. However, the undertone and true nature of what was at play here were clear for all to see if they looked closer. It was a classic case of the 'haves and have nots.' I might be dressed the same as the rest of the rich snobs in this courtroom, but unfortunately, I could never fully get rid of the poverty-line stench.

It was something I'd been fighting my whole career.

Poverty disparity was a walking, talking, breathing thing. It followed me everywhere I went, and no matter how hard I worked or succeeded in my career, I would never gain their respect because I hadn't been born into this. It stuck to me like a second skin, unable to be shed.

When your circumstances worked to keep you in your slot in life, it felt impossible to break free from the impediments keeping you there.

The lie the rich told themselves—they were *helping* the less fortunate. They threw million-dollar fundraisers to appease their guilt for the ridiculous things they bought. They didn't care about the cause, only how it made them appear to their peers.

I knew I was lumping them all together, and that wasn't fair. Mitzi and Loren were two exceptions I knew of without even having to think about it. But as I stared at the conniving woman I'd once professed to love and cherish until death do us part, a rage I'd never felt before surged up in me. She was *nothing* like either of them.

The self-assured smile she sent me conveyed she thought she'd won.

Brittni didn't understand the mistake she'd just made, though. She'd only known goal-driven and considerate Monroe. She had no idea about the life I'd led before her, the pain and suffering I'd experienced. Nor the person I had to be in order to survive, or what it took to stay alive.

The time to prepare my case had been limited, the emergency hearing being called within an hour of me being given notice. Now that all of her cards were on the table, I'd sweep the river and go all in. I wouldn't take this lying down.

Brittni would soon learn why I was once known as the Komodo Dragon. I was resourceful, patient, and most importantly, deadly when I needed to be.

I gritted my teeth as she walked out with her lawyer, and I didn't miss the way his hand slipped to her ass. Ah, so that was the play here. I didn't like Larry, nor did I owe him anything, but I wondered if he'd be the ally I might need in this fight.

Brittni underestimated the love I had for Levi. I'd go to the ends of the Earth for him. I would even open a door I'd long thought closed.

Maybe I'd been kidding myself all along, thinking I could be Mr. Nice Guy and live the American dream. That *life* was a farce, but I saw one I wanted, and it felt obtainable. Unfortunately, it happened to include the two people I now had to stay away from.

Jamming the files into my briefcase, I tossed my coat over my arm and stalked out of the courtroom, immediately dialing my contact with the state. I needed to see Levi as soon as possible, so whatever I needed to do in order to get these visits set up, that would be my first step.

Everything else would come in due time, but I'd never let my son think I abandoned him. Brittni would use the opportunity to fill his head with lies, and it wasn't something I could risk. Thankfully, she picked up after the second ring.

"Hey Karen, how are you today?"

The sweet older lady began to babble about her grandchildren. While I wanted to rush her along, I cooed and responded appropriately, knowing she'd be my biggest asset in getting the services I needed. I hated using my status and wealth to circumvent rules, but there was little I wouldn't do for Levi in this scenario.

"Make sure to give them my regards. I'll have to take Levi to that place. I think he will like it," I responded. "So listen, I'm at the courthouse, and there's been a miscommunication between Brittni and me, and she's filed for temporary full custody. I need to get visits set up. I don't want Levi thinking I abandoned him, you know."

I hadn't meant for tears to break on the words, but they had, and I knew it would help my case even if I hadn't intended for them.

"Oh dear, that's so tragic! I can't believe she'd do

such a thing. Sure thing, Monroe. I'll send out a request the second the orders come across. Top of my list."

"Thank you, Karen. You're the absolute best. I don't want to abuse my position, but I need to see him. I'll talk to you later. Thanks again."

I hung up, some relief filling me with her support. Spinning, I was surprised to find Brittni waiting for me. Her blonde hair looked faker than usual, her face tight, and I wondered if she'd had botox done. She crossed her arms, huffing when I didn't immediately start begging her.

"Brittni. You know this was out of line."

"Maybe, but it's in motion. Now everyone will see the immoral man you are."

"The only thing the court will see is the truth. I'm a great father. No way you twist it, will change that fact. I warned you not to do this, but your arrogance knows no bounds. You'll be the one looking like a fool by the end. From this point on, send all communication through my lawyer. I want nothing to do with *you*."

Turning to leave, I began to put my jacket on as I walked, my phone in my hand as I hurried out of the courthouse.

"If you know what's good for you, you'll stay away from *her*," she yelled, stopping me. "I saw her, you know. She was with some big tattooed guy. So she's either a cheating whore or a liar. Either way, she's not someone I want around Levi. If I find out you're around *her*, I will destroy *you*, Monroe. Stay away from Loren."

I stopped on the stairs, but I didn't turn back to her. I was likely to strangle the cow if I had. Fury bubbled up, and I kept walking. Her words had no value, but they still traveled and landed on my heart, striking the insecurities I hid there. Bypassing my office building, I detoured to a downtown pub instead.

The thought of working right now was impossible. I needed to get my head straight and figure out my game plan. Until I knew when I could see Levi, I was afraid nothing else would get done.

Sitting at the bar, I ordered two shots of tequila. The bartender looked at me strangely but slapped two shot glasses on the bartop, pouring the *Patrón* efficiently. Taking two lime wedges, he placed them on the rim and scooted them over. Quickly, I threw them both back, not even bothering with the lime.

I needed to feel the burn.

Motioning for another, I pulled out my phone to message my kryptonite. I didn't want to risk Loren or Wells being brought into this crossfire, nor did I want to believe Brittni had any power over their lives. But if I'd learned anything from my youth and being married to that twat, it was to never underestimate someone. She'd already shown me she was willing to do whatever it took to get what she wanted.

I'd just have to be smarter.

The tequila settled into my bones, the liquid fire coursing through my bloodstream. With a shaky hand, I texted Loren first, knowing she'd be the hardest to push away. Wells had taken himself out of the game again, so distancing myself wasn't an issue currently.

But *Loren*. God, how could I let her go? Only the fear of what Brittni might do had me considering it.

Flipping through my photos, I landed on a picture from a few nights ago. Levi and Jude were on one side, Loren and I on the other, a board game in between us. I held my arm out, smiling at the camera as we all crowded in.

That was my future.

With resolution, I slipped back into the Komodo, my emotions dulling as I sent the hardest text of my life, praying it would only be temporary.

ME: Brittni did it. She found a judge willing to grant her temporary custody. She's taking Levi from me. I've just left court. I need to get on top of this. I won't be able to make it to dinner tonight.
Loren: Of course. I'm so sorry, Monroe. Let me know if there is anything I can do. I'm here for you.
ME: I think we should take some time. I need to focus on this for the moment. I'll be consumed with it. I need to focus on getting my son back right now.

Placing the phone upside down, I knew I couldn't look at it or I'd be tempted to change my mind. I threw back the last tequila shot, wincing at the burn as it traveled down my throat. It was a welcome relief from the realization my world had been stolen from me.

ONE

LOREN

The drip of the coffee pulled me into a trance, and for a moment, I was transported back to two months ago. Watching the liquid sputter out of the machine, I debated for the tiniest second if things were actually any better. Was my life any different from the void of blankness I'd been in?

Yet, while I found myself standing at the window once again sipping my coffee as I looked out across the dog park with longing, I realized it had.

For one, my coffee now had flavor. It might not seem like a huge deal, but it had been a momentous occasion for me. I no longer felt the emptiness reflected up to me from my coffee cup, and I'd added back some dimension to my coffee game.

Second, the park was no longer a barren wasteland my soul relished in. Spring had come to Chicago, and while it wasn't exactly warm yet, it was no longer the bitter cold of winter where the wind whipped through you, sending a frozen chill through your bones. Greens and pinks had started to appear throughout the city, life attempting to emerge from the frozen abyss the city had become.

But most importantly, the biggest difference from that time to now, were the sounds.

At one time, the clicking of the clock passing time was the loudest thing in my condo, but now, a flurry of noises greeted me, and I smiled at their joyous sounds. The shower ran in the background, music played on a wireless speaker, and the timer went off as the muffins finished baking. My condo had come alive in the wake of inviting a teenager to live there, and like my coffee, it now had more flavor and dimension to it.

Jude's backpack laid across the table, his school books stacked precariously next to it. His camera sat on the coffee table where he'd left it after showing me some of his favorite shots yesterday. Shoes that weren't mine gathered near the door, along with coats, hats, and scarves. A water glass sat on the island, a half-eaten sandwich next to it, almost like he'd gotten full or distracted midway.

My condo was no longer the pristine, cold environment it had once been. In fact, it was nowhere near as immaculate as it was when I'd moved in. If Jacqueline Hanover were to step foot in here today, she would turn her nose up so quick, you'd think someone farted. The scorn alone on her face was enough to make me not care, but it was the liveliness of the condo that now made it a home. I loved everything about it, and it was a visual reminder of how different my life was, good and bad.

Placing the muffin pan on the wire rack, I stood back and grinned. I'd finally done it! After too many failed attempts to count, I'd managed to make muffins. Jude walked into the kitchen a few minutes later and found me waiting with a banana-nut muffin on a plate, grinning from ear to ear. He cocked his head at me, his hair still damp from the shower as he regarded the situation. It was probably a tinge creepy with the manic smile I could feel on my lips, but as soon as he was close enough, I shoved the baked good at him.

"Look!"

"Whoa. Okay, not burnt. Good first step. I'm guessing you want me to try it?"

Nodding, I held my breath as I waited for him to report if I'd succeeded. Becoming a foster mom had presented me with several challenges I hadn't anticipated. Having to feed a teenage boy, one of them. Jude smiled in encouragement as he lifted the muffin into the air. He toasted 'cheers' to me, nodding at it before sinking his teeth into the golden brown creation. I held my breath as I watched, waiting for his declaration.

The oddness of this scene would've surprised me a year ago, hell even months ago, if I was honest. But as I watched my foster son indulge me with the taste testing, it no longer did. This was us now, the Jude and Loren show, and I found myself unable to look away. He'd filled a part of my life I never wanted to lose. I watched as he chewed, my impatience growing as I awaited his verdict. When I couldn't take it any longer, I caved, asking.

"Well? How is it? Tell me, Jude! I'm *dying* over here."

He grinned, laughing at my discomfort, and I knew he'd intentionally dragged it out. The change in him since he first arrived was astounding. Jude joked and laughed now. He played around and did goofy things with me. Having safety and stability in his life had allowed him to relax and be a teenager. Jude didn't have to worry about surviving through the night or where his next meal would come from anymore, and it felt nice I'd been able to give him that.

"It's good, Lor. I think you finally nailed it." He smiled wide and reached for another one. Doing a happy dance, I spun in the kitchen, probably looking like a hyperactive rabbit as I tried to mimic the twerking meme.

"Oh yeah, I'm the bomb!"

Jude laughed, shaking his head. "I'm pretty sure if you have to announce you're 'the bomb,' it disqualifies, you know, being the bomb."

"I don't care. I just baked my first successful batch of muffins. Those stuffy moms at the bake sale won't know what hit them."

Jude snorted, shaking his head as he ate another muffin. "If I didn't like the school so much, I'd tell you to transfer me just so you didn't have to deal with those um, moms."

"You can call them bitches," I laughed. "Lord knows, I do."

"Okay, well yeah, those bitches."

He gave me a toothy grin, and I laughed at our inside joke. "Yeah, I'd conveniently forgotten that prep school moms were the worst. They sure didn't put *that* in the handbook."

"I can see it now. 'Not only do we have excellence in

the arts and music, but also our helicopter moms are top-notch. Sign up today to relive your glory days through your child.' Yeah, I don't think it'd sell."

Spluttering, I almost spit out my hot coffee onto the floor, the comment taking me by surprise. "Oh, wow. That was priceless. They really should come with a warning. I'm beginning to think my mother offers how-to classes. Speaking of which," I cringed.

Jude groaned, his annoyance echoing my own. "Is that next weekend?"

Nodding, I took another sip of my coffee. "Unfortunately. I'm sorry, kiddo. But hey, maybe they'll be on their best behavior with you there."

"Yeah, because that helped so much last time."

He rolled his eyes, finishing up his food. I watched as he grabbed the glass and sandwich he'd left and placed them in the sink. Jude wasn't necessarily messy. He was just a teenager. He always cleaned up after himself eventually, so I never nagged at him to do it. Plus, I liked seeing his stuff around. It reminded me I wasn't here alone anymore. It was a nice feeling to be reminded of.

"Yeah, well, we'd been ambushed."

The day in question he referred to was right after I'd been released from the hospital. Jude and I were watching a movie when my mother showed up unannounced. She'd assumed I'd want her company, needing assistance to recover. When she discovered I'd decided to foster a kid without her knowledge, well, Jude had gotten the full Jacqueline Hanover tantrum. What had been worse was she still hadn't apologized for the dinner fiasco with Sax and blamed *me* for the explosion.

Sure, that made sense. I'd somehow controlled the psycho who placed a bomb at the restaurant I was eating at. Because, you know, I wanted to lose all the men in my life in one fell swoop. Sure, Jacqueline, that seemed logical.

Shaking off the loneliness and sadness at the reminder of what I'd lost, I grimaced as I walked to the sink. "At least it's my cousin's wedding, so we won't have to be alone with her. Besides, there are some family members that aren't completely horrible."

"Yeah, okay."

"Also, I told you that you didn't need to go. I'm perfectly fine going on my own."

"I want to go. Well, let me rephrase that. The idea terrifies me, but I want to be there for you, Loren. *That* is something I want to do."

"Have I told you that you're the sweetest kid yet today?"

"Well, it's only 7 am, so probably not." He grinned, his face heating slightly, and I pulled him into a hug.

"Thanks, Jude. It means a lot to me. We can hide out at the dessert table and make funny faces in all the pictures."

"I can get on board with that, and you're welcome. You've done so much for me. With the whole dating thing being weird, I didn't want you to go alone. I know I'm not a perfect replacement for Monroe or whoever, but I'd like to be there for you."

"You know what I think, kiddo?"

He shook his head, only a tiny amount of fear and doubt remaining now anytime I broached a vulnerable topic. "I think we were meant to find one another and help each other learn what it means to have a true friend, a family. We're like two little lost penguins now braving the storm together."

"Penguins?" He lifted his brow at me, moving away to shove his books in his bag. Folding my arms as I leaned against the counter, I nodded.

"Yeah. They're adorable and seem like they'd be misfits. Plus, they walk all cute and are always ready for a party." Mimicking a penguin, I waddled over to the table. "No?"

Chuckling, Jude shook his head. "No, but I'll let you keep the dream alive in your head. Misfit penguins in action."

"Ah, so kind of you to indulge my crazy fantasies."

"It's the least I could do," he snorted, finding himself amusing.

Slapping him on the shoulder in jest, I walked out of the room to finish getting dressed. "Have a good day at school. Let me know what you end up doing afterward, okay?"

"Yep. You home for dinner tonight?"

"It'll be later. I have a late session and then barre class."

"Okay," he paused before asking the question he really wanted to know. "Has she, you know, returned?"

I stopped my trek to my room, turning to take him in. "You know I can't divulge anything. But if you're asking if I had any new female clients or ones returning, the answer would be no, I haven't." I debated sharing the next part, but felt he was owed it. "I miss her too. If I were to ever hear from a person I missed, then I would be inclined to share that information. Completely hypothetical."

He nodded, the sad look I would catch at times clear on his face. "Yeah, okay. Thanks."

Jude collected himself, then nodded as he headed toward the door. I knew he was struggling with Immy's abandonment. It'd been two months since I'd seen or talked to Nicco, Atticus, Sax, or Immy. Their ice out and disconnection from my life had been more challenging than I'd imagined. It only reiterated how loose I'd gotten in my boundaries with them. I wasn't supposed to care this much, or feel this much, for them.

I'd had clients disappear before, and it was always sad, hard. But eventually, a new client would take their spot, and I would move on in my head, filling the place they'd inhabited. I'd wonder and think about the old client at times, something reminding me of them, but then it would be gone, and I'd go about my day.

I couldn't seem to do that with Immy. Or the men she was connected to.

Atticus had always intrigued me, but he'd been so far out of my reach I didn't have as deep of a connection to him. I was curious about the sexy man, sure, but it stopped there.

Sax had entered my world, making no apologies for himself. He made himself known with his swagger and domineering presence, leaving me breathless. We'd only kissed, but it had been scorching, our chemistry so magnetic it had been hard to tear myself apart from him. The room seemed emptier without his reassuring presence taking up the wall space, observing, always watching for signs of threats. I'd felt safe with Sax, unlike any man I'd ever been around before. He might scream danger, but he wasn't the one I was worried about. Sax would vanquish anything or anyone who tried to tear me down and then carry me out of the room and fuck me against the wall to remind me I was his.

Or, at least, that was how the fantasy played out in my head.

It was Nicco who'd been the hardest to try to forget. I knew now I'd been falling in love with him. Perhaps I still was, in a sense. My heart ached every time I thought about never seeing him again. He was a piece of my heart that was gone, and I didn't know if I'd ever get it back. Nicco hadn't just helped me rediscover my sexuality; he'd awakened this carnal need in me. He'd effortlessly helped me balance the dark and the light, the recklessness and the seductive nature of my desires, and gave me an outlet to try them.

With Nicco, I'd felt freedom unlike anything I'd ever witnessed before. And now it was gone, and I missed it.

I could feel the darkest parts of me bubbling up inside, teasing me with their impulsive charm and lure. The danger was calling out to me, and I didn't know how much longer it would be until I caved.

I wanted to hate them all for leaving me, but I'd become so used to being dismissed, I didn't blame them. Of course, that was the lie I believed to cover up the truth—I wasn't worth remembering.

Deep down, I knew it hadn't been real, just a passing fancy to occupy their time. I was one of many, and I didn't even cross their minds now. I'd been forgotten, my purpose served, and now I was left discarded with the trash.

Looking in the mirror, I wanted to slap myself at the pain and fear I saw there. I didn't want to be that person, but she was still there, lurking, waiting for her chance to return. That was the thing about depression; it sometimes felt like a layer of skin you had to scrub off to fully shake it. You had to go through the refining process in order to come out the other side. Some days, I still didn't even feel like trying.

That was a truth no one ever told you. Depression wasn't something you could smile your way out of, or fix with a few positive affirmations. It was hard work, and not every day was a win.

Squaring my shoulders, I challenged myself that it was only the weakness talking, that it didn't matter if I hadn't meant anything. They had to me, and I could miss them. But I wouldn't let their departure affect me, because I chose to no longer be weak.

I ignored the fact I was lying to myself. Because which part was the lie?

The fact I thought I had a choice? Or that I'd ever been strong to begin with?

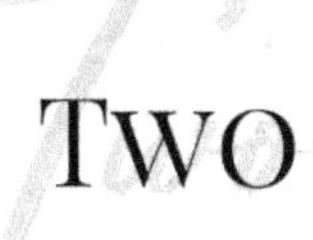

Two

Nicco

Paint splattered onto my hand, the flick of my brush against the canvas aggressive, resulting in more excess than usual splashing back. I wiped my brow, inevitably spreading paint there, but I didn't care right now. I'd been in the zone, painting out my frustrations for the past hour, though, based on the fatigue in my arms, it might've been longer.

Stepping back, I took in the canvas. It was dark and angry, my emotions bleeding onto the surface. But woven through, I saw the gold along the edges, and I knew it was her.

She was in every thought, every breath, every goddamned step I took. Loren haunted me, and I yearned to return to her. When Mas disclosed everything, he knew I would be steadfast in my commitment, wanting to do anything necessary to save her and others like her—the good, the innocent, the pure.

I never imagined it would take longer than a week, a month tops. We were hedging over two months, eight weeks, sixty days... whichever way you cut it, it was too fucking long. As much as I wanted to blame and rage at Mas, I couldn't.

It was clear how much this weighed on him as well. I could see it in his stance; his shoulders were tight, the weight becoming heavier every day. He barely slept and when he did, it was fitful; the shadows under his eyes, a clear giveaway to his lack of rest.

And so, that was why I found myself painting out my frustration, my anger needing an outlet. I'd sparred with Sax a couple of times, but it didn't have the same effect on me. Art and creation were my passion, and without my outlet, I'd been struggling. Being away from the shop was also rough. I knew it was in good hands with Cassandra, but I wanted to be back there. Ignite was the place I could be myself without any facade.

That was the thing with pretending. It eventually got old.

Having to be the fun party guy had exhausted me after the first week. The other family members had noticed my shift in personality, but no one had braved asking about it yet. My elevation in the family hierarchy could be the reason no one did, or perhaps it was the permanent scowl on my face. Being Mas' underboss automatically came with a certain level of respect, intrigue, and fear.

It was hard to get used to. People bowed in my presence now or scurried out of the room when they saw me. It made it easier not to pretend to be the person I wasn't, but the part of me who'd grown up with these people and considered them friends, he was hurt by their aversion.

A lot had changed, and it was taking time to get used to.

"I'm still angry with you, Nic, but I need a favor, so I'm going to talk to you while it benefits me, and then maybe I'll forgive you."

Imogen's voice called out from the shadows, and I inwardly cheered that she'd finally, *willingly*, talked to me. I'd missed her but understood her anger. Atticus had kept things tight-lipped around her. It was a hard line to know where to draw. She knew our lives and the things we did, but did she need to know the nitty-gritty details? I worried we were all trying so hard to protect her that we would inadvertently push her toward the enemy.

If she took a step toward me for help, I'd take it as the life raft it was meant to be. This could be my only chance.

"Anything, Immy."

She exhaled, her countenance easing from the fight stance she'd expected to need. She'd been ready to go to battle for whatever she'd wanted. This was important then.

She moved forward, now a little timidly, and I waited until she met me. The mafia side of me knew I needed to let her do things and not make it easy for her. The cousin and big brother part of me wanted to wrap her up in a soft blanket and hide her away from everything bad.

The Mascro fate wasn't to hide away, though. Our family lineage was filled with men and women rising up to do whatever it took for the family. So today, I needed to be Nicco, the underboss, and not Nic, the friend. It broke my heart, but it was necessary for her survival.

"No one will tell me anything, and part of me doesn't even care about being out of the loop. The part that does have an issue is the one where I've been disconnected from the things that were helping me heal. It took me a while to see past my anger, and now all I feel is bitterness and pain. I was getting somewhere with Loren. And while I get our protocol, she isn't like other people. She can be trusted. I know it. She didn't deserve how we treated her. Nor did Jude."

Nodding, I folded my arms as I listened. I'd assumed it would be about them. Lord knows it was all that consumed me too. Or at least the Loren portion.

"So while I accept I can't see them or text, I was wondering if you could get a message to Jude for me. I know you won't let me see Loren when we can't tell her anything, and I figure Jude will be easier to find anyway. He attends a prep school now and has a photography club after school. He'd be easy to intercept."

I studied her and realized we'd underestimated her. "How do you know all that info?"

She shrugged one shoulder before responding. "I hacked my jackass tutor's phone."

I couldn't help it, and the underboss mask slipped, and I bent over laughing at her words. The sound had her joining me, and when we stood back up, I knew it had been needed.

"You're smarter than you've led us to believe if you're able to hack his phone. I know for a fact it's encrypted and swept before and after he leaves."

Immy grinned, twirling back and forth on her feet with her hands locked behind her. "Maybe."

"Oh, you are so busted. Fine. I'll see what I can do, but you have to promise to tell Atticus. If he knew what you were capable of, he might not coddle you so much."

"Maybe," she shrugged, not looking at me.

"Hey, come here."

I pulled her into a hug, the action being severely missed over the past month. "I'm sorry about everything that happened and the circumstances that led us here. I don't like it either, and it kills me to not tell her. I can't even imagine what she must think of us. But we will make this right, MoMo. We will."

I felt her head nod in my arms as I kept her close, needing the comfort as well.

"Thank you, Nic."

I kissed her cheek and sent her on her way, needing to clean up my mess anyway. So much for keeping it professional between us. I'd only been kidding myself with that anyway. Immy was my soft spot.

Now, I just needed to find a way off the property. It should be simple enough, considering I'd barely left in two months.

"Mas, I need to check on something at the shop. Anything you want me to check on while I'm in town?"

He'd been working on something on his laptop, a furrow in his brow as he took in the screen. Leaning casually against the doorframe, I inspected my fingernails, and even had a little whistle going as I waited for his answer. I was going for the whole uninterested vibe, attempting to throw him off.

"So, Immy finally got someone to cave, huh?"

My eyes snapped to his, and I caught the smug expression spread across his face. Dropping my act, I slumped into the office and took a chair.

"I don't know if I should be more offended that I'm not the only one she asked or that I caved first."

Mas let out a sound, a cross between a chuckle and a huff at my statement. "Well, Sax was a day away from caving if it makes you feel any better."

Laughing, I leaned back, steepling my fingers. "So, what's the verdict then?"

"I think we can come out of hiding. There hasn't been any other chatter that we've seen, nor has Rawles received anything. Our pieces are in play now to move forward with our plans as well. I was going to suggest we move back to the city this weekend as is, but if you want to make amends with Immy, I'll allow you to go today."

Nodding, I accepted the answer and knew it was time. Despite the fact that I was going stir crazy cooped up in this house, we couldn't do anything else from here. We needed to be seen and show we weren't afraid.

"And, where does that leave Loren?"

He leaned back in his chair, regarding me. "I haven't changed my mind about her involvement in the family, but that being said, Nicolai, I don't own you. I'm not the Grim Reaper, and I won't take your choices away from you. I know she's the only reason you stayed here this long as is, and it would be remiss of me to think you'd stay away forever."

I nodded, relief for the first time in months flooding me.

"But," he started, waiting until I was looking at him again. "I think our lives are far too dangerous to involve her. If you continue seeing her, then her death is on *your* hands. The next few months will determine how this war plays out and how many casualties we end up with. For your sake, and even Immy's, I hope she isn't included in that number. Do you understand?"

I nodded, the underlying reality of our lives threaded through his words, but I also heard his own fear and perhaps some disappointment at having to keep her at arm's length.

"Noted."

"You're not going to stop seeing her are you?" he sighed.

I smirked, rubbing my jaw in thought. "Where's the fun in that, Cous?" Sitting up, I dropped the act and leaned forward, my elbows on my knees. "Though, it's all dependent on her. She's not like other women, Mas. Something I think you're aware of. I'm going to have to do a lot of groveling without revealing a whole lot of truth. Loren might take herself out of this game on her own."

I knew it was a real possibility, but it was a reality I didn't want to face. So even though I said the words, acknowledged them out loud, I found it hard to believe. I'd had a lot of time to think since the bombing, and the one thing I knew to be true was I needed Loren in my life.

Now, I just had to convince her as well, and grovel my ass off.

"On another note, does that mean we're set to return to the fights this weekend?"

"Yes, I've been coordinating with Lucca, and he's replaced you with Domino. I think it would be wise to still make an appearance and officially pass the baton to him this week. You won't need to be at them all moving forward, but stopping in from time to time would be expected of the underboss."

I nodded, some fear and excitement mixed in his words. I'd willingly accepted his offer, a chance to protect Loren and live the future I wanted. Despite knowing that, it still sent fear through me every time he called me out as the *underboss*, reminding me of my role in the family now. I'd continued my classes from here while we were sequestered, but the dream no longer felt viable. Despite wanting to be an art teacher and leave this life, I didn't know if I could now.

At least not until Darren was taken care of.

Until then, nothing was safe, and any future I tried to build would be made of sand, crumbling under the pressure. *I wanted more than that.*

So, patience would need to be my friend because until it was clear of danger, none of us had any future—not even a dream one.

"Right, I'll plan on being there and speak with Lucca to see if he needs anything."

Mas regarded me, a solemn expression on his face. "I

wish it was different, Nicolai, I do. It's the future I want for us as well, and I think together, we can build it for us all. Chicago is under attack, and we need to protect our city from the poison. No one is safe until we do."

"I know, Atticus, and it's why I agreed with your plan. It doesn't mean I don't have moments when I wish it wasn't different. I'll pack my things and head into town. I'm guessing I need to take Beau with me now?"

"Yes, and take our new friend as well."

Sighing, I didn't miss the grin that spread across Mas' face. Wells had been training out here a few days a week, preparing for our new venture in fighting. Mas had shared some of his plans and how he wanted to legitimize our more significant endeavors in an effort to not only give us more clout as a family but added protection. While we'd still host the fighting rings, it would be our amateur auditions for the big show.

The fighting arena and training facility were still being built, but would be ready in about a month for our soft opening, the grand opening being over the summer. By taking betting away from Delgado, Mas hoped to draw him into our trap and cut one of his profit windows out. Uncle Seth hadn't spilled too many secrets, but so far, it seemed Darren was making plays for other families' sources of income to claim as their own. Taking out Crash had been his first attack, hindering us and allowing his guy to face a weaker opponent, ensuring a win and a big payday.

I'd been reaching out to contacts worldwide to find some top-billed fighters for the grand opening showcase. It would be a weekend-long event, ending with the

Grand Prix show. If Delgado hadn't made a play by then, it was our attempt to change the board in our favor.

The players involved might be secret right now, Darren keeping his pieces close to his chest, but we were taking back control. If they didn't know which game they were playing, they couldn't cheat. Now, we just had to hope our mole problem was exterminated, or we would all pay for it with our lives.

Standing, I made my way out of his office, excitement coursing through me at the chance to make things right with Beautiful. Mas's final words stopped me at the door briefly.

"Good Luck."

Smiling to myself, I continued on my way to my room, ready to set the course in motion. It was time to get my girl back, no matter the cost.

THREE

LOREN

The week passed by and I realized how much of a routine Jude and I had fallen into. The best part was how much I liked it. We had breakfast together just about every morning before he left for school, and on the nights neither of us had anything, we would make dinner together, always remembering the special ingredient of doing it together.

After we ate, Jude would work on his homework, and I'd help him when I could. The kid was smart, taking a lot of advanced classes, and I loved watching his enthusiasm for learning. We really had become a family together, and we'd even begun a chore list, trading off who did what. I was at the point though, where I wanted to hire someone.

The amount of time we were home was limited, and I didn't want to spend it scrubbing the toilet. Granted, meals and laundry would still need to be done, but those things were more enjoyable since we often did them together. Laundry had become our binge-watching time. We were taking turns picking shows to introduce the other person to and in between episodes we would change over the laundry, fold, and put away. We could sit there and do four or five loads, and it never felt tiresome.

So far we'd watched *The Boys*, which I'd enjoyed, even if it had been a tad bit gory for my taste, *The Originals*, and *Mindhunters*. Our next choice was mine, and I hadn't decided what I wanted to start, yet. I was debating on going with either a classic sitcom or a drama.

Tonight, I'd run late from my workout, so I'd stopped and picked up some food for us. Juggling the takeout bags along with my briefcase and gym bag, I attempted to press the button for the elevator. When a hand reached over and hit 18, I looked up in surprise.

"Monroe, hey."

"Loren. How are you?"

I leaned against the elevator, my heart racing as I tried to figure out how to answer that question. "Oh, you know, living life I suppose." I inwardly cringed; my attempt at small talk hadn't improved at all in the past few months. It was so awkward with Monroe to begin with. I never knew what to say or how much to ask. We went from, 'hey, I'd like to swap spit with you' to 'did you hear that toaster strudels are on sale this week?'

Quite frankly, it sucked.

I'd confronted Monroe a few days after his Dear John text. Or well, I'd intended to. He'd been so distraught and exhausted that I didn't have it in me to be angry with him.

If I removed the feelings of being cast aside, I couldn't blame him for his choices, even if it hurt. So, I chose to honor his request. Levi was important, the most important, and I couldn't be selfish in this case or angry he'd chosen his son over me. He should, especially in this situation. So all the arguments I'd prepared in my head to shout at him, stopped on my tongue, and I hugged him instead.

"It seems you and Jude have gotten into a routine."

"Yeah, I guess you could say that." I nodded, my head wobbling around like I'd had too much sugar with how exuberantly I moved it.

"How's um, everything with you?"

"No changes yet."

"That's too bad."

"Yeah." He shifted, his posture not necessarily relaxed, but also not uncomfortable. It felt like he wanted to reach out, but was holding himself back. It gave me a small spark of hope he was struggling with keeping our distance as much as I did.

"How's um... the twins?" I amended, wanting to avoid Levi unless he brought him up.

"They're good. I haven't gotten to spend as much time with them as it conflicts with my visiting hours with Levi."

"I bet that's hard. I'm sorry, Monroe."

"Yeah, well. It's Levi, so."

I nodded, understanding what he meant. I hadn't known Jude as long, or birthed him, but I loved the kid fiercely. The ding sounded, announcing our arrival, and I both felt glad and sad. At least the awkward ride was over, but it also meant my time with him was too.

We walked slowly down the hall together, almost as if

we both didn't want to leave, but not sure what to say. When I got to my door, I waved, my bags obscuring most of my arm, but he got the message, smiling as he waved back. Entering my place, I wondered if I was doing this all wrong.

I'd given him space, but what if he wanted me to fight for him? As Jude and I sat around the coffee table eating Chinese food, and watching *Buffy, the Vampire Slayer,* I made a commitment to myself to try harder.

Maybe I could be his Monroe, pushing him to let someone in. I didn't have anything to lose, only everything to gain.

Decided, I settled back and watched the show with Jude, a new determination in my spirit.

I STOOD behind my door a few days later, peeking through the peephole to the hallway. Monroe had started varying the times he left for work, making our morning elevator rides inconsistent. Today, I planned to stake out the hallway until I saw him leave. I'd been able to persuade George down at the front desk today to tell me if he'd already left. According to him, he hadn't, so I had a window of time before I'd need to go and not miss my appointments.

My feet were starting to go numb, the high heels unforgiving after standing in the same position for hours on end. Okay, so twenty minutes tops, but it definitely felt longer.

I was about to call it when I saw his door begin to

open. My heart rate picked up, my breath hitching at the opportunity before me. Playing it cool, I waited until he'd just started down the hall. No quick escape back into his apartment for him!

Slowly, I opened my door, attempting to play it casually as I strode out, locking it. I held my phone in my hand as I meandered down the hall, my heart now hammering in my chest as I continued down the corridor. He was already waiting at the elevator bay, and I knew the moment he saw me, his small inhale my clue.

I kept my head down, though, my eyes conscious of my steps as I walked. When I drew closer, I lifted my head and acted surprised to see him.

"Oh, hey, Monroe."

"Hey, Lo."

I grinned at the use of my nickname this time, doing a fist pump in my head. I went back to my phone, though, attempting to act disinterested. Cami and Nat swore by this technique, but I felt silly doing it. It was hard to act like I didn't care when all I wanted to do was throw myself at him.

They were the ones with dating history, though, so I figured I'd try it out. It wasn't like it could make anything worse. "How's your day going?" I asked, the elevator pinging with its arrival. He smiled, holding it open for me now and allowing me to take the corner. The motion made me blush, my face heating at the simple gesture.

"Can't complain. The weather is nice today."

"Yeah, it is. The city is coming alive."

Hitting the button, we settled back against the wall.

This morning, I didn't hate the superficial comments, choosing to see them as small wins. He could have ignored me, but instead he tried to include me in his life in the ways he could. It was nice, and for a few short minutes of the day, I got to speak to him and be in his presence, especially in the elevator, where his cologne wrapped around me, leaving its kiss on my skin.

"How's Jude doing today?"

"Jude's great. He likes his new school. Thanks for the recommendation."

"Of course, he's a good kid and deserves the chance."

"Have you talked to Wells?"

He shook his head, sadness creeping over his face. "No, I haven't. I went out to his place, but he either didn't answer the door or wasn't there. He's still not at the gym?"

"No," I frowned. When I'd been cleared to return to light exercise activities, I'd been excited to get back to the gym. But Mr. Surly was nowhere to be found. When I finally dared to ask the front desk girl, she'd smugly reported he'd taken a leave of absence.

I'd been forced to return to barre classes in the meantime. I'd become friendlier with Katie, but I didn't have the connection with her as I'd developed with Cami and Nat, or even Stacy, the dressing attendant from the Boutique. We'd all hung out a few times, and she'd gotten along well with both of them. We were all going dancing soon, something I was both nervous and excited about. Katie was still a friendly face for class at least, making it not as scary.

We fell silent after that, and I regretted my question.

The elevator stopped and picked up a few people a few floors below, causing Monroe to move closer to me, his arm brushing against mine. I figured this might be my one chance, so I took it, choosing honesty and vulnerability.

"I miss you, Monroe."

My voice had him turning to me, and I saw the emotion reflected back. He grasped my hand, squeezing it as he spoke.

"I miss you too, Loren. And I'm sorry I'm putting you through this. I never wanted to hurt you, and I know I've probably blown my chance and ruined everything, but I didn't know what else to do at the time. The only thing I could think about was Levi, all my energy and time centered around him. I thought it would be easier to let you go. Both to protect you from Brittni and, well, me."

"Was it? Easier, I mean?"

"No, Lo. It's been miserable. In the few moments when I wasn't thinking about how to get Levi back, I thought of you. The times I got to see you were the bright spots of my day. I missed you, and you were only a few feet across the hall, but I could never make my feet get up and go, too scared I'd messed it up, and I couldn't bear the thought of that. It was easier to imagine a possible future someday, than to face the reality it was over, that you didn't care."

"Oh, you stupid man." Without thinking any more about it or the fact tears had streamed down my face, I kissed him.

Pulling him to me, I wrapped my arms around his neck, sinking into the feeling of his body pressed against mine. He eagerly met me, our mouths desperate as we tried to heal the pain and distance between us. He lifted my leg up, and I found myself grinding into the hard cock pressed against his slacks.

A throat clearing brought us out of our lust-filled haze, and in a moment of clarity, I remembered we were in the elevator, a now *empty* elevator. A blush spread across my face, and Monroe and I laughed when we realized we'd been busted. I peeked around his body to find George looking in at us. He winked before speaking again.

"Sorry to interrupt that beautiful moment. But are we getting off or heading back up?"

His smile twinkled at me, and I laughed, dropping my head onto Monroe's shoulder. "Sorry, George. We'll be exiting now. Thank you."

George dipped his head and moved back to give us room to exit as he held the door for us. Monroe adjusted himself before turning and grabbing my hand, pulling me out with him. He bobbed his head at George but kept walking, suddenly in a hurry to get out of the building.

"Whoa, slow down. I stood at my door for twenty minutes waiting for you to leave, and my feet are killing me."

That caused him to stop, turning back to look at me. "Did you really?"

"Yeah. I wouldn't make that up."

Laughing, I caught up to him, and we walked side by side, still holding hands. "So not to be the therapist, but what does this mean now?"

Monroe blew out a breath. I wanted to hate myself for

asking, but I couldn't live in this ambiguous state anymore. He peeked over, catching my eyes as we walked. "My situation hasn't changed, Lo. If anything, it's more stressful than before, but I don't want to push you away again. If you can be patient with me, I'd like to try. I know we were just starting to date, but I felt something real with you. I'd like to get back to that place."

"I can agree to that." I smiled, my heart lighter at finally having some direction. "I don't want to pressure you or make you feel you have to choose me over Levi. I'd never want that. I just don't want to be pushed out, forgotten."

"I could never forget you, Loren."

"I like hearing that."

"Good, because I have some ground to cover in order to redeem myself."

"That's not necessary, Monroe. I understand. I do."

"The fact you do is why I want to do it. You deserve for someone to show you how amazing you are. You're a rare woman, a beauty among a lot of toads. I think I just need your goodness around me to remind myself there are still good people out there."

"Well, I mean, if you want to romance me, I'm not going to stop you."

"Good. I don't know what this will look like, but I'm glad I have you to figure it out with. Can we have dinner together soon, and I can update you on everything?"

"I'd like that."

"Okay, perfect. Now, let's get some coffee and try to forget George saw us making out in an elevator like two randy teenagers."

Laughing, I followed him into Bean Paradise, happiness filling me again. I pushed back my earlier doubt and held onto this hope. I wanted to feel this as long as possible, reminding myself good things could happen.

 ⁕

THE DAY HAD BEEN LONG, but for the first time in months, it hadn't dragged. I knew it had to be because of things improving with Monroe, but I didn't want to be one of those girls whose mood was based on how her love life was going.

So, I convinced myself it was because I'd finally convinced Jude to watch one of my favorite shows and had taken a chance. It sounded better when I looked at it that way.

Finishing up my note for a new client, I quickly tucked Jill's chart away and headed to the front to meet the last one. I was so jazzed today, I didn't even care that my last client was Dayton. He'd been a hard one to crack, something about him not adding up, and I found myself frustrated as I tried to pull things from him.

I chalked it up to not working with adult men as often, and the poor timing of his intake. It had been the day I'd been practically dumped, clouding my judgment of him. Today, I was determined to turn it around, hoping my positive outlook would flow into the session. Peeking out my head, I smiled in greeting.

"Dayton, you can come back now."

He nodded meekly, shuffling his feet as he followed me. Perhaps it was his demeanor that bothered me the most. He was a tall man, fit, and had a dominant energy about him. Yet, in sessions, he acted submissive and cowardly. Dayton was always polite and well-spoken, another congruence to his countenance. He spoke with confidence in his tone, his body language belied his mood.

Dayton Mascro was a contradiction of terms, and I couldn't figure out why the act. I was confident it *was* one at this point, and I needed to find the answer to the game he was playing.

This was the part I loved, though. So despite his sourness at times, his discrepancy in motivation, he was a puzzle I wanted to solve. If I could figure out his game and call him on it, then I'd be halfway to his root problem.

All behavior had a purpose, after all, even the shitty ones.

"How has your week been, Dayton?"

"Oh, it's been okay, Mrs. Carter. Thank you for asking."

"Yes, of course. Did you do anything over the weekend?"

This was the thing about Dayton; it always felt like I was pulling teeth to get any traction.

"No, I just stayed home."

"Oh, well, that's nice sometimes to be inside and recoup. Did you try any of those activities we talked about?"

"No, it didn't seem like the right time." He stared directly at me but tugged at the cuffs of his dress shirt.

"Hmm. When do you think would be the right time?"

"That's an interesting question, Mrs. Carter."

My earlier attempt at changing my attitude evaporated, and I found myself slipping into a defensive pose. Intellectually, I knew if he made me feel this way, odds were he made others feel the same, with his attachment style being a bit disorganized. I could also recognize that not every client and therapist were a perfect fit. I spoke of this often in intakes, an advocate for finding the right therapist for them. And logically, I recognized his lack of effort frustrated me since he was taking a spot from a client who might be more engaged.

I knew all of these things, but I couldn't separate them personally from me for some reason. He got under my skin in a way a client never had before, and I didn't like it. Breathing deeply, I channeled my inner meditative self into staying present and not letting my emotions control me.

"It is an interesting question, you're right. Something else I've been wondering about, Dayton. You sought me out because you said you wanted help and had some family problems you were working to resolve. Yet, it's been five weeks now, and I feel like I'm doing all the heavy lifting. While everyone's progress is different, there does have to be effort, and I'm just not sure if it's there on your part. There comes a time in each therapeutic relationship where you have to ask yourself if it's the right fit for you. I think we're at that point, Dayton."

His faux fidgeting had stopped, and he watched me, no emotion on his face, not even a fake one. I leaned forward, my elbows on my knees as I clasped my hands together. "Do you think this is the right therapy relationship for you, Dayton?"

He didn't answer right away, and I watched every movement he made, looking for any clues of real emotions. When a smile spread across his face, I sat back, the expression jarring.

"You're right, you're right, Mrs. Carter. I apologize. I guess you can say I've been holding myself back, afraid of judgment." He babbled now, a complete opposite to before, more of the manic energy I'd felt from the first session leaching through.

"You see, Mrs. Carter. I did a bad thing. I hurt my family, and I'm worried they won't forgive me."

Calming myself, I steadied my breathing as I took him in. "It's common to feel like you've done something unforgivable, and I find that once people share the thing they're so worried about, not only do they feel lighter, but they're able to heal from it. Would you like to start small today and give me a tiny detail?"

"Hmm," he paused, rubbing his jaw. "You make a valid point. I guess the problem started for me when my father shot a man in front of me on my eighth birthday."

Shocked at his disclosure, I struggled to keep my face neutral as I tried to dissect what he'd given me. "That had to be scary, something that big happening at such a young age. What do you consider to be the problem that started from there?"

"Ahh, you're good." He pointed at me, his finger waving in the air as he exuberantly smiled in my direction. "I expected you to react in shock or fear. You surprised me, Mrs. Carter."

"It takes a lot to shock me, Dayton. I've heard a lot inside these walls, and I've never judged a person for the choices they've made."

"Hmm, I imagine you have heard some things. Anything good? Juicy?"

"I'm sorry, Dayton, but you know the rules. I'm not allowed to discuss my other clients with you. Let's focus back on what you consider to be the problem."

"Nah, I'm good for today."

He leaned back, crossing his leg at his knee, his arms splayed on the back of the couch. It was an odd pose, but nothing about Dayton made sense, so it fit with his whole dynamic. I wasn't sure how I felt about things. We still hadn't moved forward or made any gains, but he'd shared something with me. I couldn't punish him now by terminating sessions.

When the hour finally ended, I was exhausted, the emotional roller coaster he'd taken me on having drained me.

"So, have you decided if you're going to keep seeing me, Mrs. Carter?"

"Well, Dayton, I think that remains to be seen. You made a step today, and I'm proud of you for doing that. We need to use this momentum and keep pushing forward, okay?"

"Sure thing, Mrs. Carter. I'm glad our time together doesn't have to end yet."

I smiled, the gesture strained as I walked him out. Something about today gave me the heebie-jeebies, and I wanted to shower it off my skin. Closing down everything, I found a lighter in between the couch cushions. It had some sort of crest on it and the initials D.M. Assuming it was Dayton's, I placed it on my desk, so I'd remember to give it back to him next week.

Feeling exhausted, I opted out of Barre and headed home. Texting Jude, I told him I'd pick up dinner on my way, the action making me happy to know I wasn't alone anymore. If all the pain I'd endured for the past five years resulted in me finding Jude, then I could bear it.

Jude made it worth it.

FOUR

LOREN

It was Friday night, and I found myself at the gym, nothing else going on in my life. Which sounded lame, but after the week I'd had, I was looking forward to a quiet evening, even if alone. Jude was at a school lock-in to fundraise for a club he was interested in. They were doing a game-a-thon, a modern twist on the dance-a-thon to raise money. He'd been excited about it, and I hadn't wanted to admit how lonely I felt with him gone. Monroe hadn't been able to do anything either since he had to work late. We were finally able to make plans for dinner tomorrow night at least, so it gave me something to look forward to.

The music stopped as the instructor finished her cool-down instructions, and I exhaled a breath, rising up from the stretch. Barre class was nice today. I still preferred kickboxing, but I'd learned to appreciate the mindfulness I could enter in these classes. Picking up my gear, I sanitized everything and waved to Katie.

"See ya at the next class."

"Have a nice night, Loren."

"You too."

Walking out, I opted to toss on my sweatshirt and shoes instead of changing today. It was a lovely night for walking, and I didn't feel like putting my work clothes back on, or more importantly, my high heels. I smiled at the front desk girl, my new commitment not to judge other women unbiasedly and win people over one smile at a time. She ignored me as usual, but I felt better knowing I wasn't falling into the mean girl category.

The cool air greeted me as I walked outside, and I took a deep breath in. Something about the spring always brought a sense of rejuvenation with it. The trees were budding, and when April greeted us in a week, I imagined we'd finally start to see flowers. I was so focused on the trees and enjoying the scenery, I didn't notice the man leaning against the wall.

His voice called out, and I stopped, apprehension building in me as I turned my head to look at him.

"*Gorgeous*, we meet again."

The man was just as attractive as I remembered, his cocky swagger on full display now that he wasn't sitting. He looked me over from head to toe, his eyes taking in every detail, and I regretted not changing. Not because I wanted to look nice for him, but both times I'd met him, I'd looked like I'd just run a marathon, the sweat thick on my skin, my hair frazzled and askew, my face still red from exertion.

But honestly, I think it had more to do with my mask being harder to project in this state. The bedraggled state of my outside for once matched my inside, and I didn't feel as strong.

"I'm sorry, do I know you?"

I decided if I couldn't be professional Loren, I'd go with dismissive. He thrived on dominance and control, something I'd clocked about him from our first meeting, so perhaps I could turn the tables. The advantage being, I wasn't trapped on a train with him this time.

Crossing my arms, I jutted my hip out as I hardened my features. Maybe if I went all basic bitch on him, he'd lose interest?

"I highly doubt that, gorgeous. I'm not the type of man one forgets. Especially when a woman holds my nuts in her hands."

I didn't miss the way his nostrils flared or the heated look that crossed his eyes. He both hated and loved what I'd done last time we'd met.

"Yeah, sorry, dude. I think I'd remember that. You've got the wrong girl."

Turning to leave, he volleyed his following statement, freezing me in fear.

"Well, that's too bad, Loren Carter, foster mom to Jude Franklin and partial owner of New Horizons."

My breath hitched, my back to him as I focused on keeping my breathing steady, my racing heart and rising panic threatening to take over. *Shit, shit, shit.* How did he know so much about me? Was he *stalking* me? What was I supposed to do in this situation? *Quit panicking and think Loren!*

First, calm your breathing so you can think clearly.

Almost as if I was out of my body, I could hear my own voice when I spoke to clients, and I listened to myself, following the steps. Slowing down my breaths, I counted in my head to stay focused. Once I felt the fear recede, I thought through how to best deal with someone like him. I needed to perceive him like a client—a narcissistic, entitled one who thought they were the smartest person in the room. When I had this mindset, I felt better.

Spinning on the balls of my feet, I hardened my features as I met his eyes, finding a strong thread within me. Clapping, I threw him off as I watched his face change from smug to confused to a quick rage before he locked it away. My guess had worked.

"Congrats, you can Google. You've successfully developed the skills of an eight-year-old. Is this supposed to scare me? Or are you a misguided asshole who thinks this counts as flirty?" Scoffing, I rolled my eyes, crossing my arms to hide my shaking. *Keep it together, girl!*

His jaw clenched, and he took a step forward, his hand reaching out for me. My window of surprise was running out, and it was time to get myself out of this situation.

"You know what? I take it back. Your skills are more like a five-year-old that can't spell because you didn't dive deep enough, it seems. I have the chief of police on speed dial, approach me again, and I'll have you arrested for harassment. I don't know you or have any interest in knowing you. So, do us both a favor and leave me the fuck alone."

Turning swiftly, I took off in the other direction, needing to get away before I broke out in tears, the adrenaline leaving me as my entire body began to shake. I needed to find someplace to stop and gather myself. I didn't think I'd make it home in this state. I turned the corner, but I heard him make a final statement, chilling me even more to the bone.

"Tell your *boyfriend* my next threat won't be as subtle as a bomb."

I sucked in a breath, the implication clear. *He'd* been the one to set it. Or at least he'd been the one to give the order. It was clear he was some sort of leader, and I doubted he got his hands dirty. But what did he mean about my boyfriend? Nicco? He'd been the one I was with that night. Did he have something to do with it? Was that why he hadn't sought me out? Had I been thinking about it all wrong this entire time?

My thoughts spun out of control, the fear finally taking over as I barreled through throngs of people, not caring if I ran into them. I took a corner, no clue where I was anymore. My only focus was on escaping and putting space between me and him.

After about five minutes, I noticed the sidewalk wasn't as populated, and I worried I'd gone too far. Looking all around for something familiar, I turned my head at the next cross street when I smacked into a body. I felt their arms wrap around me and I panicked. My reflexes went into overdrive, and I attempted to kick them in the shins, my arms having been secured to my side.

"Ssh, ssh, Kitten. It's me."

Blinking, I looked up and found chocolate eyes looking down at me and his familiar smell of leather and mint breaking through my fear. "Wells," I breathed out, my body finally relaxing into his hold. He held me close, pushing my head against his chest, and I went willingly, wrapping my arms around him. I didn't care that I was pissed at him. Right now, he was safe.

I started crying, not even knowing it, but everything had come to a head, and it bubbled out of me. I'd stood up for myself, but I wondered if I might've made it inevitably worse in the process. Nothing made sense.

Who was that man? Why did he threaten me? Had he been the one to hurt me? Why? Why? Why?

The 'why' was all I could think of as it swirled around in my head on repeat.

"Kitten, I don't know what happened, but I'm guessing it was big because I know how fucking strong you are. You're safe now. I'm going to take you somewhere safe. Do you trust me?"

I felt his words through his chest, the sound a dark rumble against my cheek, a little deeper than usual. I wanted to laugh at the absurdity of this moment. Standing on a street corner, wrapped in Surly's arms *willingly*. His grip was solid, his hand on my head and his arm banded around my waist, and even without thinking about it, I knew it was true. I did trust him.

I might hate him at times and become so angry with him that I wanted to throttle him, but he'd never made me fear him. If anything, he'd helped me find my strength. Even during our disastrous kiss, he'd been protective, stopping me from doing something I might've regretted.

I hadn't seen it that way at the time, our usual stubbornness fighting against one another, but he'd protected me from myself that day. Not every guy would've stopped. Wells was surly, rude, and a massive pain in my ass 98% of the time. But I think I could see the version of him that Monroe loved. The man he was in those moments when it mattered.

It wasn't enough to forgive everything between us, but it was enough for right now.

Without even lifting my head, I nodded, his hand moving with the motion, and I said an honest truth. "I do."

I felt his body relax, a tension I hadn't noticed until it was gone at my response. His hand smoothed over my hair, and I could've sworn his lips brushed my temple, but it was gone before I could question it. He let go, and while I knew he'd have to, I missed being cradled in his arms. Wells had held me like I was the most precious thing in the world, and it was a heady feeling.

"Come on."

He grabbed my hand and pulled me around the corner, a bike parked there. He lifted the helmet and gave it to me before straddling the hunk of metal. And it *was* a hunk of metal. It wasn't pretty like Nicco's had been. Instead, it was an assortment of mismatched parts with multiple colors.

"We don't have all day, Kitten. You said you trusted me. *Prove it.*"

His voice snapped me out of it, and I slid the helmet on before straddling the seat behind him. Wrapping my arms around him, I settled in, thankful this wasn't my first time. For some reason, it felt like Wells would rub it in if it had been. His hand came down on mine, briefly caressing them before pulling them tighter.

The engine roared to life, and again, I noticed it

wasn't as quiet or smooth as Nicco's, but it sounded strong, and I relaxed against his back. We took off, whipping around the city, and I held on tight to him as we went. He started to head out of downtown, and I wondered where we were going, a little anxiety creeping in.

After all this time, maybe he'd led me into a false sense of security and was taking me out to kill me somewhere. What if he'd been involved with that man? What if...

Shaking it off, I reminded myself of all the things I'd realized earlier. This wasn't time to start catastrophizing and thinking of the worst-case scenario. It seemed my present state was already dangerous enough for me. I might even need to tone it down on the murder mystery shows if I was beginning to see everything as a conspiracy.

When we started down a gravel road, we slowed until we came to an end where an old house sat in complete darkness. Wells parked the bike, kicking out the kickstand before getting off. I looked up at him, taking him in for the first time.

He looked good. His injuries had healed, and his muscles even looked bigger. Wherever he'd been, it had done him well. Licking my lips, I watched as the edges of his lips lifted in a crooked smile, and holy hell, it was sexy.

"You know the helmet doesn't have a visor, right?"

It took me a second to realize what he was asking. He reached down and unclipped the strap, and I instantly understood. Heat crept up my neck at not realizing the intensity of the moment and fear having muted some of the details. My processors weren't firing, having been spent on dealing with the sleazy stalker douche.

"I know," I scoffed, rolling my eyes to hide my embarrassment. "I can still appreciate the whole bad boy thing you have going on even if I don't like you." I waved my hand in front of his body, and he caught it, using it to pull me off the bike and into him.

Leaning down, he seductively whispered into my ear. "If that's what you have to tell yourself, Kitten, go ahead. But we both know you'll be moaning out my name tonight when you touch yourself."

He dropped my hand and took off, leaving me standing with my mouth open, and maybe a little wet between the legs. Wells had the sexy asshole thing down. Sleazeball could learn a thing or two from him. Scratch that. I didn't need the creeper improving his skills to hit on me.

When I didn't immediately follow, he stopped, sighing before turning back.

"Loren, come on. I need to do something before we can talk about what happened. Can we make something simple for once? The dogs get antsy if I don't come in right away."

His bravado was gone, and I could see the real man under it. I assented, realizing he'd called me Loren. As much as I'd hated Kitten when he'd initially called me it, I kind of hated not hearing it from his lips now. What a tangled web we weaved. When his words penetrated my brain, I picked up my speed, passing him as I ran to the front door.

"Eager there, Kitten?"

He smiled genuinely, the light reaching his eyes, and I realized it was part of what had changed about him. Wells wasn't as pissed off as usual. He even appeared lighter, not as mad at the world.

"Um, you said *dogs*. It just so happens, I'm a big fan of dogs. Seems you might have a redeeming quality, after all, Surly."

He barked out a laugh, unlocking the door and holding it open for me to pass under his arm. "Is that so? Well, come in and meet the crew. Just watch—,"

Before he could finish speaking, I ducked under his arm and raced into the house. Clicks on the hardwood greeted me as loud paws sounded on the floor. I realized what he was saying too late and found myself in a massive lick fest as one of the dogs tackled me to the ground, the others clambering over one another to get to me next. I sat up, not caring, as I tried to love on all of them at once, speaking in baby cooing gibberish.

They were beautiful, and it made me realize how much I'd missed this, missed Barkley.

Wells whistled, and the dogs immediately backed down, sitting at attention, and I looked up at him, impressed. He laser focused his glare on the dogs, a look of disapproval on his face, and I watched as they hung their heads, whining. God, that was hot, and so adorable at the same time.

"Koda, Nova, you two know better. What if that had been an intruder? Are you going to attack them with your licks? Was that your plan?" He huffed, planting his hands on his hips as he stared them down. I couldn't help the giggle that slipped free.

I watched in amusement as the two bigger dogs pawed at their faces, begging forgiveness. Wells' face changed, and he patted them on the heads. He turned to the smaller two, one not even sitting anymore but playing with its feet, laying on his back. Wells hung his head, sighing loudly as he looked at the misbehaving mutt.

"Fort, I swear you'll be the death of me. I've never met a dog as stubborn as you." The dog rolled over, almost looking like he asked, 'what, me?' Wells went over to a tall cabinet and began to scoop out food into four bowls. I watched in fascination as he acknowledged each dog, beckoning them to come to their bowl. They waited in front of it like good little soldiers until he clicked his teeth in a sound, nodding for them to eat. I could hear the hungry inhales as the first three scarfed their food, and the little one waited, struggling to stay still. He didn't move from his spot, though, and a little whine escaped him before Wells gave in.

"Okay, Fort."

I watched in amazement as he pounced, shaking his little doggy butt as he ate. When they were all occupied, Wells walked over to me and offered me a hand up. "I tried to warn you," he cringed in apprehension, assuming I'd be upset.

Grabbing it, I got to my feet and shook my head, smiling. "I'm not mad. I loved it. I'm kind of not sure how to take you now."

"Well, don't let it go to your head, Kitten. I'm still the surly asshole you love to kick in the balls."

Laughing, I followed him as he led me to the kitchen, opening a fridge and pulling out two waters. He handed one to me, and I took it, again surprised at his kindness.

"Now, I really don't know how to take you."

"It's just a water bottle, Kitten. It's not a proposal. Drink it or not, but I figured you'd want one after being out on the road. Always makes my throat dry."

He turned the bottle upside down, and I watched in fascination as the water traveled down his throat. A stray drop here and there ran down his jaw, and for a second, I debated licking it. The crackling of the plastic broke my stare off with the drop, and I uncapped my own water and drank some to distract myself.

Wells stayed leaning against the counter and waited until I was done before he began his questions.

"Do you need to call someone, Monroe, perhaps?"

"Oh, um, no. I'm good."

"What about your foster kid? Jude, was it?"

"He's at a school thing."

The dogs had finished eating and meandered their way around the kitchen, sniffing me, curious about my presence. I sat down on the floor, not caring if it was clean, and found myself loving on the mischievous Fort. Patting him, I looked up when Wells hadn't asked me anything else.

He had a soft smile on his face as he watched me pet the dog.

"He likes you."

"Well, I like him."

Wells walked over and sat across from me, and one of the bigger dogs plopped down on him, practically knocking him over. "Koda! You big lug, watch it."

He shoved the dog off him, but the dog tried again, landing in his lap this time. Wells rolled his eyes but allowed it.

"You going to tell me what happened earlier?"

Sighing, I looked up, some of the fear returning at having to recall it, but I knew it was necessary. "I think the man who's responsible for the bomb, I think he approached me tonight with a message. Though it was more like a threat. And now that I think about it, it wasn't the first time either."

"Kitten, slow down, and start from the beginning. Tell me everything. Including what's been going on for the past two months."

Taking a deep breath, I acquiesced and shared how my life had been the past two months with him. I got lost in my story as I stroked the now sleeping dog in my lap, my voice a soft lull as I shared. In a moment of odd clarity, I realized that sitting on a kitchen floor with my surly trainer, surrounded by dogs, and telling my woes wasn't the worst Friday in my life.

In fact, I'd say it was probably in the top ten best ones.

FIVE

WELLS

Kitten sat on my floor, petting Fort, and I almost blinked to make sure I wasn't imagining things, but I wasn't. The simple fact we were *talking* alluded to this not being a dream. I hoped my dream imagination was more creative than sitting on the floor in a pool of dog saliva. Preferably with a whole lot less talking and clothes, the saliva… well, I could be game for that if it was the human variety.

The past two months have been a life-changing experience, in the best possible way. The biggest change had been gaining a life worth living for. Atticus had done as he promised and paid my debt to the Delgados, getting them off my back. The simple feeling of being able to breathe without it hanging over my head was life-altering. I still had moments of self-loathing, my choices haunting me with each step I took, but it felt manageable now. I was no longer drowning, but more like I was finally able to doggy paddle in the deep end.

I wasn't delusional enough to believe I wouldn't have any other hardships in life. I'd been around the block too many times to trust an easy out. I still had shit to deal with, only trading one mobster for another, but Atticus seemed different. And I was holding on to that hope with everything I had, it would be different this time.

"So yeah, other than tonight, not much else really. Just healing, working, and hanging with Jude." She shrugged one shoulder, but I could tell something else was bothering her. She'd mostly stayed staring at Fort, lost in petting him as she spoke.

"That's a lot to process, Kitten. Do you know the man from tonight's name?"

"No." She still didn't look up, softly stroking Fort. It seemed meditative at this point. He was out in her lap, the stillest I'd ever seen him.

"You know what this means, don't you?" That had her snapping her eyes up at me finally, the emotion hidden in those depths everything I'd wanted for months, staring at me.

"What?"

I hated how small her voice sounded, and every time I remembered how much she'd been shaking when she ran into me, I wanted to go track this asshole down and send my fist flying through his skull.

"Means we're going to need to add self-defense to your lessons."

"My lessons?"

"Yep." This had her smiling, and I wanted to hide how pleased I was to receive one.

"Oh? I guess I could get behind that."

"Good. I'm back now, and we can start up our training again if you'd like."

"I would, actually. I've missed it," she blushed, and I

wanted to see the rest of her that color. "Same nights? I might need more flexibility this time. I have Jude now. "

The foster kid in me warmed at her consideration for hers. She was the type of foster parent we'd all dreamed of meeting. I stared at her, forgetting I was meant to respond when she tilted her head, watching me. Smiling, I nodded. "Possibly, but we won't be at the gym, so flexibility is doable."

"I don't… understand. Would we work out here?"

"I work for someone new now. We'll train there."

"Okay." She bobbed her head, biting her lip before I watched her steel herself. "You know this doesn't mean I'm not still mad at you for bailing on me, right?"

"I know." I agreed, surprise filling her face at my easy acquiesce. It seemed to bolster her, and she sat up straighter, squaring herself toward me.

"In fact, I think it entitles me to a few free sessions and snuggles with this precious dog whenever I want." I covered my laugh with my hand, pretending I was considering it. I couldn't let her know how much I wanted what she was offering. I'd train her for free any day. Getting to spend time with her was the payment.

"Is that so, Kitten?" I growled, not intending for my voice to take on a heady edge to it, but it poured out of me anyway, rolling off my tongue.

She gulped, nodding her head, and I swear goosebumps covered her arms.

"That means you'll have to see me more, you know?"

"I know."

"And you're okay with that?"

"I'm finding myself not hating it."

"Well, I think that's a win in my category then," I paused, watching her. Nodding to the stubborn dog in her lap, and an idea struck me. "He seems to really like you. I've had a difficult time with him. I'll tell you what," I mused, despite already planning to give in to whatever she'd wanted. "Help me with his training, and I won't charge you for self-defense."

"Training? What kind of training do you mean?"

"You aren't the only thing I train, Kitten. Don't let it go to your head. In fact, the dogs are usually a lot more agreeable than you were. None of them ever kicked me in the balls." I leveled her with a knowing look, my eyes full of heat.

"Well, that's only because you control their food, and I'm sure if they could, they would totally do it."

Laughing, I shook my head at her. I hadn't realized how much I'd missed our banter, her fire a soothing balm to the storm that raged inside me. I still didn't think I was good enough for her, but I wanted to be. For the first time in a long time, I really wanted to be. A silence fell between us and I found myself wanting to fill it for once, the sound of her voice a welcoming relief in my home. I used to enjoy the silence, but being around a family, even if they were criminals, had shown me people truly could care about each other. If it wasn't for the dogs, I didn't know if I'd be staying out here. I'd never felt as lonely as I had the past few nights sleeping here all alone.

"So, I noticed in your recount of what's happened over the past two months, you didn't mention Monroe, and earlier when I asked if you needed to let him know where you were, you said no. So, Kitten, what's going on there? Is he… okay?" I tried to ask nonchalantly, but her small smile told me I didn't get away with it. There was no way to disguise the pain and worry in my voice for him, never had been. How he'd ignored it all those years had always baffled me.

"Well, um. I don't really know." She looked up, and I saw the sadness return to her eyes again, and I wanted to do whatever it took to make it go away, a fierce protectiveness washing over me. "We hung out every day until one morning he, um, texted me saying he couldn't commit to anything. It was my first day back to work, actually," she rambled. "Monroe said Brittni had found a way to get a judge to grant her full custody."

"She what?" I hadn't realized I'd squeezed the water bottle until I watched Loren jump in front of me. Slowing my breaths, I attempted to release the plastic from my death grip as I tried again. "Come again, Kitten. What the fuck did Brittni manage to do?"

"I don't know the full story. Monroe asked to cool things because he needed to focus on his case. It hurt, but I understood. I would see him in the hall at times, occasionally on the elevator, but we didn't go past the superficial chit-chat. I'd finally had enough and kind of ambushed him this week, and he um, well," she stopped, a blush rising to her cheeks.

"He what, Kitten?" I inched a little closer, skating my hand down the side of her face, tilting it up towards me.

"He kissed me in the elevator. We even got busted by George." She laughed in the sexiest way I'd ever heard. Her breathy chuckle had me wanting to lean forward and erase all the space between us, but I wouldn't. Not yet.

"I bet you gave Ol' George a good show."

She shrugged, but her eyes never left mine. "That still didn't answer my question." She licked her lips before trying again.

"We're to have dinner tomorrow, and he's going to update me then. I don't really know much else other than that."

I smoothed my thumb over her cheek before dropping my hand. It was too tempting to keep touching. "Say bye to Fortitude. It's time we head back to the city before it gets too late."

"Fortitude?"

"The sleeping menace in your lap. He's named for strength, but he hasn't earned it yet, so he's Fort for now." She smiled big, her whole face lighting up, and damn if that didn't have my cock hardening and my heart taking off at rocket speeds.

"I like it. It suits him." She lifted the sleepy dog's head and brought it closer to her face. "Okay, Fort. I'll be back, big ole meanie Wells promised. I'll see you again, okay?"

Kitten talked to the dog like he mattered, and I realized how attractive it was. She didn't once complain about his slobber or dog hair when the dogs had jumped all over her. In fact, it had been the happiest and lightest I'd seen her. I guess it wasn't because of me, but the dogs. Whatever the reason, I'd use it if it got her to keep looking like that. She'd always been delectable, a craving I couldn't ignore. But watching her shed some of the darkness, or perhaps even embracing it, made her strong. Her confidence shone through now. It didn't surprise me that Kitten and Fort had connected, bonded even when I thought about it. They were a lot alike and would be suitable for each other.

If I couldn't give her anything else, I could give her that.

She kissed the dog between his eyes, and he licked her nose when she pulled back. The giggle that escaped was addictive, a pure lighthearted feeling. Reaching down, I offered her my hand and was surprised when she took it, my eyes going wide.

I'd blame that for the over-exuberant pull I did, bringing her flush with my body. Her breath caught, and she clutched my shirt. I didn't say anything; I just watched her. Kitten's face was open, and I saw the lust there. I could take it right now, and she'd willingly give it to me.

But I wanted more.

I heard the way she talked about Monroe. I remembered the way she looked with Nicco. And I wanted it for myself. It might be greedy or even stupid on my part to hold out instead of seizing the moment in front of me, but I owed it to myself to wait.

"You ready, Kitten? Do you need to like, I don't know, use the restroom before we go? It is a bit of a drive."

"Oh, um, sure. That'd be smart. Where is it?"

She stepped back, and I missed her already. Covering my longing, I slipped back into my surliness, as she called it, lightening the tension between us. "Well, most people just call it the outdoors, Kitten."

She sputtered, and fuck, it was beautiful. I couldn't help it, and I full-on belly-laughed. "I'm just kidding. But you should see your face. Here, follow me."

I directed her down the hallway, flipping on the light to the guest bathroom. It was, fortunately, one of the rooms I'd completed. I stepped back so she could enter and I couldn't help but take pride in how her eyes lit up at the space.

"Wow, this is gorgeous." She ran her hand over the marble countertop, looking all around. It was white and grey with black accents. I wasn't one for decorating, so it was minimal, but the room itself had been hard work.

"I'll meet you in the kitchen when you're ready." She dipped her head in response, and I pulled the door shut and headed back. Picking up our trash, I picked up the few things we'd used. Fort laid in the same spot, looking toward the opening, waiting for her to return. Bending down, I patted the dog's fur, intrigued by his change in behavior.

The rest of the dogs were already sprawled out in their beds, no longer interested in the visitor, but Fort waited. It was something to note. Maybe he was more of a girl dog owner than a male one. I didn't give credence to that in most cases, but he had been rescued from a horrible situation as a puppy. The Underdogs had asked me to take him to see if I could help. It had been a diffi-cult learning curve, to say the least, and I hadn't been kidding when I said I needed help.

He started to wag his tail, and I knew it meant he heard her returning. Glancing up, I watched as she walked into the room, and he sprinted for her. Even though she'd already said goodbyes, she bent down and gave him some more affection. How people treated dogs said a lot about them, in my opinion. I didn't think I could like her more than I had, or maybe I was just accepting it now, but as I watched her, I realized I didn't hate her anymore. Never had, in fact.

The block of needing to push her away had gone, and a burning desire to earn the things I wanted swelled forward in its place. For the first time in my life, I wanted more from a woman.

Standing, I grabbed the extra helmet and jacket, handing them to her; it was colder out now, and the wind would be brutal if she didn't cover up some. Loren accepted it, smiling up at me as we headed out, slipping her arms in the oversized leather jacket.

I wouldn't admit to her how good she looked in it, but damn did she ever. She even fit perfectly behind me, her body pressed tight to mine. I had to drive the whole way downtown with a cock as hard as steel. Visions of fucking her on the bike didn't help either. When we finally rolled to a stop near her building, she looked oddly at me when I walked in with her.

"What, Kitten? Don't think I can be a gentleman and walk you to your door?"

"No, it's not that, it's just. Well, actually, it is that."

"I should be offended, but I know I didn't paint the best version of myself either when we met."

Snorting, she looked at me, a softening in her eyes. "No, but I probably didn't either. I was in a dark place, and as much as I grumbled about you, I think you actually helped me."

"Helped you?" I asked in surprise. She nodded, pushing the button for her floor as we entered the elevator.

"Yeah. You gave me someone to fight. All the demons in my head I couldn't, but you helped me concentrate that energy outside of myself. And, it made me feel stronger." She turned to look up at me. "I don't know if you know this about me, but I'm a therapist. And I felt like a failure, unable to help myself. The training sessions with you gave me a focus, a way to calm the racing thoughts and begin to internalize the strength I was feeling."

"I have no clue what you just said, and no, I didn't know that about you, but it makes sense. When you're not kicking me in the balls or throwing barbs my way, you do have this sense of calmness about you. I think it's what Fort felt too."

"I do like that dog."

The elevator dinged, and we walked off. "Well, um, not to be weird, but this feels like an awkward date now." She commented, fumbling with her keys in front of her door.

Crowding her in, I watched as her breath hitched, her eyes wide as she looked up at me. "Don't worry, Kitten. You're not ready for me yet, so you're off the hook tonight. Besides, it's time I had a conversation with Monroe."

I pulled myself away from her before I gave in to the temptation and walked across the hall. Knocking, I glanced back and found her in the same spot, her eyes watching me. I didn't want to believe it, but it looked like longing and a little disappointment in her eyes before she blinked and righted herself.

"Right, okay. Um, you'll message me when you know the days to train?"

Nodding to her, she smiled, did a little wave, unlocking her door. Monroe still hadn't answered, so I banged a little louder. "Monroe, open up."

A few seconds later, the door opened, and a bedraggled Roe stood in the opening. "Wells." He crossed his arms but made no move to let me pass. Okay, so he was pissed, and I deserved it. I just worried I'd finally used up all my chances.

"What? That's all I get?"

"What do you want? I don't have time for this."

Leaning against the doorframe, I brought our faces impossibly close to answer him. "What do *I* want? Well, for starters, I want to fuck Kitten up against the wall while you watch. Then, I want to fuck you while you eat her out. Perhaps after that, a little sixty-nine, or double penetration. The sky's really the limit with how many things I want, Roe. But right now, I just want to talk. So, let me in."

He sucked in a breath, licking his lips, and I didn't miss how his eyes dilated, or his breathing quickened. Monroe hesitantly stepped back, finally allowing me entry. I didn't miss how he adjusted himself, either. A smirk curved up my lips, and I purposefully brushed against him as I walked by. His moan had my own cock hardening, and I debated pushing him up back against the wall. Who needed talking anyway?

My earlier resolution, the things I'd been fighting for

the past few months, and the promise I'd made to myself earlier were the only things that stopped me. He walked into the kitchen, putting some space between us, but I wouldn't let him off the hook that easily. Now that I'd allowed myself to feel the things I did for him, I wasn't hiding it or backing down.

Monroe busied himself at the sink, his back to me, and if I had to guess, he was using it to avoid me and taking time to collect himself. He turned around a minute later, setting the lone glass he'd been washing on the drying rack before looking at me. Leaning against the counter with his arms crossed, I took him in from head to toe. He looked thinner, and exhaustion plagued him, dark circles underlining his eyes. The place was spotless, and the lack of Levi's things was a sobering reality of how much of a bitch Brittni was.

"I'm sorry," I blurted, needing to get it out there. "I shouldn't have pushed you away. You've always been the best thing in my life, and I treated you like shit. You didn't deserve that."

He accepted my statement but didn't say anything else, and part of me was glad he hadn't made it easy on me. Approaching him, I bracketed my arms around him, closing him in on both sides. It seemed I wanted to torture myself tonight as I kept dangling the carrot in front of my face.

"No, I don't think you heard me, Monroe. *I'm sorry.* Truly sorry for everything. My whole life has been a shit show of disappointment. I've made bad choice after bad choice, and I never wanted to admit they were my own. I didn't steal the money like I was accused of, but I allowed myself to be put in that situation to take the fall. I was so caught up in giving a big middle finger to the world that I lost mine. I lost you and who I was."

"Wells, that's not—."

I stopped him, placing my finger over his lip. "Ssh, let me talk, Roe." I didn't miss the way his body shuddered at my touch or how I'd inched ever so microscopically closer, brushing our lower halves together.

"I did. I lost you and wasted so many years being angry at the world instead of who I should've been angry at, *myself.* I let fear control me, greed consume me, and failure ruin me. I don't deserve you. To be honest, I never have. But I want you, Roe. So damn much. I need you in my life for so many reasons. To remind me of the person I can be, the person you see me as. Please give me another chance to show you."

My walls were down, and it was the most vulnerable I'd been in my entire life, and maybe that was why it hurt the most when his eyes shut, a shudder wracking his entire body, and I knew I'd lost him.

"I *can't,* Wells. Not right now, anyway. Not with the case and Brittni. The judge, well, he mentioned you by name. I think he was part of the group that lost money, and it's like his personal vendetta to take me down to get at you."

My stomach soured at the realization my rottenness had spread to him. Maybe this was a bad idea? *He would be better off without me.* The familiar voice whispered to me my fears, the self-loathing loud and clear. I stepped back, giving myself some space to consider things. His clean cotton scent had permeated my brain, making it difficult to think straight.

I wanted to both rage at him, and to beg, but the memory of Loren on the floor with a sleeping Fort stopped me.

"Then I'll be the friend you've needed for years, the one you were to me. I'll be that person now for you, and I'll prove to you I'm trying, that I'm not going anywhere this time."

"I don't even know if that's a good idea. I want to, Wells, more than anything. But Levi…"

"I know. Levi's what matters, but don't lose yourself either. And you're not getting rid of me that easily. I'm going to become that fungus that seals itself to you."

He scrunched up his nose, and fuck, if it wasn't cute seeing Roe all confused. "Fungus? I don't think you want to be a fungus, Wells."

"Hmph," I shrugged. "Well, I never claimed I was good at Biology outside the human body."

"I believe that's called anatomy."

"You just proved my point."

Something about my statement had us both laughing, the tension easing, but I knew I had my work cut out for me to be worthy of two people.

Two people who needed me to show them I could be counted on. Two people who were the best in the world and deserved nothing less. Two people who had glued me back together again. Two people, I'd come to realize I would burn the world down for.

SIX

JUDE

Finding myself willingly at school at 2 am blew my mind. The fact I was laughing and having fun, even more so. I'd always liked school for the most part. Mainly because it was the safest place I had to go and get at least one meal. Kids picked on me at times, the poor foster kid was always an easy target, but I'd learned long ago how to make myself as inconspicuous as possible. Even when I didn't need to be invisible anymore, I still found myself falling back into the habit. At one time, it had been the only thing that had kept me safe, becoming a way of life.

My peers' laughter rose around me, all high on caffeine and sugar, and we took turns playing video games and board games. I hadn't been sure if I'd wanted to come when my new friend, Dean, had invited me. I'd never been asked to events before, so I wasn't sure if I wanted to trap myself in one single place all night with the kids I went to school with. Loren had talked me into it, and I was glad she had. It was the kind of teenage experience I should be having instead of being arrested.

I never thought one of the worst nights of my life would also lead me to the best.

Meeting Loren had changed my life in too many ways to count. For the first time, I felt like I had a family, someone who cared. She didn't like to think of herself like my mom, more of a big sister type role, but whatever you called her, she'd shown me what it felt like to be cared for by another person.

I've been introduced to so many new things already. Having my own room and bathroom was a big one. Buying clothes with the tags on them at full price, and that actually fit, another one. All the food I could ever want was available at all times, a million devices and streaming services, but most importantly, someone who cared where I was. It all made my list.

They were normal things other kids took for granted and yet, they'd been a culture shock for me. Some of it was still hard to accept, but each day, I trusted Loren when she said there weren't strings attached. Having routines and inside jokes filled me with more hope than I ever thought possible, and the only thing she wanted from me was honesty, which I could give to her.

Another huge opportunity I now had was being able to attend a school that valued the Arts. It required uniforms, had teachers who were passionate about teaching, and had donors for their funding. It was completely different than the public school #27 I'd attended prior that barely had 1-ply toilet paper.

As nice as everything was, I often felt like Dorothy, waking up in Oz. The feeling I'd wake up tomorrow, and it would all be a dream and taken away from me, still lingered, a fear I worried I'd never lose. My history had been so unstable, I didn't know if I could ever learn to trust it. Imogen disappearing had felt natural, par for the course. Anytime something good happened in my life, it had to be balanced with something terrible. It was how things in my life worked, though. Usually, I got a whole bunch of bad.

Meeting and connecting with Immy, a girl who laughed at my lame attempts at jokes, who was beautiful and kind, had been too much good in my basket, and the world made sure to even the score. The itchy feeling under my skin was starting to rise again, the fear that something else big was on the horizon, just waiting to kick me to the curb.

Loren was healed now, at least physically, and back to her regular routine, so it was bound to happen. My life had been consistent in one thing, and it was to expect the bad the moment when you got happy. I didn't want to be cynical for the rest of my life though, so in the spirit of believing in the good and Loren, I came to this lock-in. So far, it hadn't been a bad idea.

"Jude, do you have any sheep for wood?" Olivia asked, a twinkle in her eye.

"Oh um, no, I don't, sorry."

"Too bad. I was hoping to see your wood."

I blinked, not sure what she meant. The way she looked at me, and the other kids laughed, I had a feeling it was something sexual, but I was clearly missing it. I'd never played this game before, Settlers of Catan, so I hoped it was just something related to it.

"Sorry." I inwardly cringed, heat creeping up my

neck as the girls around the table giggled louder, and the guys laughed at my ignorance. Jonas leaned over toward me.

"Dude, she just said she wanted to see your one-eyed willy."

"One-eyed willy? Isn't that a character from Goonies?"

"Your dick, bro. She wants to see your dick."

Of course, Brad had to shout it across the table, everyone else in the vicinity turning to look and laugh. Olivia shrugged, not denying, and I found myself heating even more. I'd never had a girl flirt with me before, and her overt attempts made me feel uncomfortable. When you had to survive through each day just to have a place to stay and food to eat, it didn't leave much time for dating.

"If you want to sneak off to the janitor's closet, I'll cover for you, man," the ever so helpful Jonas whispered.

"Oh, um. Thanks, that's cool of you. But, um, I'm seeing someone."

I lied in my panic, hoping Immy wouldn't mind me using her as my fake girlfriend. It was doubtful I'd ever see her again as it was. He was about to ask another question when Dean walked up, interrupting him. I'd never been so happy to see him. Having friends was more challenging than it looked. Sharing things with others had me breaking out in hives, and I wondered if being sociable was all it was cracked up to be. Perhaps, I was more of an introvert than I'd realized. Hanging with Loren or Immy had been fine; *this* was a little much.

"Jude, man, there's someone asking for you at the front. I'll take over for you."

"Oh, uh, thanks, Dean."

Standing, I placed my cards down and smiled at the table. Olivia gave a little wave, her friends laughing at her bold behavior. Feeling out of my league, I waved back but quickly walked out the door. Once I was in the hallway, I realized how strange it was for someone to be asking for me. It could only mean a few things.

Trepidation filled me, and I wondered if my prophecy was happening now. Had I thought it into existence? Was the bad about to hit the fan?

When I turned the corner, surprise stopped me in my tracks. I hadn't guessed him at all.

"What are you doing here?" My voice rang out strong, an edge of steel threaded through I hadn't realized I possessed, and I wanted to congratulate myself on it.

The tattooed guy smiled at me, apparently finding my pissed-off stance funny. He looked the same as the last time I'd seen him. Black jeans ripped at the knee, a faded t-shirt, and a leather jacket. His hair was a little longer, his jaw lined with stubble, but it was his eyes I noticed the most significant difference in. He still smiled, the carefree guy on display, but his greyish eyes looked more haunted than before, the blue barely visible.

"You got spunk, kid. I like that about you," he acknowledged, grinning at me.

"Yeah, well. I can't say the same about you, I'm afraid, Nicco."

"That's fair. I owe you and Loren an apology at the

least, an explanation at the most. I can't get into that right now, but," he paused, exhaling. "I promise, I plan to make things right with her. Neither of you deserved what happened, but until I can actually tell you what occurred, I don't want to make things worse by making excuses."

"Then why are you here?"

"Immy."

I dropped my arms and rushed forward to him. "Is she okay?"

"She's… managing. She's not injured, but she's not fine either. She's pissed as hell at Atticus for keeping her from contacting you. It wasn't her choice, neither of us, but it's harder to explain how I wasn't able to reach out as an adult. But believe me when I say, Immy was innocent. She did everything in her power to communicate with you, even defying her brother to ask me."

Relief and a giddy exhilaration filled me at hearing his words. Everything with Immy had felt so magical, almost too easy, so it had to be too good to be true. In fact, I'd worried I'd imagined it all, and it had been one-sided. To hear she'd fought to get in touch, attempting different ways made my pulse race.

"Can I see her? Or talk to her?"

"Not yet, I'm afraid. But she sent me with something to give to you. I don't know what it says," he paused for a second before starting again. "There are things she shouldn't tell you to keep you safe, but I don't know how much she cares about following the rules at this point. So, I'd take anything you read with a grain of salt, and keep it to yourself."

"What's that supposed to mean?"

He scrubbed his hand over his face, and for once, I saw some real emotion. Exhaustion and perhaps frustration lined his movements. "Fuck, I'm making it worse. Listen, Jude, you're a smart kid. I'm sure you know about things that go on underneath most people's knowledge. This might be one of those situations where the information will self-destruct after you read it if you catch my drift."

"Um, not really, but I promise to not put it on blast to all of my three followers if that helps."

Nicco chuckled, "I see why Immy likes you. You're a funny kid." He pulled out an envelope from his back pocket, and I had to stop myself from reaching out and snatching it out of his hand. My fingers tapped against my leg as I waited for him to stretch it out to me. He stopped midway, keeping it just out of my reach. "How is she? *Loren*?"

I narrowed my eyes at him. "You mean after you left us for dead in a restaurant after a bomb went off? Or how she covered me with her body and suffered fractures, burns, and was in a coma for a week? Or how about when she woke up, it was to find the guy she was dating nowhere to be seen? If you want to know how she is, then find the courage and ask her yourself. I'm not going to be used for information or allow you to wuss out."

"She's lucky to have you, kid. You're right. I need to quit trying to take the easy way." Nicco handed me the letter but didn't let go, and I sighed, rolling my eyes up at him.

"What?"

"Remember, I'm letting you get away with talking to me that way. Lesser men have had their noses broken for less, their knees capped for more. Don't mistake my kindness toward you now for weakness. Immy is my little sister, and if you ever hurt her in any way, you'll have a whole bunch of scary-ass looking men and *me* to contend with. Enter into this knowing that. Do you understand?"

Swallowing, I nodded, and he finally let go of the envelope and headed back out of the entrance. I didn't want to think about how he found me, too excited to read her words. The envelope was a light pink, surprising me at the girliness of it. Looking around the hall, I didn't see anyone and found a spot to sit alone. I knew I wouldn't be able to wait, and there was no way I could do it in a room full of my peers.

Carefully, I lifted the flap and slid out the matching paper. A floral scent wafted out, and I inhaled it, shutting my eyes for a moment as Immy's presence invaded my senses. Letting out a breath, I opened them back up and unfolded the paper.

Dear Jude,

It's weird writing a letter. I can't even remember the last time I've written something longer than my signature, but here it goes.

I've been fighting with Attie, screaming at him to let me contact you, and yet now I sit here, I don't even know how to say it in a damn letter.

Mostly, I don't know how to start because how do I tell

*you what happened, or why I can't get in touch? The truth…
I can't. And I'm sorry for that. It's not fair.*

*What I can tell you… I miss you. Gah, I sound like such
a girl, but I do. I hope you miss me too.*

*I know it's weird. We'd only known each other for, what?
A few weeks? And yet, it feels so much longer. I kind of want
to slap myself for sounding so cliche, but I guess cliches are
what they are for a reason. When we met, I was finding who
I was again. Still am, if I'm honest. Some bad shit happened
to me, and I'm not done dealing with it. That's what I'm also
upset about.*

*Loren had been helping me, and then bam! I'm back to
being locked up in a fortress, a constant reminder of him. I
hate it here so much.*

*But you've also given me something to fight for. I wanted
to give up at first, fall back into the depressive black hole I'd
been in for months, shutting out everyone and everything.*

*But then I'd hear a song you sent me or a funny joke I'd
want to tell you, and I would be reminded it wasn't all bad.
Because what world could be evil when there was a Jude
Franklin out there? The kindest, most precious boy I'd ever
met. And I mean that in the best possible way.*

*I know you don't think much of yourself. I struggle with
this too. So maybe hearing it from a self-proclaimed loner
will have some merit.*

*Now that I got the gushy stuff out of the way, some
truth, or as much as I can (again, see above).*

*My family is complicated. There are so many secrets
entwined it would take a Ph.D. to unravel them all.*

What I can tell you is this:

I promise we will see each other again. I'll do everything in my power, at least. Granted, as a seventeen-year-old girl, that isn't much, but I won't always be seventeen.

I promise that when I can, I will tell you everything. But only when it's safe. I care about you and Loren. I'd never want to put you in danger; going out to eat with us already did enough.

And lastly, I promise to finish that conversation we started before everything blew up.

Until then, I hope you gave Nicco a hard time. Tell Loren I miss her and that Nicco had no choice. I promise he wasn't to blame. Even Attie isn't to blame, though I'm the maddest at him; he's only doing what he thinks is best. But Nicco, he's a good one. I hope she gives him a second chance. I'll admit though, it will be fun to watch him sweat.

I'll try again to reach out, if not in person.

Your friend,

Immy

SEVEN

LOREN

The air fryer beeped, and I hurried over, excited to see how the potatoes had turned out. I expected Monroe over any minute, and I wanted everything to be perfect. The air fryer was my favorite discovery so far, making cooking simpler for an amateur like me.

"That smells good," Jude mumbled, walking into the kitchen rubbing his eyes. He'd been sleeping most of the day since he got home from the lock-in.

"Let's hope it tastes good too."

He laughed, having tried many of my crazy concoctions over the past month as I tried to teach myself how to cook. Baking had been the first thing I'd succeeded at so far. Nat had recommended this recipe, though, and promised me it was both simple and tasty.

A knock at the door had me jumping as I tried to finish up the food. When the phone rang as well, I felt like a chicken with my head cut off as I rushed to shake the potatoes and answer both the door and phone. Jude laughed at my distress and I threw him an accusing stare which only made him laugh more.

"Uh, can you get one of them, please?"

He picked up my phone and made a face before setting it back down. "I'll grab the door."

Sighing, I knew that meant it could only be one person. My mother.

Jude slid off the stool, a banana in his hand as he went, and I chuckled at the sight. Once he'd gotten comfortable, I rarely saw him without food in his hands. It made me happy to learn these little quirks about him and be the one to offer him stability. I'd found it was the simple things he appreciated more than the fancy stuff anyway. Jude really was a special kid.

Setting down the potatoes, I answered the call, steeling myself to deal with whatever shit she was about to spew. Jacqueline had increased her invasion of my life since the 'incident' stating it was an obvious cry for help and my life was in a state of disrepair. She called and stopped by all the time now. To the outside world, it looked like she was a caring mother; to me, I knew what it was—a ploy.

I had a bad feeling she and Brian were up to something. I just hadn't figured out what yet. There was no reason for them to engage with one another otherwise. They'd never been that close to begin with.

"Hello, Jacqueline."

She huffed, not pleased with the way I now addressed her. "Seriously, Loren. I think you need to have your head examined again. You've clearly lost it."

"How can I help you, Mother?" I exhaled, trying not to let her ruin my date.

"I need you to—" she didn't get to finish as Monroe walked in.

"Wow, Lo, everything smells wonderful here."

Turning, I placed the pan in the sink as I smiled over at Monroe, trying to ignore the irate woman on the phone who had begun ranting the minute she heard him.

"Is that a man in your apartment, Loren? Who is that?" I rolled my eyes at her, Monroe laughing when he realized I was on the phone.

"Did you call for a reason, Jacqueline, or do you have a radar that tells you when to ruin fun things for me? Hmm?"

"Of all the things, Loren! I don't know why I bother. You're the most ungrateful child there ever was. And after all I did for you, the sacrifices I made—"

"Yes, yes, you were the perfect mother. Now, can we get to the reason you called so I can get back to my dinner?"

"I do not appreciate your tone, young lady!"

"Good thing you don't have to then. I'm 32, not much of a young lady anymore, Mom. So, get over it."

"Agh! And to think I called to see how you were and to invite you over for brunch!"

"I told you I was done with those. Until you accept the choices I'm making, I don't care to be berated by you over my eggs benedict. If there's nothing else... "

"Fine. Then I won't tell you about Brian."

Dropping my head back, I pulled the phone away from my ear. This was what she did. When she didn't get her way, she used manipulation and gaslighting. Jacqueline Hanover was a fucking pro at gaslighting. Once I was calm, I placed it back on my ear.

"For the last time, Mother, I have no interest in Brian

or what he is up to. He's my ex. Part of my past for a reason. If that's the only reason you called, then you clearly don't care about me. Please refrain from calling in the future. I'll see you next weekend at the wedding, only because I have to. And if you're rude to Jude for one second, then we're out of there and I'll let everyone know it was because of you."

Quietness greeted me, and I smiled smugly. "Bye, Mother."

"It's about Barkley."

I stopped mid-motion at her words, the one thing she could say that would have me pausing.

"Brian's willing to negotiate if you meet with him. Here, tomorrow for brunch. There, I shared the message. Please try to be more grateful in the future."

She hung up, and I stayed staring at the sink, shock coursing through my body. Of course, she had an ace up her sleeve. It was naive of me to assume otherwise.

"Everything okay, Lo?"

Monroe's voice broke through my shock and I gathered myself, forcing a familiar smile to my lips.

"Yep, just my mother being her usual nasty self." I fiddled with the dish and finished putting the potatoes together. My hands were shaking, but I ignored them. By the time I turned around, Monroe was staring at me, his brow furrowed.

"I'm good, I promise, and thanks for the compliment earlier. I've been trying to learn how to cook more. Jude's a good sport about taste testing things for me."

"I'm sure it'll taste wonderful."

Jude and I looked at one another, laughing as we both

cringed. "Yeah, no. Not necessarily. It's been very much a hit or miss, with definitely more misses. *But,*" I stressed, raising the food, "I think I'm finally getting the hang of it."

"You are getting better. Nothing's been inedible, just not always the best tasting."

"That's putting it nicely since you eat almost anything."

He shrugged, and Monroe laughed with us, looking between the two of us. "You two have gotten closer."

I know he hadn't meant anything by it, but it reminded Jude and me why it was the case, both of our expressions falling.

"Yeah, well." I shrugged, not wanting to think about it. Jude didn't hold his punches, though, and said it out loud.

"What Loren isn't saying is that, while I'm a lovable teen that she's been happy to spend time with," he preened, placing his hand on his chest before dropping it. His face turned serious as he addressed Monroe. "It wasn't by choice since all the guys in her life decided to flake on her when she needed them the most."

Part of me wanted to give him a look for talking impolitely to our company, the bigger part of me was proud of him for speaking up. He'd grown so much into himself, at least with me. "Jude." I shook my head, unable to say anything else because he wasn't wrong.

"No, he's right, Loren, and I'm sorry things turned out the way they did."

"It's okay, Monroe, I know. Levi's important."

"He is," he agreed, "the most."

I didn't miss the way his eyes glossed a little, and I knew he'd been missing not only Levi, but me as well. It hadn't been easy for him. Something about that knowledge had me softening even more.

"It doesn't mean you're not either, or that your feelings weren't hurt in the process. I know I need to make up for it even if you do understand." He'd moved closer, ending with his hands on my hips as he spoke, looking down at me. Monroe displayed remorse and the last shred of doubt I'd had left me.

"You're right. I am important," I smiled, "and I'm glad we're getting another chance." Leaning up on my toes, I kissed his lips softly, mindful of the teen still in the room, who decided to pipe up, reminding us as well.

"Kid in the room. I repeat, kid in the room."

I stepped back and looked at Jude, sticking out my tongue. "That was so PG. Even Disney has spicier kisses."

"Nope, don't want to hear it!" he laughed, covering his ears.

Rolling my eyes, I handed him the bowl of potatoes across the island to set on the table. He took them with no complaints, and I turned back to grab the chicken. Monroe smiled at me, the gesture sweet and crinkling the corners of his pale green eyes.

"What?"

"You're both cute together. I'm simultaneously beating myself up for missing it, jealous of what you two have built, and glad you had each other."

I didn't know what to say to that, so I dipped my head in acceptance before handing him the chicken and picked up the bread as we moved to the table. Quietly, I scooped out food and passed it off to them. I didn't know why I felt so awkward about what he'd said, but his honesty had affected me more than I'd been prepared to deal with.

"So, um, Jude, I didn't get to ask you about how the gaming night went. Did you have fun?"

He'd taken a bite, so he chewed, nodding, before glancing down at his plate, pushing his food around. "Yeah, it was fun. It was nice to go, so I'm glad you talked me into it." He paused, taking a breath before he looked up. "Something kind of happened, and I didn't know if I should say anything, but I don't want to keep things from you."

Placing my fork down, I brushed my hands on the napkin and nodded. "Okay, what is it?"

"Someone showed up asking for me."

Before he could finish, I cut him off. "Are you okay? Was it your brother?"

"No," he smiled before it dropped off. "It was, um, Nicco."

I gasped, my hand covering my mouth at the name. I hadn't expected him to say that name at all. So many thoughts rushed through my head, and I didn't want to admit it wasn't the angry ones. I'd been worried about him and Immy, my first thoughts about their wellbeing.

"Are they, are they okay?" The sound croaked out of me, my throat tight with emotion.

"Yeah, I think so. I was kind of a jerk to Nicco, giving him the cold shoulder for how he treated you. He'd been sent by Immy to give me, um, a letter."

"Oh?" I smiled, the cleverness of her to get her way. I was glad she'd seemed to be holding onto her strength, the months we'd missed not sending her backward.

"I didn't want to tell you this because I think Nicco should fight his own battles, but Immy pleaded for his case as well. She told me a lot without telling me a lot, and it sounds like they didn't have a choice. As much of a cop-out as that sounds, I think I believe him."

Nodding, I picked up my fork to return to my food, thinking about this new development.

"You're not mad?"

His question had me lifting my head, and I noticed the concern on his face. Shaking my head vehemently, I reached across and placed my hand on his, clutching it. "No, honey. I'm not mad. Thank you for telling me. I would've understood if you hadn't, but it does feel nice to know they're okay at least."

"Was he the one you were dating?" Monroe asked, shocking me. I turned at his question, having forgotten Monroe was there. Nodding, he prodded no further, and we all returned to our food. After a few minutes, Monroe spoke up again, this time making us all laugh.

"You know, this isn't half bad."

It was so out of the blue, we couldn't help but chuckle.

"Thank you. Yeah, I'm pretty impressed with myself as well."

Dinner conversation returned to safer topics after that, and soon, Jude excused himself to his room, offering Monroe and me some privacy. We were washing up the dishes and putting away the leftovers when he finally broke.

"So, Wells, huh?"

Chuckling, I turned to him. "I wondered how long it would take you to ask. He, um, kind of saved me last night from this guy who I think threatened me. Wells drove me out to his place, and I got to meet the dogs. He seemed… different."

"Someone threatened you?"

"Oh, yeah. The guy from the train, the night I picked Jude up. He was waiting outside the gym for me."

"Are you okay? That had to be terrifying."

"Yeah, it was. I'm okay now. Wells is going to teach me self-defense."

"You know, that's the second time you've called him that."

"Hmm?"

"*Wells*. Before, you always called him Surly."

"Huh, yeah, I guess I have been. I guess he finally earned it."

I smiled, the thought was a nice one to think. Things had improved between him and me. "So, did you two talk? Did he give you the answer you've been wanting?"

Monroe sighed, his face dropping. "He did actually, and I think for once, he meant it."

"Then why do you look like your daddy took your T-bird away?"

Monroe laughed at my joke before shaking his head. "Because I told him… no."

Shock covered me, and I wondered if I heard him

right. "But, why?" I sputtered. "I thought that's what you've been wanting."

"Yeah, I know. I woke up this morning wanting to punch myself, but I couldn't put myself through it right now. There's just too much at stake. I have to trust he'll still be there when I'm ready this time, like all the times I waited for him."

Nodding, I grabbed his hand, trying to comfort him. He returned it, and I figured it was the perfect time to dive into it all.

"Would you like some wine? We can sit on the couch and talk."

"Yeah, that sounds nice."

Pouring us both some, I handed him his glass, and we walked over to the couch, both getting comfortable. I watched as Monroe took a sip and then placed it on the coffee table.

"I don't know how much detail you're wanting or where to even start since it's all a jumbled mess in my head. But I can tell you what's going on now."

"Of course."

He rubbed the back of his head before turning toward me and lacing his fingers with my free one. "I'm working with another lawyer friend of mine to have the judge removed for conflict of interest, and I've also built my case against Brittni. I'm waiting to hear if I can get the hearing moved up. They'd set it out originally for six months, and I've been attempting to get it sooner, but I keep hitting red tape. I'm just hoping I'll hear something soon. I think I have enough info to at least convince someone I deserve partial custody. I don't know if I could take her rights away completely."

"That's a tough decision to make, and I'm hoping you do hear something soon. Is there anything I can do?"

"Just be you." He beamed before sighing again. "Nothing in this case has been handled correctly, so at the least, I should be able to get his ruling reversed. There's no way she'd be able to get anyone else to believe her. The hard part, though, is that the damage is already done. I've missed two months of Levi's life and been estranged from the people I care about, believing it was easier, or perhaps better, to push you away."

"All we can do is move forward, Monroe. Regrets have a tendency to weigh you down just as much as fear, if you're not careful."

"You know, I keep expecting you to be angrier at me."

Laughing, I took a sip of the wine before setting it next to his. "I was angry at first. But once I thought it through, I couldn't fault you. I just missed you a lot."

Monroe moved closer, sliding his hand into my hair as he brought our faces together. "I missed you so much, Loren. And I know I've already said this, but I am sorry."

"Then show me." It was a whispered plea, but he understood my meaning, sealing his lips to mine.

Monroe's fingers tangled more in my hair, pulling me toward him. His other hand slid up my leg, and I yearned to be closer. His kiss was both sweet and passionate, our tongues caressing one another in a tangle. My body begged to touch his, to rock against him, and I wanted to explore that.

A laugh down the hall reminded me we weren't alone, and I pulled back, our breathing heavy. Fluttering open my eyes, I took in his flushed cheeks and smiled, liking I affected him as much as he did me.

"May I make a suggestion?"

"Please, do," he hummed as he started kissing down my neck, and I knew I needed to stop this before it went too far.

"Perhaps it would be better if we relocated to either my bedroom or even your apartment?"

"I like the way you think. Come on."

He pulled my hand, dragging me down the hall, but I stopped him before we got to the door. "One second."

Jogging, I knocked on Jude's door and waited for him to call out before opening it. "Come in."

Inching it open, I stuck my head in, trying to find the words to not make this creepy. "Just wanted to let you know I'm going across the hall. Text me if you need anything, but I'm assuming you'll be fine."

"I don't want to know."

Rolling my eyes, I shut the door, trying not to laugh. There were moments where I felt like his mom, but most of the time, I found myself falling into the big sister role, our banter playful and fun, and I loved it. Walking back down the hall, I found Monroe leaning against the wall, his sexy confidence oozing out of him.

"God, you're gorgeous."

I stopped, his words were filled with so much emotion, they almost knocked me over. Monroe's eyes were full of fire, and when he reached out his hand for me, I found myself willingly accepting it.

Pulling me into his body, I melted into him, wrapping my arms around his neck as his hands drifted down to my ass, bringing me flush with his body, his hard cock nestled against me.

He started to bend down to kiss me again, but I stopped him. "If you're wanting to do the things to me I want to do to you, then I suggest we pause for three seconds to walk across the hall."

"I can make it in two."

He lifted me up, and I squealed, wrapping my legs around him as he bounded through the door, managing to shut mine and unlock his before I could blink.

My back landed against his door as it shut, his mouth back on mine. This kiss was frenzied, our passion rising to the surface. It felt so good to be kissed like a woman again, to feel desired and wanted by a man.

We started moving, and this time my back landed on something soft as he laid me down on the bed. Monroe traveled down my body, lifting my shirt as he did, placing kisses on my stomach. His fingers grazed my waistband, skirting against my skin, sending shivers over my body.

"Ahh," I moaned, the sensation making my skin sensitive.

He slowly lowered the zipper, pulling my jeans over my ass, and lifted me, dragging them off me. Monroe left my panties on, dropping kisses on my thighs. Everything was overwhelming, and I found myself unable to focus on anything but his mouth as he pleasured me.

"Lo, I've been dreaming about tasting you. I want you so bad, but I don't want to rush this. So many things in my life are up in the air, and you're the one thing keeping me grounded. When I take you, I want there to be no doubt between us. So for right now, let me do this."

Nodding, I had no words, needing him to do what he stated. The minute his fingers breached my silk panties, my body almost convulsed on the spot. His touch was confident as he moved his finger up and down between my folds, my wetness making it slick for him.

Monroe breathed over the silk, his hot breath hitting me right where I wanted his mouth to be. His finger left me, and I whimpered, missing it before realizing he was pulling my panties down and sealing his mouth over my clit. His fingers returned, pumping into me, and I unconsciously threaded my fingers through his hair, holding him to me.

He moaned, liking the touch, and I pulled him tighter, rubbing myself on his face. Monroe added a finger, scissoring into me now, and I lost track of all the tingles coursing through me. Throwing my head back, it flitted from side to side. My moans echoed out around us, and I was glad I didn't have to censor myself or worry about being overheard. Within what felt like seconds, I was coming hard around him as he pumped three fingers into me, sucking my clit in quick succession.

"Fuck, oh God. Yes, yes, yes."

My legs tightened as I held him to me, my cry strangled as I had the best orgasm in months, my legs shaking. Monroe eventually lifted his head, my fingers loosening from his hair, and I watched as he grinned in complete satisfaction with himself.

"You taste better than I could've imagined, Lo."

Releasing him completely, I fell back to the bed, my lower half officially jelly. "Uh-huh."

He chuckled, sliding up to me, turning my face to his. "That's just the beginning, Lo. There's so much more I want to do."

Kissing him, I found myself lifting my leg over his hip, his hands sliding down my bare ass and pulling me into him. Monroe's kisses were a currency I could never have enough of, his passion making me insatiable for him. We made out like two teenagers home alone for hours, and when I walked across the hall later, I found my heart skipping at what might come, ignoring the sense of dread that had started to build since my phone call.

Eight

LOREN

Waking up this morning, I felt like I'd gone backward in time. It felt too similar to the beginning of the year when I *had* to attend brunch with my parents, where even the thought of a shower exhausted me. My depression had improved since then, I definitely had more positive days than sad ones, but it was still there, simmering under the surface, waiting for the perfect culmination of things to strike me down. The ugliness inside me was a living, breathing monster. Thinking of it any other way only minimized the destruction it could cause.

And it would destroy me if I let it.

I'd ignored it for too long, thinking it would go away or fix itself. I knew better, but the mere thought of putting on socks some days was too much. Now, anytime someone made a derogatory comment about depressed people, I wanted to slap them. Depression wasn't something you could fix by "getting over it." I wish there was a depression-suit people could wear for a day to know what it felt like. They made fake pregnant bellies; surely they could do this as well. If people understood it, maybe they would be kinder.

Who was I kidding? People were shit most of the time, even when they did know.

Okay, wow. Dark thoughts there, Lor. The effect my mother and Brian could have on my mood was startling, their energy sucking the life force from me. It made me realize how long I'd silently suffered under their oppression.

Heaving myself out of bed, I stumbled into the bathroom, all the positive endorphins from last night's orgasm having left me. Shuffling into the kitchen, I started the coffee since I forgot to prepare it last night and then headed to the shower. Jude's door was still closed, so I tiptoed past, not wanting to wake him. The kid finally got to be a teen, and I wanted to let him enjoy it and let him sleep in as much as possible.

Once I showered and dressed, I grabbed my coffee and checked my phone. I was trying to be better about it. I had to be with Jude in my life. It looked like I'd missed a few messages already based on the number of notifications I already had. Taking a big gulp of the hot liquid, I opened my messages.

Monroe: I just wanted you to know how amazing tonight was, and I can't wait to have more. Thank you for giving me a chance and not hating me for having to step back.

Ah, okay, that wasn't too bad. I'd text him back later

or stop by after my punishment brunch. On to the next one.

Mr. Surly: If Tuesday still works, we can start this week. Just let me know soon. I can't wait around forever.
Mr. Surly: Sorry, I don't mean to sound like a dick.
Mr. Surly: But let me know today.
Mr. Surly: Please. Kitten.

The usual anger I felt when I texted him was missing, and instead, I felt the flirty banter that had been underneath the surface of our barbs. I decided to text him now since one had come in about twenty minutes ago.

ME: That could work. Just depends on if you're gonna bring your A-game.

Okay, I flirted. Go, me! The dots started to dance, and I held my breath, the adrenaline of it all exciting me as I perched on the stool; my coffee neglected.

Mr. Surly: Oh, Kitten, you're the one who will be graded. Let's just hope you can break a hold better than you can kick, or the only A will be your bra size.
Mr. Surly: Shit. Sorry. I didn't mean that.
Mr. Surly: Your tits are great, by the way. Come on, Kitten, don't leave me hanging here. I'm still

trying to figure out this whole not-hating-you thing.

Mr. Surly: Your ass is A+ too

ME: Oh? Are we grading body parts now? For your information, my bra size is a C, and if you're not careful, you may never *see* them.

ME: Burn

ME: Jude taught me that one

Mr. Surly: I don't think you're supposed to announce where you learned things, Kitten. It takes away the effect. At least I have the knowledge that you're just as bad at texting as me. It's comforting since you're pretty amazing at everything else.

ME: Wow, I think that's the first genuine compliment you've given me.

Mr. Surly: I'm pretty shocked myself, but it goes to show you I'm not always an ass.

ME: Which you have a great one of.

ME: Wow, I can't believe I put that.

Mr. Surly: Now, who's objectifying who?

Mr. Surly: I'm glad you noticed. I work hard for these buns of steel.

ME: Well, this diverged quickly. Not that I think there's a time period for sexting, but 7 am is probably not the best.

Mr. Surly: Are you offering, Kitten? And this wasn't sexting. If we were sexting, you'd know it.

ME: I feel like whatever answer I give, will only get me in more trouble here.

Mr. Surly: I kind of like when you're in trouble.

ME: Yeah, I'm going to stop replying now.
Mr. Surly: Are you scared, Kitten?
ME: NO!
Mr. Surly: That's a pretty bold standpoint, then.
I'll leave you with this… I enjoyed our banter and
look forward to more. Have a great Sunday,
Loren.
ME: Thank you, Wells. You too.
ME: I enjoyed it too.

I couldn't help the grin on my face, and I sat my phone down for a second to take another sip. I didn't want to admit Wells had just lifted my mood. I never would've believed it a few months ago. Gearing up for the last message, I opened it, preparing myself.

Brian: Loren, I thought there was more time. I'm sorry.
Brian: If you want to say goodbye, you have thirty minutes to get here *Pic attached*

Dropping my phone, I gasped, standing up from the chair. "No, no, no." Frantically, I began rushing around the condo, looking for my shoes, bag, and keys. Once I had them all, I scrambled out of the door, barely remembering to lock it before I ran down the hallway, punching the elevator button. Thankfully, it opened, and I rushed in, hitting the ground floor agitated. I kept tapping the close door button, eager to get going. The elevator felt like it took forever to go down, stopping on multiple floors, and I regretted not taking the stairs. By the time I exited, I was flying out the door, ignoring the protest of the people behind me.

I took off looking for a taxi and jumped in the first one I found. I didn't think I could drive in this state, and I hadn't had the time to call Nat. A taxi was my best option.

"Glenview. Step on it."

The cab driver glanced in the rearview mirror, taking in my nervous state. "Yeah, sorry. It doesn't really work like that in real life, ma'am. If I speed, I'll get a ticket and lose my taxi license. I'll get you to Glenview as fast as *safely* possible."

He merged into traffic, and I looked out the window, my leg tapping a mile a minute as he began the drive. I went to reach for my phone to check the time when I realized I'd left it on the counter, dropping it in my haste.

"Fuck!"

"Everything okay, ma'am?"

"Yes, it's fine. I just need to get to Glenview, like twenty minutes ago."

"I'm trying, ma'am."

By the third time he'd called me that, my neck tightened, and my jaw twitched. It wasn't as bad as when younger girls called me ma'am, but it wasn't sitting with me today to hear it. I breathed through my nose, attempting to calm myself before I blew a gasket in the back of this cab. It wasn't his fault my ex was an asshole.

Thirty minutes later, we finally pulled up to my parents' house, and I threw some cash through the window, not caring if it was too much. I just needed to get inside the damn house. Running up the steps, I knocked on the door with urgency. My mom opened it a few minutes later, sniffling and wiping a tear from her eye. At the rate she was opening doors lately, I was beginning to worry they had to let some of their staff go. Jacqueline didn't open doors, and yet both times I'd been here recently, she had.

Either they were in money trouble, or she'd been waiting for me, and this whole tearful act was just that, an act. I didn't know which scenario I preferred.

"Mom, tell me he's still here. Where's Barkley?"

"Oh, Loren. You just missed him. We tried calling you, dear. You really should answer your phone more."

"No, that can't be right! I made it in time! Why wouldn't he wait? This wasn't about him! What even happened?"

"Loren! Stop shouting on the stoop and come in for some breakfast. You're embarrassing me!"

Ice water ran through my veins, the grief turning to ice-cold fury as I took in my mother. "No, Mother, I don't think I will. You clearly think so little of me that you wouldn't even wait five minutes for me to get here. I'm so sick of playing your games. I don't know what's going on here, but I'm done. If I could divorce you as my mother, I would."

Turning on my heels, I started walking down the driveway, her shouts at me to turn around disappearing in the wind. I didn't care that I didn't have a phone or that the odds of finding a taxi in the burbs were low. All I cared about was getting the fuck away from that toxic hellhole. It was so clear now how much of a setup this had been. I didn't know for certain it was true, or only a ploy to get me here for whatever convoluted reason she'd schemed with my ex.

It was official, they were in cahoots together. Whether it had always been that way, and they'd acted like acquaintances while we'd been married, or only since she ambushed me, I didn't know yet.

But I *would* find out.

Jacqueline Hanover had just made an enemy out of me.

My whole life, I'd been taught to do the right thing, and good things would come. If I hadn't learned that lie was a crock of shit years ago, today would've cemented it firmly. I was sick and tired of people taking from me. My choices, my dreams, my hopes, my life, my marriage, my child, and my future… and now *this*.

No. It didn't get to end this way. Not this time. I would find out the truth one way or the other and deal with it then. But I no longer accepted the lies they spewed as facts. If the shit I'd been through had taught me anything, it was that I could survive this.

I'd probably walked twenty minutes before I realized I was getting close to the small shopping area. I could probably find a phone there. Picking up my speed, I nearly jumped out of my skin when a horn sounded behind me, honking loudly. Fucking hell!

Gasping, I clutched my chest and turned around to see who would get my wrath next. Instead, I sank in relief at the welcome sight of who it was behind the wheel.

"Loren? What are you doing on this side of town? And *walking*?"

"It's a long story. Care to give me a ride back into the city?"

"Of course, hun. Hop in. I was headed to the center, anyway."

"Thanks, Mitzi. You're a lifesaver."

Quickly, I made my way around the car and hopped in, buckling up. We rode in silence for a few minutes before she caved and asked me what was going on.

"Feel like telling me part of that long story?"

Blowing out a breath, I turned to her. "Do you know a private investigator?"

"Okay, well, I didn't expect that to come out of your mouth. I can ask around. What's it about?"

"I need proof that my ex-husband and Mother are in cahoots to destroy me."

She laughed but then stopped, turning her head to look at me when I didn't laugh with her. "You're serious? Loren, did you take on too much too fast?"

"I'm serious, Mitzi. It all makes sense now. Right before my accident, my mother invited me over only to ambush me with Brian and his fianceé. Then, I woke up at the hospital to find them both there. Today, they sent me cryptic messages to lure me out here, only to then tell me I'm too late. Something is going on, and I don't trust either of them."

"What did they lure you out here with?"

Sucking in a breath, I prepared myself to say it. "Brian texted me that Barkley had been diagnosed with some rare disease and only had a week to live. Then this morning, he said it came sooner than they'd thought, and so he'd asked the vet to come over and take care of things. I would only have thirty minutes to get to my mother's house if I wanted to say goodbye. Yet, when I get there, they're both already gone. So, either he's an asshole, who is using my love for my dog as emotional manipulation and leverage, or he's a psychopath who killed my dog for funsies. Or worse, he lied about killing my dog. Considering there weren't any remains that I could tell, I think he's hiding her from me but wanting me to think she's dead."

"Are you sure that's just not the grief talking? Denial is the first step, dear."

I gritted my teeth. I *fucking knew* denial was the first step in the grieving process! Of course, I knew. It didn't mean just because I didn't believe *them* that I was in denial. Everything made logical sense in my head. It didn't need to make sense to her to be true. No one outside of the relationships I had with them would understand anyway. They were both accomplished narcissists. They had perfected their perceived image so well, no one would question it. Only I could see through them now. The fact that even Mitzi believed them over me told me everything. No one on this side of society would ever think differently of them. The rich did stick together, after all.

"It's not denial, Mitzi. I *promise*."

"Okay, I believe you, dear. I can get you a name if that's the route you want to take. I know someone who's used one, so I'll reach out."

"Thank you. I just want to find the truth."

She relented, but I could tell she didn't think it was a smart move. It didn't matter. I was going to do this.

She dropped me off at my condo building a few minutes later, and I had a renewed sense of strength in my stride. I stood up to my mother, cut ties with the toxicity, and had a plan to find out what they were hiding. I was done listening to their lies, accepting them as truth just because they said so. One way or another, I would get my proof and know without a shadow of a doubt.

I owed Barkley that much.

She'd saved me when I'd been at my lowest. Now it was my turn to save her, or at least give her a proper burial. I'd fight Brian on it again if I had to.

NINE

LOREN

Nat, Stacy, and Cami had all ganged up on me and decided they needed to take me to the other side of Illusion, Verity. I'd been a bit of a grouch and anxious all week as I waited to hear back from the PI Mitzi had sent me. I finally had an appointment with him, so that boosted my morale. I'd hoped to take out my frustration with kickboxing, but Wells had texted he needed to push it off for a few days as his employer was still getting things settled. I'd been more disappointed than I would've been a few months prior, and I couldn't decide if that was terrifying or growth.

My mother's calls were sent to voicemail and then promptly deleted. I'd even blocked Brian's number. If they couldn't get into my head, then I'd be one step closer to figuring out the twisted game they were playing. My dad had called once and I'd answered, and then he traitorously gave the phone to my mother, so now he was also on the 'do not answer' shit list. Boundaries were a beautiful thing.

"Come on, slowpoke!"

Cami pulled my hand, leading me into the club, and I

wondered how I let them talk me into this. The fact Cami's and Nat's faces were full of mischief scared me. Stacy hadn't been here either, but Cami had whispered in her ear after they'd decided to go, giving her a clue to what it held.

Me, not so much. *Traitors.*

"It's going to be fine, Lor! You'll love it and it will be awesome! We wouldn't take you somewhere that wasn't."

Cami had a point, but the secretive looks told me there was something they were worried about. They'd dressed me in a silky number that resembled more of a negligee than an actual dress, but with the stilettos and lingerie I had on underneath, I felt confident in it.

We came to the crosspoint, the beautiful woman standing between the two doors smiling at us. However, what shocked me was when Cami walked up to her and gave her a scorching kiss. When she pulled back, she turned to me smiling, holding out a hand for me to draw closer.

"Loren, this is my girlfriend, Lark."

"Oh my goodness," I gushed, rushing forward and wrapping my arms around her. "It's so nice to meet you." Lark hugged me back, laughing at my exuberance. It kind of shocked me as well, but I went with it.

"It's nice to meet you, Loren. I'm so happy Cams made a new friend. She talks about you all the time. I can see she's been at work dressing you too?" She lifted her eyebrow at Cami, the seductive glint unmistakable now I was closer.

"What? Lor's got a great body, and with those long

legs of hers, she can wear almost anything. She's like a life-sized doll. It'd be a crime not to."

"And I need all the help! Cami has been a Godsend. I would've been so lost on my date with…." I trailed off, clearing my throat as I realized I almost said his name. The girls looked at one another, awkwardness entering. "Well, yeah. It's so nice to meet you, Lark. And by the way, you smell amazing, like I want to rub up against you just so I can take it with me."

Thankfully, my obscure comment had everyone laughing, the awkward moment forgotten. *Like you*, the voice whispered in my head, reminding me how replaceable I was to the men in my life.

I wanted to berate it to go back to where it belonged, but ever since Jude had told me Nicco approached him, I'd secretly been looking for him everywhere, hoping he'd seek me out. It had been a week, and he still hadn't. I was beginning to realize that perhaps I hadn't meant as much as I'd assumed.

Melancholy washed over me, and I was surprised when Lark led the others over to a separate locker room. Stacy tugged my hand, pulling me out of my forlorn stupor. I pretended I knew what was happening since I'd zoned out, but when they started to undress, I couldn't stop the question from leaving my mouth.

"What the Hell?" Unfortunately, it only caused them to laugh and not answer me.

"Told you she wasn't paying attention."

Lark walked over, grasping my hands as she looked into my eyes. "Verity is all about seeing the truth, no shields. Where in Illusion your identity is hidden, offering you anonymity, in Verity, you shed the outward things that hold you back."

Peeking over her shoulder, I started to realize what she meant. All three girls stood in nothing but their high heels and lingerie, and they were smoking hot. Cami was all confidence as she sauntered over, hips swaying, and her red hair in waves around her. It accentuated her black lace bra with a low demi cut, and her panties were more of the hip hugger type and made entirely of lace, making them practically see-through. She looked terrific, and I found myself licking my lips. She was enough to make any woman question their sexual preference.

"She's smoking, isn't she?" Lark whispered, and I immediately felt terrible for ogling her girlfriend. When she saw my look, she shook her head, smiling at me. "Don't feel bad. I know how you feel. It's hard to resist her when she turns her full Cami charm on you." Lark licked her own lips, almost looking like she wanted to pounce on her girlfriend as she neared. She turned her back, taking the temptation out of our line of sight, and finished telling me what I'd missed.

"There are different rooms with varying degrees of 'truths' you can explore. Just remember that everyone is on their own journey to the truth, and it looks different for each of us. Some need to find out who they are, others, to explore a side of themselves they repress in the outside world, and some even to fall into the role they don't normally get to be. It's a safe place to do it. There are only two things to remember in Verity. Are you ready for them?"

I nodded, biting my lip as I waited to hear what I was about to enter, fear gnawing at my stomach.

"First, enter with an open mind and willingness in order for Verity's power to work and set free the part of you that's buried or chained down. And second," she leaned forward, whispering, "is the word bananas."

She pulled back, a twinkle in her eye as I considered her words. "Bananas?"

"Yep," she winked before walking over to the other three girls and whispering something in their ears as well. I watched as she skated her hands over Cami's body, nibbling her ear as she did, and damn if that wasn't hot. I found myself getting aroused from their show alone.

Nat's hip bumped mine, her purple lingerie standing out against her olive skin and brown wavy hair. "You don't hate us?"

Shaking my head, I wrapped my arm around her waist. "No, of course not. I get why you kept it a secret, but you could've told me. I wouldn't have thought anything different about you."

"We were more worried you would've chickened out. Sorry," she cringed, squishing up her nose.

Chuckling, I shook my head again. "No apologies needed. I get it. And I'd like to say I wouldn't have, but you were probably right, even if I don't want to admit that about myself. I'm feeling a little anxious, slightly turned on by Cami and Lark," I laughed, "but overall excited, I think." I shrugged one shoulder before looking at her.

"Cami strikes again," Nat giggled, and I couldn't

help but join in. Stacy walked over to us, raising her eyebrows at our behavior. She looked amazing as well in a white bra and panty set, making her look innocent despite the barely-there material. Her short hair looked sleek and stylish, a look I'd never be able to pull off, and she made it look flawless.

Looking down at my own red set of lingerie with the garter belt and thigh highs, I now realized why they'd been so insistent I go all out. "Well, at least you girls made me look hot."

Chuckling, we started to head toward the door when Cami had finally disengaged from her kiss. She looped her arm through mine and pulled me with her. She sighed a moment later, resting her head on my shoulder as we walked.

"She's just so fucking perfect."

"Lark seems pretty great. I have to admit, watching you two together definitely turned me on."

My face heated, but I wasn't embarrassed, really. Cami smiled up at me, a twinkle in her eye. "Girl, I'm gonna get you to kiss me someday, and then you won't know what hit you!"

Nat groaned in front of us, tossing over her shoulder, "Not again, Cams. You're not the Godfather of kisses."

We all laughed as we finally walked through the doors, and immediately I could tell the difference from Illusion.

"Whoa."

The place was dark, little lights twinkled throughout in various places, and a different feeling of seduction could be felt in the area. There were soft couches in quiet corners as men and women sipped cocktails, lounging in barely-there clothing, and well for some, it wasn't there at all.

Leaning closer to Nat, I whispered, "Um, I think I can see that man's penis!"

Nat giggled, shaking her head as she pulled me over. Her eyes were fixed on a beautiful man working the bar area. When he saw her approaching, he smiled wide, and I noticed how his eyes zeroed in on her. He was tall, like very, very tall, and his dark skin shimmered under the soft lights. His head was shaved, his eyes dark but open and friendly. He had a gorgeous smile that seemed to make Nat go weak at the knees as she leaned into me.

"Isn't he gorgeous?"

"He's very attractive. I take it, you know him?"

"Mmm hmm. That's Byron, my fuck buddy."

"Girl, now who's lying to themselves? You're both looking at each other like you hung the moon. There's more than *fucking* there."

Her face shut down a little, and I regretted calling her out, but she shook her head, her smile returning. "Nah, it's just lust. He's the perfect type of guy to have for the physical stuff. He's hot, his dick is huge, and he knows how to work it. What more could I need?"

"I don't know, comfort? Companionship? Intimacy?"

"Ew, gross. No, I'm telling you, dick a la carte is the way to go."

The therapist part of me could hear the lie and wanted to explore it, help her see what she was fearful of, but the friend part of me knew it wasn't my place to dig through her subconscious. Especially when we were out on a girl's night in our bras and panties. Nah, that was a conversation that required more clothing and preferably some type of pastry. Hard things always sounded better with baked goods!

Dropping it, I let her keep her delusion, knowing she'd been hurt by Mason the creep and didn't seem ready to peel that bandage off yet. Squeezing her arm, I kept it light and fun, knowing that was what she needed right then. "Well, introduce me to your favorite snack."

Nat looked at me, a laugh escaping her. "That's pretty good, Lor. We'll have you speaking the lingo in no time."

She pulled me the rest of the way, and the gorgeous man leaned down, drinking her in. He glanced at me, holding out his hand. "Ah, you must be Loren?"

"Oh wow, that's some voice you have there!" I fanned myself before remembering his hand and quickly placed mine in his. He chuckled, and it was almost just as sexy as his voice. Byron squeezed my hand softly and winked when he let go. Shit, he had one of those deep, velvety smooth voices that rolled through you like butter. I couldn't even stop the full body shudder that rolled through me. It was demanded, and well, he deserved the accolades.

"Byron's a voice actor and does this in-between gigs."

"Whoa, that's cool, and I can totally see why. I'd buy anything you sold."

He winked before returning to his role for the evening. "What can I get you ladies started with?"

Nat leaned against the bar, her cleavage even more pronounced with the move and licked her lips sugges-tively. "She'll have the special, and I'll have *you*."

Damn, Nat was bold. I kind of envied her ability to just lay it out there like that. Byron flicked his gaze to me first and then back to Nat. "One special coming up." He walked off, and that was when I could see what he wore, or barely wore as it was. He had a little bow tie around his thick neck, shirtless, and a tiny g-string banana hammock. Or maybe his anaconda was so massive it made it look tiny. His ass cheeks flexed as he moved, and when he turned back around, I wondered how in the Hell Nat could walk after riding that beast.

"You weren't lying. I think that's the biggest dick I've ever seen. I'm impressed, girl, like whoa," I whispered to Nat.

She winked before getting serious. "You'll be okay if I go have some fun? Cami and Stacy are right over there." She motioned behind me, and I turned and looked. They were at a table, two guys chatting them up as they drank.

"Yeah, I'll be fine."

"Okay, thanks, babe. Explore some of the rooms, and if you decide to go home with someone, just text one of us, so we know, okay?"

Scoffing, I rolled my eyes, nodding. "I'm not going to go home with anyone, but yes, Mom. I will. The same goes for you, missy."

"Ah, Lor, you're so cute when you try to be bossy."

I didn't get a chance to answer as Byron sat my drink down in front of me and nodded to Nat. No words were exchanged as they walked off, heading to a room around the corner. It made me think about what it must be like to work in a place like this.

Grabbing my drink, I decided to explore the area, my

curiosity getting the best of me and not feeling like being the odd woman out with Stacy and Cam. It was strange to see everyone dressed in provocative clothing, or some not dressed at all, and yet, no sexual behavior was occurring. If you put everyone in clothes, it would seem like a typical bar. Music played, and conversations took place all around me. Everyone was just in their underwear. It was an odd sight, but I started to understand the concept of Verity. If your body was open, with no barriers, then perhaps it made it easier to drop other walls as well.

If you couldn't hide behind your clothes, who were you underneath them?

As I approached the first door, I found a word on it, *Reality,* and a window to the left. There was a bench below it, and some people stood around watching whatever was inside. Walking closer, I peeked inside and was surprised by what I found.

Men and women wore VR Headsets as they mingled. There was a large screen on the opposing wall where you could see I assumed what their headsets were projecting. Everyone was a different character on the screen to who they were standing in the room. One woman looked to be a 10ft green lizard woman, and another man was a blue alien with two penises and a tail. One of the guests noticed me watching, a curious look on my face, and took mercy on my cluelessness.

"Tonight it's a virtual reality room where people can explore being any type of person, creature, or imaginary being they want. Sometimes we feel stronger or sexier being an alien, or want to explore what that would be like. This way, you can meet others who might feel the same way. Essentially, it's a role-play room, and each night has a different theme."

"Huh, that's kind of interesting," I mused, the thought of being someone else kind of appealing.

"First time?"

"Yeah, is it obvious?" I cringed.

"A little," he laughed. "But it's not a bad thing. You should walk around and check out all the rooms. Find one that fits you."

Nodding, I finally took my eyes away from the screen to look at him. "Thanks." He was a gorgeous man, but nothing sparked to life as I took him in and found myself blushing when I realized he was very naked and very hard.

People were naked, Lor! Get over it! Don't be a prude!

"I'm going to go explore. Thanks again for the explanation."

"Sure, no problem," he winked, slowly scanning my body with his eyes. His slow perusal didn't turn me on like any of the men I'd recently found myself obsessing over, but it did fill me with confidence, and I found myself striding away with a bit of a sway to my hips.

The next room I found had the word *Captivate* on the door. There was another window to the side, but this one didn't have many people watching. When I peered in, I had to blink to make sure I saw things correctly. I guess the name on the door was right because it definitely captivated my attention.

If I had to guess, this was a room for exploring curiosities or fetishes. The couples currently in there had an assortment of toys and items scattered on tables, chairs, and lounges that they were using. I watched, fascinated as one woman had on a strap-on dildo and used it on a male lover. The power and dominance she had with each thrust were unique to watch. I never thought I'd be so enraptured by watching people have sex in front of me, I hadn't even really seen pornography, but it reminded me of my time watching the couple on the dance floor, the naughtiness and explicitness calling to that darkness in me.

I blinked, pulling myself back from falling into the scene, and moved over to the next room. This one didn't have a window, drawing my curiosity even more. Instead, this one had a guard standing outside the door. He seemed out of place among all the people due to being fully clothed. He caught me staring and took it as a question.

"It's open if you wish to enter."

I started to open my mouth to say no when I found myself nodding. "Sure."

He pulled open the door, and I sat my untouched drink on the ledge before I entered, finding myself alone in a smaller room than the others. I guessed when he said it was open; he'd meant literally. There was a comfortable couch, bed, and lounge, so I sat down, wondering what this room was all about.

The minute I sat down, the lights went out, and a small gasp left me as the room lit with tiny bulbs built into the walls, ceiling, and floor. They dimmed on and off, casting a soft glow around me. Soft music began to play, and a voice that rivaled Byron's spoke.

"Welcome to *Sensation*. In this space, you can explore the truth of who you are when the world's trappings fall away. Your senses will be taken on a journey as you learn to use them anew. Sit back, relax, and allow yourself to fall into the moment of sensations."

The music grew louder, and I decided to stay and see what it was all about. I was the only one in the room, too, so there wasn't the added embarrassment of people watching me. Settling back on the couch, I was shocked when a different voice came over the system. Goosebumps erupted on my skin, and I found my breath hitching at the sound.

"Are you ready to delight your senses, *Spitfire*? Can you handle the truth?"

TEN

I was breaking all the rules.

But the moment I saw her enter, I'd been unconsciously waiting for my chance to intervene, even if I didn't want to admit it.

We'd been back in the city for a week, but Atticus was still operating on a lockdown mentality, whether *he* would acknowledge it or not. Immy being in danger so soon after the last incident had been too much for him, and he'd fallen into complete protection mode. So, even though we were back in the city, Immy hadn't been allowed out yet or given her phone. But Atticus looked to be caving any day now. I was proud of the little dynamo Immy was becoming.

Since we'd been out of the loop for two months, I'd made it my duty to check into all our businesses this week to see how things had fared in our absence. I trusted most of our people, but I wasn't as convinced the mole situation had been eradicated. Tonight, I'd found myself at Climax, and the reminder of Loren was too powerful in Illusion, so I'd chosen to hang out at Verity instead. Looked like my attempts to avoid thinking about her were thwarted, though.

I'd been doing my rounds when I spotted them, and my breath caught at seeing Loren. She looked better than I remembered, her attire revealing so much of her to me. I had to restrain myself from running up to her right then. I never expected to encounter her here, so the sudden intrusion left me off-kilter. It was good to see her, though. The anticipation and happiness rose up in me until I remembered why I hadn't sought her out yet.

She'd gotten hurt because of us, almost *died* even.

When I heard the report of her injuries, I wanted to go on a rampage, killing anyone in my way. Only Atticus had been able to get through to me and calm my anger down. That was when the guilt seeped in. It was like failing Jaz and Immy all over again.

Except, this time, I could do something about it. I could leave her alone.

I was so angry at first, battling with my desires, but once I'd realized the best course of action, I'd been able to commit. Nicco and I didn't speak of her to one another, nor did Atticus. We all pretended she was safe, happy, and living her life away from the criminal underground.

But like an addict, I checked in with the detail I'd placed on her every night. They were keeping a watch from a distance, giving me updates on her safety. Every night I lived and breathed those few moments where I got to know how she was. I knew she hadn't been seeing anyone, and I hated how pleased that made me. It was worrisome to think she might be alone, but I didn't hate it either.

Mostly, I worried whether she would forget about me.

We'd shared a moment, and as dangerous as it was, *I wanted her*. I was lying to myself if I believed otherwise.

Seeing her so free tonight was too much temptation for me to resist, so I'd hidden away in the security booth watching over her on the camera, hoping to reduce the need coursing through me to grab her up and fuck her against the wall. I was failing my job on all fronts. I wasn't paying attention to anything else in the club, and hell, I'd failed by not anticipating she'd show up here in the first place. Had I been out of it so long that I couldn't anticipate the dangers any longer? Or, perhaps I was more affected by her than I wanted to admit.

When she stepped into the private sensation room, the opportunity before me was too perfect to waste, and I let myself zoom into her room, all the other cameras no longer my focus. Here I could have her in a safe and controlled setting and watch. Here, I wouldn't be tempted to ask for more. Here, I wouldn't fall under her spell by touching her.

It was all I could have. But I wanted so much more.

I watched her settle into the couch and noticed every movement she made. The voice started telling her what the room was all about, and I snapped. No! He didn't get to touch her with his voice, getting off on the sounds she was sure to make.

Stepping out of the booth, I knocked on the door for

the Sensation room but didn't wait for them before I stepped in. The man looked up, surprised at my interruption. I could already see his delight at having Loren on the other side of the screen, and possessiveness I've never felt before surged through me.

"Break."

"But it's not—"

"Did I stutter, asshat? Break. In fact, you have the rest of the night off."

He looked stunned but stood and walked out immediately, not wanting to test my ire anymore. Smart choice. Not all the employees knew who we were, but I was sure there were rumors, and my reputation always preceded me. I was glad for it if it got me to my spitfire.

Sitting down, I found the controls and changed the camera angle. The sick fuck had it zoomed in on her cunt and nowhere else. I was going to need to talk with Mas about the hiring qualifications for these rooms. There had to be people out there that weren't perverts. Maybe we needed to do a rehaul of this place too. Dayton's touch here was still too prominent.

She leaned back and pulled her legs up to get comfortable, looking around at all the lights. I watched her face as the excitement built for her. She looked fucking stunning in her bra and panties, the thigh highs instantly making my cock take notice as it began to stiffen. The action made me suddenly realize how long it had been since I'd had sex. In fact, it was the longest I'd ever gone. I hadn't been in the mood lately, chalking it up to being sequestered away. But now, taking in *my spitfire*, I knew the real reason.

"Are you ready to play, *Spitfire*? Can you handle the truth?"

She sucked in a breath, and it was glorious. Her breathing quickened, and I watched as her skin flushed, a moan escaping me unintentionally at the sight.

"Goddamn, Spitfire. You're so fucking tempting."

"Sax?"

"Yes, Spitfire. Do you have multiple men that call you that? I'd like to think I was special."

"No, I mean, you're the only one. I'm just surprised. I haven't seen or heard from you in months. Not since… Anyway, it's me that should be wondering if I was special."

She sat up, crossing her arms, and I realized how strong she'd become in my absence, her spitfire surged forward, and I couldn't help but encourage it, wanting to see more of her fire raging, even if it was at me.

"You don't believe that for a fucking minute, Loren."

She huffed, sticking her chin up. "Loren, is it? Well, I can believe whatever I want, especially when you don't give me a reason to think otherwise. You know what? I am feeling quite angry with you now that I think about it. "

"Oh? Why are you angry, *Loren*?"

Her nostrils flared, and I found myself leaning in closer to the screen to watch her, completely enchanted with everything that encompassed Loren. My own pulse raced, and I realized what I'd truly been missing all these months. It wasn't just her body I craved, though I did want her, but her energy, her passion, and kindness were the balm to the damaged pieces in me. In Loren, I saw redemption and a purpose to be better. To not feel like the fuck up I hid away most days, constantly seeking the approval of others.

"Why am *I* angry?" she scoffed, throwing up her arms. Standing, she spun around; I assumed looking for the camera. "I'm angry because everyone left me! I'm angry because I was alone in that hospital room and I almost died. I'm angry because when I woke, it wasn't to the men I'd been getting to know, but the asshole ex-husband who took so many things from me already. I'm angry because you made me doubt how I felt and who I was. I'm angry because you made me feel like *I didn't matter!*"

She shouted the last part, and I realized she was crying, and I snapped. I was out of my chair and in her room within seconds, scooping her up off the floor and into my arms. She tried to fight me, hitting me with her fists, but once I had her cocooned in my grip, she fell into me. Sitting down on the couch, I sat back and attempted to soothe her as best I knew how. I didn't usually stay around for this stage of comforting someone.

"I'm so sorry, Spitfire. That was never my intention. You can be angry all you want at me. I deserve it."

I held her close, smoothing her hair as her body shook with emotion. I felt like the biggest ass in the world. Fuck! I'd screwed up. We'd all screwed up.

"I know this doesn't matter now, but I thought it was better to let you go. I thought I was doing you a favor. I didn't want to dirty up your life or make it too complicated. And honestly, I didn't think you'd notice. We'd only shared a kiss. I thought you'd be okay."

She lifted her head, her eyes shiny from tears, and looked me dead in the eyes. "It's not up to you to decide what I can and can't handle. And it might've been only a kiss, but we both know it wasn't *just a kiss*."

I nodded, accepting her answer. "I kind of like seeing this side of you, Spitfire. You're right. It wasn't fair to make that choice for you without your input. Everything happened so fast, I made it out of fear. The thought of failing another person was...." I shook my head, unable to say it, dropping my head down into her neck, breathing her in.

Her hand went to the back of my head, and she dug her nails into the short hair there. Fuck if it didn't feel amazing. I loved that in her own pain, she was still trying to comfort me.

"I like it when you tell me things. I think this is the realest conversation we've had. Usually, you saunter in spouting off dirty things, and I go all gooey, forgetting everything else."

"I make you gooey, do I?" I whispered into her neck, her skin soft against my lips.

"You make me more than that, and you know it."

"I think you need to tell me more, Spitfire."

Lifting my head, I took in her eyes. They were clear, with no inebriation in sight, and full of heat. "There are still a lot of things we probably need to discuss. I'm not discounting that. If I promise to tell you more later, can I show you what this room is all about? I really had intended on doing only that. Let me take your mind off things."

She debated my words, looking at my face, before

slowly nodding. "I was kind of intrigued about this place. Will you show me?"

"I'd love to, *Loren*."

This time when I said her name, I felt her tremble, and I had to remind my dick to stay in my pants for now. "Usually, it's over the speaker, so I can go back to the booth and watch from there. Or," I paused, watching her closely, "I can do it from here in the room. Which would you prefer?"

Loren chewed her lip, and I didn't know which one she would pick. "So, you're not going to touch me?"

"No. Not with my hands, at least. I'm going to caress your body with my words, using all of your senses."

This time there was no hesitation as she answered. "Stay."

Her voice was breathy already, and I used all my might to stand and lay her on the couch. Thinking clearly for a second, I sent a text to security to turn off all the cameras in this room. We didn't need to record any secrets here. Nor did I want to violate her privacy that way.

But really, I didn't want any other man to watch her and get off on her sounds or body. I might not be able to have her just yet, maybe not at all, but it didn't mean Spitfire wasn't *mine*. I could accept sharing her with Atticus if he ever got his head out of his ass, and hell, even Nicco. The grumpy fighter and the good guy, I was still on the fence over, but those had been her choice, and I was done taking that away from her. I'd learn to deal with it if I had to, if this developed further.

But I fucking wouldn't let anyone else touch her. Loren had just become mine. It didn't matter if I never got to have her, she was mine, and I'd die to protect her, especially from myself.

So if this was the only night I got, I would take it and make it the best night.

"Lay back and get comfortable, Spitfire. Close your eyes, and let go. Don't hold on to anything in your mind."

I found the control panel in the room and hit the sound button creating a soft beat. Clipping on the microphone, I decided to use it anyway to utilize the acoustics and speaker placement. Next, I adjusted the aroma, making it more similar to my smell, and kept the temperature a little warm for now. I hadn't done this before, but I'd helped create the concepts for the rooms and knew how they all worked on the primary level. There was a script to use in the booth, but I'd improvise if it meant staying with Loren.

"Before I get started, Spitfire, do you remember the word given to you?"

"Mmhm."

"Good girl. You're gonna wanna use that if you ever feel uncomfortable or like you can't go any further, just say the word. Okay."

"Mmhm."

"I need to hear you say it, Spitfire."

"I understand."

"Good. Now, keep your eyes closed. If you need help, I can always cover them for you." She gasped, and I almost wanted to do it. "Now, you must listen to my voice and do as I say. If you stop at any time, then so will I."

"Okay." Her voice was soft and a little breathy, already falling under the spell and seduction of the room.

"Spitfire, I want you to take one hand and trail it up your arm, very delicately. I want you to imagine it's my hand, softly caressing your arm. My fingertips brushing against your soft skin, bringing goosebumps to the surface. Now, trail your hand over your belly, the same pressure, and gently around."

I moved closer and blew on her skin, her breath catching, and I had to hold myself back from touching her. "Now, brush your hand over your breast, Spitfire. Cup it and show me what I'm missing."

She placed her hand in her bra and drew it down, and I groaned at the sight. "Fuck, Spitfire. You're making it hard not to touch you."

"Tell me," she breathed, rolling her hand over her nipple. "Tell me how it makes you feel. I want to know."

"Oh, do you now?"

"Yes, please, *Mr. Sax.*"

Groaning, I leaned in and blew on her nipple, tempting me to stick my tongue out and lick it; it was so close and perfect.

"I've been hard since the moment I spotted you walking in. I've been watching you as you explored, determined not to interfere, thinking it was better. But the moment you stepped in here and I heard his voice talk to you, I couldn't bear the thought of another man getting to touch you with their words," I growled.

Her breath caught, her hands stilling at my confession.

"You think about me?"

"So damn much."

"What… what kind of things do you think about?"

"I'll tell you, but you can't stop touching yourself. Deal?"

"Ok-aa-yy…" she moaned.

"Imagine as if your hands are doing what mine want to do, Spitfire."

"Mmhmm."

"You're such a good girl, Spitfire," I purred as I watched her hands trailing over her body. I rubbed my palm on the outside of my pants, a groan escaping at the touch. Leaning closer, I let my breath fan over her skin as I spoke, still wanting to incorporate the sensations of the room.

"Mostly, I think about your smile, your sass, your fire," I admitted. "But when I'm alone at night, I think about all the things I wished I'd done the night we went out. All the things I wanted to do to get your face to look like it did the night in the club."

"What?"

"Oh yes, Spitfire. He'll kill me for saying this, but the first time you came to Climax."

"Yeah?" she asked, her voice breathless.

"The two men up top you chatted with in Illusion, well, I was the first one, and well… Atticus…." I trailed off.

"Was the second one?"

"Yes. I was so mad at him when he made me switch places but even more excited when he didn't realize it was you afterward. He saw a beautiful woman coming undone by the sight of two people enjoying themselves on the dance floor, and he gave in to his baser urges."

"He… didn't… know….?"

She could barely get any words out through her pants, her hands pinching her nipples hard now.

"No, Spitfire, he didn't. Did you like having his fingers in your dripping wet pussy?"

She sucked in a breath before an imperceptible nod could be seen. "Yes."

"Well, when I'm alone at night, I think about that scene, but instead, it's me touching you. I slipped my hand around your front and in between the high slit you had, and I grazed your thigh. I would think about how my hand would travel to your hot wet center, and how soft your skin would feel. The smell of your hair in my nostrils, the press of your body against me as I rubbed my hard cock against your back. I'd think about how easy it would be to bend you over the rail and slide into you. Slipping in so effortlessly."

"Ohh, yes, can I?"

"Ah, you're learning, Spitfire. Trail your hands down lower. I want to watch you touch your outer thighs. I want to see you skirt the outside of your panties and feel the wetness dripping there. Then I want you to tell me how it feels."

"Um, I've never really talked about it before."

"Nothing to be scared about, Loren. Just use your words to describe it to me, let me know."

"Okay, I'll try."

"Slide your hand down lower, yes, just like that. My dick is so hard right now just from watching you. I don't think you understand the appeal you have, how fucking sexy you are without even trying."

"I like how you see me."

She moved her hand lower and did as I'd instructed, her fingertips brushing along the lace.

"Spread your legs wider, baby. Then touch yourself, and tell me how you feel."

"I feel… so very wet. Um, your voice makes me curl my toes, and thinking of you touching yourself to thoughts of me arouses me so much."

"Mmm, yes. I thought about how easy it would be to fuck you on your desk, against the wall, in my shower, and even between Atticus and me. Would you like that, Spitfire? To be taken by two men at once?"

I leaned closer, my lips barely touching her skin as I spoke the last part. Her breath hitched, and I watched as her skin flushed at my words. She was still tracing the outside of the lace, so I gave her a little push.

"Dip your fingers in, Loren. Let me see how wet you really are. Let me hear how turned on you are by what I'm telling you. I think there's a dark side of you that wants all the naughty things, who relishes the thought of bringing two powerful men to their knees."

She slowly slipped her finger under, and I watched as she hesitantly ran her digit up her slit. I needed to up the stakes, so she wasn't thinking so much. Moving off the bed, I grabbed a feather before returning between her legs.

"Loren, can I remove your panties? It's okay if you don't want me to."

"Um, yes, you can."

Carefully, I unsnapped the garters, and slid her panties down, running the palms of my hands down her skin deliberately. I leaned in, trailing my nose up her thigh, breathing her in. "Fuck, Loren. You smell incredible. I just want to devour you."

Once I had her legs free, I tossed the fabric on the floor and laid down between her legs. It would look perverted to anyone else, but I wasn't there to peep. That was just a bonus. Using the control, I selected the speakers on the couch and added the effect of vibrating. Now anytime I spoke, she would feel it everywhere on her body.

Using the feather, I brushed it against her leg as I started again, trying not to thrust myself into the couch. "My favorite thing," I started, pausing as she gasped, the vibration and bass now active. "Was to imagine you walking in on me touching myself and then screaming out your name. You'd walk over, give me a saucy wink and then drop to your knees and clean me up. Then you would make me watch you, just like this, as you screamed my name."

"Oh, oh, that feels so good, Sax."

"Yes, just like that, baby." I rubbed the feather along her skin, heightening her senses. "Now, I need to watch you plunge your fingers into yourself, pulling them back slowly. Do it for me, Spitfire."

"Yes, *sir.*"

She slid her hand back down, the bass decreasing now as I stopped talking, and I watched as she slid one finger in. "Yes, Loren. Go deep, coat yourself. Now, pull it back out slowly, and tease your clit for me. Teach me how you like to be pleasured. I want to learn all of your buttons. *Show me*," I purred, the rumbles running right up her legs into her cunt as she gasped but thankfully didn't stop this time.

Her moans were intoxicating, and I sat up, no longer able to lay there without giving in.

"Spitfire, you have me so hard right now. I want to touch myself while you're giving me a show. Is that okay with you?"

"Yes, please."

Not taking another second, I unzipped my pants and had my cock out, instantly moaning as I wrapped my hand around my shaft. "Oh, fuck, Spitfire. Your hand is so wet. If that was my dick, I would slide in so nicely. I'd fuck you so deep and hard, you'd forget your name. I'd make you see stars and wouldn't stop until you came so hard around me, you'd squeeze my own orgasm out of me. Our skin slapping together, your hot cunt wrapped around my cock. Oh, I can see it. *Fuck.*"

"Oh God, I want that. I want it so bad."

"I want it too, baby, but not tonight. Not like this. I want to be able to fuck you for hours and take my time enjoying you. Playing out all the different ways I imag-ined it."

"Tell me more… about… me with you… and… "

"Ah, Spitfire, are you turned on by the thought of

being between Atticus and me? Well, we've shared before, you know. We like having a woman between us, making it about her pleasure, bringing her to the ultimate orgasm. I'd lay down, and you'd ride me, your breasts bouncing with each thrust, and Atticus would fuck you from behind, and you'd feel so full. Just thinking about how wet you'd be, has me almost cumming right now."

"Fuck, Sax. That's hot."

"Mmm, you're almost there, Loren. Tell me more so I know what to envision. My hand is wrapped around my cock right now, and I'm stroking it as I watch you. Open your eyes, and watch me."

She did, looking at my eyes first before traveling down to my hand. She licked her lips, and it fucking killed me. A bead of precum developed at my tip from the look alone. I squeezed myself hard, choking my cock so she could see the slit.

"I want you, Sax. *Please*, I need to feel you in me. I'm so desperate and needy. It's not going to happen unless it's your cock inside me. *Please*."

I watched as she begged me, her pleading ripping my heart in two. She shouldn't have to beg. Loren was a fucking treasure and didn't need to. Was I taking her choice away again by putting my wants and demands on her?

"Fuck, Spitfire. I want to, so much. Are you sure that's what you want?"

"Yes, it's the only thing I want. I need you."

The moment she said she needed me, I pulled her legs to me and lifted her up before slamming her down on me. She barely had time to wrap her arms around me before she was screaming out at the move.

"Oh, fuck. Oh, fuck."

"Hearing you cuss is the most beautiful thing. You feel better than I could even imagine. This is going to be quick, and then I'm taking you somewhere I can fuck you senseless. No running away."

"Then fuck me already, Mr. Sax."

Sealing my lips to her in a crushing kiss, I leveraged her up and down my cock, the sensation so mind-blowing I knew I'd be ruined for any other woman. Loren was perfection. The better move was to forget about her, let her live her life with one of the men who'd keep her safe. But by having a taste of her, feeling her wrapped around me, I knew I'd never be able to walk away.

I was only kidding myself to think I ever stood a chance in the first place.

Within a few seconds, we were both coming so hard, our moans and screams rang out through the room as our breathing began to finally slow. Her head laid on my shoulder in contented bliss. I brushed her hair aside, gently rubbing her cheek as her eyelids fluttered open.

"Hey."

"Hey."

"Was that okay? Not just an in-the-moment thing?"

"It was everything I wanted and needed, thank you. You don't have to keep up your claim, though. I don't expect you to do anything more. I begged you."

"Oh, Spitfire. That's where you are so wrong. I only have one question for you."

"Okay…"

"Your place or mine?"

She smiled, my breath catching more from the sight alone, and I knew I was done for. There was no turning back from here, and as much as that ought to scare me, I only found myself happy for the first time in months.

ELEVEN

ATTICUS

Leaning against the shower wall, I braced my arms as the water rolled down my back, pooling at my feet. I barely slept last night. The worries of protecting the family and keeping everyone safe haunted me. Especially after Wells reported the encounter Mrs. Carter had. Darren was proving to be more nefarious than I'd given him credit for.

The realization I might not be up for this fight hit me. Inadequacy at not being able to root out Delgado's plan assaulted my every waking moment. Everywhere I looked, I saw the casualties, my ineptness at distinguishing risks and pitfalls. I was failing.

I was meant to be better than this.

I'd been groomed my entire life to be this badass, ruthless mafia boss searing fear into his foes, and yet I'd run scared, hiding away while Delgado flourished even more in my absence. I'd been a fool, playing into his hands.

It had been a most grievous mistake. One I was now paying for.

Despite pretending things were better, and moving us

out of lockdown, I still had no clue about the actual game or players.

But I was done being weak.

It was time to strike out and maneuver ourselves into a position of power. I might not know what board we were using, but I wouldn't find out by hiding in the corners. I needed to play in order to gain any traction. I only hoped I could live with the consequences.

Lifting my head, the water sluiced over my face, the scalding temperature a welcome relief to the ice I felt in my veins. Steam billowed around me, and I found comfort in the obscurity. I used to be safe in my home, able to drop the mask and be free.

Now, the only place I could do that was here, in a four hundred square foot bathroom. It was the only place without cameras, the only place I was ever truly alone. The only place I didn't have to be everything and have it all together.

Even in my home now, I'd been relegated to being 'the Suit' and everything the moniker implied. It was no longer acceptable to just be him 90% of the time. Lives were lost in the moments I wasn't completely on guard. I couldn't lose anyone else. The image of Mrs. Carter lying broken in her hospital room was enough to remind me what was at stake.

She haunted me now.

No matter how much I tried, I couldn't get her out of my head. The few short moments I'd been in her presence played on a loop. I'd become fluent in her mannerisms from those few encounters. The most significant one being the time I hadn't even known it was her. Thoughts of her against me, my fingers in her dripping wet center, had me squeezing my straining cock each time I recalled them, even now.

Every time I jerked off to thoughts of her, I hated myself a little more, but I couldn't stop. I'd never admitted it to Sax, or fuck, even Nicco, but I was jealous of them. They could be with her when I couldn't. A stolen moment in secret was all I had, so I allowed myself to indulge the fantasy even if it only made me want her more.

My obsession had become so bad, I swear I'd heard her moans in my sleep last night. Soon, I wouldn't be able to breathe without hearing her.

Thinking about her body, the way her curves felt against me, I squeezed and trailed my hand up faster. I imagined what it would be like to be inside her, my cock growing thicker from want. I regretted not taking the chance last time before things became complicated. Stroking even faster, I squeezed the base as I imagined fucking her between Sax and me. Taking her ass while he plunged into her pussy, the ultimate feeling of tightness as she squeezed around me. This was it. My breathing quickened, my hand a blur now as I chased my orgasm.

"Fuck."

My moans rang out around the shower, my cum washing down the drain, and I bent my head down against the wall as my breathing slowed. Coming down from the orgasm, I pretended not to hate myself. The sad part was, these forbidden moments in my shower were the best of my day.

Shutting off the water, I grabbed the towel and dried

myself, gearing up for returning to the Suit. Guilt had already begun building for taking brief moments to shed everything and indulge in the escape Loren brought me. I was beginning to realize they'd become as necessary as eating. If I stopped, who would I become, if not my father?

I didn't want to travel down the same paths as him, and having people I cared about kept me firmly cemented in knowing what was at stake. I wouldn't put her life at risk by getting involved with her. Because I knew if I did, I'd be all in, becoming a possessive alpha hellbent on nothing but protecting her. And maybe that wouldn't be such a horrible thing, but I wasn't selfish enough to do it. Yet.

Loren had a life that wasn't mafia. She had a job, a family, and other lovers that could give her things I couldn't. I wouldn't take it away from her just to satisfy my hunger. Because as much as I enjoyed thinking about her between Sax and me, I didn't know *if* I could share, and that was turning out to be the biggest surprise of all.

I'd never felt this possessive or jealous before. It shook me to my core and altered the foundation of what I believed about myself and who I was.

It was a risk I couldn't take for a woman I hadn't spent more than a few hours with. For a woman I'd never been inside. For a woman who was too pure for this dark world.

If I hadn't found her website myself, I would almost believe she was a honeypot, sent to distract me from the Delgados so someone else could sweep in and disarm us from the inside out. I'd done extensive checks on her, though, and knew her history backward and forward. She wasn't meant to be anything more than a means to an end. I thought she'd be safe, but Mrs. Carter was turning out to be the most surprising key to this whole thing, giving those closest to me a cause.

Dressing in a navy suit and grey button-down. I decided to opt-out of a tie today since it was Saturday, I would live a little.

The comment had me chuckling, causing the duo I stumbled upon in the breakfast nook to glance up. I stopped midway through the door, shock and disbelief covering my face before I quickly shut it down.

Fuck. Fuck. Fuck.

Sitting practically in Sax's lap, wearing only his button-down white dress shirt, was the woman I'd been imagining naked and masturbating to for the past hour, in the flesh.

"Mrs. Carter. I can officially say I'm surprised to see you here."

Sax watched me closely, his hand possessively on her hip, the other holding a coffee cup as he brought it to his lips. I didn't miss the smug smile that played there before he drank from it, either.

"Oh, Mr. Masters, um, I didn't expect to see you, um, and dressed like this."

"Spitfire, you don't need to apologize. Mas is just *jealous*."

"Mas?" she asked, turning her head to him. I watched as they got lost in one another's gaze; the jealousy and possessiveness I'd felt earlier roared to life even more. I turned, heading to the counter to get out of their sight.

Mostly so I didn't walk over there and rip her out of his arms. I had no claim on her, no place to do such an action. He was my best friend and most trusted ally. She was a single woman, no ties to me. I didn't even think she knew I'd been the one in the club. I had no reason to feel this way.

Yet my cock and heart were in disagreement. Straining against the counter, I pressed the stiff appendage into it, hoping to punish myself or gather some relief as I busied with filling a cup. Shit, I needed to think quickly or get out of here. I didn't know which was worse, though. Leaving and having them realize they affected me or staying and punishing myself in the process of my restraint.

My cold exterior helped keep me disengaged, at least, and I bit my tongue not to make a retort. If I heard her speak, I would want her more. That wouldn't do.

"So um, you guys live together?" I heard her ask. "And why would he be jealous?"

"Because of what we talked about last night," he whispered, nibbling her neck. "And, we've always lived together, or well since we've known one another, we have. Package deal."

"Package?" her breath caught, and I had to compel myself to focus on the packet of oatmeal I'd picked up to read. I could tell by her sounds, Sax was attempting to push my buttons. This was torture, actually, it was worse than torture. I'd take waterboarding any day over this. Hardening myself, I attacked, wanting to see him bleed along with me.

"I'm actually surprised to see you with Sax this morning, considering the last time I saw you barely clothed, it was with Nicco. Where is the young chap this morning?"

Sax turned and glared, his ministrations stopping as Loren tensed. She looked at me regarding her over my coffee cup, and I watched as she completely shut down. Loren slid off his lap, tucking the shirt under her, and patted her hair, attempting to tame it.

"Um, yeah, well, he hasn't reached out to me. And, actually, I think it's time I head home. I don't want Jude to worry." She turned to Sax, her voice softening now that she was out from under my watchful glare. "I'm gonna grab my stuff. Can you give me a ride, or do I need to order a car?"

He kissed her nose, smoothing down her long dark hair and tucking it behind her ears. I didn't want to admit how transfixed I was by the movement or how obsessed I'd become watching them. Sax was a different person around her, his hard edges a little softer, his gruffness more directed. When she stood and tiptoed out of the room, her hands holding the shirt over her ass as she crept by, I noticed how perfect she looked in it. Her long legs were accentuated, and her dark hair contrasted against the stark white.

When Sax cleared his throat, I knew I'd been found out. Flicking my gaze to his, I met a disappointed one. It wasn't what I expected, being prepared to deal with his smugness or anger, but Sax being disappointed in me... *hurt*.

"What?" I snapped, going on the defensive. The beast of a man stood, his muscles flexing as he did, his bare torso displaying his tattoos. It was then I noticed he was the most dressed down I'd ever seen him in the house, even if it was only 7 am on Saturday. Sax typically wore either workout clothes, black suits, or black tactical gear. His clothes had a purpose and nothing more. Seeing him in the soft grey cotton sweatpants was odd, and it stuck out to me. He walked toward the counter I still leaned against, his bare feet padding on the floor in confident strides, and I prepared myself for his attack.

"I don't have to tell you how much of an asshole you were. Whatever you're doing, stop. It won't work. Believe me, I tried and failed myself. Whatever this restraint is about, this holding yourself back you're doing for some reason, it isn't going to last. You forget I know you better than anyone. I *know* you want her. Hell, I know how much it's eating you up inside thinking about me having her. I thought you were right, that staying away was wiser, that I could save her that way. But I was wrong."

He let his words ring out, giving me time to think them over. I didn't respond. I didn't even acknowledge him, just staring at his face as I drank my coffee, acting unaffected. When he didn't get the response he searched for, he sighed, shaking his head at me. The movement sliced through my walls, and for a second, I almost gave in and answered him, but I couldn't

"I get it, Mas. I do. But answer me this… what if she isn't the one that needs saving? What if she's meant to save *us*?"

He let go of the counter and walked backward, watching me for the first few steps, before turning on the balls of his feet and heading out of the kitchen. I placed the coffee cup down and turned, barely making it into the sink when I heaved up what I'd just drank. Grabbing a glass, I filled it with water and swished it around before spitting it out.

This was my weakness, my curse, my one flaw I kept closely hidden.

The very thing my father said would be my demise because I would never have the stomach for what would be required of me as boss of the family because lying made me sick. Literally.

I'd learned ways to control it over the years, but every now and then, things would catch me off guard, like finding the one woman I hadn't been able to stop obsessing over practically naked in my kitchen. And then, my stomach would revolt, and I'd lose it. The Grim Reaper said it would be my downfall. The joke was on him when I shot him and left him for dead. I hadn't felt even a trickle of nausea then.

He was one of two people who knew, the other our family doctor. Not even Sax knew this hidden shame. Over the years, I'd discovered ways to deal with it when I couldn't control things, but having Sax by my side had meant I'd always been prepared for the unknown, mitigating the likelihood. Facing off with Sax now, lying to my family about the shit we were in, scared I'd let Immy down again, carrying everything on my shoulders, and denying myself the beautiful woman I craved with everything in me, had me blowing chunks.

I wasn't allowed to be scared. But I was. I so fucking was.

Sax's words echoed around my head, the possibility

she could be good for us, but I dismissed them. If I let them be true, then I wasn't any better than Dayton. I didn't need to be saved. There wasn't anything worth saving left in me. The only hope I had was to make it worthwhile for the people I cared about. Nothing would absolve me from what happened to Immy or Jaz. If I couldn't protect those who knew this type of danger existed, then I had no chance with someone like her.

Chugging the remainder of my coffee, I placed it in the sink, checking one more time it was clear. I slid my gun into the holster under my arm and swung my suit coat up and on. Getting into the practice of wearing a gun had taken some time. With how things were right now, it was stupid not to, even if I didn't always agree with using them.

I headed toward the garage needing to get started on my meetings now that I was back in the city. Perhaps breaking a few people today, leveraging a few secrets would be just the thing to perk me up on this Saturday.

***

"It seems we're at an impasse, Mr. Santos. I believe you have something I need and want, yet you don't seem to want to give it to me. It pains me to have to do this."

The room I was in lit up with colors as the screens around us turned on. His eyes zeroed in on the image I had displayed on the screen. As I watched him, I saw it, the first sign of fear, as he dropped his eyes back to me now and swallowed.

Violence was easy to use and typically gave you the

result you wanted. But it was messy, required no finesse, and was amateur, in my opinion. I'd much prefer to cripple my opponents at the knees and then watch them suffer as I took everything from them. Mental and emotional pain was far more reaching and motivating. Of course, I didn't need any convincing of that. I'd been my father's favorite test subject after all.

Slipping into the cold, calculated man I'd become known as was easy now. It gave me the shield I needed to wield my power and control my foes, allowing me room to flex my muscles and dive into the darker urges coursing through me.

"Ah, it seems you recognize the face."

"Of course, I do, asshole. That's my wife."

"Oh, are we at the lying stage of our show already? I was under the impression she was your girlfriend, *your mistress*. The one you don't want your wife to know about."

Simeon Santos gritted his teeth, spit flying from the corners as he spoke, no longer remaining quiet. The picture was of a young waitress he'd been seeing for six months now. Based on his lie to protect her, I think he actually cared about this one.

As I kept watching him, another picture, this one of his wife, flashed up, showing her home making dinner, the image clearly taken from outside. Interesting. His reaction to her wasn't as terrified as it had been to the younger waitress; perhaps he did love her. It clicked a few details in my mind, offering me the angle to take for the leverage I needed.

Leaning forward on my arms, I stared at him as he

sweated under the lights. His leg gently shook as he waited for me to make my demands. Simeon knew he'd been beaten but was hoping to still leave here with some level of control. He wouldn't. I'd take what I needed. His opportunity to barter had long passed.

"I asked you before if you knew how Delgado was cleaning his money. Or I should say, *my money*? You had a bit of a memory block back then. Perhaps now that you've had some time to shift things loose, is anything coming to mind?"

I flipped the screen back to the pretty waitress, knowing it was my best bet now. I zoomed in on her face, and he swallowed, unable to take his eyes off her as he kept flicking them up there. Simeon visibly sweated, pulling his collar as he attempted to find a way out of this.

The only way out was with the truth. If he didn't give it, there *wasn't* a way out for him.

Over the past few months, it had become evident that not only had my father and Uncle Sean been stealing, but using someone else to clean their money, or more likely, cleaning it themselves, taking our footing in this city away. If Delgado no longer needed the resources we provided, he would take us out one by one, leaving no one behind. It was the fear of this massacre that had kept us sequestered in the suburbs. If I knew where to start, I'd be able to regain my stronghold.

"I, uh, I may remember something now that you mention it."

Grinning, I leaned back in my chair, crossing my feet

at the ankle, and cocked an eyebrow at him, dropping all formalities now. "Oh? Please, Simeon, I'm all ears."

"I'd forgotten until you said something."

"Of course, memory loss does take time." It was bullshit, but I'd play his game until he was no longer useful.

"But I do remember hearing something about a new club opening."

My anger boiled to the surface at this news, but I held it at bay. Clubs were also our territory. Everyone was well aware, whether it be sex, dance, gambling, or even fighting, *we owned it.* If Delgado was brave enough to step outside of us for cleaning and stepped into our lane with new venues, then he had grown way too cocky. I needed to bring him down a peg.

It had Dayton written all over it, and for the first time, I wondered how long he'd planned this power takeover with Delgado. If Darren—because Austin had to be dead at this point—was able to deceive us this well, for this long, my father had to have been involved longer than I suspected. The memory of shooting him flashed through my mind reminding me he was gone, calming me even as his ghost continued to haunt me.

"Anything else you can offer, Simeon? Maybe the name of this club, where or who?"

"Um, nothing I can recall."

His leg began to bounce, and he gulped. His earlier stoic behavior had fled him the moment I'd flashed the pictures. It was time to hit him a little lower.

"Hmm, okay. Well, thanks, old chap. If you don't mind, could I borrow your phone?"

"My phone?"

"Yeah. Mine's out of juice," I deadpanned, offering him nothing.

"Um, yeah, I guess. Am I free to go afterward?"

"Absolutely. Let me make this call, and then you can head home to your wife or girlfriend. Whichever it is."

He watched me cautiously and slid it across the table. Lifting it, I wanted to roll my eyes at his gullibility. Not to mention he had no password protection on his device. If he knew anything else, it was amazing it hadn't been leaked yet with his inability to lock his phone.

Finding the number I wanted, I put it on speaker as it rang. The screen switched to a video, and Simeon's eyes jumped up as his eyes watched the woman. Almost simultaneously, someone picked up on the call I made, the screen showing the same.

"Hey baby, you headed home from the office? Can you pick up some milk on your way home?" she asked. When I didn't say anything, she stopped what she was doing to look at the phone. "Hello?"

"Oh, apologies, ma'am. This phone was left at—"

Before I could get the words out, Simeon reached over and muted the call, knowing it was too late to hang up. One, his wife would be suspicious, and two, he wouldn't be walking out of here if he did.

"I remembered something. It's on Wabash, an old supermarket. It's going to have a bit of everything, and," he stopped, swallowing, glancing up at the woman on the phone, "it's called the *Masked Kingpin.*"

Hitting the unmute, he sat back, pleading to not say anything. The woman's voice rang out once again, filling the room. "Hello? Hello? Anyone there?"

"I'm so sorry, ma'am, I must've hit the mute button with my face. I'm going to leave this at the lost and found at Nutty Brew. Will that do?"

"Oh, yes, thank you so much. My husband must've dropped it. He works around the corner from there."

"You don't say? Well, that's wonderful. I'm so glad I could help."

"You're too kind. I'll be sure to tell him when he gets home."

"You have a nice day, ma'am."

"Thank you, you too, sir."

Hanging it up, I slid it across to him, giving him a pointed look. He nodded, pocketing it, and hurriedly left. The guard at the door followed, giving me a nod before he left, understanding he needed to follow. Once I had only one guard left, I exhaled, relief settling in my bones at having finally gotten some leverage.

It wasn't the news I wanted to hear, but it was a place to start. Picking up my phone, I called the pissant who was supposed to be giving me updates but who'd lately failed to do so.

"Mr. Mascro, I was just going to call you."

"Is that so, Marcus? I'd be very interested to hear what you have to say."

"Oh, well, nothing new to report, unfortunately. They've been very tight-lipped and seem to be hiding out for the moment."

He spoke fast, a tactic to cover his lies. He'd already sealed his fate, though. This was why I hated liars. Everyone always thought they were the one in charge, getting away with something, making them feel powerful and like the most intelligent person in the room.

They were all wrong.

Lies made you weak.

"Very well, Marcus. Can you make sure to keep Darren away from *Evolve* and don't let him sniff around it?"

"Uh, yeah, sure thing, boss. Can I ask why?"

"No, you can't, but I'll tell you anyway. The remodels are finished, and we're opening the speakeasy below. I don't want Darren getting his hands on our ideas."

"Of course, Mas. You can count on me."

"Hmm. Have something for me next time, Marcus."

"Yes, sir."

I hung up before he could hang himself more. Now, I just had to wait and let him set a trap for me. Marcus had been a gamble, and while he didn't pan out by giving me insider info, he'd at least be valuable in setting the trap I needed to lay by ratting himself out.

Lies made you believe the wrong thing, the version of the truth you needed to feel safe.

I didn't need to lie to myself to know I wasn't the smartest person or even remotely safe. The only way I'd be safe was if all my enemies were kneeling at my feet, being crushed under my heels.

TWELVE

LOREN

Walking into my condo building, I sent a quick text to Jude to let him know I was home and to remind him to pick up his suit on his way back. He'd spent the night with his friend, Dean, under the agreement he wouldn't stay up all night and would be home by early afternoon to get ready for the wedding. I'd almost canceled after the ordeal with my mother and Brian, but it wasn't my cousin's fault they were such horrible people.

I would indeed hide out at the dessert table like I'd promised Jude, though, and leave as soon as socially acceptable. No sense in punishing myself just to be cordial. Nodding at George, I made my way to the elevator when a voice stopped me.

"Beautiful."

My feet quit moving, but my heart took off at a rapid speed, my breath catching. I stood stunned in the middle of the lobby, not daring to look or turn toward him. I didn't know what to think or feel. The million different times I'd imagined him finding me, it hadn't been like this. Peeking out of the corner of my eye, I caught a brief glimpse of him, and my knees went weak.

Shit. This wasn't good.

When Sax had bated me last night, my anger had surged and then quickly been replaced with lust for the man. We shared a vulnerable moment, and I felt him lower his walls to me. I felt his remorse and knew he meant it.

When all of the men who'd come into my life had pulled away, I'd understood in a way, logically at least.

Monroe had to focus on Levi. It hurt, but it was the right choice for him, even if I'd wanted to be part of it. It wasn't for me to decide.

Sax and Atticus, I missed seeing them in my office and was probably the most upset about losing Immy, but again, with Sax, we'd kissed once, gone to a disastrous dinner, and flirted a lot. The underlying tension had been there, but we hadn't popped the seal yet to what we could be, and Atticus was a whole other mystery within itself. He confused and interested me, but we were nothing to one another.

Wells, he'd always been hit or miss, and while the verbal sparring was lacking, I hadn't been emotionally attached to him yet either. We still had a long way to go if anything was going to develop past friends, but I hoped we could be that. The lust came easy, but I wanted it to mean more.

But Nicco… He'd destroyed me in a way Brian never had.

The anger surfacing last night only reminded me how much it had hurt.

"Everything alright, Mrs. Carter?" George asked from the front desk, my sudden frozen state, an uncommon sight in the lobby. It was the reset I needed as I glanced at him and nodded.

"Yes, thank you."

Spinning in the other direction, I focused on his eyes, too scared of what I'd do if I took his whole body in. As it was, his eyes were difficult enough to gaze into. Grey-blue eyes swirled with emotion, and I wanted to cave.

But I wouldn't.

If there was anything good that could be gleaned from the situation with Barkley, it was I had to be stronger and stand up for the things I wanted. It wasn't enough to wait for others to decide whether or not I was worthy. *I had to demand it.*

"Nicco."

His face fell a little, and I hated how gutted it made me. I didn't want to hurt him. He'd been the first one to show me I could be the person I was becoming. And maybe if he'd approached me a week ago before I'd talked with Monroe, Wells, and Sax, I would've accepted him back with open arms. But each of those men had reminded me of what I was worth and deserved. I didn't know if I could risk it anymore with Nicco.

"Can we talk?"

"I don't have anything to say to you that I haven't left on your voicemail or the texts I sent, but if you feel the need to say something, then I'm all ears."

I turned fully toward him, crossing my arms. When he started to approach me, I realized I didn't want to have this conversation in the lobby but didn't want to invite him up, afraid I'd cave easier.

"Let's go to the cafe across the street. You can at least buy me a coffee."

"Of course, yes, thank you." He sighed, looking relieved.

Rolling my eyes, I spun around and stalked out of the place. That was until I remembered what I was wearing. A borrowed shirt and pants, presumably of Atticus'. Shit, I couldn't go out like this. It was fine for the cab ride and then walking into my building, but not around others. I could feel him behind me, his body heat pressing into my back, and I pivoted quickly to turn in the other direction.

"Actually, I need to change, and I'm on a schedule, so I guess you can come upstairs, but don't take it to mean anything else."

"Understood."

I hit the button, and thankfully it didn't make us wait long as the doors opened, a few people exiting. Pushing the button for my floor, I leaned against the wall, arms crossed, as I stared off with him, taking him in fully.

He looked good, like *really good*, and I hated him a little for it.

His hair was pushed back, freshly shaven on the sides, the blue of his grey-blue eyes sparkled under his dark lashes, and his muscles even looked a little bigger. Nicco wore a simple black t-shirt partially tucked in one side with his belt showing, black jeans with strategic holes on the knees, and black boots. He had a leather strap around his wrist and a few silver rings on his inked fingers. It was simple, and yet he was drool-worthy.

It was a crime really how good he made black look.

A new tattoo peeked out of his collar, and I was curious about what it was. Nicco leaned against the wall casually, letting me take my fill of him, a crooked smile on his face. Silence hung between us, neither of us breaching it in this small space. When the elevator came to a halt, the ding sounded, announcing our arrival, but we were locked in a stare-off. It wasn't until a throat cleared that I dropped the hold he had on me and looked.

Of course, it would be Monroe standing there, holding the doors open.

"Hey, Lo. I just knocked on your door, but you obviously weren't there because you're here. Um, yeah," he chuckled, nervously. "I was headed to grab some lunch and wanted to see if you wanted anything."

He glanced between Nicco and me, taking in the other man. When he looked back at me, I panicked, not knowing what to do.

"Yeah, that would be great, thank you!" I chirped. " Just um, get me whatever you're getting. I'm sure it will be wonderful!"

My voice came out all high-pitched and squeaky, and Monroe smiled at me, softening my nerves. He stepped in and held out his hand to Nicco, his good-guy nature rising to the surface.

"Hey, I'm Monroe. I live across from Loren."

"Nice to meet you man, I'm Nicco."

"We're just, I don't know, really," I babbled, dropping

my hands awkwardly at my sides. When the elevator started to beep, I jumped, remembering we weren't standing in the hall but still on the cursed thing. Rushing forward, I made it even more awkward when I tried to squeeze under Monroe's arm as he shook Nicco's hand with his other.

Grabbing his hips as I squeezed by, he jumped at the unexpected touch, letting go of the doors and stepping forward. So in what could only be a comedic parody of my life, I slid out into the hall while Monroe stepped forward, trapping Nicco and him together as the doors began to shut. Neither of us seemed to know what to do as the doors closed, opposite sides from one another. Monroe turned right before they shut all the way, an odd expression on his face as he still gripped Nicco's hand. Hand covering my mouth in shock, I couldn't stop the giggle that flooded out of me.

Both men looked at me, a smile on their face at the sound before the door shut completely, taking them away from me. I watched as the floors descended and waited, leaning against the wall. When it got down to the bottom, the elevator stayed for a few minutes before it began to ascend again. When it stopped on 18 again, I held my breath, unsure what to expect when it opened, only releasing it as they slid open and he was there.

Nicco's head lifted, snaring my eyes with his, and my breath caught. Fuck, this was hard. He slowly walked forward, approaching me with caution.

"I wasn't sure if I'd find you here."

Scrunching my brow, I tilted my head at him. "Why? I told you I'd listen to you."

"You did, but then one of the most attractive men I've ever met, and nicest, by the way, was offering to bring you lunch, and I realized how out of my league I was with you. Not to mention how I royally screwed up. I should've tried harder. I'm so sorry, Loren."

He gripped my hands, and his face had the most heartbreakingly beautiful expression. A door opened and closed in the other direction, and for the second time in his presence, I remembered we were in public.

"Come on, let's talk inside."

I pulled his hand, and when he linked our fingers together, I didn't have the heart to drop it like I should. It felt too nice. Our fingers hooked together with ease as tingles zipped up my arm at the small gesture. My resolve to hold strong was failing, and I knew I needed to put some space between us when we got inside, or I'd end up fucking him on the kitchen island.

Dropping his hand to unlock my door, I took some deep breaths as well, gathering myself. I had to keep it together, so I didn't fold easily. I sat my stuff down on the console table, kicked off my shoes, and then turned to address Nicco.

"Um, do you mind if I change real quick?"

"Of course. I'll just wait here."

Heading toward my bedroom, I shouted over my shoulder, "Help yourself to the fridge or whatever. I'll be quick."

Rushing, I discarded the clothes and turned on the water to the shower, hopping in before it warmed so I could rinse my body at least. Grabbing my loofah, I squirted soap and ran it over my body quickly, rinsing and jumping out in record time. Drying myself, I hastily dressed in clean clothes and ran a brush through my hair. I sprayed some spritz on, not wanting to smell like another man but also not wanting it to look like I tried all too hard.

Slipping on some socks, I hopped out into the hallway and smoothed my clothes down as I walked casually back to the man who had slowly awakened my heart. I found him leaning against the kitchen island, a water bottle in his hand. When he heard me, he looked up again, and almost like in the elevator, I was hooked in his gaze momentarily. Shaking my head, I took a seat on one of the stools, keeping the island between us. It was probably for the best.

He moved closer, leaning over the other side, bringing his intoxicating smell closer to my vicinity. Fucking hell, that wasn't fair. I kept getting lost in his eyes, so I dropped them, fiddling with the sleeve of my shirt, before looking up, avoiding his hypnotizing gaze this time.

"So, what did you want to talk about?"

I folded my arms, my defenses being triggered, and I wanted to throw up my walls and shield the pain. Nicco sighed, the sound agonizing, but I held firm, reminding myself of all the hurt I'd felt and hadn't deserved. He could've called, sent a text, wrote an email, or even sent a fucking carrier pigeon! He could've done anything but ghost me.

"There's nothing I can say that will ever make not reaching out to you okay. I want you to know that first. Atticus prohibited any outside contact, that's true, but I don't know, seeing you here, being in your vicinity, and feeling this, I know I should've tried harder. I'd convinced myself after a while that it was for the best. Perhaps he was right; it was easier to let him be the bad guy because by then, I knew I'd messed up, that I'd lost the best thing. And the only one at fault was me. I raged and fought, but I gave up. You're not someone who anyone should give up on. If I never see you after today, I want you to know that at least."

"All your words are pretty, Nicco, and there's a part of me that understands and wants to welcome you back with open arms."

"But?"

"But, they're just words and you hurt me, *deeply*. I've had to have this conversation a lot in the past few weeks, but it's the hardest with you. I woke up alone, surrounded by people who I've come to realize possibly hate me, having to learn I'd almost died and had been in a coma for a week. Maybe I could overlook that, and forgive you, with the understanding that you weren't able to reach out to me, even if it doesn't make any sense to me."

Looking up, I met his eyes this time, tears filling mine, a truth rising to the surface I'd been ignoring.

"But you didn't just fail me; you failed Jude too. You knew how much he meant to me, and in the chaos of everything, you were the only one who might have known what was at stake and going on. And well, you left him on his own. You didn't reach out, and he was taken to a group home. I don't know if I can forgive you for leaving me yet, but I definitely can't for you leaving

Jude. It's my job to protect him now, and I can't have someone in my life who doesn't see that."

Tears streamed down my face, Nicco's eyes holding them as well. He nodded, wiping them, acceptance coming over him. The part of me that had held out hope he would fight for me fell, dying on the spot. I hadn't realized the response I'd wanted from him until that moment when he didn't do it.

I wanted him to fight for me, to fight for us, to show me he'd meant everything he said, and that I wasn't just a hookup. But he didn't.

"Fair enough. I *did* fail you, Loren, and Jude. And I can't apologize enough for that."

Nodding, I slid off the stool, prepared to show him out. "I'll show you to the door. Thank you for coming."

My words held no emotion, falling flat as I deflated internally. I took a step forward, headed to the hallway. I'd only taken two steps when his hand sealed over my bicep, and for a moment, my breath caught, the move reminiscent of Brian grabbing me when I failed him in some way. I froze, my body going rigid as I tried to calm my heart. When Nicco felt my body tense, he thankfully let go, moving around in front of me instead.

"I'm sorry, Loren. I didn't mean to grab you. I just wanted to stop you."

His hands were held out in front of him in a placating gesture as I slowed my heart rate, grounding myself in the present.

Taking a step back, I saw his eyes fill with pain. I hadn't meant to make him feel that way, but I needed space right then. I had to put my own safety first for once. It was something I couldn't sacrifice anymore. Nodding, I waited for him to say whatever he needed to say that had him reaching out for me.

"I wasn't finished, Loren. I *did* fail you. I don't deny that, but what I also want you to know is that I'm going to prove to you that I'm worth taking a chance on. If I can only be in your life as a friend right now, then I will. It will kill me, but it's better than not having you in my life at all, Beautiful. Can I at least have that chance?"

"I don't know. It's not just me I have to think about."

"If I could interject," Jude said from the corner, stepping into view, a sheepish Monroe behind him with a bag of food.

"Sorry, we didn't mean to eavesdrop, but we also didn't feel like we should intrude on that personal moment," Monroe clarified.

I smiled, wiping my eyes more as they both walked toward me and realized we were about to have another pileup in the hallway. Taking a step back, I pivoted until I was back in the kitchen. The guys followed, Monroe placing the food on the counter and made himself at home getting drinks together. Nicco observed him, and I couldn't decide if he was angry, jealous, or just intrigued.

"Lor, I've had a week to think about Nicco and everything that went down. Immy's letter was vague, but I could figure out enough to know it wasn't a conscious choice, neither one of them was able to do anything about it. Whether or not you want to believe him, I guess that is up to you. But from my perspective, I do, and I forgive him. I've been around a lot of liars and fake people, and I know the difference. Nicco isn't lying. So whatever you want to do with my two cents, there it is. Just don't make a decision because of me. I appreciate it and love you even more for it, but this isn't a time where I think it matters."

"You love me, huh, kiddo?" I asked, the words coming over his tongue so easily, I couldn't help but call them out.

His cheeks reddened, the admittance apparently slipping freely. "Yeah, I do."

"Good, because I love you too, Jude."

Pulling him into a hug, I held him in my arms for a second, knowing he was wise beyond his years, his life teaching him to know those things. And while I hated it for him, I couldn't dismiss it just because I was scared of being hurt. It would be unfair to use him as an excuse and then discount his experiences and feelings in the process. When I pulled back, I noticed Monroe and Nicco watching us. They stood next to one another, and I didn't want to admit how good they looked side by side.

One was all light, golden hair with pale green eyes, the other was dark hair with stormy eyes, and tattoos covering his bronze skin, bad boy written all over him. And yet, while their exteriors differed significantly, I knew they were both nice guys, *good guys*, the kind that had hearts of gold. The packaging was just slightly different.

Sighing, I wiped my face again, knowing I'd need to do some type of mask to get rid of all the puffiness before the wedding, or everyone would think I was crying for other reasons.

"Fine. Jude makes a valid point. I don't know if I

can trust you yet, Nicco. You abandoned me when I needed you, and that hurts. Out of all the people who left, you were the one I'd connected to the most. I can't promise that things will move in that direction again, even if my body wants to. But I'd be remiss if I didn't say I haven't missed you or wished I could talk to you."

"So, are you saying you'll give me a chance?"

"Yeah, as friends."

"Okay, I can accept that, and I'll show you that you can trust me again. I promise. I'll be the best damn friend you've ever had."

"Don't make a promise you can't keep. The lie hurts too much."

I'd whispered it, but he still heard it, striking his heart. I didn't mean to keep hurting him, but it was true, and I needed to remind myself of what was at stake. He nodded, swallowing. Monroe walked back over, having set the table with Jude and giving us a modicum of privacy.

"I hope it's not too presumptuous, but I grabbed a few extra sandwiches if you want to join us, Nicco, and if that's okay with you, Lo?"

I glanced at Nicco, hope shining in his eyes. "Yeah, if it's okay with you, I'm good."

"I'd love to."

So that was how I ended up having the weirdest lunch ever with an ex-booty call, my 'has potential' neighbor, and foster kid. It wasn't as odd or uncomfortable as I expected, making me wonder for the first time if something unconventional could actually work. Wells and Monroe seemed to think so, but did that apply to others too, or only them?

As we all laughed at a story Jude told us over deli sandwiches and chips, a picture began to form in my heart, one I wasn't ready to acknowledge, but one all the same, and I was surprised who all it included.

THIRTEEN

Smoothing down the navy fabric of my dress, I turned to the mirror, checking all my angles to make sure everything looked okay. Peering over my shoulder, I caught my reflection, the expression of insecurity catching me off guard as I bit my lip. I hadn't cared what I looked like in so long; the feeling had become foreign to me.

In reality, it was the first time in forever I'd felt confident about my body. Yet, the conditioned response lingered after years of emotional abuse. Thoughts wanted to rise up, my subconscious mind fearful of not meeting expectations. How many times had I wanted to feel like I was good enough in the eyes of my mother? Brian? Classmates and colleagues even?

It was a heavy thing to realize you'd spent so many years trying to measure up to others' expectations of yourself, that you'd forgotten what was important to you.

Staring at my reflection, I realized I didn't know myself. Not anymore.

But unlike before—when I'd been so depressed, the

weight blanketed me into an empty void making me unrecognizable—this was a good change.

My hair was clean and shiny, no longer hanging off me lifelessly. My complexion was clear and dewy, something I'd worked to achieve for years, and now looked natural. I had a nice color to my cheeks, the sun bringing out my olive complexion and was no longer the oily and pale pallor it had become. My shoulders were set back, my posture confident, and I could feel a difference in my stance. Yet, it was my eyes that had the most glaringly obvious transformation.

No longer empty, I didn't see fear, self-loathing, or contempt for life staring back at me. Instead, I found a brightness I'd never seen before residing there. I wouldn't deny there was also some mania, a hint of rebelliousness edging in. Mostly, though, a strength I'd never known before stared back, challenging me. My mask had cracked, and I shone through.

And quite frankly, it terrified the shit out of me.

Perhaps, that was an odd reaction because I should want to be happy and strong, and I did. That wasn't the issue. But if I no longer had the 'perfect Loren' mask to hide behind, who did it make me? Would people like this 'real' Loren?

But maybe most importantly, how long did I have before someone tried to take it? Without the mask, the wall shielding my emotions, I was open and vulnerable to any attack. And if I didn't think I was currently in a battle forged between the past and the present, I was deluding myself. I was on a precipice, the odds shifting with each win and loss.

Brian wouldn't want me to look or feel strong, especially without him. Jacqueline wouldn't either. I had to accept the fact they were narcissists, and unless they controlled me, they wouldn't back down. The extreme reaction with Barkley only proved it. They were a live grenade I would need to handle delicately, or I would lose more than the light I'd cultivated inside me. I could lose Jude, too.

A few months ago, I would've said the men I'd grown close to, the ones I didn't want to admit I pictured in my life, were the reason for this change. But I didn't believe that anymore. I'd already lost them and survived. It had been hard, and part of me feared I was only setting myself up for failure, trusting them again, but if anything, I'd proven to myself I could do it on my own.

I needed to own my strength and validate my own achievements, or I'd never change.

"Lor, can you help me with this?" Jude asked, breaking me out of my thoughts. He stood in the doorway, staring down at the tie he had wrapped around his neck, looking at it in confusion. Chuckling, I walked the short distance and took the long strands from him. Almost as if no time had passed, I found myself folding and tucking the tie into a crisp knot. I didn't have to do it often for Brian, he'd been proficient, but every now and then, it had been an intimate gesture I'd do. The sudden intrusion into the moment had me clearing my throat as I stepped back.

"There you go. You look really nice, Jude."

"Thanks. It's not horrible," he joked. "I've never worn

something this nice before. Hell, I've never worn a suit before. I'm nervous I'll get something on it and ruin it."

Grabbing my earrings, I put them on as I answered him. "Nonsense. It's just clothes. They can be dry cleaned, or if it's something crazy, then replaced. I know you're not going to be some spoiled princess who's careless and doesn't take care of things because they know no value. So, don't stress over something that, at the end of the day, is meaningless."

"Huh, never been happier to not be a spoiled princess before."

Sticking out my tongue, I shook my head, laughing. "Well, I didn't say you weren't a nuisance."

"Yes! Means I'm doing my job as a teenager."

"You're hilarious." I walked over, grabbing his hands in mine. "I'm happy you're here. Thank you for going with me."

"Yeah, no problem." He shuffled on his feet, the emotion making him uncomfortable.

"I know, I know, too much emotion. Come on, let's see how long it takes my mother's head to explode."

Placing my arm in his, we laughed as we made our way to the door, ready to take on the evils of the world. Well, okay, maybe just the evils of Chicago's upper echelon.

WALKING through the hotel with Jude, we made our way to the ballroom where the wedding would take place. We turned the corner when I came to an abrupt stop at the sight before me. Blinking, the image didn't clear, and I turned to Jude, whispering to him.

"You see it too, right? I'm not hallucinating?"

Jude laughed, shaking his head. "No, Lor. You're not stroking out or whatever. I see them too."

Releasing a breath, we kept walking toward the strange duo leaning against the wall. I didn't want to make it obvious, but the slight licking of my lips had one of them smirking, his ice-blue eyes flaming with his intentions. When I left him this morning, I'd pushed down the doubt, ignoring the thought it would be only one night. I didn't see Sax as the type of man to be tied down, but seeing him here now, it made my insides flutter.

His wall companion also had my heart kick-starting, and I felt myself caving even more to him. I hadn't thought he would work this hard for it, never having anyone do it before, especially after he'd seemed to cave earlier. Brian had never tried, and when I didn't give him what he wanted, he went and found it himself. And yet, Nicco stood there as well, hands in his pockets with a sheepish smile on his face.

And I didn't hate that he was here, no, not at all.

They both looked delicious in their suits, and fantasies of what they could do to me with their ties, *together*, had me clenching my thighs. Clearing my throat, I pushed the thoughts out of my head, not wanting to get turned on with Jude right next to me, nor with my family within close proximity. Some societal limitations were harder to get rid of than others, and keeping it PG around certain crowds was apparently one for me. It was good to know your boundaries.

"Hey, what are you guys doing here?"

Sax smirked, lifting his eyebrow like the answer was obvious, and based on the way his eyes trailed over my body, I supposed his intentions were. When he didn't give anything up, I turned to Nicco, hoping he'd be more forthcoming.

"I, uh, wanted to make good on what I said earlier, and when Monroe mentioned he wasn't able to join you, I decided I would. I know we're technically crashing, but I made a few calls and was able to get your cousin an upgrade, and in return, she was kind enough to extend the invitation."

I looked between the two, Sax still undressing me with his eyes, and Nicco with hope that I wouldn't turn him away. It *was* a sweet gesture, and I knew my cousin wouldn't mind.

"That was kind of you. I'm sure you made Jo very happy."

"Joe?" he gulped, looking at Sax, apprehension building in his gaze before he looked back. "Your cousin is named *Joe*?"

Before I could tease him a little more, someone outed me. "Don't let her razz you. She means Josephine. Loren's just the only one who can get away with calling her Jo," my aunt offered, joining our circle and causing Nicco to relax.

Pouting, I turned to my aunt. "Ah, come on, Aunt Lorrie, don't ruin my fun!" The older woman rolled her eyes, giving me a rueful smile. Dropping the act, I folded her in my arms, a broad smile on my face. "It's so good to see you."

My Aunt Lorrie was my favorite relative and, fortunately, my dad's sister and my namesake. She was the coolest, and her daughter Jo and I had been close growing up, despite the age difference. Jo really was like a younger sister to me.

"You too, dear. Now, Josey called me in tears today when this one here called to offer her the Rose room and whatever upgrades she wanted."

My aunt beamed at me before walking over and kissing Nicco and Sax's cheeks. It was cute watching Sax bend down for her. They both preened under her affection, beaming smiles my way. She turned back to me, taking in Jude.

"Ah, this must be the famous Jude I've heard so much about."

I watched as he blushed when she patted his cheek and squeezed his hand. I knew she wanted to hug him, but she'd always been conscious of body language, believing hugs were earned and not expected.

"Nice to meet you, ma'am."

"Now, none of that. It's Auntie Lorrie."

"Okay. I've never had an aunt before."

It was an innocent comment, yet my insides wept at the life he'd lived up until now and rejoiced we could make it better.

"Well, I'm honored to be your first. This means I have a lot to do to show you the benefits of having a Great-Aunt."

"Aunt Lorrie, you are the best. But who have you

been getting all your gossip from? I know my mother hasn't been praising him." I looked at her curiously as she smiled wide, a hint of mischief at play.

"Ah, well, I believe that is surprise number two." She looked over at Nicco and Sax, and they briefly bowed their heads, smiling wide. I wanted to think how cute it was that they were all in on a secret with my aunt, but the suspicious part of me had anxiety creeping up at the unknown.

"Well, Beautiful, I didn't want to come empty-handed, and since roses are a little too ordinary for you, I brought something that will hopefully make you smile and soften you toward me."

Cocking my head, I looked at him, unsure what he could bring me.

"That's a pretty tall order."

The door to the bridal suite opened, pulling my focus, not realizing it had been so close. Jo exited, her white satin gown flowing around her as she talked animatedly to someone on the other side of the door. When she saw the group gathered, she spotted me and stepped forward, making her companion visible.

"Jude! Loren!" Imogen's voice rang out, and she bolted toward us before quickly stopping in front, not sure how to proceed. Taking the step for her, I pulled Immy into a tight hug, so happy to see her. Her brown hair was swept up, and she wore a dress. It was the most put together I'd seen her, and the thought eased me, the worry I'd held for her dissipating some.

"Oh my goodness, Immy. It's so good to see you. I've been so worried." I pulled back, running my hands up and down her arms, as I confirmed she was really here and okay. Stepping back, I tried to ease the awkwardness between the two teens. "And this one," I joked, knocking Jude's shoulder with mine. "I don't think he will believe it's you unless you hug him."

She smiled and reached across, and Jude opened his arms to hug her back, both of them relaxing in the gesture before pulling apart. My aunt, in her perceptiveness, could read a room better than anyone and covered the awkward silence that had fallen.

"Imogen's been a huge help. She's a delight, a true treasure."

Immy blushed, her smile radiant as her pale blue eyes sparkled, and despite not seeing her for months, I could tell she'd grown stronger. Her eyes still held some darkness, but she wasn't hiding any longer. In fact, she stood tall, and that was significant progress. My cousin walked over, hugging me as well, joining our huddle.

"Loren, it's so good to see you. I'm sorry I haven't reached out as much since everything with Brian. I've been worried about you," she whispered before pulling back. Shaking my head, I dispelled her guilt.

"I'm good, and I'm so happy for you today. I can't believe you're getting married, Jo."

"Me either!" she squealed, "But speaking of things you can't believe." She wiggled her eyebrows before looking at the group that had gathered to the side. Nicco, Sax, Jude, Immy, and my aunt all spoke in hushed whispers.

"Jude? I know, it was a surprise, but the best thing I've done."

"No, silly. The hot men you have that were willing to schmooze me just to get an invite." Her smile was wide as she delivered the news. "I'm not one to turn down an upgrade either, but just so you know how much effort it took on his part," she whispered, leaning in further. "I'd tried to get the Rose room a year ago, and the bitchy lady told me it was booked out five years in advance and I should plan better. So, whatever strings he pulled to make it happen… like *damn*!" Her eyes went wide with her statement.

Butterflies erupted inside me, and I looked at Nicco again. He was talking with the others, but his eyes were on me. When he caught my stare, his lips lifted up on the side, a softness entering his eyes, and I couldn't deny he was trying. Mouthing, "thank you," I turned back to Jo.

"Wow, that is something."

"Yeah, *they* are." She giggled. "The bearded one hasn't taken his eyes off you since I stepped out here either, and before, he'd kept your mother away, so winning! If I wasn't marrying the love of my life right now, I'd be jealous, girl." She squeezed my arms, her smile radiant as she turned back to everyone. "Speaking of, I think it's time you all took your seats, so I can walk down that aisle and get married!"

"Oh yes, of course. You look gorgeous, by the way. Congratulations, Jo."

"Thanks, Lor. And I do look great, don't I?" She spun, striking a pose. "Imogen saved the day with a quick makeup fix." She winked at the teen, then grabbed her mother and made her way to get in position. Jo stopped after a few feet, looking back over her shoulder. "Oh, beware your mother's warpath. She's been on one since she arrived, and didn't like not getting her way." She briefly flicked her eyes to Sax, and I briefly bowed my head in understanding.

Aunt Lorrie huffed, rolling her eyes. "That's saying it kindly. She's pissed Nicco showed her up by procuring the ballroom. She was prepared to brag all night about how she wrangled the Lilac room for Josey. I think for irritating your mom in the process, he should get bonus points." She winked before they continued on their way to the ballroom, leaving our little group standing awkwardly as we regarded one another.

"Well, I guess it's time to take a seat."

Sax sauntered over, sticking out his arm to escort me, giving me a naughty wink as I placed my arm in his. The rest followed us into the room, an usher directing us to our seats. I caught my mother's scowl as we sat, but I ignored it, too focused on the way Sax and Nicco's bodies felt next to me. Because, of course, they both squeezed in close, not allowing an inch between us. Sax laid his palm on my leg, effectively wrapping it around the bare skin visible when I crossed my legs.

It was a possessive grip, and I sucked in a breath, peeking over at him from the corner of my eyelid. His lips lifted up slightly, but he continued to stare straight ahead, a look of innocence on his face. Nicco shifted, his leg brushing against my other side, and when Sax's thumb began to softly caress me, I could no longer focus on anything or anyone around me. The music started, and we stood as the bride walked by, but once we sat again, they both went directly back to what they were doing. It was going to be a long ceremony at this rate.

SOMEHOW, I'd managed to dodge and avoid my mother for the past hour as I greeted my family with my trailing shadows. Jude and Immy had found a safe place to hide away and were chatting while sharing a plate of hors d'oeuvres. They both had wide smiles on their faces, and I was glad they'd been reunited. I hoped it meant they would be able to continue their friendship now, though I wondered if there was potentially something more brewing between them. I might need to talk with Jude about making sure not to rush things based on Immy's history. I didn't want to see her be triggered and have it ruin their relationship.

Arms wrapped around me, and his now familiar smell greeted me. His tall frame cocooned me in him, and even with heels putting me close to 5'10", he was still a good five inches taller than me. Tilting my head up, I found the sexy neanderthal staring down at me, a softness around his edges as he did. It was something I'd started to notice. When he was in his zone, everything was locked down, and he scanned the room looking for all possible threats, but in the tender moments with me, I was his focus, and he showed me past his walls.

"Hey."

"Spitfire, have I told you how radiant you look tonight?"

"No," I said, a smile in my voice.

"Well, you are, even more than the bride."

Shaking my head at his nonsense, I looked back to the room, not wanting to lose sight of Jacqueline and be ambushed when I was actually enjoying myself. Sax's hands slid back to grip my hips, pulling me harder into him. His breath skirted my neck as he bent down to whisper in my ear.

"Believe it, Loren. You're sexy as fuck, but tonight, there's a shiny confidence coming from you too. I think my dick changed you last night."

Guffawing at him, I tried to distract him from the fact I wanted to rub myself against him like a cat in heat. The way he could say the sweetest and dirtiest things together, making my heart and pussy respond simultaneously, blew my mind.

"What I wouldn't give to take you somewhere right now and remind you, if you've already forgotten, *Spitfire*."

Sucking in a breath, I watched the couples dance on the floor and smiled at how happy my cousin looked. Sax didn't let my distraction impede him, though, and thrust the thick appendage he kept speaking of against me. The hard length rubbed against my ass, reminding me of all the pleasure he had given me.

"Do you remember how dripping wet you were? How when you begged me to fill you, I picked you up and impaled you on me in one go?"

Shit. He wasn't stopping or backing down, and I really didn't want to moan out loud and have my family look over and see the blatant look of lust on my face. Taking his hand, I pulled him until I stopped in my tracks, realizing I couldn't leave Jude vulnerable for someone to approach in my absence.

"Nicco will watch them."

Sax must've known what I was thinking and when I looked over, I saw Nicco staring back, his grey eyes hooded, and he nodded. There was a look of pain and longing on his face, but surprisingly, no jealousy. I found it odd, but my arousal didn't have time to linger on it. Once I knew they were safe, I regained my footing and took off. Out in the hotel, I looked around as I kept pulling him, searching for an appropriate place. They always made it seem so easy in books and movies to find random hookup spots. I guess there was the bathroom, but I didn't really fancy having to maneuver around a toilet or have others hear us.

Finally, I spotted one of the rooms the bridal party had used to get dressed in. Cracking the door, I found a sitting room with another door that opened into a smaller space for the bride or groom to dress. Walking toward it, I barely made it inside before Sax had me up against the wall, his lips on my neck.

"I haven't been able to stop thinking about you all day, Spitfire. When you're not there, your hands are like little ghosts I can feel all over my body, haunting me with the pleasure they can bring me."

Moaning, my head fell back against the wall as his palms shoved up my dress, the tight material bunching around my hips. Now that my legs could move, he hitched them up, wrapping them around him. The move brought me closer to his lips, and I took them in a bruising kiss. This was the thing about Sax. He made it okay to want.

Nicco had taught me it was okay to explore and find confidence in sexuality, making it comfortable and safe.

Sax, he showed me how to take it.

He was dominating and possessive, but he let me control it at the same time. It was an odd combination, but it was exactly what I needed.

His hands gripped my thighs, pulling me tighter to his body as we kissed like there was no tomorrow. When his fingers brushed over my panties, I moaned loudly into his mouth; the feeling felt so good. There was no denying how turned on I'd gotten from his dirty talk and the small ministrations he'd edged me with throughout the ceremony.

Sax gripped the edges of my panties, and before I could protest, he ripped them right off me. Gasping, I pulled back, shock covering my face.

"Why would you do that? I happened to like those a lot."

He gave me a rueful smirk, nothing but pure sexual mischief in his eyes. "Oh, Spitfire, your reaction was half of it, *this*," he plunged up in me, pausing as we both moaned and caught our breaths, "was the other."

Sax had apparently freed himself in my lust haze and started to pound into me at an unforgiving pace, but it was what I'd wanted. His cock filled me up, his girth what I'd needed as he pulled me down onto him. The only sounds were our moans and grunts, accompanied by the delicious sound of our skin slapping into one another. I was so close already, my pussy soaking him with each thrust, that when he bent to kiss me, nipping my lip a little, it was all it took to send me over.

Moaning into his mouth, he accepted my offering greedily, swallowing down the sound. When he stilled a few seconds later, holding me tightly to him. We stared into one another's eyes as he pulsed in me. Our breaths were heavy, mixing with one another as we stayed entwined, sharing the moment. Intimacy had never felt so effortless.

Our timing couldn't have been better as we heard the other door open in the first room a few seconds later and heard people enter. Shock covered my face, but Sax held a finger over my lips, and we stayed perfectly still, his cock staying hard in me as we listened. The door was open next to us. We hadn't made it past the threshold before Sax had slammed me against the adjacent wall. As long as they didn't walk into this room, we would stay hidden. I was thankful his finger was over my mouth in the next second when the voices started.

"You're running out of time, Jacqueline! My patience is running thin."

My eyes bugged out at the sound of my ex's voice and my mother's name. Sax, apparently more adept at subterfuge, raised his eyebrow at me but didn't make any other sound. There was some whispered shouting that followed, and I could only catch partial sentences.

"… I told you I was taking care of…"

"You're lying!"

"I want what I'm owed. Or… I don't think…"

"We still have the… if all else fails."

There was a sound of feet shuffling, and then we could hear them clearly.

"You promised!"

"Well, it seems I'm not the only one who lies, Jacqueline. We're supposed to be in this together, but don't think I won't sell you out if it benefits me too, that is, if you don't hold up your end of our agreement."

"I'll get it. But, don't forget who you're speaking with, *Brian*. I brought you in on this. I can take you out just as easily."

"You know, I used to be scared of you, but you've lost your touch. You're running out of time and credibility."

Movement could be heard again, making their words fade as they moved. The last thing I could make out was "vum," but I had no clue what it could mean.

We heard the door shut, and I went to ask a question, but Sax hushed me, making sure to wait until we were positive they were both gone. Anxiety coursed through me, wondering what they were up to. But hope surged forward, replacing it at the realization I'd been right. The confirmation of that outweighed everything else, taking back some of the strength they'd both stolen over the years.

When a few minutes had passed, Sax dropped his hand, and he gave me a knowing look before quietly releasing my legs from the death grip around him. He dropped them back to the floor and slowly pulled out of me in the same breath. While I smoothed my dress down, he'd managed to find some tissues, winking as he gave them to me. Cleaning up, I watched as he did the same before tucking his cock back into his pants and zipping up. I wasn't even sure if he had boxers on since it was dark, but the idea of him being that readily available started to turn me on again.

My stare down with his dick must've been noticeable, and he chuckled as he pulled me out of the room. I knew we needed to go, the voices having confirmed our time was up, but a part of me was sad there wouldn't be a round two. It only proved how different I was becoming and how much I enjoyed my new freedom.

FOURTEEN

NICCO

Being near Loren all night after months of wishing I could hold her, yet knowing I wouldn't get to touch her how I wanted, was torture. It didn't help that she looked radiant, causing me to physically hold my hands down each time she was near, so I didn't reach out and grab her. It was a pain I would gladly bear, though, if it meant I got to be back in her life.

When Monroe had mentioned the wedding on our awkward elevator ride, I was shocked he'd willingly help me. I realized how nice of a guy he was and someone I wanted to become like.

Doubt had crept in for the tiniest second, making me want to walk away, to take the easier route. But I couldn't do that again. My heart wouldn't let me give her up so easily this time, no matter the reason. So instead, I vowed to emulate him and hoped my actions showed a more mature version of myself. The only way I would walk away this time was if she sent me.

Sax and I still hadn't talked about our feelings or what it meant for us. But when he uncovered my plan, he insisted on joining me. I hadn't realized their relationship had escalated. It had almost made me want to give up, too. Instead, I thought of it as the slap in the face I needed. If I wanted the reward of having Loren in my life, then I needed to quit giving in, wanting to escape with the easy route, and accept the risk.

Hell, I was supposed to be fighting for her!

And for once… I wanted to. So, I needed to show her.

There wouldn't be any more backing down or attempting to walk away if things got difficult. Because life without her was worse. It was as simple as that, and I needed to show her I was serious and someone she could depend on.

"You should ask her to dance when she gets back," Immy whispered to me, giving me a soft smile.

She knew I had feelings for Loren and how hard the past few months had been with our forced isolation. Immy had high hopes that things could be fixed easily with an apology. Her naivety was something I loved about her, her belief that things could be fixed if you wanted it bad enough. With all the things that had occurred in her life, I was glad she could still view the world with such hope and openness, even if it meant it wasn't that simple for me.

Seeing her tonight, it was the happiest I've seen her in a long time, and it made me proud. I was beginning to see parts of the old Immy emerge, transforming into something new with a layer of strength she hadn't possessed before. It confirmed how much she'd grown and the woman she was growing into.

Mostly, it reminded me I couldn't underestimate people, including myself.

I was beginning to realize I'd relied on Atticus to make decisions for me for so long, I'd forgotten I could make them on my own. Even my plan to leave the family to teach hadn't been entirely mine. I hadn't officially done anything with it because I held on to the fact I wouldn't be able to leave, the fear holding me back. Even in my rebellion, I hadn't made a decision. I thought I'd been thinking for myself, but I'd covered it up, pushing off the blame, and allowing myself to be controlled under the lie. It was just the way it was.

I didn't want to only be a pawn in someone else's game plan; I wanted to drive my future, and that started with figuring out what I wanted to do with my life. And perhaps more importantly, who I wanted to be at the end of the day.

What Atticus had told me about the family and Loren being targeted did change things for me. A future I hadn't envisioned flashed before my eyes, and she was at the center of it. I just had to figure out how to make it happen now.

"Maybe." I shrugged, not making eye contact with her. "We'll see how she is when she gets here." Immy shook her head, knowing I was making excuses, but it was all I had at the moment.

"She'll forgive you, Nic."

I nodded, hoping to appear like I was listening as I scanned the room. I found her mom watching us, casting dirty looks at our table all night. I had a feeling she was up to something. Jacqueline hadn't taken her eyes off us. Sax had pointed her out when we got here, waving as she walked by. The way she'd blanched at his appearance was comical, but I didn't miss the once-over she did of me, disgust lingering in her eyes as she tossed her hair, dismissing us. It was only a matter of time now before she came over, making her move. I hoped she left Loren out of it for once, but it wasn't likely, based on what I knew.

"Anybody want more cake?" Jude asked.

"Yeah, sure. I'll go with you." Immy turned to me, a question on her face. "Is that okay, Nicco?"

"Yeah, yeah, just hurry back," I responded, distracted. I turned and watched as they walked off, all shy smiles as they regarded one another. Immy was happy, and it was good to see them reunited. It made me want to believe in first love. They made it seem so hopeful, and it was nice to see Immy still believed in it after everything she'd been through.

Glancing back around, my constant need to survey the room for threats overrode me, so I wasn't surprised when she struck. Her staying away up until now had been too good to be true. I knew it had. In a way, though, I was thankful she waited until they were gone to descend upon me.

"I don't know what you're doing here with my daughter, but you won't be getting anything from her." Her voice was smug. Her nose turned up as she delivered her threat. Jacqueline was practically vibrating with anger as she stood at the end of the table, waiting for me to make a scene. When I stared at her, not giving in to what she wanted, her face became redder.

"You seem to be mistaken, lady. The only thing I want from your daughter is to be in her life."

"Well, you won't be getting any of *that* either," she huffed, crossing her arms. Rolling my eyes, I sat up from the leaned back position I'd been in and leveled her with disinterest. Jacqueline's returning look told me everything she thought about me. Clearly, she knew more, based on the smug way she stood, her fists planted on her hips. The way she cast her eyes at me, scanning me from head to toe, let me know she thought I was worse than the gum on the bottom of her shoe, not that she would ever allow such a thing to occur. She attempted to degrade me with her words and demeanor, her power play to anyone she deemed lower than her.

It wasn't the first time someone had made snap judgments based on my appearance, and quite frankly, she was nowhere near as scary as the people I dealt with regularly at fight nights. I didn't care how she viewed me, but her actions spoke of how she thought of Loren, and that was something I wouldn't let stand.

"Interesting. Last I heard, your daughter wanted nothing to do with you. So, I think it'd be best if you left before I decide to make a scene, embarrassing you in front of all of your peers that you try so hard to impress."

Her face turned a shade of purple that couldn't be healthy, and I wondered if I'd unintentionally killed her. It wouldn't bother me, but killing the mother of the girl you wanted wasn't a good look. Even if the mom of said girl was a bitch, it probably wasn't good form.

I watched as she warred with herself to put me in my place or to maintain social manners. The neighboring eyes won out in the end, keeping her in check. Jacqueline smoothed down her dress, turned in a dramatic flair, then stopped a few feet away. She didn't even deem me worthy of a full turn, as she glanced over her shoulder to deliver her scathing blow. The method of choice with women like her was to hit you when you thought you made it out safely. There was always something underhanded going on under the surface with women of her stature. They had too much free time and money, allowing them to stick their noses into situations they didn't need to. I didn't doubt she'd go away easily.

"Might want to reconsider your devotion to her considering she's been slutting it up with the big tatted one."

The sneer on her lip conveyed how she thought about Sax, and I laughed, her words not hitting the target she'd intended. Rolling my eyes, I didn't care what else she had to share. She was attempting to stir up trouble, but she didn't have all the information for once. The fact was, I did know she was with Sax, and when I thought about it, it didn't bother me like she expected. The fact was, I was happy for them both, even if jealousy also raged within me. The overarching emotion, the one that stood out the most, was acceptance, because Loren needed to be loved.

I knew what that meant for my life, too. Loren was someone I was willing to figure things out with, no matter what it looked like. I didn't know how it would work, but it was a path I would explore for her.

Immy and Jude walked back, plates in hand, big smiles on their faces as they flirted with one another. Jacqueline stomped off when I didn't respond, passing them. I could only assume a scathing look was directed at them, and I watched with pride as Jude rolled his eyes at her. Apparently, there was no love lost there either. I would need to ask him about the situation later to make sure there wasn't something I was missing.

The thought had surged up unencumbered, but the reality of it warmed me. My protective gene had been triggered, wanting to make sure both Jude and Loren were safe. She'd been right earlier that I'd failed him, and in turn, her. I had known the full scope and could've called Ignite to find him a temporary place, but I'd neglected it, more focused on my own wants and what I'd lost. I'd been self-absorbed.

The fact I'd forgotten about the youth center also riled me up. It had become a secret passion project of mine after all. When I heard about the troubles there, I couldn't standby and let it disappear. It had always been a good place, even if the name had suggested otherwise. When I was younger, it had even been a haven for me. While I'd been taken in by Dayton and the family when my mom died, it was still hard to feel like I belonged.

Surprisingly, it was Dayton who had encouraged me to go. He'd been on the board at that time, and it had turned out to be a good suggestion. I found resources and support there to encourage me with my art. Before long, I had friends outside of the family, giving me a safe place to belong. It showed me there was life outside of the mafia. I just had to dream it.

When the scandal broke, and the potential closure of the place, I stepped in. People in this city needed a place for kids to learn and feel safe. I hoped by staying anonymous, by keeping the Mascro name separate, it might be able to be the place it was meant to be this time. I'd intentionally hired Mitzi to run it, hoping her connection with the Chicago elite would help draw in donors and give it prestige, helping it in the long run. So far, it seemed to be doing well under her management and supervision.

The first things I'd changed were the board of directors and name, needing something new to be reborn in the fire. I hadn't intended to name it after the shop, but it was also my rebirth, representing the better parts of me, the life outside the dark crime world.

Ignite Youth Center was a thriving place, and lots of kids were able to get the support, safety, and resources they needed to thrive. It felt good to be responsible for that. Seeing Jude as part of it was confirmation I was on the right path.

I didn't mind that no one knew I was responsible for it, well, I guess Atticus knew, but I liked it better this way. I didn't have to worry if people were only friendly to me because of it or wanted something from me. I'd been left with a large sum of money from my father, the Mascro family trust switching over on my twenty-fifth birthday, but it felt wrong to use it. At least this way, I could give back, and it felt better used.

It was a slippery slope hiding behind the name in obscurity, and I knew I needed to tell Loren, but I didn't want her to change her mind about me only because of that. I didn't want to sway her with it. For some reason, it felt like cheating, using something that should be done out of merit, not for praise. It would be the easy option, and I wanted to win her over because of who I was and not only the good deeds I'd performed. But I guess there was also a tiny part of me that worried it would be seen as a betrayal, and I didn't want that either.

There were already too many secrets between us; I didn't want to add another.

Sax and Loren walked in a few moments later, and I could tell what they'd been up to. Loren's complexion was rosy, and her body looked more relaxed as she held his hand, walking toward us. Jealousy surged again, but it wasn't an all-consuming type. In fact, I think I was just jealous of the time they got to spend together, not of Sax, not of what they'd done.

Weird.

Maybe this relationship would work better than I thought. But first, I had to get her to forgive me, to give me a chance.

A slow song started to play, and I decided to take Immy's advice. Jumping up, I gave the two teens a look to stay at the table until Sax returned. Immy rolled her eyes, but Jude nodded, accepting my demand. I was beginning to really like the kid, and what he brought to both Loren and Immy's lives.

Striding toward them, I took my shot and used all the cocky swagger I had in me as I approached. "Beautiful, can I have this dance?"

They both stopped, Sax smirking at me with his crooked smile and knowing eyes, but he didn't try to derail me. That said something.

"Hi. Yeah, okay, I guess that would be okay. I, um, sure, uh-huh."

Her stutter was adorable, lifting my lips at the corner, knowing I still affected her, hoping it was a good sign. Taking her hand, I pulled her out onto the dance floor before she could regain her composure. I almost sighed with relief with how good it felt to have her in my arms.

Pulling her close, Loren's smell surrounded me. Dropping my head into her neck, I breathed her in and sighed out loud. "God, I've missed you, Beautiful."

I didn't miss the way she melted in my arms at the sound, her body melding to mine. I knew I would never be able to walk away from her again. How I'd done it the first time was a complete mystery.

The music played, and we swayed in our position, two bodies joined together almost indecently for a wedding, but I didn't care. Her arms felt too good around me for me to care about offending some rich white women.

For a moment, I could believe it was just us, that we were on this dance floor dancing and had come together tonight. She entwined her arms tighter, spurring me on to believe that all wasn't lost between us. For how could it be when she held me like this? There was no way she didn't care about me. I *had* to believe it, at least.

I was at the point that even if Loren decided she didn't love me, that she couldn't be with me, I would be in her life regardless, in any shape or form. It would hurt to see her be happy with others, but I would rather be part of her world than nothing. The things she brought to me were irreplaceable. Loren didn't realize the light she had. She was a comfort, a dream, a purity that was difficult to find. She was the way out of the life I had always felt damned by.

All the darkness I'd been around, all of the violence and cruelty, it disappeared when she was with me. Loren was a soft caress, a gentle smile. She was enjoying your favorite pizza and laughing at stupid things. With Loren, everything felt natural.

"I missed you too, Nicco."

Her words were whispered, but I heard them, breaking through the last layer I'd held onto. I'd always thought I used a shield to hide the mafia part of my life from everyone else, but perhaps, I'd hidden from life instead. After experiencing the freedom to be 'Nicco' without having to be 'crime family Nicco,' or 'art teacher Nicco,' or even 'tattoo shop owner Nicco,' and simply be me, I could not only see the difference but feel it. Loren taught me how to just be and accept the parts of me I hadn't ever wanted to face.

I could see Loren doing that with Immy as well. I knew Immy still had a lot to learn and process, that she wasn't healed completely. But she was no longer shriveled up in a ball crying in the corner, metaphorically speaking. Imogen now held herself together, and I could see the strength emerging in her that she would need for this life. And perhaps, that was what I realized the most.

Twirling her around, I held her close, needing to feel her and know it wasn't a dream. "You're a great dancer,

Beautiful. I almost want you to pinch me so I know I'm not dreaming." Loren looked up at me, a soft smile on her lips, but I could still see the hurt and fear lingering there, and it gutted me.

All the dreams I'd ever had were about running away, about having something separate from the family and leaving that responsibility behind. But why couldn't I have it all together? Why did the mafia have to be separate from my other dreams? Immy had said it perfectly— life and family were complex no matter who they were. Why not enjoy having the people around you that you wanted. Especially with the power we had. Why did I keep feeling like I had to choose? What if this was a perfect 'why choose' moment?

The music changed, and the emcee came on announcing for all single ladies to head to the floor. I watched as Jacqueline smirked near the emcee and had a bad feeling she had something planned. When I felt Loren tense, her panic palpable, I fell into my white knight mode.

Wrapping her up, I pulled her away and off the dance floor. She didn't need to be out there on the floor, reminded of her marriage, an outcast amongst her family. I stepped out through the ballroom doors, peeking over my shoulder for a brief moment. Sax confirmed with a nod he had them. With a breath, I pulled her along, Loren going with me willingly. I walked far enough away, so we didn't have to hear and I felt her body begin to relax.

"Thanks, Nicco. I kind of forgot about having to deal

with those types of things and didn't, well, I wasn't prepared, to say the least."

"Yeah, no problem. I kinda wanted to get you away anyway."

"Oh?"

"Yeah. I wanted to see how you were feeling about everything." We were stopped against a wall, my thumbs brushing small circles in her palms as I listened.

"Generally? I mean, not bad." She looked at me quizzically, not sure what I was asking. To be honest, I didn't know what I was asking either. I just wanted to talk to her when an idea popped into my head. Smiling down at her, I mischievously asked her the thing I'd been dying to know.

"Actually, I have a question for you."

"Okay."

"So, Cassandra was telling me this story..."

"Oh, God. No, please." She groaned, causing me to chuckle.

"So, is it true?"

"Well, I guess it depends on your definition of the truth," she hedged, dropping her eyes.

"Hmm," I crowded her against the wall, speaking low as I lifted her chin. "Did it happen, Beautiful?"

"Yeah," she grumbled, sticking out her lip, and I wanted to nip it between my teeth. Our bodies weren't pressed together, and I struggled not to lean into her, to show her how she affected me.

"Then it's the truth. Don't tell me pretty lies, Beautiful. They're too dangerous to believe."

"It's not so much a lie, as it is wanting to save face, Nicco." Loren's face heated at the admittance.

"Your face is beautiful. I don't know what you need to save it from." Loren softened, a smile highlighting her face.

"I've missed your sweet talk, Nicco."

"I've missed you, Beautiful." She laid her head on my chest, and I pulled her close. After a while, I smiled into her hair as I prodded her again. "So… did you really come down to the tattoo shop?"

"Yeah, a moment of weakness."

"I have to say. It kind of gives me hope."

"Why's that?"

"Because it meant maybe you still felt something for me. That it was as strong as I remember feeling about you."

She pushed me back, looking at me this time as she spoke. "That was never in question, Nicco, because I did feel for you strongly, hence why I went down to the shop. Why I was so upset when you left me, it's not about not missing you or not feeling things for you. It's about being hurt."

"I get that, I do. I never meant to cause you pain, Loren. I thought I was making a better choice. It was miserable every day staying away from you, not calling you. Fuck, I even almost punched Atticus once."

"You did?"

"Uh-huh, it was interesting."

Laughing, she nodded. "Yeah, I could see how that might be complicated."

"Complicated. Hmph. That's a good word for it.

There's just," I paused, trying to find my words, "so many things you don't know about our family yet."

"I'm starting to get the idea."

"Oh?"

Loren rolled her eyes, and fuck if it wasn't the cutest thing. "Well, yeah, I mean, I got blown up, and there's always all those scary beefy guys around in suits. And, of course, the blackout SUV with the magic drivers and the fighting ring. I'm not… I'm not stupid."

"That's one thing you aren't, Beautiful. You're right there."

"But… I also don't want to say it out loud because then it makes it true. And I don't know if I'm ready to accept it."

"That's fair. Because I think once you do, life will change even more."

"Yeah, I've had a lot of life changes lately. Speaking of, I should probably get Jude home. It's getting late, and I promised him we wouldn't stay forever."

"Yeah, okay. Um, do you guys need a ride?" I asked hopefully, not ready to leave her yet.

"Yeah, sure. That'd be great." Loren smiled, and my whole world lit up. How could her smile make me feel so happy?

We walked back into the ballroom, and thankfully, they were cutting another cake or some nonsense. They had three cakes. Seriously, who needed that many cakes? Well, I didn't know why I was suddenly angry with the bride. She was lovely and nice. I suppose I was taking my frustration from Jacqueline out on her.

Nodding to Sax, I indicated we were ready to leave, not

wanting to enter any further. He motioned to the two teens, and they headed toward us. Taking the chance, I grabbed Beautiful's hand and pulled her. When she linked her fingers with mine, my whole body soared, content filling me. I slowed our pace as Sax, Jude, and Immy caught up.

"Are you guys ready to go?"

"Yes, thank God. If I had to listen to one more crappy wedding song, I think I was gonna poke my eyes out with a spoon."

"Dramatic much there, Jude?"

"You said the same thing, Immy!"

"What? I would never," she sassed, and they both fell over in laughter.

"Come on, you crazy kids. Maybe if we ask nicely, Nicco or Sax will stop and get us ice cream," Loren offered, winking at me. Fuck, I'd buy her the whole store if she kept looking at me that way.

"Oh, yes, ice cream!" They chorused despite having devoured plates of cake just a second ago. They took off walking toward the parking garage, bumping into one another as they flirted, the three of us trailing behind. When we got to the garage, we all clambered into the vehicle that was idling for us.

Thirty minutes later, full of ice cream and laughter, we pulled up to Loren's building. She paused before opening the door, looking at us. "I wasn't expecting you guys tonight, so I wanted to say thank you. I know my cousin appreciated it. And it was nice to have the backup. I successfully avoided my mom all night too."

"Yeah, about that..."

"Nope. Don't tell me," she shook her head. "It's been a nice night."

"Well, I do feel like we should talk soon about her. She's up to something. I don't trust her."

"I know. We, uh, overheard something," she glanced at Sax and then the teens, who appeared to be focused on a phone screen. "But I'll unpack all that later. I just want tonight to be this."

"So, that means there will be a later?" I asked, that familiar feeling of hope rising up.

"Yeah, there's going to be a later."

She smiled before leaning over and kissing me on the cheek and turned and kissed Sax on the cheek, as well. She hugged Immy before climbing out of the car. Jude stopped, blushing, and I realized he didn't know what to do or how to act in front of us. Finally, he awkwardly waved and followed Loren out.

When the door shut, Immy turned to me, a stern look on her face. "If you break her heart again, I will punch you in the junk myself."

I looked at her, all seriousness, nodding to show I accepted her words. "If I break her heart again, I'll *let* you punch me."

Grunting, Sax added, "If you break her heart, I'll just shoot you."

His comment sent us all laughing as the car pulled away, and I sat back, thankful that things might be changing.

"So, are you guys gonna talk about the fact you both like the same girl?" Immy mentioned casually, throwing it out there for us. I looked at Sax as he peered up at me, and I shrugged my shoulders. "Nah."

"Isn't that weird?" she questioned. I was surprised when Sax was the one to answer this time.

"What's weird about it? We both like her. She likes both of us. As long as we all know and are happy with the arrangement, why can't we? Life's too short to live in the confining rules of the world. The mafia should've taught you that, princess."

"I guess when you put it like that."

"Besides," he continued, stretching out his long legs, "benefit of being in the mafia, she's more protected this way. More men to make sure she's always covered. Can't say I don't sleep better at night knowing that."

I didn't say anything. But inside, it made sense. I was envious. Of course, I wanted to be the only one she needed. Thinking more realistically, though, perhaps, Loren deserved more.

Settling back, the rest of the ride was quiet as we drove home. Before we pulled in, Imogen asked one more question. "So, does this mean I can go back to therapy?"

"Yeah. I think we could talk to Atticus about that."

"And can I have my phone?"

"Now, now, princess, don't push it."

"Ugh, you guys are the worst! Like, seriously. How can you expect a teenager to live like this? It's absurd." She continued to rant as she walked inside, leaving Sax and me behind. Chuckling, I shook my head, "I'm so glad she's a typical teenager, after all."

"Yeah, me too."

The night hadn't ended with any grand sweeping promises of love. But the night ended with me understanding what it truly meant to love someone.

And while I wasn't ready to say the words out loud yet, or even admit it to myself, I had started to come to the conclusion that I did, or at least I could.

And that was something I had never imagined before.

FIFTEEN

MONROE

Sitting in the quiet restaurant, I shifted again in my chair as I waited, hopeful this would be the turning point I needed. I'd already been denied a new court date, the hope I'd had earlier in the week flaming out. The only benefit was it gave me more time to gather all my weapons because now I was preparing to strike. My meeting tonight was the lynchpin I'd been waiting for.

I'd been attempting to schedule a meeting with him since Levi had been stolen from me. Finally, there had been an opening in his schedule. I didn't quite know everything he did or what his job entailed, but I knew he was the best, a rare good guy in the midst of assholes.

We'd met several years ago randomly through hockey and kept in contact. I'd helped him out a few times with some legal stuff, and he'd always told me to call him if I ever needed help, my last Hail Mary, so to speak, and he'd be there. I hadn't ever needed him until now.

The timing just sucked, making me once again have to choose something over Loren.

Thankfully, things there had started to improve, and

were headed back in the direction I wanted. Staying away from her had been hard, but I knew it had been necessary. Not because Brittni had threatened her, but because I knew if I had let Loren get involved, she would've either come to resent me when I inevitably pulled away or lost herself in my fight. She'd changed so much and had enough on her own plate. I couldn't bear to burden her with mine right then.

Jude had mentioned the wedding to me earlier in the week, and when the date mirrored my meeting, I felt hopeless. When I'd met Nicco in the weird elevator ride, I'd seen the solution. I hadn't known what he'd meant to her until I saw it on her face, and I realized it was an opportunity to make amends and give her what she needed.

It was then I understood the luxury of her dating multiple people at once. I didn't have to be everything or do it all. I couldn't anyway, not with Levi, nor did I think she would ask me to. It didn't stop me from wanting to, though. At least this way, I could be part of her life without feeling like a constant failure.

I'd always imagined the perfect relationship including Wells anyhow, so including more guys wasn't a big leap for me. Nevertheless, I wasn't certain whether or not that feeling would last once I had my life back in order. Would I be jealous when she was with the others? Would I feel like I was constantly waiting on the sidelines, only called in when I had value? In theory, I was on board. It would be interesting to see how it played out in real life to know if it was viable.

Nicco seemed like a decent guy, though, and I could tell he cared for her based on how he responded to my questioning. I felt compassion for the guy in the end, and I decided to help. I mentioned he could earn brownie points by attending this wedding. I only hoped he took me up on the advice. I guess it would be a test of whether things would be successful or not. Could we help one another or would we let jealousy get in the way?

When I finally spotted my friend walking through the space, I stood to greet him.

"Monroe. I'm glad we were finally able to find some time." He reached in to shake my hand, pulling me into a hug, slapping my back with his other hand.

"Me too, Logan. Thank you for coming to Chicago."

We took our seats, the waiter immediately appearing to take our drink order before quickly walking away to fill it. The service here was exemplary.

"I apologize it's taken so long. Things have been a bit chaotic with the new company getting off. I'm still closing out some of my old assignments as well."

"Ah, yes. How is all that going?"

"It's good, weird," he grinned, "but good. I feel lighter in a lot of ways than I have in years, but there's still that lingering feeling that the other shoe will drop the moment I stop worrying about it."

"Oh, yes. I know that feeling well." I chuckled just as the waiter sat our drinks down, and we ordered, sending him on his way.

"So, from your message, your ex has taken full custody of your son?"

"Correct. She's claiming neglect and violation of the custody order when I had my neighbor watch him."

"What have you gathered so far? Knowing you," he smiled, "you've been thorough."

The confirmation was nice to hear. "I have documentation proving she was having an affair long before our divorce, as well as who spent the most time with him parenting-wise before and after. And while that should be enough to sway any judge, this one has either been bought or has a grudge to prove."

"You said you believe the judge was part of this investment scheme your friend was connected to?"

Nodding, I took a sip of my drink, the hidden shame I felt for Wells' involvement rising to the surface. I didn't like to admit that part of me was angry with him for falling into the trap, wanting to take the easy way out to get the life he'd always wanted. The more significant part of me, though, felt responsible for his downfall. I'd always been the one to stop him in the past, his voice of reason, but when he'd pushed me away, I'd been hurt and wanted him to miss me.

It wasn't something I liked to admit about myself, that I desired to feel needed to feel worthy. Classic foster care kid syndrome, I suppose. I found a way to survive when it became dependent on others. If you made yourself useful, *invaluable,* they wouldn't want to get rid of you.

It had transitioned over in my teen years into social relationships, and I'd become so used to being everything for everyone else, I forgot what I needed. In a way, it was how the Komodo side of me was born. The times I needed to be relentless and unforgiving to survive, over-riding my natural instincts to sacrifice myself for others. It was rare, but the few times I'd been pushed too far, I found the coldness comforting as I struck my foes down, avenging all the wrongs done to me.

It wasn't my natural state or something I took plea-sure in doing, and the one time I needed Wells to step up, to show me I was worth fighting for, he hadn't. Worse, he'd ruined his life in the process.

I loved the man, but resentment and disappointment now coated the one thing I never doubted before. A part of me feared that once I was no longer of use to him, I'd be discarded just as easily. Wells' inability to make a commitment, to follow through on what he said, trig-gered all my insecurities. If he hadn't been able to give it to me before, why would he now? Logan's question had inadvertently stirred up a lot of things I hadn't been ready to face, especially Wells' admission of feelings the other night.

Swallowing another gulp, I placed the glass back down and looked up. "While he wasn't charged officially with anything, the damage had been done. The company named him in the scandal, wanting to have a scapegoat and separate themselves from the fallout. Wells was caught up in the blowback, losing everything in the process. Because nothing could be reaped back, everyone connected lost millions, and I think the judge sees this as a way to take his pound of flesh. He might even be getting some compensation from Brittni, I don't know. It's hard to prove anything. She either covered it up well and has been playing dumb this whole time, or she hired someone to do it for her. Who knows what they're doing. She's definitely sleeping with her lawyer, and I've debated telling her husband to see if he could be an asset."

Logan watched me, a thoughtful look on his face the whole time. He started to answer when our food arrived, interrupting him.

"Here you go, gentlemen. Let me know if you need anything else, and I hope you enjoy your meal."

The steaming food was a welcome disruption, and I used it to wash away the emotions that had sprouted up, not ready, or wanting to deal with them yet. After we'd both taken a few bites, Logan began again. I couldn't even taste what I was eating, the movements mechanical as I speared my fork and placed it in my mouth, my thoughts whirling a mile a minute.

"I think I might be able to help you there. I had an associate of mine look into things after you called," he paused, taking a bite. I rested my utensils on my plate, too anxious now to take another. It felt like an eternity while he chewed, and I found irrational irritation bubbling up in me. When he'd finished his bite, he wiped his mouth politely, taking a sip of his water. It might have been only a minute, but it felt like an eternity while I waited, holding my breath for what he had to share.

"I believe I have enough to help you. The question you have to ask yourself is, how far do you want to take it?"

His question took me by surprise, and I swallowed, understanding what he was asking. The cold exterior of the Komodo fell over me as I debated my recourse. It wasn't comfortable, a mask I wore out of necessity, the weight heavy with doubt, fear, and desperation. The more time I spent with Loren, though, the tighter the strain on it felt, reminding me it wasn't who I was.

I didn't like the person I became in those moments, but I'd accepted it, believing it was the only choice. I'd thought I was past it, but here I was, finding myself warring with the desire to turn off my emotions and crush Brittni, and my heart understanding she was still Levi's mother. I wasn't confident I could be the one to take her away from him. But if it meant her or me, I'd choose Levi every time.

"To get my son back, whatever it takes."

He dipped his head in understanding, and something that looked like respect reflected back in his eyes. He reached into his pocket and pulled out a card, sliding it across the table to me.

"I'll let Cohen know you'll be in touch."

"Thank you."

Logan nodded, and the conversation fell to trivial topics as we finished our meal. He told me about reconnecting with his niece and how he just started a new security company with a friend, Alpha Security Solutions. When I laughed, he only grinned as he continued to talk.

"So you still have your foundation, H.M.E? What does that stand for anyway?"

"Ah," he chuckled, "it stands for Hail Mary Enterprises and it's a conglomerate of entities I oversee. I'm the guy people call in when they're on their last Hail Mary."

"That explains why you're so busy," I mused, smiling at him. "Makes sense how it connects to the security one too. Do you even have time to play hockey anymore?"

"Not very much, unfortunately. I try to get in some slaps of the stick when I can, but up until a few months ago, I'd been focused on a project. Now, things are beginning to thin, and I think I'll have more time to live life."

"I'm guessing that might have something to do with your niece?"

"Yeah, you could say that."

"Funny how kids change things."

Logan chuckled, signaling the waiter for the bill. "Well, she's in her twenties, so not much of a kid, but yes, I want to spend time with her. I was very close to her mother, and while she's not biologically related, I care for her deeply. It's like getting Victoria back to some degree just by being in her presence. If you ever find a woman who makes the bad things not seem so dark and the good things a million times more, then do whatever it takes to hold on to her. I was young, naive, and I thought I had time or would meet someone else. But now I'm in my 40's, an eternal bachelor, and know the young love I felt for her was the most honest love I've ever found."

"You know, I'm starting to understand what you mean. Before everything with Brittni, I had started to see a woman who made me smile even when she wasn't around. I paused things to focus on Levi, and while I don't regret the decision because he deserves all of my attention, I hate it had to happen. It makes me resent

Brittni even more for the moments she's stolen from me, not only with Levi but Loren too."

"Then, you're doing the right thing. I can tell you're willing to do it, and the only reason why I gave you the card. But I can also see your guilt and fear over what you might have to do. *Don't*, Monroe. I've known you for years, and you're a good man. You've helped me out of a few situations and a few of my clients. You're not someone who maliciously attacks others. And to be honest, I wondered if there was someone new in your life because you do seem different. You're more confident, and there's this happiness that, based on the circumstances, shouldn't be there. I expected to come here tonight and get you drunk while we plotted your ex's demise, but you're a man who is focused and knows what he is fighting for. I'm happy for you. So don't feel guilty. Brittni started this, and if there's one thing I'm good at, it's ending things. Grab hold of the life you want to live and don't let anyone else take it from you."

I nodded, his words penetrating the fear that had wrapped around me. He was right. I didn't need to feel pity for her or guilt. She made her choices, and there were consequences for them. I also couldn't wait for others to decide my life was worth living for me. I had to do that on my own as well.

I had hoped to come out of this dinner with a solution to my custody battle, and instead, I left with not only that, but a declaration on my heart to fight for myself. I had to stop being scared I wouldn't be enough and embrace it. I had it wrong all along.

My life wasn't about pleasing others and being

needed. It wasn't about being the Komodo Dragon either to get what I wanted. It was time I accepted all facets of myself and just be me, Monroe Miller.

A devoted father who loved learning new things to do with his son.

A divorcee who was learning the difference between lust and love, but most importantly, that he was worthy of love being reciprocated.

A lawyer who could be ruthless but knew where to draw the line.

A dork who was awkward but found a kindred connection in Loren.

A fighter who was learning he could be strong without sacrificing himself.

And mostly, a man who could want two people and be brave enough to risk it all for the life and family he'd always dreamed.

Waving goodbye, I set off in a direction I knew well, but with a renewed sense of hope. Things were going to change.

And it all started with me.

Sixteen

LOREN

The car rolled to a stop outside the building I had left just yesterday morning. It felt like a week—or perhaps even a month with how my life had changed—had passed since then. It had been dark when we got here on Friday, and I'd been too sexed-up to notice the place Saturday morning. Looking at it now, I took it in more. It was a massive building with multiple floors, very modern and upscale. Though in this area, that wasn't uncommon. They were only about a fifteen-minute drive from us, and Nicco's comment about family being in the area surfaced, making sense.

A door opened the second we came to a complete stop, and I jumped back a little in surprise. I turned to Jude, my eyebrows raised. The exclusivity of the situation made me wide-eyed. He chuckled at me, nudging me to exit. Stepping out onto the sidewalk, I waited for him before following the burly men inside.

They were quiet but respectful as they escorted us across a threshold that beeped, and I eyed the lobby with a new interest. A few people were dressed similarly in the foyer, but they all looked to be guards, no other guests mingling about, and I became even more curious as to who they were to have this type of operation. I had to assume it was all owned by them.

Just who were they? Oil Tycoons? A hidden Prince? The secret love child of a Russian mob boss?

The facts were staring me in the face, but I ignored them, my ignorance providing me with comfort for the time being. It might be naive, but I wanted to live in my bubble of ignorance until the moment I could no longer. My plate was full, and I was only beginning to manage it.

"Whoa, this is intense," Jude mumbled. The man leading us smirked at him before holding the elevator open for us to enter and then keying a floor for us.

"Yeah, it kind of gives a whole new meaning to them not being able to contact us," I grudgingly admitted.

Wells had surprisingly texted me this morning, stating he would like to start training today. I was even more surprised when he told me it was Atticus' place. I hadn't known they knew each other, much less that he was his new employer. Though, the most shocking thing had been when he mentioned bringing Jude along so he could hang out with Imogen while we worked out.

Jude had been over the moon with the news and hadn't let me make any excuse to decline. Not that I would have, but it was cute he was so eager for the opportunity. I think we were both feeling the anxiety of them leaving again, and in his attempt to thwart it, he wanted to spend as much time as possible, soaking it in like a sponge so he had enough to last.

It was a positive thing for his life, and I couldn't deny

I hoped to see Sax and possibly Nicco too while we were here. Getting a more in-depth look into Atticus' world wouldn't be a bad thing either. My brain hadn't let me process the information Sax had told me in the sensation room yet, either. I think if I did, I would become even more of a slobbering mess in front of him. I didn't know what it was about Atticus that made me so tongue-tied or weak at the knees in his presence.

Especially when I wanted to hate him for keeping the people I cared about away from me. Yet, his domineering and commanding presence in the kitchen had me weak at the knees, and I'd been sitting in Sax's lap at the time. Looking down at the workout clothes I wore, I suddenly felt underdressed with all the opulence surrounding us. When the elevator dinged, announcing our arrival, we both stepped forward and were greeted by a butler as we exited.

"Welcome, Mrs. Carter, Mr. Franklin." The older man bowed his head at us, and unsure of the protocol, I found myself wanting to curtsy, but I reigned it in, pulling forth all the years of being a Hanover.

"Thank you." Okay, so maybe that was just common courtesy, but the confidence on how to engage in these situations was there. I nodded, awaiting his instruction as I held my hands clasped in front of me.

"Mr... Atticus would like to speak with you, Mrs. Carter, before your session. Mr. Franklin, I will show you to Miss Imogen on the way."

"Oh, thank you. You can, um, just call me Jude."

"Of course, Jude."

The man bowed, turning and walking down a long

hallway. I grabbed Jude's arm as we followed, taking in the place with each step. It was elegantly decorated in dark colors and had a modern look about the place. I hadn't been on this floor last time, and I found it to be homey despite the dangerous, dark vibe about it. It suited Atticus with his designer Armani suits and blacked-out SUVs.

Before we made it past two doors, we were stopped by a grinning bearded man.

"Spitfire, can't get enough of me, huh?"

My face flamed at his comment, and I shuffled uneasily on my feet. The movement drew Sax's attention to Jude, who I hadn't been able to bring myself to glance at. For the first time ever, I saw the giant's face flame a little at being caught out by the teen. His embarrassment helped to cool mine.

"Well, this isn't awkward at all," he mumbled.

"Mr. Wessex," the butler interjected, "I was showing our guests to Miss Imogen and Master Atticus."

"Thank you, Bernard. I can show them the rest of the way."

"Very well."

The older man turned, the tailcoats—I'd just now noticed—fanned out behind him as he went. Sax motioned for us to continue, joining me at my side. His body bumped into mine with each step, his tell-tale smirk giving him away. It seemed that once Sax had allowed himself to open up and touch me, he couldn't stop doing it.

His hands always found a way to me, and I found myself wanting them. I had never been a physical touch person before. Mostly because touches were sparse growing up and only used for punishment or out of obligation. I could see now how much physical intimacy had lacked in my marriage, especially in the small touches.

Maybe my experience was normal, and Sax and the others were the exception, but that didn't seem right either. Especially after meeting the girls. Cami was the touchiest person I'd ever met. While I could almost justify it with how flirty she was, Nat and Stacy still displayed more than anyone in my life prior. It led me to believe it wasn't them, but me, who was the outlier. I didn't know what to believe.

Before we came to a room, the sounds of a piano could be heard. Sax stopped, causing us to halt with him, and I watched him for a brief moment. The sound was beautiful, the playing brilliant, and I wondered who it was. He closed his eyes, almost like it both pained and excited him to hear the music. After a deep breath, he opened them again, and this time he grabbed my hand and pulled us along. I looked to Jude, who only shrugged as well, not understanding the reaction to the music.

"Who is that? It's amazing."

"It's uh, Immy. She hasn't played very much in the past year. It's just nice to hear again."

"It's lovely."

"Yeah, it is."

He smiled down at me, and I could see the love he held for the girl there, almost like a father. When I first met him, I thought he was arrogant, brash, and a bulldozer. Or, at least, it felt like he'd bulldozed into my life with his cocky swagger. But I was beginning to see the sweet undertones and protectiveness that made up Sax. It made him even more irresistible, and I found myself facing a difficult decision soon.

A few weeks ago, I'd been alone, managing life on my own, happy to shuffle through it with Jude figuring it out as we went. I'd pushed aside the pain I'd felt, not wanting to spiral back into my depressive fog, but I wonder now if I'd done myself some disservice. Once again, I'd forgotten that ignoring sad things didn't make them disappear. The fear I was falling for this man who had the potential to hurt me slammed into me, along with the fact he wasn't the only one I was falling for.

I was going to have to choose at some point and lose the others. It seemed simple at first, dating more than one, exploring and learning about myself. But now, I wasn't so sure. How did I even begin to make that decision?

Before I could ponder it more, we stopped at the door the music came from. I found Imogen sitting on a piano bench, her back to us as she poured herself into the song. Her hands flew across the ivories, her delicate touches on the keys, a beautiful caress as she played. Imogen's body swayed with the song, her whole essence flowing into the music. It was breathtaking to behold, and I knew it was a special moment to witness. None of us interrupted, not wanting her to stop until the end.

When the last note played out, I couldn't hold back any longer. Pulling my hands free, I clapped softly, not wanting to surprise her.

"That was beautiful, Imogen."

She turned at my voice, tears on her face as she smiled softly. Quickly, she wiped them free and slid off the bench.

"Thank you. I didn't realize you guys were here. I, uh, yeah…" She held one arm across her body, holding it with the other, her shields down, and I could tell she felt exposed at us hearing her pain. I started to fall back into my therapist role, wanting to step in to comfort her, but halted when Jude stepped forward.

"Ims, that was amazing. I can't believe you play that well. Would you show me?"

Her arms dropped, and she grinned, nodding. "Yeah, I guess I could."

They headed to the bench, and I turned to leave with Sax, stopping before I made it two feet to address Jude. "I'll grab you when my session is over. Um,… be good?" I cringed, not knowing what to say.

Jude laughed at my lame attempt. "Yeah, sure, Lor. I'll try not to break anything."

"Well, okay, so you're not a toddler. Just, I don't know." Throwing my hands up, I laughed and walked the rest of the way out. I found myself stopping right outside the door for a second, Sax giving me a knowing grin as we listened.

"Do you really want to learn?"

"Absolutely. I've always been interested in music, I just didn't have many opportunities, I guess."

"Well, cool. How about I show you, and you show me yours? Um, no, I didn't mean it that way." When they both laughed, I decided to leave, not wanting to overhear anything else. I'd been concerned Imogen wasn't emotionally prepared, but apparently, Jude had comforted her in his Jude way, and I needed to let them figure everything else out on their own until they needed me.

"Satisfied, Spitfire?"

"I just wanted to make sure she was okay."

"She's good. Really. Immy has come a long way."

"That's good. I worry about her."

"She asked to go back to therapy, you know."

"She did?"

"Yeah. I was going to call you today about it."

"Oh. Well, I would love to see her. I just worry now with our relationship and Jude," I stopped, touching his arm. "Things were already difficult for me before we started, you know, and I'd already blurred the boundaries with her, but I could justify it because it was in the office and still so new. But I don't think I can reason with myself anymore that the relationship with her is strictly therapeutic. It pains me to say that, but I don't think I'd be the best fit for her."

I hadn't realized we'd stopped right outside an office, so when Atticus spoke, I jumped, turning to find him in the doorway.

"Perhaps that's something we can discuss along with another matter this morning, Mrs. Carter."

"Sorry, I didn't see you there, Mr. Masters."

He stared at me, taking me in from head to toe. "Please, come in."

Atticus stepped back, motioning for me to enter, and I looked to Sax first, apparently seeking his permission.

He dipped his head, the corner of his lips lifting, and he waited for me to step forward into the space. Once I cleared the door, I felt Atticus move to shut it, Sax's foot stopping it.

"You won't be needed, *Saxon*." I watched the stare-off between them, uncertainty filling my belly at being alone with Atticus.

"I think Spitfire would prefer for me to be present, *Atticus*." I didn't miss their exchange with one another, tension filling the space.

"Last I checked, Saxon, I had the title of boss."

I watched as Sax's jaw twitched, not liking this development. If I was honest, I wasn't sure how I felt either. It was strange seeing them standing off. The last time had been at the fight, but this one seemed even more intense. Perhaps because I was the one involved. My need to be the peacemaker rose, and I found myself intervening despite my better judgment.

"I'll be okay, Sax." His crystal-blue eyes broke the stare-off, lifting to meet mine. I nodded, and he watched me for a moment before turning and stalking off. I didn't think he'd go far. If I knew him, and I felt I was beginning to, he'd want to be close by if I called out. You know, assuming this room wasn't soundproof and Atticus didn't plan to off me or something. The thought shocked me, and I berated myself for giving in to my darker fantasies. He had a dark and dangerous vibe about him, but I didn't need to entertain crazy ideas like he was an assassin kingpin, mob boss or something.

Besides, he was well-mannered, professional, and kept his boundaries way better than I had. If anyone needed to be questioned, it was me, not him. Despite my earlier jokes, I knew he was a respected businessman, and I needed to quit romanticizing the danger. Clearly, I've seen too many shows lately filling my head with nonsense.

"Would you care for any breakfast? Coffee?"

Atticus indicated to a cart that was laden with pastries and a pot of coffee. It looked scrumptious, but between getting ready to work up a sweat and being in his presence, I didn't think I could stomach the sweet baked goods well. The coffee, on the other hand, might be helpful.

"Coffee would be lovely, thank you."

I'd slipped back into the role my mother had ingrained in me my whole life. It had been natural, the politeness seeping out of me, and I found myself shivering, not liking how easy it had been. I didn't want to be *that* woman. Atticus noticed my reaction and stopped, a wrinkle developing between his eyebrows.

"Are you okay, Loren?"

I didn't miss the fact he'd dropped the formality, and it made me feel more at ease, the pretentious fakeness dissolving around me.

"Yeah," I swallowed. "I know you don't know me, but I've been going through sort of a transformation over the past few months, and well, I'd slipped back into the person I didn't want to be for a second, and it grossed me out, if I'm honest."

"And who do you want to be?"

His question struck me as odd, and even one I would ask a client. He stared at me, waiting for me to respond, and I found myself giving into his magnetism. Seriously, I needed to have a proper talk with myself. I'd been lamenting how I would have to choose soon, and it was already hard enough with three men I'd become close to. Not to mention, I was angry with him for blocking me from them. And yet, my eyes locked onto his, my body relaxing as I stayed snared in his gaze, waiting for him to tell me what to do.

"I'm still figuring it out, but someone who isn't afraid, someone who fights for what she wants and knows what she deserves."

"And what do you deserve, Mrs. Carter?"

He dropped my eyes this time as he finished pouring coffee into a mug, walking over to my chair and handing it to me. I reached out for it, my hand touching his as I wrapped it around the hot beverage. Atticus didn't let go, though, and I found myself looking up at him in question.

He towered over me, and his dominance shone more as he waited for me to answer the question. Licking my lips, I fought to push the lusty thoughts back and remember what he asked me.

"To be given a choice."

Atticus didn't let go right away, watching me as I waited to see if my answer would be satisfactory. When he relented, his fingers grazed mine, and I found goosebumps breaking out across my skin, an electric shock heading straight toward my clit. Swallowing, I pulled the mug close to me, opting to go with black in order to avoid any more of that. Taking a sip, I used the moment to gather myself. I wanted to deny the flash of heat I saw in his eyes at my reaction, but I couldn't. Not when he looked at me like that. But just as fast as it had come across, it was locked away, the cold mask returning.

Once I had a few sips, my face no longer on the verge of overheating, I glanced up. Atticus was leaning against the desk, his hands in his pockets as he watched me. It was a weird combination of relaxed while still giving off commanding vibes. I sat up straighter at his notice, my thighs rubbing together unconsciously at the heat I felt.

"You surprised me, Mrs. Carter."

"Oh, how so?"

"You're nothing like I expected."

"You know, you're very good at answering questions without really answering questions. Immy does it too sometimes, but she's not as skilled as you, yet."

He smirked, pleased with my assessment. "Ah, well, habit, I'm afraid."

I watched as he lowered his shoulders, some of his tension fading, and I found myself unable to sit any longer under his scrutiny. Standing, I roamed around the space, taking in the decorations. Walking over to a bookcase, I pursued the titles of the books, but most were business-oriented and meant nothing to me. Noticing an antique chessboard, I sat down, intrigued by the pieces.

"These are gorgeous."

They were wooden, all hand-carved and stained to be lighter or darker to represent black and white. Atticus watched me as I admired them before moving over and taking the piece from me. I worried I'd broken some unspoken rule at first, but then he spoke, and it felt like he revealed something fundamental about himself.

"Thank you. My grandfather gave them to me. They're a family heirloom."

"Wow, that's pretty amazing. Do you play?"

"I do. What about you, Mrs. Carter?"

"No. It always seems too complex for me."

"It can be, but I found it to be mostly about planning ahead."

"Huh. That makes sense." Standing, I poked around some more on the bookcase, the proximity to him too much. The next thing I found was an antique record player. I opened it up and saw a record. Peering close, I spun, my mouth open as I gaped at him. "You listen to the Beastie Boys?"

He leaned back in the chair, his leg propped on the other as he watched me. At my question, his face transformed into amusement. "Am I not allowed to?"

"No, it's just, I don't know. You don't strike me as the type, that's all." Shrugging, I dropped my eyes, embarrassed at my reaction.

"What did you think I listened to, *Bellezza*?" He purred the question, the forbidden word he'd called me that night, falling off his tongue, and I found myself sucking in a breath. A finger lifted my chin, and I came face to face with Atticus. I hadn't even known he'd stood. His hypnotic umber eyes seared into me as he stared down.

Licking my lips, I whispered, "Jazz, or something like classical, maybe."

He chuckled before asking another question. "Can we get to the reason I asked you here, or do you need to look through the rest of my stuff?" he teased. I was surprised to find a slight smile on his lips, and I involuntarily licked mine again. Heat flashed hot in his eyes for a second, but then he dropped my chin, stepping back, and it was gone.

I assented, cheeks flaming at the question, and walked back over to the chair. I grabbed my coffee and downed the rest of it, using it as something to distract me from the fact I'd just made a fool out of myself. Once I was done, I looked up and spotted Atticus sitting behind his desk now, the space adding to the wall I'd felt slam down between us.

"Mrs. Carter, as you stated in the hallway, things have changed since we last were in your office. While I don't doubt your skills, I do worry that not only is Immy growing attached to you and Jude, but that it's also not safe. The bombing was a big reminder of what is at stake. I've also been informed you were approached again by the man who had tried to take your phone on the train. The one you told me about the night we picked you up at the police station?"

"Oh," scrunching my nose, I hadn't thought the conversation would go in this direction. "Yes, that would be correct. He mentioned something about the bombing, but I haven't seen him since that night. What does that have to do with this meeting or Immy's treatment?"

Atticus leaned forward on his arms, locking his knuckles together. "Because I believe these experiences are connected to me, and your connection to Immy unintentionally placed you at risk. I'm sorry about that."

Nodding, I couldn't answer, wanting him to keep

talking. When he didn't, I opened mine to ask, but he started again, and I stopped myself, shutting my mouth.

"I'd like to propose an alternative."

"I'm listening."

"Instead of meeting in your office and paying you, what would you say to meeting with Immy here and I pay you with Sex?"

"What?" I screeched, jumping up, forgetting I still clutched the mug in my hand. It fell to the floor, crashing on the hardwood, and the next second, the door was wrenched open, and Sax barreled in, ready to fight something. He assessed the room for threats, checking Atticus briefly before looking at me. His eyes crawled over my body, taking in every inch of me. When he was happy nothing was wrong, he released a breath, looking between us both, lifting an eyebrow toward me.

"He said he wanted to pay me with sex!" I shouted, my hands aggressively going between the two men. Atticus' face blanched, and he stood quickly, attempting to calm me. Except when I heard the growl, I realized it wasn't me he was placating, but the possessive man behind me. Sax froze for a second at Atticus' gesture, and we stood in a weird triangle, all looking between one another with uncertainty.

"My apologies, Mrs. Carter, but I think you misunderstood me. I said, *Sax*, not um, sex."

"Oh." I deflated, sitting back in my chair until I realized I still didn't understand, my face flaming. "But how? Do you, like, own him? I'm still confused. I can't take a person from you."

Sax moved over and took the position Atticus had at

the beginning, leaning against the desk, placing his back to his boss. His long legs reached me, and he kicked my foot, getting my attention.

"No one owns me, Spitfire. But I'll let you own my dick if it means I get to be deep in you every day."

Gasping, my face reached critical limits, and I worried it would be permanently red from here on out. I crossed my legs, squirming as I tried to ignore his words and how it now sounded. Atticus rolled his eyes behind the brute, causing me to laugh, the emotions escaping from me. It was the funniest thing I'd ever seen him do, and it made him a little more real. "Sax, you can go back out in the hall. I'm almost finished."

"I'm good right here, actually." He crossed his arms, his stare firm on me, with no intention of moving.

I looked between them both, biting my lip in worry. I didn't want Sax to get in trouble for going against his boss's orders. "Sax, it's fine. Just a misunderstanding."

I remembered the mug, and I looked down at the shards at my feet. I knelt and started to collect them, when hands gripped mine, pulling me to my feet. "Leave it, Spitfire. You don't want to cut yourself. Let's hear what Atticus has in store for me."

He sat down in the chair, pulling me onto his lap, and I stared at the well-dressed man across the desk. He cleared his throat, narrowing his eyes at the man behind me, but when Sax made no move to leave, Atticus sighed and focused back on me.

"As you can see, it seems my number 2 has become more enamored with you than doing his job. So, for the time being, I'd like to offer him as protection until some things in our lives calm down. With that, you could meet with Immy here, train with Mr. Young, and still be safe. Now, I understand your concern with Immy, so perhaps it could be unofficial? Maybe more like a mentorship or confidant? I heard what you said that day about connection and relationships, and I'm glad that Immy could connect with you on her first try. But I'm a man of numbers, and the likelihood she'd be able to reproduce that bond or be willing to try again are slim. So if that means we change the dynamics of your relationship to make it work, I'm good with that. It's important that you keep whatever secrets you may uncover here or with her to yourself. That is vital."

I thought about what he was saying, and I could understand where he was coming from. Part of me knew it was still very blurry, and I was allowing my feelings on things to cloud my judgment, but I also knew I would never be able to walk away from a girl who was hurting and needed my help. If it had to be more of a casual thing, I still thought it would be better than nothing. I didn't want to be another person in her life leaving her either. But the implications that it was dangerous had me hesitating.

"How dangerous?"

"I think you know the answer to that, Mrs. Carter."

Slowly, I nodded because he was right. I was in a bombing. Some man had waited outside my gym and accosted me. Not to mention the train. Evidently, I'd been in danger longer than I wanted to admit. I wanted to run away, hide Jude and myself somewhere the evils of the world wouldn't touch us.

But that wasn't life. It wasn't even a reality. Evil was everywhere. There was no escape.

Good things didn't happen just because you wanted them to. The death of my baby was a painful reminder of this fact. I caught myself rubbing my stomach at the thought, and I immediately stopped, but not before Atticus' eyes had dropped there. Clearing my throat, I focused back on the present, hoping to distract him from asking the question I didn't want to answer.

"I have a feeling even if I asked, you wouldn't tell me who you are." I paused, but he didn't say anything, just stared at me, gauging my reaction. "But I'd be naive to believe you didn't have some type of power. And while I appreciate the offer of *Sax*," I giggled, before pulling myself together. "The concept weirds me out, and I'd rather propose a different exchange."

"I'm listening."

"My ex-husband kept something from me, and now he claims that it's gone. I hired a private investigator, but they are giving me the runaround now. I was meant to meet them today, but they canceled at the last minute. This coming after Sax and I overheard something last night, well, I'm starting to think there's a bigger picture. My mother, my ex-husband, and perhaps even Monroe's ex are connected and plotting together. Help me figure out what's going on there and stop them."

"That can be arranged." I sighed in relief. The disappointment I'd felt this morning at receiving the notice washed away. Another idea popped in my head, so I decided to go for it. It was time to practice demanding what I deserved after all.

"One more thing, or well two."

He approved my request with a nod, but I swear his lips lifted, a pleased expression wanting to emerge. Atticus' eyes even seemed to have softened at the request.

"The thing my ex kept was my dog. Help me get her back, and Monroe his son."

"Monroe, he's your neighbor?"

I nodded, not surprised he knew. Atticus seemed like the type to know everything about a person.

"Done." The corners did lift a little more this time, and I decided to push for more. All he could do was say no. "Anything else?"

"Actually, yes."

"Go ahead, Mrs. Carter," he said, offering me the chance, a full smile on his lips now. "I have to say you're more of a businesswoman than I gave you credit for."

"I think you'll find you've underestimated me in several ways, but that's beside the point. Jude," I breathed. "I want to adopt Jude officially. I've started the paperwork, but if something happened to me, *promise me* you won't let him be lost to the system again. You owe me *this* for keeping the people important to me away for months with no contact." A tear slipped through, and I quickly swiped it away, never dropping my eyes.

He nodded, solemnly. "You have my word."

I exhaled, the tension ebbing out of me completely as I relaxed into Sax's arms. "Thank you. When do you want to start?"

"Tuesday work?"

"If we do it in the evening, then yes, I have clients until 5 pm."

"I'll make sure we can."

He dropped his eyes, picking up his phone, and I felt the dismissal from his posture. Standing, I started to walk out, Sax right behind me, when he spoke one more time.

"Thank you, Mrs. Carter. I hope you keep surprising me."

I didn't turn back, but the smile on my face was wide as I walked out.

Seventeen

Wells

The music blasted through the speakers, and I set the last practice dummies up in the gym. I'd thought the house out in the suburbs had been grand, but Atticus' place in the city was more impressive, in my opinion. Maybe it was the modern feel to it or the fact he had a whole building that made it stand out more with floors devoted to different activities. But I enjoyed the amount of time I spent here.

Atticus had held up his end of the deal and proved he wasn't like Delgado. It gave me hope that other people could be different too. Maybe I'd only been around the wrong people my whole life or only chose to see people that way. Whatever it was, it was nice to know people weren't all bad. He'd given me a room here, but other than keeping some clothes to change into after working out, I hadn't done anything with it.

I still had the dogs to look after, and I knew if I got too comfortable, then I'd lose myself, allowing someone else to do everything for me instead of earning it. In the past, I would've been all for that. I felt owed for the life I had to live, the right to be given things easier, but it had only ever ended in disaster. My vow to be better was a reminder on my heart to push forward through the pain and earn it this time. Change wasn't easy, but I wanted to work for it.

I knew their trust was worth it.

Atticus had been appreciative of me informing him of Loren's encounter the night she ran into me. He still hadn't told me everything, but being around the family and fighting in the underground rings, I'd picked up on things. There wasn't any love lost between the Delgados and the Mascros. What I'd pieced together from overheard conversations, what he'd done to Imogen was reprehensible. It seemed I'd finally picked the right side. My life was changing, and I was in charge of its direction for once. Fighting had always been an escape and outlet, but it was becoming my life force now.

I could finally make something of myself.

Funny, it was going to be with my fists since they'd always gotten me in trouble as a youth.

The door squeaked, and I looked over my shoulder to see who it was. Atticus had asked to speak to Loren before we started, so I assumed the noise wouldn't be her yet. So, when I caught sight of her, I hadn't been prepared for how beautiful she would look, catching me off guard and stopping in my tracks. Swallowing, I greeted Sax, who took up a stance against the wall. He eyed me but didn't show any other emotion, content to watch from his post.

"Hey, Kitten. You scared to be alone with me now?" I teased, turning to face her. Crossing my arms, I smirked as she approached. Her hips swayed, and I wanted to put my hands on them so badly. This was going to be more challenging than before, and I briefly berated myself for suggesting this. Still, the thought of her being unprepared or in a similar situation again propelled me to tuck my lust away.

"Oh," she turned, noticing Sax hadn't left, her face heating up, "um, it's not a problem, is it? I can tell him to go away. I think he's just curious." She fumbled for her words, and I found it endearing. Smiling an honest smile, I shook my head, dropping my arms and walking closer, my body language open as I approached. When I was near, I bent down, whispering in her ear, unable to help myself.

"Guess we'll have to keep the extracurricular training for later."

I didn't miss how her skin raised in goosebumps, but I kept walking, picking up the last cone and placing it where I wanted. She followed, a question now on her face. "Extracurricular?"

"Well, I figured you didn't want me to say out loud in front of your wall partner there how much you like to be held up against them."

She stopped, shock on her face before she recovered, a smirk forming. "Oh, he knows, seeing as he fucked me up against one last night." Kitten sauntered over to the bench, placing her bottle of water and towel down. When she spun around, she winked and started to wrap her hands.

Chuckling, I broke my frozen stance and walked over. "Kitten, you never cease to surprise me. I think it's my favorite thing about you."

"You have things you like about me? Enough to list them?"

She looked at me with disbelief, her nose wrinkled as she stopped with her hands midair. Walking forward, I took the material and finished the one she had left to do, tucking the fabric in. "There are so many things I like about you, Kitten. It was just my stubborn ass keeping me from admitting it before."

"And now?"

"Now, I hope to show you I might be more than, what did you call me, *surly*?"

"Yeah, that was *one* of them," she grumbled.

Smirking, I moved in closer, not able to help myself. "Oh, there were more?"

"Mm-hm, but I don't think you've earned the right to know yet."

"Fair enough, Kitten. Well, I hope to show you that I can, that I want to. I'm not going to be nice like Monroe, he's one of a kind, but I'll try not to be such a brooding asshole all the time."

"I kind of like the asshole." She grinned softly, and something passed between us.

"Good, because he kind of likes you too. Now, let's get to work. I need your help with Fort, and I doubt he's gonna manage where he is for long before he's causing trouble." Dropping her hands, I watched as her grin spread, lighting up her whole face. Her eyes weren't as sad anymore, and the strength she used to muster with me seemed to be more prominent now, not just bursting out of her when she'd had enough. Loren was emerging, and I found it enchanting to watch.

"Fort's here?"

"Yep, and he's been a complete nuisance since you left. I was desperate, so I brought him with me. Let me tell you, the drive, not fun."

She jumped up a little, clapping in her excitement. "Oh, I can't wait. Come on, let's do this." Kitten took off in a jog, warming up her muscles, and I watched as the giant tracked her every move. I'd need to be careful not to catch his ire. I wouldn't want to be hit by his fist for crossing any lines. I didn't know the status of her relationships, and perhaps I was too late to be a contender.

I didn't want to think that way, but it was a possibility. I knew I couldn't only change in hopes of getting to be with her. I wanted to be a better person for me too, without the caveat of her as a reward. Loren made me want to be better because she deserved it and spurred me to believe I could. If I were only her trainer and occasional friend, then I would learn to accept it.

"Okay, punches first."

We fell into an easy routine, and despite the few months since she'd been in a training session with me, she hadn't fallen behind.

"Have you been training with someone else?"

"No," she panted, hitting the glove in an upper strike. "I had to take barre, but I practiced my punches at home. It helped to picture some of your faces and take out my aggression that way." She hit the gloves three more times before I called it. She bent over at the waist, catching her breath. When she peered up, her smile radiated through her whole body.

"Gah, I've missed this. Kicks now?"

"Sure, Kitten."

I agreed, despite wanting to go over some other moves. If she was excited about doing some kicks, then I'd let the woman do some damn kicks. Better than have her kick me in the balls, anyhow. Once she had her breath again, I lowered the gloves and had her start in on her kicks. Her legs moved as gracefully as before, and after a few practice ones, she fell back into the rhythm of the kicks just like no time had passed.

When she reached twenty for each leg, I stopped it, dropping the gloves.

"Good job, Kitten. You're showing improvement even without training over the past few months. I'm impressed."

"Wow, I can't believe you just gave me a compliment without hurting my feelings first."

"Ha! And you thought you weren't funny."

Kitten pushed my shoulder, her giggle sending a bolt right to my dick. I turned my side to adjust myself out of view. Sax noticed, smirking at me, the cocky fucker. Moving into self-defense, I started with the basic hand and hair holds, and we practiced getting out of them for the next thirty minutes.

"Like this?" She asked, moving down to make my arm go slack, allowing her to maneuver out from under it.

"Exactly, Kitten."

She beamed at me, and I got lost for a minute. Locking it down, I lifted a brow. "You ready for more? Or are you good for the day?"

Kitten bit her lip, assessing me. Unfortunately, before

she could answer, the door opened and Fort raced in, a guard behind him, and I knew our time was up. The scoundrel ran straight for Kitten, almost toppling her in his exuberance.

"Sorry, he got away," the guard wheezed. I waved him off, running my hand on the back of my head, blowing out a breath. When I looked back at Loren, she was on the ground, playing with the mischievous dog.

"Oh my goodness, Fort. You've gotten so big in a week." He barked, sitting up on his hind legs, preening at her words. "You're the most handsome doggo." She rubbed his head, petting him all over, and he took it, knowing where the good stuff was. He flopped down, opting for a belly rub.

"Well, I guess that settles it. Let's move this outside where we have more room."

"Oh, yay! I'm so excited."

"Hopefully, you'll be saying that in the next hour."

"I should have Jude come out too. He'd get a kick out of it."

"Yeah, sure."

I started to pick up all the training material, wiping down the items that needed it as she fawned over the mutt more than she'd ever had with me. When I slammed a cone down, I realized I was jealous of a dog. Shaking my head, I finished the rest, remembering who the alpha in this relationship was.

Sax had come over and looked at the dog with suspicion, and I felt moderately better that Fort didn't like him either. Guess it was just a Kitten thing.

I grabbed my stuff and motioned for her to follow.

She stood, clapping her hands to get Fort's attention, and he agreeably walked with her, happy to be in her presence. Sighing, I accepted the fact that perhaps not every dog liked everybody, and if he were going to like someone, he'd picked a good one with Loren. She was hard not to like, after all. I'd tried for months, and I still ended up here, not able to get enough time with her, now having to share it with a dog.

For the next thirty minutes, we spent time outside going over some basic commands. Regrettably, he did listen to her more than he had me, but he still wasn't consistent. When he ran after the ball but refused to give it back, I couldn't help but laugh out loud at Kitten's frustration.

"Fort! Come back. Here!" When she heard me laughing, she turned to me, placing her hands on her hips, her chin sticking out. "What?"

"Not so fun when he does whatever he wants, huh?"

"I'm sure he's just tired. It's fine."

"Uh-huh."

"Ugh, fine. He's stubborn, but I still like him."

Jude and Immy started playing with the dog, so I took the chance to pull Loren over to a swing on the patio. "Come on, Kitten. That's enough for today. Swing with me."

She didn't resist, and when we sat down, I placed my arm behind her back and gently pushed with my feet. We watched in silence as the two teens ran around laughing with Fort for a bit before she broke it, turning to me.

"Wells, thank you for teaching me. I know I still have

a ways to go before I can successfully evade an attacker, but I already feel more confident. That man scared me more than I want to admit, and it's been troubling me. You've given me back some confidence."

"You're welcome."

"Huh."

"What?"

"I expected more of a sarcastic comment or sexual innuendo, not an actual answer."

"I can be polite!"

"You know Monroe once told me you weren't completely housebroken, and I thought it fit. It's even funnier now knowing you train dogs."

"Oh, you think that's funny?" I turned, leaning over her, trapping her as I engulfed her on the swing.

"Yeah." Her answer was breathy, and I wanted to kiss her. She licked her lips, and I started to lean forward when a door banged, saving me from rushing things. Placing a kiss on her forehead, I moved back, allowing her to straighten.

We sat there, swinging for a while longer, not needing to talk. I kept my arm around her shoulders, though, my thumb rubbing small circles on her exposed skin. I could almost pretend this was a scene out of a movie, the happy ending where they watch as their perfect life unfolded before them.

It was a perfect moment, but I knew it wasn't my ending. I still had some treacherous paths ahead of me, some obstacles to overcome on my course there, but it was a step and a reminder of what it could be like. I just hoped Monroe would be part of it as well.

Eighteen

LOREN

Despite being ghosted by the PI over the weekend and not gaining any traction on the whereabouts of Barkley, I'd surprisingly still been able to have fun. It was enlightening in a way. From the moment I'd learned about my dog, it had been all I could focus on, needing to discover the truth. I'd gone a bit obsessive over it, and the distractions had been precisely what I needed. I felt more hopeful now with Atticus looking into it, and I knew he'd find something. Yesterday had gone well, and I'd enjoyed myself around them all.

My time with Atticus had been interesting, and I'd begun to see some of the seductive man behind the suit I'd encountered in my first meeting. Perhaps it was because now that he wasn't attached to my client, I felt more freedom to explore my attraction. Whatever the case, I'd started to see him as a person, and I found him fascinating. However, it presented a whole slew of new problems. I still hadn't been able to acknowledge he'd been the mysterious stranger. Only so many mind-bending things could be processed at once.

Training with Wells had been better than ever. Our

typical abrasiveness toward one another had evaporated, leaving a budding friendship to emerge. He was still surly at times, but it was more in jest and no longer carried the hatred I used to feel from him. And, of course, *Sax*. The embarrassing moment with him and Atticus still made my face redden, but everything else had been bliss.

Today would be the first day since Friday I hadn't seen him, and I found myself longing for him in a way I hadn't been prepared for. It was official, my heart had gotten attached, and now, I worried I wouldn't be able to handle everything that would follow. In theory, casually having sex seemed like an easy plan, but maybe I wasn't that type of person. Sex meant something to me, even when just physical. It was like a part of me latched onto them. I wasn't sure if that was healthy or an attachment issue. Therapist problems—when you psychoanalyze all of your choices.

The best part had been seeing Jude laugh with Fort. He and Immy had played with Fort for so long, and I wasn't sure who was more tired when we left. We made plans for the rest of the week, giving both Jude and me some solace that they wouldn't disappear again. He'd been smiling more ever since, and I think spending time with Immy would be good for him. I didn't want to admit that he also appeared to enjoy the guys' company as well.

It seemed like things with him and Immy were good, and I cringed when I thought about having to have 'the talk' with him soon. When I thought of how he would take all the uncomfortable topics, it made me laugh at his discomfort, making my own not seem as bad. It was necessary, though, and I advocated for mental health and sex-positive topics with teens. Informing them of safe practices and helping them understand the consequences had a far more reaching impact than telling them not to do something.

Monroe had been busy on Sunday, but had texted things were looking up. He expected things to move forward in his favor finally. He wanted to come over for dinner tonight, so I was looking forward to it. I hadn't seen Nicco at Atticus', but I shouldn't have been surprised since I knew he didn't live there. Nicco had also sent a message saying he was thinking about me and hoped we could get together soon.

He was trying, showing me he cared, which I needed. It was hard to trust my emotions though, because I wanted to dive all in with Nicco. But I needed to be more cautious with my heart this time. I could admit I wanted to get there again with him, but I knew it couldn't only be about getting naked together. No matter how much my hormones screamed at me, I would have to keep my horniness at bay.

Besides, between sex with Sax, raising a teenager, work, and training, it wasn't like I had much time. The thought re-emerged of having to choose soon, plaguing me again, but I pushed it aside, wanting to hide in my delusion for a while. Even if I knew sex was beginning to mean something to me, I was enjoying it too much to stop. I felt I owed it to myself to try as many dicks as I wanted anyway, even if that meant I was 'whoring around'. My mother and Brian could sniff some carbon monoxide for all I cared. It was my vagina, and if I wanted to ride as many men on the dick train as I could until I puked, I would.

Doris poked her head into my office, breaking me from my thoughts on dicks, geez. "Loren, your client's here."

"Thanks, I'll be right up."

Nodding, she walked off as I focused back on the note I'd been staring at for the past five minutes. Glancing over it, I reviewed it quickly before submitting. Having more going on in my life had me daydreaming all over the place. I needed to rein it in and focus on my clients while I was at work. When I looked at who was my next one, a pit formed in my stomach. I'd come to dread sessions with Dayton. He continued to evade my questions, offering no concrete information or disclosures. I was at the point where I needed to terminate and refer him, whether he liked it or not. It wasn't benefiting either one of us if I felt this way about his sessions.

Shutting my door, I locked my belongings up and stuffed the key in my pocket. I didn't often do it, but I'd started to for *his* sessions. Dayton appeared to fixate on me, searching for information about my personal life. I walked out of the last session to grab something I printed for him and found him hovering over my desk when I'd returned. When I'd questioned him, he brushed it off, stating he'd been looking for something he'd left. I remembered he had, so I pulled it out of my drawer and handed it to him. Despite having a valid reason, it still felt very *off* to me.

Walking through the lobby door, I assessed his

appearance before he noticed me. As usual, it didn't match his affect or energy. He was a tall man and had an air of dominance about him. I could tell he liked to control situations and was used to others doing what he said. But yet his demeanor continued to want you to believe otherwise. Today, he shuffled his feet as he sat in the chair, his hands clasped loosely in his lap as he stared at the floor. It was driving me insane that I couldn't figure out his game.

"Dayton, are you ready?"

He poked his head up, nodding before standing, and shuffled through the door. I rolled my eyes when I turned my head. The overkill of his behavior was too much for me to bear today. Irritation bubbled to the surface, and I found myself needing to take a calming breath before I followed. This wasn't good if I couldn't control my own emotions. Our sessions would never be productive at this rate. Shutting the door, I took my seat.

"Mrs. Carter, how are you today?"

"I'm well, thank you for asking. How are you today, Dayton?"

"I'm, I'm good," he stuttered, "thank you."

Dayton began picking up things off the side tables as he usually did, turning them over and looking at them before placing them back down. He was acting more manic today, which was odd. Usually, he was controlled and would avoid eye contact. Today, he babbled to the point of stuttering.

"How's your week been so far?"

"Oh, it's been go-od."

"Can you tell me what's been good about it?"

He sat back, crossing his legs over his knee, and I felt something change within him. The behavior stopped, and he looked me directly in the eyes. "Well, I've acquired some new information about my son."

"Oh? The one that you've been trying to get in touch with?"

"Yes, the very one." He said it slowly, emphasizing words, and I wondered what his intention was behind the action. It clearly had a purpose, but to what extent.

"How did you come across this new information?"

Dayton watched me, assessing my question before he answered. "Let's just say, I have a *new* friend."

I wanted to roll my eyes again at how evasive he was, but I kept my face blank. "Making new friends is always a positive thing."

"Yes, very positive."

"What do you hope to gain from this information?"

"Time will tell. Time will tell. It's hard to know if I should act now… or wait until a more *opportune* time." Again, his words were slowly drawn out as he spoke, and I knew he was deliberately doing it.

"Interesting. What is it about this information that you feel will help you?"

"I think I finally understand my son's motivation."

"Okay," I nodded, grasping for something to expand the conversation. "Do you feel comfortable talking about what happened with you and your son now?"

"We had a bit of a disagreement on how to run the family business."

"Families can be tough at times. Especially when parents and children have differing opinions."

"Yes, I think my son has become *weak*."

"Interesting word choice there," I commented, but it was almost like he didn't hear me and kept talking.

"I'm not sure if he has the *stomach* to do the things that are required of a Mascro."

"So your family name is important to you?"

"The *most* important."

"It's good to have connections to our family history."

"Do you know anything about *your* history?"

Confused, I looked up from my computer where I'd been typing. "I'm not sure that's relevant, Mr. Mascro. We're here to work on *you*, not me."

He assessed me thoroughly this time, and it weirded me out. The way his eyes rolled over me made me feel uncomfortable.

"Did I ever tell you I have a daughter as well?"

"I think you mentioned it once, but you've not spoken of her. Is your relationship with her any better?"

"She's a little bit easier to manage. But she's sided with her brother at the moment."

"Well, maybe it's important to them. Perhaps you could sit down and talk with both."

"I don't know if *talking* will get us where we need to be."

"I found in my experience that most things can be resolved if people sit down and discuss their wants and expectations. And then you can find a compromise."

"I don't know if I'm willing to compromise on this."

"Well, do you mind sharing what it is you're struggling with? Then maybe we can find a compromise together. I've been told I'm pretty good at finding solutions."

"I'm sure you are Mrs. Carter. In fact, I think you're *very* flexible with some of your solutions."

Quirking my brow, I tilted my head at him. Dayton was being cryptic, but he was more open than he'd ever been. "I don't understand what you're implying or are referring to, but I'm glad to hear you're open to new possibilities."

This time he leaned forward, bracing his elbows on his knees. "*Possibilities*. Yes. Oh, the *possibilities*." Again, it felt as if we were having two different conversations, his words holding a different meaning than what they traditionally did. I decided to redirect and get the conversation back on track and under my control.

"Have you been experiencing any symptoms of distress lately?"

"I was very distressed, yes. But like I said, once I gathered this new intel, I'm now feeling a lot more confident. Soon I think I will have my life back the way I want it to be with no barriers or distractions."

"It's good to focus on goals and be able to visualize what we want them to look like."

"Yes, I agree. Goals are fundamental to me."

"Could you share with me what your goals are? And how do you feel you have been improving on the goals we set?"

He leaned back now, an assured smile on his face as he braced his arm on the back of the couch. "I'm feeling very confident about how things are. You could say that I'm feeling very *energized* to succeed."

"That's great. I love to hear when clients are feeling better. What have you changed in your life to bring about this new energy?"

"Did I ever tell you about my wife?" He asked, changing the subject abruptly.

"No, I don't believe you have. You've only mentioned you were no longer married."

"Yes. Well. I'm a widower, actually. My wife unfortunately died last year." He dipped his head, but I didn't see any grief or sadness portrayed in his features, just an obligatory reflection of what he felt needed to be displayed.

"I'm so sorry to hear that. How are you doing with it? I'm sure it's been difficult."

"It was," he agreed, nodding. "Yes, it was very challenging, but it was time."

"Oh, was she sick? Had she been diagnosed with something?"

"You could say she was sick."

A weird feeling formed in my belly, the confusion in his statement sending tendrils of apprehension through me, alerting all my red flag sensors. "How have you been dealing with your grief?"

"Well, actually."

"Oh? And you've gone through the grieving process and landed on acceptance?"

"Yes, I have accepted her death."

"Can you tell me the importance of bringing her up today?"

"Oh, yes, yes! Let me get back to my story. So, my wife's death. It was supposed to be the start, the turning point of my new next chapter in life. But instead, my son ruined it all. And I'm not sure I can ever forgive him for that."

"It sounds like you carry a lot of anger and hatred towards your son."

"Affirmative."

"Anger is one of those emotions we only really feel on the surface. Usually, under our anger are other emotions such as hurt, sadness, or betrayal. Perhaps that's what you're experiencing?"

"Definitely betrayal. I taught him better. I raised him to be a man, to be a *certain* way, and then the moment I needed him, he turned his back on me and chose *them*."

"Sounds like his choices upset you?" I leaned forward, his emotion for once appearing real.

"Of course, it fucking upset me!" He roared, causing me to jump back at his outrage, my emotions showing for a split second before I pulled my blank mask back on.

"It seems like a lot of tension stems from this relationship."

"I want to make him pay," he spat, the vehemence in his words palpable.

Swallowing, I breathed in for a second, calming my heart. "I can understand how that might feel like the answer, but in my experience, revenge isn't the only option, nor the best solution. I believe it was Socrates who said, 'He that would take revenge better dig two graves' so perhaps we can find a different outcome."

"In *my* experience, Mrs. Carter, that phrase is only relevant if you're not the one holding the shovel." His voice had become cold, calculated, and for once, he matched the energy and vibe he presented. I guess Dayton had decided to quit playing the game.

"What do you mean exactly?"

"Well, you see, *dear*. If you have the shovel, then you can smack the other person in the head and bury them."

Fear began to course through me at his statement. My heart rate increased as I searched my tools and training on how to deal with something like this. He didn't appear to be joking or one to speak in hyperbole. "It sounds like you have some strong emotions around this. Would you say you're feeling violent towards your son?"

"Violence is such a mild-mannered word, dear." I dismissed his continued use of dear, focusing on what he was implying.

"Do you feel you might harm your son if you were to come into contact with him?"

"I want nothing less than to crush him between my fingers," he seethed, his face distorting.

"Have you thought about this often?"

"Every damn second of every day since he betrayed me."

"It sounds like you've put a lot of thought into it. Do you have a plan?"

"Oh, I know the perfect way." He flicked his gaze up to mine, the coldness seeping into me from his look, and I shivered, unable to stop my body from reacting. "Do you have the means to put your plan into place?" My voice came out small, the last question of assessing his homicidality locking into place.

"Not yet. But I'm close."

"I have to say, Mr. Mascro, the information you're

telling me is concerning. If you remember at the beginning, one of the reasons for breaking confidentiality is homicidal ideation. And I'm worried that you might do something you'll regret."

"Oh, I won't regret this."

"I'm starting to think perhaps more intensive services are needed here. I applaud you for opening up more today, and I appreciate your willingness to share. But I'm concerned you're not safe to leave my office. I think it's in your best interest to notify someone and create a safety plan to help reduce the likelihood of you following through with your plan. That way, when you leave here, you won't make choices you'll regret later."

"Oh, you thought this was real? I thought this was the place to share my fantasies? But of course, dear, do whatever you need to ensure you feel comfortable. I don't even know where my son is."

His whole posture changed, and he fell back into the bumbling idiot act, dropping his eyes. My skin crawled, and I wanted to rake my hands over it, dispelling the way he made me feel, but I held it in, not wanting him to know how much he'd affected me. Swallowing, I took a few minutes to collect myself.

"Okay, well, what are some high risks we can identify?"

Dayton was agreeable for the rest of the session, willing to work on this safety plan, and gave me the appropriate answers. For the rest of the session, he kept his perfect mask of non-emotion on. There was a moment where I wondered if he had dissociative identity disorder, but I knew that wasn't right. His switches were purposeful, controlled. It was abundantly clear there was more going on here. The question still remained of why?

"I would like to refer you for some testing if that's okay?"

"Sure. Sure. Sure. Can we talk about it next time, though? I need to go." He'd already gotten up and headed to the door before I answered.

"Yes, of course. I have you for next week at the same time. Does that still work for you?"

"Yes, yes. Thank you, Mrs. Carter. I will. I will speak with you then." He walked out quickly, and I worried I'd made a huge mistake letting him go.

NINETEEN

LOREN

After Dayton's session, I found it difficult to focus on my next client and was grateful when lunch was next, allowing me ample time to regroup. Typically, I ate at my desk and scrolled through emails or Pinterest, but today, I felt the need to escape and hopefully clear my head in the process.

Gathering my belongings, I dipped my head to Doris as I passed and headed out, the ability to even small talk expended at the moment. The cool spring air greeted me, and I breathed it in, already feeling better as the oxygen cleared my head. I loved spring and how the earth started to come alive again. Seeing all the flowers beginning to bloom and the budding of the trees as they began to emerge was a good reminder of how things come in seasons.

Walking the streets aimlessly, I took in the city's sights, remembering how beautiful it was at this time of year. A few minutes later, I found myself on a familiar block, one I hadn't been on in months. When I noticed the sign was on for Ignite Ink, I made an impulsive decision and decided to see if Nicco was free. Popping into the place next door, I grabbed some tacos and hoped he wouldn't mind a lunch date. Entering the shop, I took a deep breath and greeted Cassandra. She welcomed me, and I tried to hide my embarrassment from our last encounter.

"Well, hello, darlin'. It's good to see you." She smiled kindly at me.

"Yeah, you too. How are you doing, Cassandra?" Despite my attempt, my face heated anyway.

"Things are good, but I doubt you're here to see *me*."

Smiling, I nodded. "Is Nicco in? I was hoping he was available for lunch."

"Yeah, sure. Let me go grab him."

Nodding, I walked over to the wall and checked out some of the new designs he'd put up. When I came to a particular piece, I stopped in my tracks. It caught my focus so intensely, I didn't hear him approach from behind me.

"It's beautiful, isn't it?"

"I'm just in awe, Nicco. It's amazing."

"Thankfully, I had something amazing to go off of. It was the only way to get you out of my mind. I thought about you every day."

"Wow. I don't know what to say." I turned, taking him in. Sincerity rang true in his eyes, the grey-blue mesmerizing as always. He'd framed a sketch drawing of me laying on a pillow, my hair billowing out behind me, my features were soft, his hand cupping my cheek. It was elegant and breathtaking. I almost didn't believe it was me.

"I'm happy to see you, Beautiful. What brings you in today?"

"I had a weird session and needed to get some air. Somehow, I found myself here. I hope that's okay."

"Of course, anytime."

"Okay, good. I grabbed some food and hoped you hadn't had lunch, thinking maybe I could crash yours and surprise you with tacos."

He grinned wide, his whole face lighting up. His dark hair was disheveled, and he wore glasses today, making his eyes softer somehow. I'd been able to push how attractive he was out of my mind over the past few months, but standing in front of him, it was like being smacked with a gorgeous dude in the face, knocking my breath out of my chest.

"Who doesn't love surprise tacos? Come on, let's go to the back."

He grabbed my free hand and pulled me along. All the memories of my last time here with him flooded me, and I found my face flooding with heat for a different reason this time. It would be hard to see his desk and not want him to throw me down on it. Thankfully, when we got to the back, he directed us to the couch and pulled over a little table for us to set the food on. Setting my stuff down, I turned to him, amazed I was here. It still felt surreal.

"I didn't know what kind of tacos you liked, so I got a bit of everything."

"Beautiful, it's *tacos*. How can there be anything wrong?" He beamed, relaxing me.

"True, true," I conceded. "Tacos are a staple of life."

We both dug in, taking a few bites, letting the quiet settle around us. After a few minutes, he set his taco down and looked at me, a serious look on his face.

"Do you want to talk about whatever brought you here?"

Wiping my mouth, I swallowed before nodding. Nicco noticed my action and stood and grabbed some water from the mini-fridge. I didn't realize how much I needed it until I'd drank half of it.

"Thank you. Those are spicier than I expected."

"You're welcome." He leaned back against the couch, giving me space to talk or process.

"So, yeah, I guess I want to talk about it. I mean, I can't really tell you too much." I fiddled with the napkin in my lap, focusing on it to find my words. Looking up, his eyes settled me like they always did, and I found my voice. "It was just… strange. This client has been confusing from the beginning, and I feel like he's playing a game. But I don't know what his purpose is, and it frustrates the hell out of me."

"What's going on?"

"He's so disorganized and all over the place. He comes in each session, and I feel like he's somebody different. It's always faked and forced, and there will be moments where I feel like the real person slips through. But it's more that he's trying to confuse me or make me think he's crazy."

"Wow, that sounds interesting. What's he there for?"

"That's one of the things he doesn't ever talk about. He's vague and will say he had some problems he wanted to work on whenever I ask him. He never really shares with me."

"Sounds like maybe this person is more difficult than they need to be."

Chuckling, I picked up my taco, taking a few more bites before answering again. "That's definitely one way to look at it."

After finishing, I picked up my trash, placing it in the bag on the floor. Nicco did the same and then turned his body more towards me, his arm going to the back of the couch as he rested his head on it. His leg was bent at the knee, laying across the cushion, and it made me want to turn into him and have him fix everything for me. Staying where I was, though, I twisted only a little, facing him.

"Is there somebody you could tell? Or, I don't know how it works, but can you change therapists? I mean, if I don't like who cuts my hair, then I go to somebody new."

Chuckling at his cuteness, I agreed. His other hand had grabbed mine while he talked, playing with our fingers. His touch against my skin was electrifying, and I had to focus on what I wanted to say. Nicco was far too charming, confusing my thoughts and reservations.

"Yeah, I should do that. It would be better to staff it with someone I work with, even if only so they know what's going on. He left today, and I felt really weird about how things had ended, and I'm just not sure what to do."

"Aren't there protocols in place for stuff like this?"

"Yeah," I confirmed, smiling at how engaged he was.

"I went through all the steps for risk assessment, and he didn't present as 'at risk'. But I also felt, like, maybe he was telling me what I wanted to hear."

"Someone you could call and have them keep a closer eye on him?"

"No. He's an adult, and his wife's deceased, and apparently, he doesn't talk to his son or daughter, so I don't really know who else in his life I could call. He didn't list an emergency contact."

"If you're that worried about him, could you go visit him at home?"

I thought about it but then shook my head no. "That crosses the line of what I feel comfortable doing."

"Fair, but I wonder if you're this worried if maybe you should call the cops and have them check?"

"I don't know. Maybe?" I shrugged. "I'm not really sure how I feel about it or how to gauge it. Do I only feel this way because he weirds me out, or is there something really there? I think that's what's bothering me the most, that I can't figure out the puzzle."

"I'm sorry, Beautiful. If I know anything, though, it's that you won't give up, and this person has the best therapist looking out for them."

"Thanks," I smiled. Shaking my body, I physically tried to dispel the weirdness that had been coating me. "Well, anyway, let's talk about something else because I'm getting into my head more about this, and I want to shake it off for the rest of the day."

"Of course. So, I heard you had fun at the house yesterday?"

"Yeah, I did, or *we* did," I confirmed. "I was surprised

when we got invited after the whole ordeal. It's a gorgeous home, though. I still can't believe Atticus owns the whole thing."

"Mas' place is pretty awesome. If I didn't like my own space so much, I'd be jealous. It's too busy there for me. Living at the estate the past few months almost drove me insane on top of missing you."

"Yeah?"

"I wish I could show you the inside of my mind and how many times I thought of you and how angry I was." He scooted closer and cupped my cheek. I'd laid my head on the side of the couch, his palm following me. I found myself falling into his eyes. Clearing my throat, I lifted my head, his hand falling away.

"It was beautiful. He has a floor for everything. I don't even know what someone would do with that much space. And that backyard, I was impressed," I rambled. "The back area was incredible, and we got to play out there with Fort."

"Oh, yeah! You got to play with the dog. Now, I'm jealous I didn't come over."

"You'll have to come next time. Wells is bringing Fort with him each time. He hopes I'll be able to help train him, but I don't think I'm very good at it," I admitted, laughing. "I mostly just patted the dog and let him lick my face. But it was fun. Jude and Immy seemed to enjoy themselves as well."

"That's incredible. Immy deserves some fun."

Nodding, I found myself relaxing again; the conversation having returned easily between us. "Atticus wants me to meet with her and talk again. It'll be informal, but I'm happy to be back in her life."

"Really? Well, go, Mas. I didn't know my cousin had it in him. I'm glad, though. I know she's missed you. That was one of the hardest things about the lockdown, not being able to talk to you or Jude. It gave us something we both could commiserate with each other over." He paused, and I realized his fingers were still looped with mine, his thumb tracing over the top one. "I warred with myself because, at the same time, I understood the reasoning and wanted to keep you safe."

"What was the reasoning then?"

"It's hard… so hard to keep it from you. I want to tell you, I've never wanted to tell someone in my whole life more than I want to tell you. But doing that opens you up to more danger than I would ever want to put you in. I already feel so much guilt for what happened to you with the bombing, and I would never want you to be hurt like that again."

Dropping my eyes, disappointment filled me. While I understood something was going on, and I didn't want to deal with that knowledge, part of me needed the answer to verify if I mattered to him or if it was just pretty words, pretty lies he was telling me. Dropping my head more, I picked at my pants, brushing off some nonexistent lint.

"Yeah, that was intense," I stated, my voice coming out shallow. "I'm still not sure I fully processed everything. It was more about focusing on healing and Jude. And then, you know, dealing with the fact that all the men in my life left me." I hadn't meant to put it out there like that. I didn't want to keep beating him up, but it slipped, the pain of those moments filling me with grief.

"Yeah," he said, accepting my agony, reminding me of how he'd been when I told him my darkest confession in this very room. Something in me shifted, the pain and hurt lifting a little and allowing me to see the truth of what I felt plastered on his face. "Beautiful, I can never be apologetic enough for what happened. I know it sounds like an excuse, but in my heart, I believed it was what was best. I wanted to give you protection, and I'll never not be sorry for that. I'll say it until I'm blue in the face if I have to."

"I might regret this too, but what do I need protection from?"

He hesitated, debating what to tell me, and I knew it was a precipice for us. When he began to answer, the breath I hadn't known I was holding released.

"There are people in my family's world that want to hurt us, and you'd be the number one way to accomplish it. You're not just connected to me, but Immy and Sax, now. It makes you valuable, and hurting you, inevitably would hurt Atticus."

"You're kind of freaking me out now, Nicco. People want to hurt you? I thought this was some business competitor, but it sounds like something deeper... *more.*" I knew I was grasping at straws, and if I really thought about it, a bombing attempt was extreme because they were angry about a sushi restaurant. Still, the mind did curious things when presented with truths you weren't prepared to believe yet.

"I told you, my family... is *complicated.*"

Agreeing, I nodded. "I'm starting to understand that even more, now. I don't think I want to know anything else at the moment." I bit my lip, worry filling me. I didn't want the people I was beginning to care about to be under attack either, but I was at my limit, and I knew it.

"It's probably better that way. Honestly. The less you know, the safer you will be."

"There's a curious part of me that wants to pull the string, you know? I don't know if I'm more worried about what I'm getting myself into or for you. I guess I wanted a choice, but I don't know what that choice should be. I'm starting to agree with your reasoning to stay away even if it hurt."

Nicco moved closer, with no hesitancy this time, and cupped both my cheeks. "Beautiful, listen, I don't know if there is a right or wrong decision. All I know is that I need you in my life, and I'll do whatever it takes to make sure that it happens. Life without you was miserable. I don't want to live that way if I don't have to. Do you understand?"

Nodding slowly, I didn't drop my eyes from his. They were so earnest and full of strength. I wanted to be that certain about something, and I wanted to be part of whatever he was offering. This was the Nicco I'd fallen for, the one who had told me he had me when I was falling apart in his arms after sex. The one who said he'd be my tour guide and took me on a journey of self-discovery.

"I understand, and I absolve you of any guilt. It was a greater kindness you did, and I see that now. I think… at this point, I couldn't walk away even if it was for the best. All of you have entrenched yourselves into my life, and it was empty without you. I'll listen and do whatever is needed. I'm trusting you to have *our* best interest at heart because Jude and I, we're a package deal."

He dropped his head to mine, his breath fanning over my face, and I closed my eyes, soaking him in. Nicco pulled back, and I noticed his eyes were glossy. "Beautiful, I don't make promises I can't keep. So hear me when I say this, I promise with my life to protect you and Jude, and while I know I still have to make up for the pain I caused, and things are still up in the air for us, I want you to know I'm okay with Sax. I was jealous at first, but I accepted it because I didn't fight hard enough. But then I got to thinking how it made perfect sense. So, if we ever get back to that place, I won't make you choose."

I sucked in a breath, his words echoing the fears in my heart. "You're not mad or disgusted?"

"No, Beautiful. I told you before I wanted you to explore, and I would be here for you in whatever capacity that meant. I stand by that."

"Thank you," I breathed. Pulling back, I needed some space from the intimate moment before I kissed him. "You know, I'm enjoying getting to discover who you are on a real level. Don't get me wrong, the sex was phenomenal, and you helped me figure out who I am becoming as a woman. I just don't want to lose myself again."

"I don't want you to lose yourself either."

"I'm glad we can have these types of conversations. That was one of the things I missed the most about you, Nicco. You were someone I could talk to openly with, and then you were just gone. I didn't know what to do with that."

"I'll never be able to say sorry enough."

"I know, and I don't want you to feel like you always have to apologize; that's no relationship either."

"I don't, Beautiful. I look at you, and mostly, I'm angry I missed out on months of your life. On time I could've been getting to know you more. I used the excuses, and it was cowardly of me."

"I'm just glad we're here now," I affirmed. "I think if we take things slow, I'd be ready for more. But, right now, I need a new topic. I don't know if I can handle any more emotions."

"Sure. How about we discuss the tattoo you owe me?" He smirked, a mischievous look on his face.

"The what now?" I asked, attempting to deflect.

"Oh, I'm sure you remember our little bet at the fight? I said if everybody wasn't enamored with you, then you won, and I'd have to do anything you wanted without complaint. And if I won, then you had to get a tattoo. Based on the fact that not *one*, not *two*, but *three* men were at that booth drooling over you that night, not to mention every man in that VIP section, means I win." He paused, a smug look on his face. He leaned closer, whispering, "So, *Beautiful*, what tattoo are you going to get?"

"Wow, I didn't think I was gonna have to go through with it."

"How about this?" Nicco offered, knowing he won. "You pick where to place it, and I'll design it myself."

Sighing, I gave in to his demands. "You promise not to do something offensive?"

"Come on, Beautiful. You wound me with your doubt!" He faked getting hit in the heart, covering his chest. "I would never want to put anything that's not as beautiful as you on your body."

Chuckling, I agreed. "I guess I do trust you in that sense. Okay."

"Yes!" He fist-pumped, grinning wide. "Perfect. I already know exactly what I'm designing. When are you available?"

"Oh, wow, okay," I gathered myself, thinking through my schedule. "How about Friday?"

"It's a date. Can you make it here around 2 pm?"

"Yeah, that's doable."

"I'll have Cassandra add you to the schedule then." He grinned wider, and we picked up the rest of the trash as we talked about his classes and what it had been like living cooped up with Atticus, Sax, and Immy for two months. Nicco kept teasing me about the tattoo placement, and I realized I had a decision to make.

When I left there and headed back to the office, I registered that I did feel better. And I was glad I'd taken the chance to spend time with him. I was beginning to learn that the rewards were better than the potential risks each time I took a chance. So I would just need to keep reminding myself that sometimes, it was more dangerous to stay in your comfort zone than to step outside of it. Each of these men showed me that while they weren't perfect, they would at least own up to their mistakes, which meant everything to me.

TWENTY

LOREN

Unlocking my door, I was surprised when my phone began to ring. Not many people called me, so the sound always took me by surprise. Creasing my brow at the blocked number, I debated if I should answer it. I didn't like not knowing who was on the other end; anxiety coursed through me at who it could be.

By the fourth ring, I was a ball of nerves, and only the thought it could have something to do with Jude had me accepting the call.

"Hello?" squeaked out, my voice sounding weak as I answered, and I hated it. Resolving myself, I straightened my spine and tried again. "Hello?"

"Good evening, Mrs. Carter." The voice instantly sent shivers racing over my body, my name rolling over his tongue. Even through the phone's tiny speakers, it still had my body wanting to bow to him, begging for more.

"Mr. Masters." It was all I could manage to get out, the name a breathy reply.

"I've called to give you an update on what we discussed yesterday."

"Oh?"

"I believe I have some information you'll be interested in. Would you be able to come over this evening?"

"Oh," I startled, surprised and shocked at his speediness. "Um, that's great, but I have dinner plans with my neighbor tonight."

He was silent for a few seconds before he responded, my lip finding its way between my teeth as I waited.

"What if I propose an alternative?" he asked, pausing and keeping me on pins and needles. "How about if you and Mr. Miller have dinner here instead? This involves him as well, and I'll have food catered in for the occasion."

The thoughtfulness of his suggestion had me smiling, a blush heating my cheeks, making me feel like a schoolgirl getting attention from her crush. Atticus was no boy though, he was all man, a commanding presence begging for obedience, and I found myself wanting to give in to his call.

"That sounds lovely. There's just one problem."

"What is it? I'm sure we can find a solution together, Mrs. Carter."

Atticus was more disarming over the phone when I couldn't read his body language. His concern had my body heating and my tongue sticking to the roof of my mouth. It suddenly had me flashing back to the sensation room when Sax was only a voice and how mind-blowing that experience had been.

"Mrs. Carter?"

"Oh, sorry, I must've muted the phone accidentally with my cheek," I lied, clearing my throat. "I haven't told Monroe yet about our agreement."

"I see."

"But, I'm sure once I do, it will be okay. Can I just check with him first?" The need to please Atticus was riding me hard, and I found myself worried he wouldn't be happy with my response, not to mention I suddenly felt guilty for lying.

"I will call you back in 10 minutes, Mrs. Carter."

"Thank you."

"And Mrs. Carter?"

"Yes?"

"There's no need to feel shame about being flustered, Bellezza, but *don't* lie to me."

The phone clicked, and I stood frozen, my face heating in embarrassment. The sudden ending of the phone call was abrupt, but I didn't find it rude. I was learning it was his nature. It felt more like he was holding himself back from saying or doing more at times. His own shields in place. Mr. Masters was a tough cookie to crack, and he had me so twisted, I wasn't sure how to handle him. A strong need to be seen as flawless in front of him was always at the surface, highlighting my failures.

But the thought, *that feeling*, was triggering, reminding me of my mother and Brian. Yet, Atticus was nothing like either of them, and when I looked deeper at the feeling, I knew it was different at its core. With Atticus, it was out of respect, not fear, or at least not the same kind of fear.

With my mother, and even Brian, I feared their repercussions and reactions to my choices in the end. I constantly found myself managing their emotions along with my own to reduce any negative response, fearful of their violent tendencies. With Atticus, the sense of danger about him had me wanting to obey in a different way. The darkness was seductive, calling to the portion of me that liked to run free. The section of my personality that wasn't concerned about societal norms or boundaries. The part of myself that scared me a little, if I was honest.

The realization I'd been standing frozen in my living room for a few minutes now had me setting my stuff down and placing my phone on the counter. It was 5:30 pm, and Monroe was due over here in an hour. Kicking off my high heels, I slipped on my moccasin slippers by the door and walked across the hall.

I could've called Monroe or texted, but this felt like something I should tell him face to face. I'd planned to do it tonight, so all this did was speed up the timeline. Knocking, I only waited a few seconds before he answered, a huge smile on his face.

"Lo! I thought we were having dinner at your place in an hour?"

"Yeah, we were. Can I come in real quick?"

"Yeah, sure." He backed up, his smile slipping some at my statement, allowing me to enter. As I passed, I couldn't help but take a deep breath, his fresh cotton scent calming me. He smelled delectable each time I was near, and I constantly found myself wanting to just place my nose on his neck, breathing in his scent. I quickly sat down on the couch, knowing I was short on time. I probably shouldn't have left my phone, but I still struggled to use it.

"This must be a serious conversation if you're sitting on the couch," he cautioned as he joined me.

Giggling, I shook my head. "No. I mean, it's serious in nature, but I don't think you'll see it as something bad."

"Okay. Now I see what you mean about dragging things out. The suspense is killing me."

Grabbing his hand, I squeezed it, smiling. "So, I kind of told you before about how I was dating Nicco before everything happened." He nodded, and I continued. "Well, I'd also met another man during that time, Saxon, or Sax. I hadn't seen either of them because of something that happened after the bombing. And while I'm not ready to date Nicco yet, he has come back into my life, and we're working on getting to know one another first. Sax and I, well, I guess we're dating. I don't know what to really call what Sax and I have. He's kind of intense in the best way. Well, why I'm saying this is because I met him through Jude's friend, Imogen."

"Oh, yes, of course. He's mentioned her. Did he get back in touch with her?"

"Yes. They came with Nicco to the wedding. Neither of us had seen them since the restaurant, so it was nice. On Sunday, Wells asked if I was ready to start our training."

"Training?"

"Oh, um, yeah, Wells offered to teach me more kick-boxing and self-defense. He apparently works for Imogen's brother now, Mr. Masters."

"Wow, I didn't realize. So much has happened in a short time. I guess I've been further in my hole than I realized." His eyes held some shame, and I squeezed his hand, not wanting him to regret fighting for Levi, ever.

"I'm not sharing this with you to make you feel bad. I'm getting to the point, I promise."

"I know, Lo. It just made me realize how consumed I'd been, in not a good way. Losing myself to get Levi back isn't what I wanted either. I'm glad we're having this dinner. I think I needed it more than I knew. We're still having it?"

Smiling, I agreed. "Yes, I'm getting there," I confirmed, chuckling. "Yesterday, when I was there, Mr. Masters, well, he wants me to do something, but I can't tell you exactly without breaking HIPAA, but he was willing to do me a favor in exchange. I guess I was feeling bold because I negotiated with him."

"What did you ask for?"

Pulling my shoulders back, I was still proud of myself for the moment. "I know you said you were meeting with someone, but I figured more help wouldn't be bad either. Mr. Masters, he has connections and means to get things. It's not that he's rich. I've been around rich people. It's more that he exudes this power and has ways to get things I don't necessarily have access to."

"Okay…"

"One of the things I asked help with was figuring out the connection between my mother and Brian. I don't believe them about Barkley, and the PI Mitzi suggested ghosted me, probably paid off by them. I overheard part of a conversation at the wedding, and they're clearly colluding. I'm just not confident on the how, or why."

"So he agreed to help? That's wonderful."

"Yes," I affirmed, nodding, "and I hope you don't mind this part, but I also asked him to help with you and Levi." I cringed, waiting for his answer.

"You did?"

"Yes, are you mad? I can tell him no if you don't want anyone in your business."

Monroe moved closer, the distance between us becoming nonexistent as he grazed his thumb over my cheek, pushing my hair behind my ear in an intimate gesture. "No, that's really sweet, Loren. I'll gladly take whatever help there is. What does it have to do with dinner?"

"Oh, God, yes," I chuckled, his hand still on my jaw. "He called me when I was getting home to let me know he had information and invited me to come over tonight."

"So, you do need to cancel."

"No," I chuckled, his concern for cancelling making me realize how invested he was in us. "The opposite, actually. I told him I already had dinner plans with *you*."

"You didn't have to do that. I would've understood."

"Can you just let me finish, Monroe?" I laughed. "You're being too nice. Always giving me an out when I don't need one."

"Okay, okay, I'm sorry. You're right." His smile was wide as he waited.

"So, I told him I had plans with you, and he mentioned the information he had to share involved you too and countered with inviting us to have dinner at his place. He's willing to have something catered in. Okay, *now* you may ask questions. That's the end."

Laughing, he nodded. "I'm good with that. As long as I get to spend time with you which I've been severely missing, I don't care if we eat at McDonald's."

"See, too nice."

He watched my eyes for a second before he leaned in, kissing me softly. How the sweetest kiss from Monroe could be as hot as the devouring ones from Sax was a mystery and a problem. A good problem, but still one when I would eventually have to choose. The reality was becoming heavier and heavier, the decision almost unbearable to make. Nicco acted like I wouldn't have to, but would they all agree?

"Selfishly, I thought if maybe you got to know Sax, and Nicco if he's there, that I, I don't know, it wouldn't be as weird. I'm just," I sputtered, "I really like you all. I don't know what to do." I found myself admitting my fears as I stared into his pale green eyes, the lightness offering me protection. "Maybe if you all knew each other, it wouldn't be as difficult. I don't know what I expected. I'm… kind of spinning right now. Maybe I'm asking for too much."

"No, Lo, you're fine. I promise. Of course, we can go to dinner there, especially if he has information on Levi. I would love that. I met with someone this weekend, it went really well. But I'm still waiting to hear back on a court date. I called someone today, and it could possibly be moved up this week. But if Mr. Masters has more information, that's even better. Never apologize for following your gut. You're always thinking about others, you know, that's what you do. You consider everyone else's needs before your own. So if this is something you need, want even, I can do that for you."

"Thank you, Monroe." I smiled until I remembered the time. "He said he would call back in 10 minutes, and I left my phone at my place. I don't know what time we're meeting. Do you want to walk over with me? And then I could tell you once I know?"

"Yeah, sure."

Monroe followed me across the hall. When I opened the door, I heard the ringtone coming from the counter. *Shit.* I took off running. I didn't know how long it had been or what ring it was on, and Atticus wasn't one to keep waiting. "Why can't I ever remember to take the darn thing with me?" I mumbled under my breath. Phones were not my friend.

"I should get you one of those watches. That way, the calls come to you even when you're away from your phone," Monroe offered, chuckling at my distress.

"Yeah, that'd probably be smart."

Picking up the phone, I winced when I saw I had three missed calls already. It started ringing again, scaring me, causing me to drop it. Bending over quickly, I stood up fast with it as I answered, causing me to be slightly out of breath.

"Hello?" I huffed.

"Mrs. Carter." He stopped, pausing for a second. "Did I interrupt something?" I didn't miss the hint of steel behind his question.

"I mean, sort of, but no, you're fine," I rambled, his tone throwing me off. "I just walked in from across the hall from talking with Monroe. I left my phone here.

When I unlocked the door, I heard it ringing, so I ran, then it stopped, but then you rang again, and I jumped, dropping it, and yeah, that's why I sound this way…" I finally managed to run out of words, and my face heated. Monroe's body shook with laughter, his fist over his mouth in an attempt to hold the sound in. Sticking my tongue out at him, I almost missed what Atticus had to say.

"Well, good to know, Mrs. Carter." His curtness had my hackles rising.

"You thought something else, didn't you?"

"I have no clue what you could be referring to, Mrs. Carter."

"Uh, huh. I'm on to you, Atticus."

"Oh, what are you on to, Loren?" This time, his tone turned playful when he answered. For some reason, when he used my first name, it rolled off his tongue differently than Mrs. Carter, making my core clench tight.

Clearing my throat, I slowed my breathing. "Just that you're not as mysterious as you pretend."

"I would beg to differ," he teased before remembering our conversation and reigning it in. "I do need to set things in motion if you are agreeable to dinner this evening."

Disappointed that the flirting had been cut short, I slouched on the barstool, answering. "Yes, Monroe said he was okay with dinner. We just didn't know what time to be there."

"It's 5:45 now, how about 7 pm? You're welcome to

arrive early, of course. You can hang out with Imogen or perhaps Saxon, but dinner will be served at seven."

"You won't be available during this time?"

My question had him pausing, silence getting to me over the line. "I'm afraid I have matters to handle until then, Mrs. Carter." Ah, so back to formality it was then.

"The time is agreeable to us."

"Wonderful. See you then, Mrs. Carter."

He hung up the phone again before I could say anything else. Looking at Monroe, I found him observing me, an unreadable look on his face.

"Dinner will be ready at 7. I'd like to go earlier to speak with Imogen, but that would leave you alone. Maybe Wells will be there? Have you two spoken a lot since the other night?"

"No, we haven't. I probably should talk to him, though. I've kind of become distant lately, pushing people away. I've been avoiding talking to him. But maybe I should try harder and give him a chance to prove himself."

"I think that'd be great. Not that I know him as well or have a history like you do. But yesterday, we actually had a lot of fun. He doesn't seem to hate the world as much. I mean, he still hates *people*," I chuckled, "but he wasn't as grumpy as normal, which was nice. We laughed a lot, and he brought Fort, so that was a blast."

"Is that one of his new dogs?"

"Yeah, he's having a little trouble with him, and for some reason, the dog likes me, so he asked if I'd help."

"I'm not surprised. You're amazing, Lo." His smile

was genuine, and I found myself returning it, attempting to not dismiss his compliment. I pushed away the uncomfortableness, reminding myself it was because I wasn't used to hearing those things, not that they weren't true.

"Well, I better tell Jude. Do you want to meet back here, in, let's say, 20 minutes, to leave?"

"Perfect. I need to change out of my work clothes. I can be back in fifteen minutes."

"Sounds good. I don't really need to do much. Let me go check with Jude."

"Okay." He kissed my cheek, surprising me, before giving me a wink as he walked toward the door. I found myself watching him walk away, focusing on the way his butt looked in those pants of his. The man wore a suit well and had a way of looking sexy and professional. There was also a layer of disheveled rumpledness about him like you could mess him up, and he wouldn't mind. It was a weird combination, but it worked for Monroe. The door shut, and I jumped back at the sound. I needed to stop getting lost in my thoughts.

Walking to Jude's room, I knocked on the door and waited until "enter" was mumbled.

"Hey, so change of plans. Dinner will be at Mr. Masters' house now. Can you be ready in 15 minutes?"

"Yeah," he confirmed, sitting up quickly. "Immy going to be there?"

"Yep, and Monroe's coming with us too."

"Oh, okay. Cool. You okay with all this?"

"Yeah," I immediately responded, but stopped when his question penetrated. "What do you mean?"

"Just seems like you have a lot on your plate."

"Yeah," I agreed, "I'm just trying to figure it out."

Jude nodded in response, an understanding look on his face. "Yeah, I can be ready in 15 minutes."

"Perfect."

Closing his door, I put his concern in a little pocket in my mind to remind myself when I was feeling lonely that he cared. Walking into my room, I realized I didn't know how we were getting there. Unlocking the phone still clutched in my hand, I saved the number and sent a message asking about transportation.

ME: We're leaving in 15 minutes. Will you be sending a car again? It's not that I expect it, but I didn't want to arrive at your house and make your magic car people wait for no reason.

A FEW SECONDS LATER, the dots popped up, and he replied. I had to admire a man who didn't make me wait.

MR. 'BOSSY PANTS' Masters: Beau will be waiting for you at 6:00 pm, Mrs. Carter.

ME: Thank you.

BEFORE I COULD STOP MYSELF, I asked another question, finding it easier through text.

• • •

ME: Should I bring wine or something?

Mr. 'Bossy Pants' Masters: Not needed. I assure you I have a full wine cellar if you're interested in some.

ME: Oh, okay, thank you. It was more of a knee-jerk reaction. Growing up, I always felt like I had to bring something.

Mr. 'Bossy Pants' Masters: Just yourself, Mrs. Carter.

ME: Okay, I'll see you in a little bit then.

Mr. 'Bossy Pants' Masters: Looking forward to it, Mrs. Carter.

DROPPING the phone on the bed, I quickly changed my clothes and found myself excited for this dinner. It would be interesting, at least. Especially if Wells was there too. I wanted to watch the dynamics between him and Monroe, only having seen them together when he was injured or at the gym. Thinking about it, I picked up my phone and sent one message to Nicco.

ME: Change of plans. Atticus called with information and invited Monroe and me over for dinner. I'm assuming Sax will be there, and Wells too. So, I just wanted to offer you the invitation. If you would like to join us, I guess, even though it's not my house. Maybe more of a, I'm going to be there in case you wanted to stop by. Okay, this is really long, and I'm rambling now. So I'll see you if I see you.

· · ·

CLOSING IT, I shoved it in my back pocket before slipping on some shoes, but then I stopped. Looking down at my jeans, I decided I wanted to spice it up. I only had a few minutes left, so I quickly went back into my closet and slipped on a burgundy dress that hugged my frame and some black strappy heels. Rinsing my mouth out with mouthwash, I brushed my hair and pulled it back, spritzing myself with some spray. Next, I put on what was becoming my signature red lipstick. Right as I finished, the buzzer from downstairs buzzed, and there was a knock at the door as well. I hurried down the hall to let Monroe in. Jude lifted his eyebrow when he caught my appearance.

"Whoa. Looking nice, Lor."

"Thank you," I beamed. Opening the door, I found Monroe looking as delicious as ever.

"Wow, Lo, you look amazing."

"Thank you," blushing, I shuffled us out the door. "Ready?"

"Yes, let's go!"

We headed down the hall and didn't have to wait long for the elevator. As we all walked into it, I realized I'd left my phone in the pocket of my jeans. I didn't feel like going back for it, so I hoped I wouldn't need it. The thought of *'who would call you?'* filtered through until I remembered it was right.

Who would call me when I was going to be with all of them? Ha! Take that self-doubting thoughts. Smugly, I leaned against the elevator wall, excited about what this evening might hold. It seemed like things were beginning to align, and I was at the helm of my life for once.

TWENTY ONE

LOREN

The drive to the house was pleasant, and I listened to Jude and Monroe talk about hockey. I was thrilled when Monroe offered to take Jude out one weekend and teach him if he was interested. Not only did it make me happy to see Jude get the opportunity to try new things, but it felt nice that Monroe wanted to be in our lives, and was making an effort. It warmed my heart, really.

There was a voice in the back of my head trying to pop up and tell me it was all too good to be true, that just when I'd gotten happy, it had all been taken away, and it would happen again because inevitably, *everyone left me.*

Yet, that wasn't the case anymore. The difference this time… I had me.

If I had written my own story, carved out a path I'd take in life, it wouldn't have included the bumps and bruises I'd received along the way. I'd be living in my suburban house with my husband and our 2.5 children and dog. I'd have brunch every Sunday with my parents, and I'd go to PTA meetings for fun.

It was a nice story, one I would've been happy to live.

But it wasn't *my* story, or the one I really wanted to live anymore.

I was learning to let go of the preconceived perceptions of the life I'd dreamed and open myself up for all the possibilities this life could give me.

No, I hadn't wanted to be divorced at thirty-two, but I also wouldn't have met Nicco, Saxon, or Monroe. It was doubtful I would've even met Wells, kickboxing not even on my radar before this past year. And while it was possible I would've still met Atticus and Imogen, I wouldn't have become inserted into their lives. Nor would I have met Jude.

The realization I could be living a life where I didn't know him, and he was left alone, broke my heart. I didn't want to replace my grief with focusing on him, filling one hole with something else, but I couldn't deny the joy he'd brought to my life, or the sense of purpose.

Not having these experiences, meeting these men, or being a part of their lives wasn't something I would ever trade now. The pain of them leaving had hurt, but I'd survived it. I'd shown myself I could be strong. It was an experience and lesson I wouldn't want to have missed.

So, yes, self, they *could* leave me. I could also get hit by a bus tomorrow. It didn't mean I was going to stop living. I'd done that already, and it hadn't been enjoyable.

The car came to a stop again, our door opening the second it did, and I found myself squeezing and hugging Jude before I unbuckled my seatbelt. He hugged me back, giving me an odd look when I pulled away.

"Everything okay, Lor?"

"Yeah."

Smiling, I squeezed his hand and climbed out of the car. Monroe stepped up next to me, and I watched him as he took in the place.

"What did you say he does?"

"No clue. It's all very secretive. I know they own some restaurants and have something to do with fighting," I shrugged. "I've found it's better to not ask questions."

"That's not foreboding or anything."

Blowing out a breath, he linked our hands together, and we followed the black-suited men inside. Sax waited at the foot of the elevator, giving me his patented crooked smile.

"Spitfire, it seems you really can't get enough of me. This is now day four."

"Hmm, I believe I was invited by Atticus tonight, not *you*."

He chuckled, his eyes promising me all kinds of dark desires. The man was not safe for my sense of decorum or panties. Thankfully, he turned his stare to Monroe before I decided to jump on him.

"Mr. Miller, it's a pleasure to meet you. I'm Saxon."

"Monroe is fine. It's nice to meet you too."

They shook hands, and I found it strangely attractive to see Monroe not be intimidated by the massive paw of Sax's.

"I'm impressed, Sax. I didn't know you had manners in you."

Monroe chuckled at my tease, and we all walked into

the elevator. Sax smirked, not saying anything, which heightened my anticipation.

"Loren, are you hanging out with Imogen before dinner? I know you'd originally said tomorrow, but since you're here now, I wasn't sure what your plans were?"

"Yes, if she'd like to." He nodded, then looked at Jude and Monroe. "Mr. Young is in the fitness arena. I can drop you both off there, or I can take you to a different part of the complex. There's a movie theater, music room, library, or even a dark room."

Jude looked at me, and I gave him a soft smile. "You're 17, hun. You don't have to stay with Monroe if you want to check out something else."

His smile lit up, and he looked to Monroe next, "Would you mind if I checked out the library? Immy was telling me about it."

"Of course, I have some things to discuss with Wells anyway. You'll have to tell me how this library is. I'm super interested in it now."

Jude grinned, and Sax hit the floor for him to exit on. Jude's simple request had me affirming my earlier thoughts. All the hard things had sucked, none of them being pleasant, but I was finding these small precious moments were just as powerful as any big moment. Watching Jude be polite and respectful, getting excited about books, and spending time with his friend made me happy, and I liked that feeling.

When the door dinged, it was to let Monroe off first, and then the next floor was Jude, who Sax directed to a guard on the floor. When the doors shut, leaving Sax and me alone in the elevator, the atmosphere shifted. The second the doors had closed, he was on me. Trapping me against the elevator wall, causing me to gasp. Sax never wavered in his feelings, always showing me exactly how he felt.

"If I had more time, I'd show you exactly how many manners I have, Spitfire. But since I only have three more floors, I'll have to leave you wanting until I can fuck you so hard you won't even be able to say the word *manners*."

He slammed his mouth to mine, hitching my leg up high on his hip. The fabric of the dress pulled some, but it didn't stop him from being able to rub his very hard cock against me. His tongue swirled around, and I saw stars. I realized it was because I hadn't remembered to breathe, Sax having stolen the breath straight from me.

Pulling back, my head dropped to the wall, a moan echoing around us. Without hesitation, his finger plunged into me, my core tightening around him. He dropped down to the ground, snagging my panties to the side as he sealed his lips on my clit and sucked hard. My fingers threaded through his hair, his beard rubbing against my thighs, leaving me with a burn I'd feel for days. I moaned, my head falling back against the elevator as I gave into him.

Quicker than I'd ever thought possible, I felt myself beginning to cum, his fingers spearing me deep as he curled them up, hitting me just right. I shuddered, my moan stuttered as I attempted to manage the sensations coursing through me. The elevator began to slow, and Sax, apparently used to the motion, dragged his finger out slowly, coating himself in my juices.

In a coordinated move, he dropped my leg, fixed my dress, and kissed me quickly on the lips within seconds of the door opening. Sax pushed me in the direction I needed to go, and I walked out in a daze, my skin feeling alive. When I turned back, I found him plunging the finger he'd coated into his mouth, his tongue swirling around it as he stared straight at me until the doors closed.

Fucking hell, the man was going to kill me.

I spotted a bathroom before I made it to where I assumed Imogen's room was, and I ducked in, needing a minute to calm myself before I was capable of talking to a teenager. While I wouldn't be her therapist anymore, I wanted to be a good resource and confidant for her, which meant focusing on her and not how I wish the building had more floors so Sax would've had more time to show me his *proper manners* between my legs.

Splashing water, I managed to calm myself, the redness decreasing from my face slightly. I debated what to do with my panties, the material soaked through from his attention. Deciding no panties were better than wet ones, I slid them off and hid them under some tissues in the trash. My skin still felt sensitive, the orgasm having heightened all my nerve endings, so each move of the dress material caused me to gasp.

Opening the door, I was distracted by the sensations, and I bumped into someone, not expecting anyone to be out there. "Apologies," I started before straightening myself. "Mr. Masters."

His hands were on my biceps, his grip firm as he steadied me. The touch had me moaning out, and I gasped as I realized it. Atticus froze, his eyes searing into mine. He didn't let go or move back, just continued to hold me hostage. The redness I'd just gotten rid of crept back up my neck, spreading across my cheeks.

Clearing my throat, I tried to get through to him. "Mr. Masters? *Atticus*?" The sound of his name had him blinking, letting go of my arms so quickly, it was like they'd burned him. He stepped back, collecting himself in the process, the mask sliding back into focus.

"Mrs. Carter. Sorry, I hadn't expected you to be there. Are you on your way to Imogen's room?"

"Yes."

He assented, nodding down the hall. "It's two more down on the right. I'll send someone up when it's time for dinner."

With that, he scurried off down the hallway in the opposite direction of me, avoiding my eyes. Flushed and confused, I turned and went in search of her room, at least knowing which one it was now. I stumbled down the hallway in a daze; the orgasm and close encounter with Atticus had scrambled my brain waves. When I came to an open door, I peeked in, finding Imogen on her bed. Knocking on the open door, I hoped what I'd just been up to wasn't written all over my face.

"Knock, knock."

"Loren! Hey, how are you?" Imogen sat up on her bed from her prone position. She'd been lying on her stomach reading a book. A smile graced her face as I walked in.

"Do you want me to leave this door open or shut?"

"Open's fine. There's nobody else on the floor."

I wanted to disagree that her brother was, *in fact*, on the floor, but it was her choice, and I figured she knew the risks. So, I left it open and walked in, looking around the massive room and taking it in.

"Where can I sit?" I asked, falling into my role, easily giving her control of the environment.

"How about we sit over on the couch?"

I looked around her room as I moved and was amazed at the size of it. It was an incredible space with two levels. Her bed was on the upper level, and then a lower section held her entertainment center with a couch, oversized chair, and a TV. There was also a bar area with a fridge, microwave, and small counter that was stocked with snacks. She had a reading window and a keyboard in the corner.

"Wow, this place is awesome. I'm kind of jealous of your room."

"Thanks. Attie let me design it when I moved in."

"Well, you did great. I love the colors."

Her room was done in soft lavender and grey. It was feminine and delicate without being obnoxiously girly. She had fun posters and paintings on the wall, a shelf of well-loved books, including her Harry Potter ones on the top. The sight made me smile, remembering our conversation the first day. There were musical notes on the walls and what looked like sheet paper framed as well. One even had a butterfly painted in watercolors over it. The room was a fun look into who Imogen was and gave me insight into what she cared about. Sitting down, I waited for her to settle.

"Is it me? Or is it a little bit more uncomfortable this way?"

Chuckling, I agreed. "Yes, of course, because at least with my office, it was neutral and obvious what the meeting was about, but here it's your bedroom. While that could be comforting, it also confuses it for you. But remember, this isn't like therapy anymore, so it doesn't have to be so formal, either. Would it be easier if we went somewhere else?"

"No, it's fine. It's just making me laugh how nervous I felt."

"Well, it's also been a few months, so you haven't had to really broach uncomfortable topics. We don't have to talk about the hard stuff today either. We can talk about whatever. I just want to be in your life, whatever that looks like. With how things have changed with other relationships in my life and yours, it just wasn't ethical or prudent for me to stay in that role without me crossing boundaries. I care about you, Imogen, and I want to help, but only with what you're willing to share."

"That makes sense," she said, smiling softly. "I'm glad you're here. I've missed talking to you."

"I missed you too, sweet girl. How have you been since I last saw you?"

"Some good days and bad days. It was really hard at first not being able to reach out to you or Jude. I was furious at Atticus for a while. I even slapped him." She ducked her head at the comment, her cheeks tinting red.

My eyebrows raised as well, "Oh, wow. How did he respond?"

This had her lifting her head, a small blush as she grinned. "He wasn't too happy about it. Though, Sax told me good form later," she giggled. I couldn't help but join her, completely seeing Sax making a comment like that. "After that, I tried to work out my anger through music."

"Speaking of, it really was beautiful when I heard you playing the other day."

"Thank you," she blushed. "I used to love music, but then after everything, it was hard to play. Once I started talking to you, getting all those emotions out, I found I could start playing again. In the past couple of months, I actually started composing some songs. It's been really therapeutic."

"Oh, that's amazing, Imogen!"

"I don't know what it means for my future, but it has been nice, at least to get that piece of myself back."

"Definitely," I agreed. "How have you been with everything else? The bombing was a pretty traumatic event. Did it trigger any of the stuff we'd started to talk about?"

"Yeah, I think that's why I went off on Atticus, because I was stressed, and what did you call it, a height-ened state?"

I nodded, confirming.

"Yeah, well at that moment, I'd cast him as my dad. I was tired of the family taking people away from me, basically. It took me about a week to finally pull myself out of the loop and remind myself he wasn't my dad. Atticus has never done anything to harm me, and he's always put my best interest first. I apologized, and he said he understood. So things are better between us."

"That's really good to hear. Again, I'm impressed."

"Really?" she asked with a soft smile, and I squeezed her hand in confirmation. "At first, it was hard to stay in the present. I did fall back into feeling helpless and weak, and I *hated* it. But in some ways, because I had you guys to fight for, it made me stronger. I stood up for myself, and I was proud of that. I didn't agree with him and I made it known."

"That's absolutely something to be proud of."

"I just hope things are stable now."

"Me too," I admitted with a laugh.

"What about you? I'm allowed to ask questions now, right?" she asked, smiling.

Grinning back, I nodded. "Yeah, I guess you are." Blowing out a breath, I weighed my words. "Well, it was hard. I woke up alone in the hospital and discovered I'd been there for a week. My ex-husband was there with my mother."

"Oh, wow!"

"Yeah, that was not what I expected to wake up to, not that I expected to wake up in the hospital, to begin with, but you get what I mean. I think the hardest thing, though, was not knowing what happened to you or Nicco. And then feeling like I'd let Jude down because he'd been placed back into a group home. I was upset with myself for not thinking ahead. Thankfully, Monroe showed up and—"

"Oh, Mo-no-roe," she sang out, blinking her eyelashes. Giggling at her, I felt my face heat.

"He's here tonight, so you can meet him later. He's my neighbor."

"Okay, I've heard Jude talk about him."

Agreeing, I confirmed. "He showed up, got Jude out, and once I was released, things were going moderately well. You know, for being in recovery. I still didn't know where you, Nicco, or Sax were. I couldn't get a hold of any of you by phone. I didn't know where you lived. I did go to Nicco's apartment and his shop, but he wasn't there. So that was hard," I shrugged, not wanting her to know how close I'd been to spiraling back. "But I had Jude."

"I hated not being able to tell you guys anything," she pleaded.

"I know, sweet girl. I don't blame you, and despite

Atticus being the one who blocked us, I don't even blame him. It was just worse when Monroe pulled back, too, having to take care of his son. That was when I felt really alone. Jude and I bonded, though, and we became each other's person. I really don't know what I would've done without that kid."

My eyes had grown teary, and I smiled a watery smile. It was hard remembering the past, but I was doing it. I didn't want to be trapped anymore by the bad memories. I knew I still needed to deal with the bombing, the memories just waiting to erupt out of me, but for the time, I was managing what I could, one thing at a time.

"He said the same, you know. I'm kind of jealous you guys had each other, but I'm glad you did. I'm sorry our departure affected you guys in such drastic ways. I hated that, that you would think we didn't care, and were just gone."

"I never thought that about you, Immy, promise."

"That's good because I really missed you guys." Her eyes were now glassy as she attempted to hide them with a smile.

"I missed you too." Without even having to think about it this time, I pulled her into a hug and let myself relax, hoping there wouldn't be any leaving this time. When I pulled back, I gave her a mischievous smile.

"So, speaking of you and Jude?" I watched as her face blushed bright red again.

"Uh, huh. What about us?" She asked, attempting to be vague, but her face was red as a tomato now.

"Yeah, that's what I thought. Is there something more going on between you two?"

"I mean," she dropped her eyes, twisting her hands in the blanket as she spoke. "We haven't said anything. We're just friends. I've never dated anyone before… never been allowed to." Her hesitancy made sense to me then.

"That's not a bad thing. I don't know Jude's experience, but based on the fact his life has been pretty up and down over the years, I bet he has the same level of experience as you." She thought about it for a moment before nodding.

"Yeah, you're probably right. It's just hard to talk about your feelings."

"Oh, I get it, girl." I laughed, nudging her shoulder. "It is hard. In my experience, which granted, until I met Nicco, hadn't been much, you'll regret not saying anything. I can share what I've learned if you like?"

"I would, but… just don't give me details about my cousin," she shivered, screwing up her face.

Laughing, I agreed. "Noted, I think I can do that. What I've found is no matter how hard communication is, it's always best to just say it. Lying or hiding things, no matter how good the intention, leads to trust being broken. Putting it out there clears up any hurt feelings or assumptions. Because no matter how perfect you think someone is, they have their own past and baggage, which filters and changes how they view things. So, while we might think we've been clear, in reality, we haven't, and over time those unspoken truths make us believe the craziest lies." I paused, the magnitude of what I'd said hitting me.

I'd accepted so many things from Brian, assuming he'd loved me, but he didn't say it, and I should've realized. Instead, I lied to myself that our life was perfect and exactly what I wanted. But if I was honest, I'd never been happy with him because I never felt free to be myself. Over time, I lost who that was, so conditioned to respond and manage everyone around me. No wonder I'd been so tired, the weight of grief finally burying me so deep I couldn't see. Clearing my throat, I focused back on Imogen.

"Unless we say it, it doesn't get heard. It's scary and it could mean being hurt, but it's better to know before you're in too deep and you feel like there's no way out anymore. Jude, he's a good kid. He's not going to make fun of you or hurt your feelings if he doesn't feel the same way."

"I think I would die if he said he only saw me as a friend, though."

"Yeah, it might be embarrassing, but you have to look at it and evaluate it for yourself. Is the embarrassment greater than the possibility of a relationship? And if so, don't say anything. You're not risking anything because the relationship isn't as important. But if not being in a relationship, if not knowing how that person feels about you, or not having the opportunity to explore a relationship is worth more than possible embarrassment, well, then you know it's just a small price to pay. Consider which one would feel worse. Not having him or being embarrassed if he said no."

Imogen considered it, chewing her lip as she thought it over. "I guess that makes sense," she sighed, not thrilled with the realization she'd have to be vulnerable. Patting her hand, I tried to instill some strength in her.

"It's hard being the one to bring it up, but it does improve things relationship-wise when you do. And I always say, if you can't talk about the hard stuff, it's not someone you want to be in a relationship with anyway."

"Yeah, that's fair. Booyyssss," she groaned, throwing her head back in a laugh.

"Don't I know it!"

"Yes! Let's talk about you now," she said, instantly sitting up, turning her eyes toward me.

"Um, I thought we already had Loren time. This is Imogen time now."

"Don't think I missed the fact you have three boyfriends currently." She eyed me, watching for me to crack.

"Hmm." I grinned, holding in my words, rolling my lip into my mouth.

"Yeah, 'hmm' all you want, Missus, I'm on to you!" She smiled, letting me know she was joking, and I relaxed. I found myself taking a deep breath, weighing my words as I tried to figure out the best way to describe my situation without it sounding like I was using her cousin.

"I'm… just trying to figure things out. I'm open with them on who I'm seeing, so we're all just exploring together."

"I think it's great. You deserve all the happiness, Loren."

"Yeah?" I was surprised by her response.

"Yeah."

"Thanks, girl. Now," switching topics while I could, I focused back on her. "What can our next prank on Jude be?"

Giggling, we put our heads together as we talked about possible ideas. Before I knew it, a guard knocked on the door, letting us know it was time for dinner. Walking arm in arm, we headed toward the elevator together. Imogen had a massive smile on her face, and I found myself with one too—a real one. I was glad I'd had this opportunity to be in her life again. She had become vital to me, and I think she was going to be important to Jude. It was a relationship I wanted to have with both of them.

The guard was quiet in the elevator, staring straight ahead as we rode. Imogen and I attempted to make faces at him, but he didn't budge. Which only meant we were laughing harder as we stepped off the elevator. We walked into the room to six guys standing behind chairs, waiting for us. Our laughter halted as I noticed them, my face heating as I took in the other men and Jude. Imogen was quiet next to me as she eyed the man she didn't know, so I took the lead.

"Hey." Wow, Loren, excellent conversational skills you have there, I scolded myself, face flaming even more.

Sax smirked, and I could only imagine what he was thinking. Shifting my legs, my dress rubbed against me, reminding me I didn't have on any underwear. I took in all the men regarding me, and I found myself curious about what they were thinking. Wells and Monroe stood next to one another, with Jude at the end. Sax and Atticus were near the head of the table, with Nicco between the two groups. My face continued to heat the longer we stood there, all the attention on me with no one saying anything, just staring.

Imogen pulled my arm, and I leaned down so she could whisper in my ear. "I take it back. I'd say you have *five* men interested in you."

Giving her a look, I rolled my eyes. "I think your tutor needs to work with you on math because I *know* you're not counting your brother in that number."

She shook her head, grinning wide, and I saw how beautiful she was when she was this carefree. "We'll see who's right."

Ignoring her comment, I found myself walking toward the long table. It was a dark cherry wood, and the surface shone under the lights. It was set for eight people, with four place settings on each side. Taking the empty seat I was directed to, I looked around the table. I was across from Sax, putting Nicco on my right side and Wells on the left. Monroe was next to Wells with Jude across from him. Imogen sat in the last empty spot between Jude and Sax. As soon as she was seated, the car magic I often wondered about transformed into kitchen magic, and the door instantly opened. Waiters carrying trays of food exited and sat them down on a sideboard along the wall. I was surprised when Wells leaned close, whispering something in my ear.

"Every time I eat here, I feel like I'm in *Beauty and the Beast*. I'm just waiting for them to break out in song and dance."

Snorting, I quickly covered my mouth, trying to tamp down my laughter. I hadn't expected Wells to be funny. Nicco leaned over, his breath skipping across me, causing goosebumps to rise.

"Beautiful, you look ravishing. I'd much rather have *you* for my main course."

His words had my laughter drying as I tried to remember to breathe. I could not be getting turned on in a room full of people that included two teenagers. Nope. Thankfully, a plate was placed in front of me, and a lid lifted off. The most wonderful smells emitted from it, causing me to groan at it.

"Mm, this smells amazing."

"Thank you, Mrs. Carter. Shall we eat before we discuss business?"

I nodded, taking his comment to mean without the teenagers, and I watched as everyone waited for him to pick up his fork to eat. Once he had, everyone else began to as well. It was so odd, like we were dining with the Queen of England instead of a Chicagoan businessman. I didn't know what he sold other than sushi, but apparently, it was a lot.

It was quiet as we ate, and I tried not to think about the fact I'd slept with two people in this room. Nope, that wasn't awkward at all. Scratch that, I realized. I'd let another one eat me out, and another one finger fuck me as a stranger in a public club. And when I *actually* thought about it, I'd let another hold me up against a wall while he pilfered my village. Shit. I *have* had sexual encounters with all five men. I just conveniently kept forgetting about the one with Atticus. It was easier to pretend that way and not want his hands on me again. Shifting, I was surprised when a voice spoke up, causing me to jump, nailing my knee into the table.

"Is the food not to your liking, Mrs. Carter?"

Atticus' voice had my face blooming even redder after the last thought I'd had. "Oh no, it's lovely."

"Is something else the matter then, *Spitfire*?" Sax smirked, lifting an eyebrow at me.

"Nope, nope." I shook my head, emphasizing my point. The guys chuckled at my response, and I wanted to fall onto the floor and hide under the table, but my conversation with Imogen came back to me, reminding me what I was fighting for.

I could do this. I would own it. I wasn't ashamed of the things I've done. In fact, I was proud of them. So, instead of being embarrassed, I held my head high, knowing that at one time or another, every single man at the table, not counting Jude, had wanted *me*.

That was a power I wanted to build on. Smiling, I lifted my head and stared right back at Atticus.

TWENTY THREE

The moment her dark chocolate eyes met mine, I had to reign in my desire. This woman continued to barge into my world like a storm cloud, no inclination of the danger awaiting her. Part of me liked the fact she wasn't scared of me anymore. It said something about the growth she'd had over the past months. She held her head high, her eyes boring into mine, staring at me straight on. Mrs. Carter was no longer flustered by my presence, and I didn't like what it meant.

If she started to fit into my world, I would get *ideas*. And the last thing I needed was for my thoughts to take off running along with my libido. A woman comfortable with this life wasn't anything more than a death sentence. Jaz had been a prime example of how being born into the criminal underground didn't make you safe.

She was and would always be a liability. Nothing more. The fact she no longer feared the danger around her only strengthened my resolve to keep her at arm's length, no matter how much I craved her.

No one else in my life seemed to understand the risk

or care about the consequences. Their constant fighting me on allowing her in had become tiresome, and I'd finally caved. If only to keep the family's weaknesses closer, and I could counteract any attacks made. It didn't mean I liked it or agreed with them, but the connection she had with Sax, Nicco, and Immy was too strong now. If I continued to push them away or deny them access to her, I'd create more discord in the family, weakening us even further. Thus, I had to be more innovative, more strategic in my moves. Which meant covering my bases and ensuring all assets were secure and ignoring how *her ass* made my pants tight, my dick weeping for her.

Instead, I needed to focus on what lay ahead.

As long as she continued to be helpful, I would protect her. At some point, though, even my protection wouldn't be enough. I only hoped they were all ready to deal with the cost of their choices.

Because there would be a cost. They were ignorant if they believed otherwise.

I wouldn't risk everything for Sax and Nicco to wet their dicks. I wouldn't even do it just so Immy had a confidant. I wasn't against those things, or even her, for that matter. I liked Mrs. Carter and enjoyed her company, something I found lacking in most women, but my family's safety was my number one concern, and I'd do anything for the people I cared about.

So, for now, I had to figure out a way to include Mrs. Carter without losing everything else in the process. Maybe most importantly, my own heart.

"Mrs. Carter, how is your job going?"

The radiant woman across from me appeared amused

at my question, her brow quirked as the corner of her lips lifted up. "It's going well, thank you for asking."

She lifted a fork up to her mouth, and I couldn't help but be mesmerized for a second as I watched her red lips wrap around the tines. My fingers tapped on the table, the only sign I was struggling with my emotions.

"Very good," I managed to utter. "How are you recovering after the bombing?"

I knew it was a shitty thing to ask, reminding her of the traumatic experience and how everyone left her, but it was reactive, a way for me to regain control. The kick I felt next to me alluded to Sax not liking my line of questioning either, my attempt to dominate the conversation not going unnoticed by him. I lied to myself that I did it to test her, to ensure she could handle things. But it *was* a lie.

"Oh," she started, stunned at the question, her face dropping slightly as she appeared to be transported back there for an instant, but just as quickly, she regained her composure. Her eyes lifted to mine again, no ounce of the fear present now. "As you can see, my cast is gone, and I had to do some physical therapy. But I'm finally getting back to where I was stamina-wise. I still have some pain every now and then, but I would say, all in all, I'm recovered."

She went to take another bite, but I found myself wanting to poke her again. I wanted to believe it was still about testing her, but something deep down had roared to life, and I didn't want to acknowledge it. "And what about from the bombing itself? That had to be a traumatic experience?"

She stiffened, along with my cousin. He narrowed his eyes at me as I watched her swallow. To my surprise, she didn't withdraw into herself but answered quietly, "I'm getting there with that one."

"Hm."

The glares I received around the table from four men as she dropped my eyes and went back to eating had me ending my interrogation. The rest of the meal remained subdued, free of conversation. The only sound that could be heard was the scraping of forks on plates.

When Immy was done, she spoke up, her anger directed at me with a scowl. If she were a cartoon, she'd have smoke coming out of her ears. I couldn't help but smirk at her attempt to be threatening, which only pissed her off more. "Attie, I don't appreciate how you're speaking to my friend. You said you would try, so try harder. Jude and I will be taking our dessert to the theater room. Next time, I expect you to be nicer." She threw her napkin down, pushing back her seat and grabbing Jude's hand. He briefly looked at Loren, who dipped her head before he stood.

"I'll text you when I'm ready to leave."

"Okay," he replied, nodding.

Imogen tugged him over to the buffet the servers had placed dessert on. I didn't miss how Imogen didn't let go of the boy's hand or how their fingers laced together, faces flushed. She grabbed a plate and handed it to him before grabbing another, attempting to bolt quickly from the room.

"Immy," I barked, her whole body freezing at my tone. "Remember what we discussed." She didn't turn, but her shoulders relaxed when I didn't scold her. Assenting to my request, she didn't turn back but made her way out of the room. I'd wanted to reprimand her. The urge my father had instilled in me to demand respect triggered, but my love and respect for her won out in the end. Plus, I was secretly proud of her for standing up for what she believed in. Immy needed to be able to do that to survive.

She still had nightmares. Though she'd stopped telling me about them. Her screams, however, echoed over our floor, a reminder of what she'd endured. Each one ricocheted inside me, a knife to my heart, reminding me of what trust in the wrong person had gotten me. My only solace was Immy becoming stronger, and I convinced myself that keeping her nightmares to herself was a sign of her strength. She wanted me to know she could handle it, and I admired her tenacity because no matter what our life became from this point forward, she would need it.

The brother in me wanted her to remain the bright and hopeful girl I've known, not becoming jaded by the darkness around us. I wanted a way for her to be both—resilient and optimistic.

Sitting back, I crossed my arms as I surveyed the table. I watched as dessert was placed in front of everyone, my observation making a few of them squirm, especially the two outsiders. Internally, it made me smile, knowing I affected them. Once the waiters were clear of the room, I nodded to the two guards remaining. They shut the doors, taking a position in front of them, blocking them so no one could enter.

Glancing at the plate in front of me, I was pleased when I found fluffy meringue and lemon. Lifting the fork to my mouth, I paused, distracted by the enchanting temptress across from me. A quick glance told me I wasn't the only one watching, as every man's eyes were focused on Mrs. Carter. Her red lips closed around the tines of her fork again, slowly pulling out as a slight moan left her mouth, causing my dick to twitch at the sound. My irritation at her continuance to entice me had my cold nature slashing out before I could stop it.

"Your ex-husband," I paused, her eyes snapping up to meet mine. "He's very successful at what he does. In fact, I'd say he railroaded you during your divorce proceedings. I've never seen an adulterer make out so well before. Did you even try to keep anything?" I steepled my hands, eyes holding hers. Sax made a grumbling sound next to me, but I ignored him.

She slowly placed her fork on the plate, crossing her hands in her lap. "You'll have to excuse my ignorance, Mr. Masters, but I believe I asked you to look into my mother and Brian and their connection. I'd think someone so concerned about confidentiality would understand the need to follow proper etiquette."

The corner of my mouth lifted before I quickly dropped it. I shouldn't be getting this much entertainment out of pushing her buttons, but I was. "It might be proper etiquette, *Bellezza*, but I never signed anything saying I wouldn't look. And quite frankly, you are ignorant if you didn't think I'd look into *everything*."

Forks dropped around the table, clanking against plates as the other men scrambled to fight for her. Their complaints rang out, but it was all background noise as I stared off with the beauty. I saw her eyes flash at my use of the pet name, her cheeks heating in remembrance of our dalliance. I leaned on the table, taking a posture of nonchalance as I tilted my head in one hand.

"And since it seems you're currently with, what? Three people around this table?" I stopped and pointed at Sax, Monroe, and Nicco, taking in their pissed expressions as I did, making my smirk grow at being the biggest dick in the room. They didn't understand her the way I did. I understood that now. She wanted to be pushed, needed it in order to feel alive. I could see the darkness flashing in her eyes, her pupils dilating as I kept going. "I'm assuming it's okay to discuss this openly?"

I watched as she switched legs, crossing her other one and taking more of a power pose as she braced herself against the chair as well. Her small hitch of breath had me curious, but I dropped it when she narrowed her eyes at me, the level of heat boiling at this point. If she hadn't been involved with three men already and wasn't Immy's therapist, I'd be balls deep in her, the fire calling to me in a way I'd never felt before. I liked her submitting, bowing at my words, but this version had me willing to burn my entire empire to the ground just to feel her.

Fuck.

Sobering, I dropped my cold mask back into place, not even realizing it had slipped, letting my true nature shine through. She'd disarmed me so delicately, I hadn't even noticed. Mrs. Carter's eyes dimmed at my change, and I almost gave in again to bring it back. But I couldn't. No one was worth losing everything for.

"If I didn't want them here, they wouldn't be. You can stop trying to put me on the spot or make me uncomfortable and deal with your own emotions, Atticus."

My eye twitched at her bravado, wanting to fall back into her pull. "It's cute you think you're the one allowing them to be here."

"Atticus!" Sax hissed, giving me a pointed look, fury on his face.

Rolling my eyes, I sighed, letting out a long breath. "Fine. Then you won't mind if I start with Mr. Miller first." I didn't wait for her to answer but turned my attention to the human version of a golden retriever at the end of the table. Though, that wasn't quite accurate. Monroe might look like the boy next door, but I'd uncovered an interesting past.

"I know you've been in contact with Mr. Hawthorne, but," I paused, purposefully drawing out the information. "I think I have something that will be helpful in your proceedings, as well as being successful in obtaining an expedited court date for this Friday. Does that work for you?"

"Yes, thank you." He observed me, not afraid of me, and I saw hints of the legendary Komodo he was rumored to be. "Can I ask who the judge is?"

"A new one who isn't biased. I'm having Judge Buchanan looked into for negligence, bribery, and fraud. If there's one thing I can't stand for, it's corrupt individuals who play with kids' lives."

"Wow, okay. Again, thank you," he choked out, swallowing. I knew I could be cold, and as a mafia boss, most people would assume I was ruthless. But there were some people you didn't touch, and kids were one of them. Using Levi as a pawn to gain the upper hand when it appeared Mr. Monroe was a good father had irritated me, and I'd gone even further than Loren had requested out of principle.

"Don't thank me. Thank, Mrs. Carter. She was the one who negotiated for my help on the matter." The words spilled from me, dismissing the credit. I didn't want the gratitude when I hadn't done much, nor did I want others to see me as soft. He needed to believe it was only because of Loren. He assented, his eyes shifting briefly to her.

"All the information I gathered is in a folder. You can verify if anything is overlapping or new with what you've already gathered." I motioned to the guard, and he walked forward, handing the file to Mr. Miller. Monroe accepted it but didn't open it, holding it in his lap. I assumed he already knew some of it and was curious if he would go down that path.

The man on paper appeared too squeaky clean to sully himself with such tactics. I didn't take him for someone dirty or scheming, but his past had me pausing, unsure which path he would venture toward. Though, if Mrs. Carter had any influence over him as she had the others, then he'd be above board. The only curveball was it regarded his son, and if there was one thing that would make honorable men do desperate, unspeakable things, it was their children.

Slowly, I brought my gaze back to the woman I'd been physically forcing myself not to look at, Mrs. Carter. I expected her to be angry, fuming as I made her wait. But instead, I found her not even looking my way at all. Her plate was cleared, no evidence of her pie remained. All of her focus, though, was on Nicco as he leaned over, feeding her small bites of fluffy meringue and lemon, making me lick my lips. They looked comfortable and jealousy speared me as I watched, my purposeful power play earlier blowing up in my face. Clearing my throat, I gave Nicco a pointed look. The cheeky fucker turned slightly and locked eyes with me.

"Yes, Cous? Did you need something? Maybe some water for that scratchy throat of yours?" He turned fully, putting the fork down, but he didn't take his hand off her leg. When I didn't answer, sitting there clenching my jaw and staring threats into him, he had the nerve to lift an eyebrow, challenging me. "Your earlier comment made me think you weren't taking Mrs. Carter seriously, and as your second, I had to make sure we were meeting her needs to fulfill the agreement you made for Immy."

His comment hung in the air, everyone watching to see what I'd do at his open disrespect. My anger spiked, and I had to take a moment to calm myself. This wasn't like me. I didn't strike out against my own. Once I had my breathing slowed, I found myself able to respond.

"You seem to have confused being second and coming in second to Sax." I regretted the words the moment they were out of my mouth, but there they were, my jealousy on full display. Sax merely chuckled next to me, shaking his head. He'd been quiet most of the night, only admonishing me or flirting with Mrs. Carter. He found it entertaining to watch me sink myself. Leaning forward, I tried to reign in the tense atmosphere and control.

"I need you to get in line, Nicco, and do the job you told me you'd do."

Again, my voice came out caustic, his hackles rising at the accusation. Nicco leaned back, not liking the threat.

"Tell me, Cous, how am I not doing the job you wanted me to do? Last I checked, I was the one who'd made sacrifices for you."

I clenched my jaw, not wanting to admit he was right and I was angry he'd been focusing on Mrs. Carter, lavishing her with attention when I couldn't.

Because that was the absolute truth.

I could disguise it however I wanted, wrapping it up in a pretty lie, but a lie was a lie. It didn't matter how deceptive it was. At the end of the day, it still wasn't true.

Loren intrigued me. Hell, she enticed me, and I knew I could never have her.

I could take her like I'd envisioned earlier. I could take her for a night. I could even take her from the men she was already with. I could take all I wanted, but I would never have her.

Besides, that wasn't me. Despite my bluster, I wanted my family to be happy, and I'd never take that from them if at all possible.

Ultimately though, I could never have her the way the others did. Because once she knew who I was, once she knew what I'd done, there was no way she would look at me the same again. I couldn't be with someone who looked at me in fear. Not like my mother had with my father.

I wanted to be the man she saw me as now, the loving brother, the businessman, the sexy stranger, and perhaps even the hero. But to be that man, I couldn't be with her and guarantee the safety of my family. Unlike Monroe, I *would* do whatever it took, even if that made me the monster in the end. I wasn't a hero, even if she saw me as one currently.

Looking at Mrs. Carter, I focused on her, dismissing Nicco, unable to discount his statement. "Mrs. Carter. I have two pieces of information for you."

She sat up, all of her focus back on me. It was a heady thing, and no wonder so many of the men around this table were willing to sacrifice themselves for her, even if she didn't know it.

"The first piece is that it appears you were correct to believe Barkley is alive. I have reason to believe she's being hidden somewhere. My associate found communication between Ms. Christine Perry and Mr. Brian Carter, along with receipts for dog food."

She gasped, looking at Mr. Miller for something.

"That's Brittni's sister, Brian's fiancee," he replied.

Loren nodded, turning back to me. "Why can't you confirm if it really is Barkley?"

I didn't answer right away, not knowing how much I wanted to commit, my debt already paid. In the end, I gave in, wanting to see this woman smile. "Two reasons. The first is I wanted to gather visual confirmation, and I have someone checking it out tomorrow. The second was whether or not to take action then, to retrieve the animal."

"Yes! Absolutely." She nodded forcibly, looking at me like I'd lost my mind for questioning it.

"While I might agree with your decision, I wonder if I might offer an alternative."

"I don't know what alternative you could give me where she stays because unless you can guarantee her safety, I want her out of there!"

I found myself smiling at her outrage. "Maybe wait to decide until you hear what else I uncovered, Mrs. Carter?"

"Okkaayy," she dragged out, not convinced. When I didn't answer right away, she became agitated, rolling her eyes. "Are you going to tell me, or do I need to dance on the table to get your attention?"

"I thought *you* were the one who enjoyed watching others dance, Mrs. Carter? In fact, if I remember properly, you liked it very much, *Belleza*." Her face flamed, but she didn't drop her eyes, confirming she knew now it had been me. Interesting. I wondered when she found out.

"Well," she started, making me realize I'd been quiet for a while, replaying the scene at Climax in my head. Clearing my throat, I refocused.

"So far, what I've uncovered is about your mother and Brian. I can confirm they're in cahoots over something to do with you. There are multiple communications between them mentioning an item and using something as bait. My guess, they need you for something and are willing to bribe or threaten you in order to get it. Your ex-husband is demanding your mother pay up soon."

"What on earth could they need me for? That's the question, but it tracks with what we overheard."

"And it will take longer for me to uncover," I finished.

"So, what does that have to do with Barkley?"

Smiling, I found myself excited to share this. "You can play it two ways, Mrs. Carter, depending on how dirty or how much you want to stick it to them. I'd suggest you use it to your advantage, assuming she's in a relatively safe environment." She started to protest; I held up a finger, stopping her. "Because taking her right now will only be temporary unless you have proper certification, and based on the fact he had her to begin with, I'm assuming you do not."

She sat back, a pout on her face at the realization. "Brian kept it all, never letting me know where it was, so when the divorce was finalized, like you said, I didn't have representation, thinking we were going for mediation. Instead, I found myself in a courtroom. He had everything prepared, and me being the mess I was at the time, just relented, wanting out of the room and away from all the staring faces. I don't even know if he has it, honestly, but it would be in his name if he did."

I started to offer a suggestion when my newest fighter spoke up. "If I might interject, Mr. Mas—" I gave him a look, and he stopped. "Atticus," he corrected. I'd gone over with him to use my first name while Loren was present, and under no circumstances was he to reveal my identity. While she was allowed into our little bubble, it didn't mean they needed to know who I was or what I did.

"Go ahead, Wells." I gestured for him to continue.

"I might be able to help with the paperwork and ownership. I have some contacts with my work. If we can procure this, would that be beneficial?"

"Yes," I affirmed, "because if you hold documentation stating Barkley is your dog, then you could have them arrested for dog-napping if you want to go that far. But either option, reporting them or taking the dog back, your claim will stand if you have legal documentation. That is, of course, unless you want to go outside the law?"

She looked at me oddly before she laughed. "Sure, just call up the mob boss and ask him for a favor. A quick double cap in the knees for being an asshole ought to do it." Sax shifted next to me, and outside of Monroe, no one else joined in. When she gathered herself, she looked at me. "I see your point. If I don't do it the right way, I'll always be waiting for them to steal her back or retaliate."

"You could always stash her at my house," Wells offered.

Loren smiled softly at him. "Thank you for offering, but I'd be waiting for the day to come, never getting to enjoy her company. No, Atticus is right. I need to do this the proper way, despite how frustrating it might be to wait. I wouldn't put it past Brian to know I took her and use it against me."

Nodding, I accepted her answer. "Precisely why we haven't acted. I suggest waiting until the moment you can ensure her safety with you, and I'll get visual confirmation it is her, and she's healthy if you'd like?"

"Yes, please."

"Her condition might sway your decision, but in the meantime, I suggest working with Wells and getting the proper documentation so you can successfully obtain her."

"Thank you, and Wells, I would appreciate any help with it."

"Of course, Kitten."

I didn't miss how his words dripped with lust, his eyes speaking of familiarity with her body, adding another man.

"Is that all you need to discuss, Atticus?" Sax spoke up next to me, giving Loren fuck me eyes. I blamed the sexual tension coursing through the room and my memory of her rubbing against me in the club for the following statement, but in reality, I wanted to stir the pot. I wanted to verify if these men were as onboard as they appeared about dating Loren together, especially if they knew everything. Loren claimed honesty, but how far did that extend? So, sitting back, I draped my arms over the chair and waited a few seconds, building anticipation before dropping the bomb.

"Just curious, Mrs. Carter, since you've been with every man around this table, who's the best?"

Loren's face went white, and uproars sounded around the table. I wasn't sure if they were at her or me, but I sat back, smiling. Maybe now, the seductive dynamite would explode on its own, taking out casualties along the way—my heart included.

Twenty Four

The urge to punch Atticus had been strong all evening, but when he uttered his last question, I had to physically restrain myself from clocking him. It wouldn't be good form to lay him out over the table, not with unknowns present and guards watching. But I didn't like how he was acting. Growling, I leveled him with a glare so cold, it could've rivaled Antarctica.

"*Boss*, is that an appropriate dinner conversation?" I hedged, attempting to steer the conversation away from things that made me want to throttle him. His eyes never left Loren's, though, and he only smirked in response, the corner of his lip lifting slightly as he waited.

"I agree with the old man, Cous. It's not really—"

Atticus lifted a hand, stopping Nicco from saying anything else, his eyes fixed on the enchanting woman across from him. The two men at the end of the table shifted uncomfortably, and I noticed our newest fighter gripped his utensil, his jaw clenched. *Interesting*. It seemed he cared more about her than just fucking.

Returning to Loren, I conveyed with my eyes for her

to fire back that it would be okay and no matter what, I *would* protect her. Ultimately, this was a test, and Atticus wanted to know if she could withstand the pressure. Despite his reluctance to have her in our life, he continued to show his hand concerning her. Eventually, he would fall to his knees, and I, for one, wanted to be there to see it when he did. He was fighting too hard for him to not care about her. Denial was his middle name.

Loren looked at me briefly, her face warm from his suggestion, before returning to Atticus, her spine straightened.

"I didn't realize you were interested in my bedroom partners, Mr. Masters. Does your fiancée know you go around asking women who they slept with?"

She took a sip of the wine, running her tongue over the rim to lick up the drop of the red liquid that had fallen. Smirking, I attempted to smother my chuckle with my fist as I watched Loren rise to the occasion. Each day with her, I began to believe in things I didn't know were possible. She softened me in a way. I just wasn't sure if it was for good or bad. I wondered if it would be detrimental in the end.

"As a matter of fact," Atticus started, but I'd had enough, and cut him off. If I could get some time with her before she left, I wanted it to be alone and not with a table of dudes I couldn't drop my shield with.

"*Sir*, was there anything else you wished to address?"

Atticus' jaw ticked, irritation evident in his actions, but he knew me well enough to know I wouldn't have stepped in without cause. Granted, my cause was mostly so I could eat my dessert, and only minimally so he didn't bury himself so far he wouldn't have a way out.

"No, *that* was all."

Atticus pushed back from the table and stalked from the room, ignoring everyone in it. The guard opened the door, following him out, and the tension immediately leaked from the area with his exit. The grouchy fighter cleared his throat, getting up to leave as well. He didn't say anything but paused before he left, briefly looking over his shoulder at Loren.

"Kitten, I expect to see you tomorrow."

He waited for her to respond, and when she smiled, nodding, his shoulders dropped as he left. His gait had lessened in the aggression, giving me pause, again. It seemed Mr. Young still felt he had a chance in this race. The thought made me laugh, surprising the table at the sound. I ignored them, though, not owing any of them an answer but Loren. It seemed my time was running out on getting on board with the other two, and I wanted to take every opportunity available to me until then.

My gut reaction was to push them away, and make them accept she was ours and move on. This wasn't the life for them. It wasn't even the life for her, but I'd do everything in my power to protect Loren. And I was starting to understand, that meant allowing her to choose who she deemed important in her life. It didn't mean I had to *like* them, though.

My circle was small for a reason. The fewer people I cared about, the better. That currently only included three people I'd go to the ends of the earth for. Four when Nic wasn't getting on my nerves, which was few and far between most days. He was the little brother, constantly pestering, but you loved him anyway.

His hand right now was asking for trouble as it kept creeping up her leg. I didn't begrudge the man for wanting to touch Loren, but there was a limit to what I could take having to watch and not join in on.

Loren cleared her throat, glancing at the three of us that remained. I gave the lawyer a curious look. He'd snuck in when I hadn't expected, and I wondered if I'd need to check into him more. He looked harmless, but he had the most access to her. On paper, he was also the best candidate for Loren. Something about that unnerved me. I didn't like thinking I wasn't good enough for her or the best person.

I knew it came with a cost, but I wanted it to be worth it. My whole life, I'd risked everything for the family, pushing my desires aside to do what was needed. This was something *I* wanted. Someone I *needed*, and I didn't want to question whether it was a good idea or not.

Because I knew it was a terrible idea, but I'd already lost that fight with myself. So here I was, wanting what I couldn't have and taking it anyway.

"Spitfire, do you have time to have a nightcap before you need to leave?"

"Um," she looked between the remaining two men, and I saw the indecision in her eyes. Needing to see her for a few minutes, I tried to make it easy for her.

"I have something to give you, actually. I promise to be on my *best* manners."

"Oh," she paused, her face heating at my innuendo, "sure, I'd love to."

She turned to the one she came with. "I'll be a few minutes. I don't know what time it is, but I just remembered I left my phone at my place. Can you get Jude, and I'll meet you up front when I'm done?"

"Of course, Lo." He kissed her cheek, and if I wasn't mistaken, he gave me a bit of side-eye. I didn't care if he thought he was marking his territory because I knew the score, but it did make me have a smidge of respect for the guy. Perhaps there was hope for him yet, and he'd show me he deserved to be included.

"I can show you where they are," Nicco offered to Mr. Nice Guy.

"Thanks."

Loren beamed as she looked between them, and it was the only thing that had me faltering for a microsecond. They both smirked as they passed, clearly seeing her joy at them being friendly. Narrowing my eyes at them, I waited until they passed by before I pounced.

Moving around the table, I had her up in my arms and over my shoulder as I stalked out of the room, my arm banded around her legs. She squealed, but I kept walking as she tried to move. The last guard pulled the door open, keeping his features forward. I didn't waste time with the elevator and climbed the stairs two to three at a time, my long stride helping me eat the space as I moved upward.

"Sax!"

"No time, Spitfire."

She huffed but gave up and quit resisting. I barreled into my room, slamming the door and locking it before I dropped her to the bed and was on her in a split second. Kissing her, I dropped my hand down to her center, and found myself shocked when I found no barrier this time. Pulling back, I smirked at her.

"Well, well, Spitfire, seems someone has been naughty all through dinner." I didn't wait for her to respond, knowing my time was limited. Wrapping her legs around my shoulders, I dove in before she could protest. Licking up her silt, I took her into my mouth as I lightly bit her clit.

"Oh, fuck, Sax," she moaned, encouraging me.

Impatient, I tugged my pants down, my dick having remained hard since the elevator. Loren was so wet, I slid in easily as I lifted her lower half up, impaling her. The moment I'd given into her, I couldn't stop wanting to feel her around me. Earlier when I'd tasted her, the wetness that awaited me was like a gourmet dessert I couldn't get enough of. Lifting her up more, I drove faster, rubbing my thumb against her clit as my dick plunged deep.

My hands gripped her hips hard, as I forcibly slid her on and off me, pulling me even deeper. Her moans rang out around me, and I knew I was running out of time. Looking down, I watched my cock pull out, covered in her, and I spotted the beard rash I'd left earlier, when I'd rubbed my face back and forth. A smug smile covered my face at the thought of the rest of the fuckers seeing it, and it had me preening. The thought of them seeing and knowing where I'd been spurred me on.

Lifting her practically off the bed and placing her

ankles on my shoulders, I held her legs to me and fucked her hard. I felt her coming around me as my balls tightened, and I spilled myself into her. After the waves of pleasures slowed, I carefully dropped her lower half back to the bed, slipping out. Loren laid in a daze, as I grabbed some tissues to clean her. She didn't move, but her leg twitched, and I chuckled, kissing her inner thigh. Loren had cum so much, I felt her gushing all the way down to her backside.

I couldn't help myself, despite knowing I was likely out of time, I dropped to the bed. I sucked her clit back into my mouth and thrust a finger in, moving another to her back door. Loren moaned, gasping as she sat up, surprised to find me between her legs. I watched to see if she wanted me to stop, but when she grabbed onto my hair, I dove back in, sucking on her inner thigh as I plunged into her core.

Running my other finger around her rosette, I felt her tense for a second and wondered if she'd ever had anyone there before. The thought had me hard as steel again, and I thrust my cock into the bed, attempting to find some relief. When I plunged a finger in both holes, she immediately detonated, covering my fingers in her cum. Her fingers pulled hard, suffocating me in her juices.

Pulling back, I was pleased with the mark I left, the beard rash also prevalent. Looking up through my eyelashes, I licked a long trail up her core as she gasped. My fingers were coated in her, and I sucked them dry as she watched, her breaths heavy as she watched me. "Mmmm, even better than pie."

Righting her clothes, I pulled her all the way up into a sitting position and moved over to my desk area, tucking myself back in. I hadn't lied, I *did* have something for her, and I snatched the small box off the top and walked over. The sight of her in a tight dress, with her fuck me heels had me wishing I could slam her against the door and fuck her until I couldn't stand for round two. Unfortunately, I'd already pushed the limits with the time frame she'd given, so I sighed, knowing I'd need to wait until another day.

"Don't make a big deal out of it, Spitfire, but I got you this so you could feel safe."

I handed her the box, my nerves getting to me as I watched her open it. I'd never bought something for a woman before. She opened the lid, and I watched as her eyes went wide and then looked up at me.

"It's beautiful. I love it, Sax. Can I ask how it's meant to keep me safe, though?"

Grinning, I pulled the ring part on the chain, and a small knife popped out. "I'll show you how to use it later, and I hope you never have to, but it's there if you ever find yourself in a situation without an escape."

I held her eyes, the seriousness of my statement penetrating her. She nodded, swallowing as she looked at the necklace a little differently this time. I knew I should mention it also had a GPS tracker in it, but I thought it might weird her out if I did. It was only live when activated by either the wearer or the controller of the account. But I didn't know if that would matter to her, so I kept it quiet, filing it away to tell her later.

"Thank you." She said again, rubbing her finger over the emblem of a cherry blossom. "It's amazing."

"It is, with the ability to be vicious if needed. Much like you," I admitted, grinning. "It's called a vicious circle knife."

She laughed, looking up. "That's hilarious. I don't think I've ever been called vicious in my entire life."

"Maybe you just had to learn it about yourself," I shrugged. "Come on, let me get you back before they come looking, or worse, I decide I don't care and fuck you against the door anyway."

Her breath caught, and I grasped her hand, pulling her to her feet. My arm wrapped around her waist, and I stared for a few seconds, memorizing how her body felt against me. My hand lowered to her back, and I turned to walk us out, leaving my hand there. We were both quiet as we descended the stairs, and I stopped on the last one, lifting her chin. I kissed her deeply, not wanting an audience for once.

"Be good, Spitfire."

I smacked her ass, sending her on her way as I bolted back up the stairs. I didn't have it in me to watch her leave tonight, and I knew exactly how to take out my frustration. I didn't knock when I made it to the top floor. Instead, I threw the door open, the wood smacking against the wall as I entered. Atticus was facing away from the opening, staring at the drink cart, a rocks glass held between his fingers. The amber liquid was low, and he swirled it before he tossed it back. He hadn't even flinched when the door knocked against the wall, alerting me to his sour mood.

"I know, Sax. You don't have to come and berate me. I'm doing it enough for both of us." He turned, and I could tell he meant it. Agony covered his face, and I knew this wasn't about Loren, not really.

"I keep pushing her away, and she keeps getting back up. She's starting to fit into this life, and I can't have those ideas. Not after last time. Please understand, *brother*." The anguish in his words had me nodding, the fight leaving me.

"Have you ever considered that it's different? We were kids, no real knowledge of how this world operated, stupid in love, and blind to the real terrors of the world. We've come a long way since then, Mas. Before you paint yourself into a corner, maybe get to know her?"

"I can't." He shook his head once, the force enough to make anyone flinch.

"I disagree. I think you *won't*."

Atticus leveled me with a glare that would've had most men falling to their knees, begging for mercy. "It's different for me. You know this," he hissed.

I sat down, the angle to play finally coming to me. "You so sure about that? I think it was different under the Grim Reaper, but you're not him, Mas. If you plan to change the family, if your whole initiative is being better, doing better, why can't this be part of it as well?"

He stared, not answering.

I assented, accepting his non-answer. "I'd intended to punch you in the junk, but I can see you're doing a far better job of beating yourself up than I could. Enjoy being alone."

Rising, I didn't miss his words as I left, pausing only slightly to even acknowledge I'd heard them.

Walking back to my room, my breaths were heavy as I debated changing clothes and punching some bags in the gym, or if it was a ride my motorcycle type of need surging up. The urge to escape rode me hard as the panic began to edge into the outskirts of my mind, and I knew I didn't have much time. Heading to the garage, I tossed on my helmet and leather jacket, revving the engine as the first memory hit me as his words took root.

"I've never known you to be naive, Sax, but you are if you think someone like her could ever be okay with the things you've done. Guys like us don't get the girl. Even your own mother couldn't hack it."

SAXON MEETS ATTICUS

"Baby, Momma's going away for a while, okay? I'm not sure when I'll be back." My mother buttoned my coat, smoothing down the fabric as she spoke to me.

"Why can't I go with you?"

"It's not a place for kids. You'll be fine. This will be good for you. You can make friends. I know Mr. Mascro has a son close to your age."

"But I want to stay with you, Momma. I promise to be good. I won't eat as much, and I'll be real quiet when your boyfriend's over. I'll apologize and everything."

"Ssh, none of that. You're a good boy. This is a good opportunity. You'll see. Mr. Mascro will change your life." She barely got the words out before she started to sob. Quickly, she swallowed the tears, wiping her face.

"Remember, strong boys don't cry. Make them want to keep you. Give them a reason to trust you. And whatever you do, don't get too close. It always ends up as heartbreak for us. We aren't like them, but you can become one of them. I know you can. You're going to make me so proud."

She pulled me close, and I tried to swallow back the tears that had started to fill my eyes. I didn't want to leave her. Her parting sounded too close to goodbye, and even my nine-year-old self could hear it. I knew things had been more challenging lately. Her most frequent boyfriend had been too handsy, and when he'd punched her, I hadn't stopped to think when I hit him with the baseball bat momma kept by the door.

That was the first time I'd met the scary man in the suit, the one who looked me over like I was his favorite new toy. I'd sat huddled against the wall as he'd come in with some others, taking the man away. He promised I wouldn't have to see the bad man again, nor would I get in trouble. I remembered how he bent down to me, handing me a handkerchief to wipe the blood off my hands.

"You did good, son. Protecting your Momma like that." I only nodded, too scared to say anything in his presence.

"Do you know who I am?"

Shaking my head no, that made him smile, and it filled me with ice. He was scarier than anyone else I'd ever met, but he looked more like the fancy people momma worked for cleaning houses than the men she tended to date.

The memory faded as I focused back on my Momma. She'd lost weight in the past week, not eating as much since the night he'd visited. I hadn't seen her boyfriend since then either, but I hadn't been upset about it. He was a mean drunk, and he made Momma cry. I hoped to never see him again.

Taking my hand, Momma led me down the stairs of our run-down apartment building, and the homeless man that snored on the stoop as usual. The black car that rolled to a stop looked out of place in our world. It was the shiniest vehicle I'd ever seen, no smudges on it at all. The door opened, the man in the suit with the cold exterior stepping out. A small boy, also wearing a suit, followed him.

He was smaller than me, but he held his head high, imitating his father. Something about his eyes, though, made me stop, taking him in. He was scared. When he locked eyes with mine, I recognized the lonely kid in him. It didn't make sense how someone who had so much could feel the same as me, but it was the first time I'd ever felt as if someone could understand my life.

Momma kissed my cheek, wiping it clean as she pushed me to move toward them. The scary man smiled, attempting to appear welcoming, but I knew too many men like him. He looked better than most, but it was the same bullshit lurking, hiding behind his fancy clothes and cars. You could dress up mean men, but I knew one when I spotted them. The boy grinned kindly at me, encouraging me until his father noticed, and he shut down his features.

I'd never seen a kid be able to do that before, and it made me even more curious about him. Glancing over my shoulder, I watched my mom wipe away tears, but she continued to encourage me. With one last look, I cataloged her features, the feeling of something terrible happening heavy in the air. It wasn't an uncommon thing in the projects, and I'd come to know it well.

"I love you, Momma."

She bobbed her head, her tears spilling faster as a sob broke loose, and she crumbled to the ground. I pivoted to return to her when a hand clamped down on my shoulder, holding me to the spot.

"Leave her. She's fine. Your future isn't here anymore, son. There's something bigger and better planned for you. Just you wait. You're gonna love it."

I never saw my mother again after that, Dayton told me she'd committed suicide a week later. I never believed him, expecting his hand in it, but I hadn't wanted to disrupt the status quo, so I stayed silent. I glued myself to the boy who'd shown kindness and had eyes like me, and I vowed to protect him. Maybe if I only focused on one person, I could be successful.

Fury at Atticus' words washed over me, and I sped around the corner, needing the feeling of the wind on my face and the motor beneath me to outrun the memories. Out here, I could command it, convincing myself I wasn't a fool.

I didn't want Atticus to be correct, and the low blow

of using my mother had been too far. The taste of Loren still on my lips was the only thing keeping me from believing him.

I'd once vowed to always protect him, but I couldn't save him from himself. This was a battle he'd have to wage on his own. And if it came down to it, I wasn't sure I'd pick him anymore. Loren was changing me, taking my hardness and breathing life into me. She reminded me of the little boy who hadn't realized he'd killed a man to protect his mother from being raped.

It might sound weird to have your girlfriend remind you of your first kill. But it was influential in the sense that my spitfire gave me hope that I could choose a different path for me than the one I'd been set on. My mother had sold me to Dayton Mascro in exchange for making the murder go away, in hopes of giving me a better future. I wanted to believe she hadn't known the dangers that awaited me or the choices I'd have to make over the years in a pursuit to keep my promise, making myself valuable to them.

Because despite all the bloodshed, corruption, and danger, I had made myself a family. The darkness I'd unleashed that night in pursuit of something good had found an outlet as well, allowing me to flourish, sealing my fate. But for the first time, I wondered if perhaps I could be more than the muscle, have more purpose in my life.

Atticus didn't like Loren being around because it made him question his stance, worried he'd have to see her as an equal, able to withstand his world and thus making him vulnerable.

The thing he was missing, the question he should be asking instead… Would I be there when it all settled?

For the first time since I was nine, I was beginning to see a future outside the family, which should terrify Atticus.

Loren was more than his equal. She was the wild card he hadn't planned for.

TWENTY FIVE

LOREN

The ride home was quiet, all of us in our own thoughts as the car drove us back to the condo building. Monroe shifted slightly in the elevator, the file clutched tightly in his hand, and I wondered if he'd looked at it yet. The curiosity in me wanted to know, but I'd let him tell me when he was ready. When we found ourselves in front of our doors, Jude looked awkwardly between us before giving Monroe a fist bump.

"Later, Monroe."

I dipped my head, communicating I'd be in shortly. Jude unlocked the door and went in, leaving us standing in the empty hallway. Distributing my weight from foot to foot, I realized I was the one now nervously shifting.

"That was an interesting dinner," I blurted, apparently feeling the need to state the obvious.

Monroe observed me, assessing my statement. When he came to some form of conclusion, he smiled slightly, nodding to me. "Yeah. I can't say I've ever had dinner with so much sexual tension in the room before."

Blushing, I didn't know how to answer his comment, so I shrugged. "Mr. Masters was out of line. If I was still

Immy's therapist… Shit," I cursed, dropping my head at my slip up. Shaking it ruefully, I lifted it, a maniac smile taking over. "Can you believe that's the first time in all the years I've been practicing therapy that I've ever slipped like that?" Rubbing my temples, I sighed. "I hope whatever is in the file can help you, Monroe. I'm tired, so I think I'm going to head in."

The exhaustion had hit me, and I knew I was at my limit for dealing with things today. It had taken all of my emotional resources to stand up to Atticus and not slip back into the simpering woman I'd been with Brian. But now, I was done.

I needed a warm bath, some soft music, and a chance to block out all the other noise and focus on centering myself again. It had become my routine in the time period I was beginning to refer to as 'no dick season' in my head. It had been simpler in a way. Monroe's warm palm cupped my cheek, lifting my face to his before I could move.

"Do you need anything, Lo?"

With one question, I melted. *No one* had ever asked me what *I* needed. Not my mother, not my ex-husband, not even friends. No one outside of work ever checked in with me to see what I needed, and even there, it was work-based, or the occasional 'how are you dealing with everything?' question. When you were the strong one, the one everyone went to for their emotional needs, you never got asked. Not in a real way, at least. There were the customary questions, those polite reflex ones, that left you feeling more empty than seen when asked.

Monroe saw me, though. He wasn't asking if I

needed help, leaving it open for me to say no. He wasn't even tossing out a throwaway one to let him know if I needed anything. He'd point-blank asked what *I* needed. It was one of the sexiest things a man had ever asked me.

Deflating, my eyes fluttered closed as I let him hold my emotions with me at that moment. Standing there in the hallway, in my heels and sexy dress, I relaxed into his presence, letting someone under the mask. I hadn't known I'd still been wearing it tonight. The facade had become so ingrained into who I was as a person, I no longer felt it on me until something forced me to take notice.

Opening my eyes, I wrapped my arms around his middle, falling into his embrace. This was what I needed —a hug.

Monroe hugged with his whole being, wrapping you in his embrace and cocooning you in his warmth. The power of a hug was a remarkable thing, and when someone did it well, it could make you feel like a different person afterward.

I let go of the fear and judgment. I let go of the worry. I let go of feeling like I had to have all the answers. I let go of so many things in that hallway on the 18th floor. But the most important thing was what I grabbed hold of. What I let in—hope.

It might have been a minute, it might have been ten minutes, hell, it could've been an hour. I didn't know how long I stood, time slipping away as I let Monroe absorb my vulnerabilities as I soaked in his strength. I knew when I pulled away, though, that something significant had changed within me, and between us, for the better.

"Thank you."

"You're welcome. I know I let you down when I pulled back despite my intentions not to do so. And while my reasons were honorable and what I needed to focus on," he said, grinning, already seeing the arguments in my eyes of what I would say to defend him, justifying his behaviors for him. "It still hurt you. You were collateral damage in this war Britt has decided to wage, and I regret not being able to see that sooner. I know you don't hold it against me, but I feel it's just as important for me to say it. You're amazing, Loren, and I want to be part of your life. If I hadn't made it clear before, I'm making my intentions known now. We'll figure everything out together. "

He kissed my nose before he pulled away, stepping toward his door. I watched him, for some reason not wanting him to leave just yet. Monroe unlocked his condo, opening it, but stopped before he stepped through. "Thank you for the help with Levi. Can we get together for dinner again?"

"I'd like that."

"Good," he replied, beaming. "I'll text you. I'll cook this time."

Nodding, I turned and entered my home, waving to him as we both shut the door. Leaning back against it, I smiled, releasing the tension even more. The bath still sounded nice, but I no longer needed it to decompress, Monroe's hug having done wonders. Giddy, I laughed as I walked in and grabbed my phone off the counter. There were a few messages from Nicco and Sax, heating my cheeks. There was one from my mother, but I cleared the notification, not wanting her toxicity to sour my mood.

Heading to my room, I stopped briefly to let Jude know I was in, noticing how he seemed happier lately, too, since reconnecting with Imogen. I didn't want to admit I'd been feeling the same, too scared of what it meant or how they could hurt me worse this time if they left.

When, the thought whispered.

Shaking it off, I prepared a bath, deciding to pamper myself. As I slipped under the water, I thought about Monroe's hug. If it had been this rejuvenating and powerful, I wonder what else his hugs could do for my body? My cheeks heated as my core throbbed with need, and I wanted to be at the top of that sign-up sheet.

"How have your flashbacks been this week?" I asked my client. Jill had started coming to me a few weeks ago. The trauma and ordeal she'd witnessed was extensive, and she had a lot of work ahead of her.

"Not as bad. It helps to be at home now. It's hard, though, when the oddest things trigger me. I'm finding new ones each week, it seems. It feels impossible at times like I'm never not going to hear his voice… or feel his touch."

Nodding, I gave her a reassuring look. "It's understandable it feels that way. You experienced something horrific, and triggers don't always make sense. The brain catalogs everything in those moments, even if we're not aware of them at the time. Without getting too technical, when the brain starts to experience similar things, they rear up. You could be doing something completely opposite of the traumatic event, but if it has a similarity, it's triggered. Your brain does it as a way to protect you, throwing up the red flags, so you don't get hurt again."

Jill nodded, a look of contemplation on her face. "That makes sense. It helps me think about it as something my body is doing instinctively instead of not being able to hack it."

"That's a really great reframe. Finding the strength in what's happening instead of focusing on the negative aspects. The brain doesn't care about context. So maybe someone wore a red bow tie, now when you see red bow ties, trigger. But what we don't expect is how the brain generalizes as well, so now, not only red bow ties, but maybe the color red in general, or any bow ties can be loosely associated."

I watched as she contemplated this, some tension loosening around her. "My point is, you're not weak or broken. It's part of the process, having to retrain your brain to what is the danger and what isn't."

"Training, that's something I understand," she said, smiling softly.

"I bet. That's something you can use here. You've focused and trained for something in your life at sixteen that most adults haven't achieved. I think this week, I'd like you to track your triggers so we can see if there's a pattern. Then we can formulate a "training program" together. Do you still have your journal, or do you need another one?"

"I still have it. Thanks, Loren. This has been helpful today. I'm glad I listened to my coach and tried therapy again."

"Me too. I'm glad that we seem to have connected. Sometimes you gotta try out different therapists until you find what you need. Nothing wrong with that," I acknowledged, getting up. "Don't forget to grab your candy, and I'll see you next week, Jill."

"Yes! My favorite!" she cheered, finding the flavor she wanted. Chuckling, I knew she'd keep fighting. Finding joy in the small things was a good sign.

Checking my phone, I found a message from Wells needing to move our session, and he wanted to know if I was available on Friday instead.

ME: I'm um, getting a tattoo… Nicco won a bet. I'm not sure where. So, I could be in pain?
Mr. Surly: Why did that make me want to cancel just to watch that?
ME: Because you like seeing me in pain?
Mr. Surly: If that's what you need to tell yourself, Kitten.
Mr. Surly: I'll check with the kid.
ME: Why do you all call him that? You make him sound like he's 18! He's almost 30. I'm only 32. I've had pizza older than that.
Mr. Surly: That doesn't even make sense, Kitten. And he is a *kid.*
ME: You don't make sense! How old are you?

You're acting like you're 80!

Mr. Surly: 35. He hadn't even gone through puberty by the time I'd graduated, had my first job, and heartbreak.

ME: So is that what makes a person "mature"? And heartbreak? I find it hard to believe you weren't the heartbreaker. You seem like the type.

Mr. Surly: I've broken many hearts, but it doesn't mean I haven't also had mine broken.

ME: You're right. I shouldn't assume you don't have feelings just because you rarely show them.

Mr. Surly: Ouch, you wound me Kitten. You got your claws sharp today.

ME: Sorry, it just sometimes comes out with you.

Mr. Surly: I so want to make a joke there.

ME:?

Mr. Surly: I'm trying to be good, Kitten.

ME: That must be hard for you.

Mr. Surly: Seriously, it's like you want me to be mean. I will not break, no matter how many sexual innuendos you keep making.

ME: I don't want you to be mean! I think your translator is broken because I'm not making any sexual comments.

Mr. Surly: *Okay*, Kitten.

ME: I'm not! What did I say then?

Mr. Surly: That you sometimes cum around me, and I'm hard. I'd rebut that first part that it's not sometimes, but always. The second one is right, though. I am hard when around you, Kitten. Always.

ME: I don't even know what to say to that. Are we at this point in our friendship?

Mr. Surly: Do you often flirt with friends?

ME: I don't know. I haven't had many friends I was sexually attracted to.

Mr. Surly: See, I knew you found me hot.

Mr. Surly: I want to be more than friends, Kitten. I'm just trying to show you I'm worth it first.

ME: Oh.

Mr. Surly: But if you don't want to, I'll back off. I just thought we had a spark.

Mr. Surly: I didn't mean to do this over text either. I had a whole plan and everything to woo you and charm you over to the "Wells isn't a dick" side and then make you find me irresistible.

ME: I think I'd like to hear this plan, but I need to finish work first.

Mr. Surly: I look forward to sharing it with you then, Kitten. I'll check with Nicco and let you know about the tattoo. If not Friday, then Sunday. I'll be ready to strangle Fort by then anyway. I think he's going through withdrawal from you. He's become a mopey dog, and when he's not moping, he's tearing shit up. I can't win with him.

ME: Ah, my poor baby.

ME: Okay. We will touch base later.

ME: Bye, Mr. Surly.

Mr. Surly: Bye, Kitten. Be good.

Smiling, I shoved my phone back into my purse, looking at the time. Shit! I'd taken too long flirting with

Wells, and now I was going to be late to pick up Jude. Nevertheless, when I got to the lobby, I stopped, surprised to find Atticus waiting for me.

"Mr. Masters, what are you doing here?"

"Mrs. Carter. I was wondering if I could have a moment of your time?"

"Actually, no. I'm on my way out. There's a thing at school for Jude, and I'm already running late."

I made to move past him, not wanting to play his games today. There were moments when I enjoyed the challenge, but I was beginning to get tired of the back and forth; it no longer had any thrill. He reached out, clasping my hand gently, halting me. I didn't turn around, my breathing fast as I tried not to think about what his hand was doing.

"I owe you an apology, Mrs. Carter. Perhaps I could make amends by giving you a ride there, and it would also allow us to chat."

I counted in my head, closing my eyes as I tried to center myself. Turning, I tried to drop my hand, but he held on, not letting me. Lifting my eyes, I found myself snared with his magnetizing eyes. The umber color was so deep, always trapping me in their depths, but it was the gold tinges that captivated me. It felt like his eyes were trying to show me he had those pockets of light; you just had to look for them. I evaluated his gaze, searching for any deception. When I didn't find anything but sincerity, I assented. It would save me from having to track down a taxi or taking the L.

Atticus turned his hand, keeping our palms together, and led us through the building out to a side alley I'd never even known was here. He opened the door, motioning for me to slide in first to the SUV. Climbing in, I was surprised to find it empty, half expecting to find Sax there. Once I was situated, Atticus climbed in, and the car took off. He didn't slide down the divider or take out his phone, so I wasn't sure how he knew where to go, but at this point, anything was possible with the mysterious man.

He was quiet for a few minutes. I fought the urge to ask him what he wanted, feeling since he'd sought out the meeting, he could be the one to share. A few minutes later, Atticus cleared his throat, turning to look at me.

"Loren, I'm sorry for my behavior the other evening. I was out of line and unprofessional. You are a friend of our family, and I treated you like an enemy. It's not an excuse, but I've been more on edge since Immy's attack and the recent bombing. It wasn't fair of me to speak to you in such a way, to invalidate your feelings or choices. I know I have a long way to go to earn your forgiveness and trust, but I would like to try. It's evident you're important to the people in my life, and I need to accept it and not fight against it. Sax gave me an earful, along with Immy."

"I appreciate you saying that and acknowledging my feelings, but it feels you're guilted into having me around. I don't know about you, Atticus, but I don't make it a habit to be around places I'm not wanted. Your words are pretty, and all sound lovely, but I've heard enough flowery words and apologies to last me a lifetime."

He gritted his jaw, his fist unclenching as he stared

hard at me. It hadn't been the response I think he'd wanted, or expected, used to everyone allowing his behavior. Perhaps a few weeks ago, I would've accepted it, but I'd been learning things about myself and coming to terms with what I wanted in life. I didn't have to take what he said just because he'd said it. I wanted to believe him, but he'd given me whiplash so many times at this point I didn't trust he wouldn't strike out at me again when he felt backed against the wall.

"What can I do then to earn your trust?"

"Show me. Apologies are just words unless they have actions backing them."

"As you wish."

I laughed at the phrase, catching him off guard. He gave me a perplexed look, clearly exasperated he hadn't been able to sweep in and make a pretty speech, and I'd fall at his feet for the crumbs it was.

"Pray tell, why are you laughing at me?" He sighed.

"*Princess Bride.*"

He gave me a look, his eyebrows raised in confusion. "That clears up nothing for me."

My jaw dropped. The notion he hadn't seen a classic movie was truly shocking. "You haven't seen *Princess Bride*?" I asked, despite Atticus just saying it.

"If it's a movie, then no."

"We must remedy this."

"I do not care for movies."

"I don't even know who you are right now!"

"What do movies have to do with knowing me, Mrs. Carter?"

"Everything!"

"Hmph."

He didn't say anything else, and I remained shocked the rest of the trip. We pulled up to the school, and the door opened for me a second later. Seriously, magic. As I began to exit, he clasped my arm, stopping me. "I forgot to mention I looked into Barkley."

Turning, I found our faces close. He'd moved across the seat to grab my arm, bringing our noses almost touching. I stared into his eyes. This close, they felt more like a black hole I could fall into and never escape. Darkness and brokenness swirled within. When he realized I stared back, he shut it down, closing off the vulnerability I'd seen.

"What did you find?" I finally remembered to ask.

"She is with Christine but appears to be in a safe environment and is fed. Since she's not being mistreated or in danger, I'd advise waiting until your Mr. Young has the paperwork and then make your move."

"Thank you. I will."

He let go of my arm, and I slid the rest of the way out, pausing before I shut the door. "That's something that shows me who you are more than your words ever will. Thank you for getting back to me."

He appeared shocked for a mere second before he relented, facing forward. Sighing, I shut the door, and the car immediately pulled away. It had to be motion sensored or something. I was determined to figure this out. Shaking my head, I made my way into the school, excited to be here to support Jude.

Everyone else could wait.

TWENTY SIX

MONROE

The file Atticus had given me, along with the information Logan had, sat atop the booth I currently sat in. The day I'd been waiting for over the last three months was tomorrow, and I had a decision to make. Did I remove Brittni from his life for good? Or did I salvage the relationship because she was his mother?

The Komodo part of me wanted to make her bleed, ruining her life in the process and protect Levi from a potentially toxic relationship. The kid who grew up without parents, and my instinct as a father, wanted to make sure Levi had the choice and didn't feel like he had to choose between us. It was the overriding fear and need to protect him as a parent that said differently.

I'd gone back and forth so much, I no longer knew what I wanted or thought. Tomorrow was the court date, and I had to choose. So, I decided to reach out and see if he'd meant what he said the other night.

"Hey, Roe."

Lifting my head at the greeting, I didn't hide the shock that he'd shown up quickly enough, and Wells met my eyes with understanding, a tinge of hurt as well if I looked closely.

"Hey, Wells. Thanks for meeting with me."

"I told you I'd be there for you, and I meant it. I know my track record isn't the best, but I'm working on it. So you need me, I'm here. I even canceled with Kitten."

Shock filled me again, and I swallowed. Wells had never put me first before. "Wow, thank you. Though, I feel bad for Loren."

"Don't. She was cool with it. We even flirted a little."

Nodding, I took a drink of my water, not sure what to say now. I knew he liked Loren, and he said he wanted us all to be together, but it seemed too good to be true. I didn't want to be hurt again, so I was trying to be realistic despite my inclination to grab ahold of him and run away into the sunset. *Trying* being the optimal word.

"That's good. I'm glad she wasn't upset."

He smirked, knowing I wasn't saying everything I wanted. "So, what did you need help with?"

Blowing out a breath, I tapped the folders. "The information Atticus gave me, along with the things I'd procured from Logan, are inside. I don't know how far to push things. Do I detonate the atomic bomb, irrefutably ruining any chance Levi has at a relationship with his mother? Or do I do the bare minimum, getting back my son, but letting her stay in his life?"

"Even without looking at the evidence, I'm going to say, detonate. Brittni has been nothing but a bitch from day one. I know you probably want to preserve that relationship, but is it worth it if she screws him up? If she's doing more damage in his life, isn't that a reason to monitor it? She needs to be held accountable for her actions, something I don't think Britt ever has been in her whole life."

Humming, I digested what he was saying. It had merit and gave me a little peace in my decision. Perhaps there was a way to make her accountable for her actions and held responsible for her future interactions with Levi. I needed to figure out how to be a hero without having to be the villain first.

"That's actually insightful and helpful. Thank you."

"I'll try not to take offense at the *actually* part," he smirked, setting my heart racing. Thankfully the waitress came over, saving me from having to respond.

"Hello, fellas. What can I get you started with tonight?" She eyed us both but didn't overtly flirt, and I liked that about her. We both ordered burgers, and once she left, quietness descended around us. Clearing my throat, I found myself playing with the fork as I attempted to figure out what to say.

"So, you mentioned the other night you were working for Atticus? How is that going?"

When Loren had gone to talk to Immy, and Jude had gone to the library, I'd found Wells. I made awkward small talk with him there, skirting the issues in our relationship.

"He, uh, came to me after the bombing with Loren. Said he'd help me with my debt if I helped him with some information on the Delgados."

"Wait. He paid off your debt? Wasn't that like…"

"$250,000? Yeah."

"Whoa. That was generous of him."

Wells snorted. "Yeah, well, I was suspicious at first if he'd do what he said. But he has, despite who he is."

"Who are they?" I whispered, leaning forward.

"I... Don't ask me that, Roe. *Please.* I don't want to lie to you, but I signed an NDA and was forbidden the other night from saying something. I don't want to be dishonest with you ever again, so please, just don't ask."

I sat back, shocked. Narrowing my brow, I took him in. Wells looked serious, his face taut with anxiety as he pleaded with me to let it go. Exhaling, I consented, not wanting to put him at risk. If Loren trusted Atticus, then I would too. Plus, so far, he'd been helpful. Both with her issue and mine. If he'd also helped Wells, then I didn't want to throw suspicion on him.

"So the job then?"

"I used to fight for them before the night I was beaten. It was the only way I made the monthly demands the Delgados enforced. He's opening a fighting venue. They already own a few other establishments, such as Climax and Evolve. Atticus brought me on to train some of the others and is giving me the chance to fight. It could be the opportunity I've been wanting."

"I'm happy for you, man. Just don't get your ass whooped by younger guys, or you'll never hear the end of it."

"Hey!"

We were laughing when our food arrived, and the tension that had been surrounding my heart over the past few months fell away. I'd missed my friend. It was easier once we'd gotten the big feelings out of the way, our conversation falling back into our comfortable familiarity.

"Loren and Jude were telling me about Fort. He sounds rambunctious."

"Ha! He's a pain. I've never had a more stubborn dog. I'm at my wit's end with him. If he hadn't bonded to Lor, I don't know what I would've done. I just hope he can be somewhat amenable to training. I've been thinking," he paused, looking up at me through his eyelashes, "about maybe giving him to her for a therapy dog if I can get him to cooperate."

Smiling, I agreed. "I think she'd like that."

"Phew. I worried it might be too much."

"Nah. Not with Loren. She's not like the women we've dated before. She's different."

"Yeah, I'm starting to see that."

Finishing off my food, I placed my napkin on my plate, wondering what to say next. Wells surprised me again, offering his own vulnerability.

"I know the other night, I made some claims and said some things, but are we going to talk about liking the same girl, who also happens to like a few other people, and the fact we like each other?"

"I think that's the most vulnerable words you've ever said in one sentence," I joked. Wells softened, and it encouraged me to be vulnerable too. "I told her when I realized I liked her months ago that I also had feelings for you, but that you often had your head stuck up your ass, so I didn't know what, or if anything, would ever become more between us."

Wells snorted, agreeing. "Accurate, even if it does sting a little. How did she respond?"

"Well, actually. At first, she thought I was just waiting to be with you, but I admitted that ideally… it would be all three of us together."

He sat back. "You thought that before I even admitted I liked her?"

"I knew you liked her from how hard you were resisting, dumbass."

"Oh, yeah." His lips lifted slightly in a crooked grin. "She didn't freak out?"

"No," I chuckled, "quite the opposite. It's hard to see her with Nicco, and even that big scary one, but I see how Lo is with them, and I know I could never ask her to choose. That was my problem all along. Having to choose between you and a woman. I could never let you go, and in the end, it never worked because I couldn't give my heart fully to someone who didn't also see you as an extension of me."

"I think that's the most romantic thing you've ever said to me. I kind of wish we weren't in a crowded restaurant with a booth between us right now so I could show you how incredibly sexy I find you when you go and get all territorial."

Gasping, I locked eyes with him, and I saw he meant every word. There weren't any walls between us, and he was showing me himself. Wells' emotions were on the surface, and for once, I didn't have to guess how he felt.

He was showing me. Grabbing my water glass, I downed the rest of it.

"I kind of wish the same, but I also know if we're going to actually make this work this time, have a real relationship between us, then we need to take it slow. I can't give you my heart for you to change your mind in a week when things get tough. I'm sorry, I know that probably hurts, but if I'm going to have a chance at the future I always dreamed of, then I want to do it right."

"I accept that because I know you're right, even if my dick says otherwise."

Groaning, I shifted my own growing erection at his dirty talk. He smirked, watching me.

"I'll break down your walls, Roe. Just like you did for me countless times. And when you can trust *us*, it will be better than you ever imagined. I promise to give you that."

I gripped the table, keeping myself seated. I feared otherwise I'd throw caution to the wind and kiss his stupid, handsome face. Clearing my throat, I closed my eyes and counted, my breathing slowing as I centered myself on ignoring the lust coursing through me.

"So we both want Loren, and I told you how I felt about the others. What about you? How do you feel about them?"

Wells blew out a breath, leaning back in the booth. "The possessive idiot in me wants to claim her. I see her with them, and I want to break their hands. The realistic side of me knows I should be grateful. More dicks in her life means I have less opportunity to mess it up. I might actually be capable of having a relationship with her if I'm only on for 25% of the time."

"I think you're underselling yourself, but that's an interesting way to look at it."

Before expanding on it more, the waitress came over with our checks and cleared our plates. I was kind of sad the dinner was over, enjoying seeing my friend again. Even if he also made my pants tight, leaving me with blue balls. An idea came to me, only briefly thinking about it being terrible, and I decided to follow my heart.

"I'm headed to Levi's hockey game. Since they're technically supervised," I growled, flexing my jaw, "I can go to them even though they're not on my assigned days. Would you… would you want to come?"

He smiled, nodding. "I'd love to. I miss the dork."

Snorting, I tossed some money down and slid out of the booth, and Wells did the same. We walked out of the restaurant, and I took his hand, hoping he wouldn't push me away. When he linked our fingers together, it felt like teenage me was getting to finally live in the light, hope coursing through me that this was the start of my new beginning—the real one.

TAKING A DEEP BREATH, I pushed through the doors, ignoring the opposing side of the courtroom, and focused only on my lawyer. Last night had given me a lot to think about, but mostly it gave me the courage to do what I needed to do. Wells had been right. If Brittni was a good mother, she wouldn't have taken him away from his father for being better at it than her. She claimed it was neglect and my sexual orientation, but when I thought about it, it was because she didn't like not winning.

It was time she learned what it felt like to lose everything.

I caught Larry sitting on the right side from the corner of my eye, and I greeted him. He hadn't been such a bad guy, in the end, just having the unfortunate misfortune to be swayed by Brittni too. When I'd told him what she'd been doing, he'd quickly asked what I needed. He might be older, but he wasn't a fool, at least not twice.

Adrenaline pumped through me, the Komodo rising to the front as I accepted my role in this. My lawyer smiled when I sat, checking to make sure I was ready.

"You ready for this?"

"Yep. Did you get the other cases filed?"

"Yep. I have them right here. Once we present the information for the custody case, I'll present our other evidence to the Court and serve Brittni with the papers."

"Perfect."

Exhaling a breath, I sat back and looked around the room. My eyes met Brittni's for a brief second, and I hid my confidence. She appeared smug, though, assuming she'd win. Since this was a family case, this courtroom was open, providing a bigger stage for Brittni's fall. I did a double take when I spotted Loren and Wells walking in. I blinked, but a smile came to my face at their show of support. The last bit of courage I needed filled me, and I turned forward. I happened to catch Brittni's glare as well when she saw them, crossing her arms like a child who hadn't gotten her way.

The bailiff walked in, calling us all to rise seconds before the door to the Judge's chambers opened. I was glad to see it was a new judge, and a woman even. I'd looked into her, and she was fair, giving me hope that with the information presented to her, I'd be granted what I asked for with no bias.

She took a moment to look over her notes before addressing Britt's lawyer. "Mr. Reynolds, do you have any information to add to the evidence presented?"

"Yes, Your Honor. We'd like to push forward with full custody and terminate Mr. Miller's rights."

"On what grounds, Mr. Reynolds?" she asked in surprise. "As far as I can tell, Mr. Miller has performed exceptionally for all the requirements placed on him, that quite frankly, I'm appalled we're even given in the first place. There is nothing to support the original custody claim, much less give Mrs. Kimpton full rights over Mr. Miller. Do you have anything to add to the evidence?"

Relief rushed through me that Atticus had been right in finding this judge and that Brittni wouldn't have anything to stand on now that I'd had time to prepare. I watched her lawyer swallow as Brittni tugged on his arm, giving him a look.

He stood, brushing off her touch, and I wondered if he'd realized his career could be impacted by his booty call and was reevaluating if it was worth it. A smile crept up, and I covered my face with my hand to hide it as I watched it unfold. My lawyer caught my eye, his own smile tilting up. When I'd contacted Brandon, a friend from law school, he'd been flabbergasted that the case had made it to court back in January.

"The plaintiff would like to present a new piece of evidence. It has come to our attention that after a visit with Mr. Miller, the child, Levi, was covered in bruises."

Fury rose through me, and I had to stop myself from yelling in outrage. The judge might be reasonable, but there wasn't a judge around who accepted disorder in their courtroom. The lawyer handed her a picture, and Brandon tilted his head to me.

"Do you know when this could've been?" Shaking my head, I didn't trust myself to speak. He nodded in understanding and focused back on the front.

"This is a pretty big claim, Mrs. Kimpton. Are you sure this is accurate information? Did you report it to CPS? Where was the visit supervisor during this? Where are their notes?"

Her questions eased me, knowing she didn't buy it just because there was photo evidence. The lawyer swallowed, clearing his throat. "It was only brought to my attention this morning. I believe it occurred last night, and with the case being moved up, my client hadn't had time to file the appropriate paperwork."

"This goes against proper procedure, Mr. Reynolds."

"I am aware, Your Honor. My client felt it was important enough to bring to you first."

She hummed, turning to us. "Mr. Warner, does your client have any information on this photo?"

"Your Honor, my client hasn't been informed of any concerns of this nature. When is the date in question this alleged abuse occurred?"

Brandon turned his head toward Brittni, waiting for her to answer. The Judge looked too when she didn't answer. "Mrs. Kimpton, we're waiting."

"Last night, Your Honor."

I wanted to roll my eyes. This screamed desperate. Pulling Brandon close, I whispered to him, "Let me speak." He dipped his head in understanding, turning back to the judge.

"Your Honor, my client would like to say something about these claims."

"Go ahead, Mr. Miller."

"Thank you, Judge Jones." Standing, I buttoned my suit coat as I pulled myself to my full height. "May I see the picture?" She consented, handing it to the bailiff who brought it over. Instantly, Brittni started furiously whispering to her lawyer. Looking at the picture, I grinned.

"First, Your Honor, last night I only saw Levi at his hockey game. It was full with about a hundred or so people. I wasn't even alone with him. When I saw him after the game, I gave him a hug in the hallway. I was accompanied by my friend, and Brittni's husband, Larry, was there. I've joked with Levi about being Captain America, but I'm not, in fact, him. I'm in no way strong enough to have put these bruises on him in the brief seconds we hugged. I would argue that they were even from the hockey game, but that isn't the case either. This picture is at least 2 years old and from when he went dressed up as a Dalmatian for Halloween. Except, I didn't read the instructions properly, and the dye bled onto his skin. If you were to see the full picture, you'd see his costume in his hand, a bag of candy, and him laughing at being what he called 'a human Dalmatian.' I never have, nor will I *ever*, lay hands on my son."

I paused, emotion coursing through me as I thought about how much I loved Levi, and the thought of hurting him was so obscene. Clearing my throat, I returned my eyes to the judge. She watched me with a critical eye, but it wasn't hard; if anything, it was understanding.

"I'm a good father, and the reports from the supervised visits can attest to that. I followed all the rules, had all the inspections necessary despite believing the claims against me were false. I've done everything and would do it a million times over for Levi because I love him, and I would never want to not be with him."

"Thank you, Mr. Miller. I find your statement both compelling and interesting." She turned and addressed the other side, where Brittni still furiously tried to get her lawyer's attention. His jaw was tight, but he ignored her. Smugly, I sat down, a smile on my face that it was almost over.

"Mr. Kimpton?"

"Yes, Your Honor?"

"Is Mr. Miller's claim true about the extent of his interaction with the minor?"

"Yes, Ma'am. I was there the whole time. In the brief time I've been married to Brittni, I've never seen Monroe do anything I would consider neglectful or harmful. He's a good father, as he states."

"Thank you. I'm surprised you're willing to go against your wife's claims."

"Yes, well. It seems my wife might be the one who needs to be under review and not Mr. Miller."

"I see." She looked shocked at his admittance before addressing Brittni. "Mrs. Kimpton, some strong accusations and reasons for doubt have been brought to my attention today. What do you have to say for yourself?"

"I'm just a concerned parent, Your Honor, and want the best for my son. I *don't* believe Monroe is a good father. The people he's kept company with and exposed Levi to are awful people, and how he flaunts his sexuality is just perverse. I don't want Levi to be around it. I stand by my claims. I want full custody."

"Hmm. I see."

"Counselor, do you have any advice to give your client to drop her claims?"

"No, Your Honor. She is set on keeping them."

"Very well."

"Counselor," she directed toward Brandon this time, "do you have anything else to add?"

"Yes, Judge, we do. We would like to petition to close this case against Mr. Miller and open a case against Mrs. Kimpton for full custody. We have documentation spanning the past four years which demonstrates that my client has been the custodial parent and the one involved in Levi's life more than Mrs. Kimpton. We've filed papers with the Court this morning to bring a claim against Mrs. Kimpton for defamation of character. We've also passed documentation to the relevant federal agencies demonstrating that Mrs. Kimpton has committed multiple counts of fraud and tax evasion. I believe there are federal agents waiting outside the Courtroom to speak with her when we're finished here."

The courtroom was quiet for a minute before everything erupted. Brittni began screaming, to the point the judge had to yell "order" and have her taken away for contempt when she wouldn't stop. Once she was gone, the judge looked at us, and I didn't know if I imagined it, but she smiled briefly at how the tables had turned.

"Mr. Miller, I grant your request to dismiss this case. I will also be speaking with the District Attorney to recommend adding charges of obstruction of justice in the case and falsifying evidence. I will expedite your request for full custody. We need more fathers like you, Mr. Miller. Have a good day. Dismissed."

The gavel slammed down, and I sat back, the bang sealing the confirmation I needed this time. The sound echoed around my head, validating the hope within. The Komodo simmered, smirking at having watched Brittni self-destruct like she did. He stepped back into the darkness, knowing I didn't need that part of myself at the moment. It felt nice to know I could be strong without losing myself in his depths. It wasn't a 'this or that' situation. I could be both at once.

Brandon nudged me, the sound around me returning as I relaxed, smiling up at him in appreciation. "Thanks, man. I couldn't have imagined a more perfect ending."

"You're welcome. But I feel like you did most of the work." Shrugging, I didn't care. Levi was coming home.

"Does that mean you won't charge me by the hour then?" I joked.

"Funny." He packed his stuff, patting me on the shoulder as he walked by. "Congrats on getting your son back."

Nodding, I placed all the information I had back in

the file and noticed Larry was waiting for me. "Hey, Larry. Thank you for what you said."

He nodded, shaking my hand. "Thank you for the information you gave me. I could've lived with the affairs, but her trying to steal my money and put me at risk of losing everything, I couldn't stand for that. Plus, I meant what I said to the judge. You're a good father, and Levi's a good kid. He should be with you, even if I am going to miss him. Let me know when you want to stop by and grab his stuff."

"Thanks, I will." Shaking my head, I shouldn't have been surprised he was more concerned about his money, but if it got me his support, I wasn't going to question it. Wells and Loren were waiting for me outside the courtroom, and they both rushed me. Loren hugged me tight, and even Wells gave me a good solid three-slap hug. It was the kiss on the cheek afterward that took me by surprise, a blush rising to the surface.

"I'm so happy for you, Monroe."

"Me too. I'm glad it's finally over. And now, I'll get Levi full-time. As much as I hated taking Brittni away from him, she had to be held responsible for her choices."

"Hmm, I guess a wise person told you that?" Wells chided, giving me an all-knowing look, bumping his shoulder with mine.

"More like a wise-ass," I teased. "Thank you guys for being here. I hadn't expected it, but it gave me the last bit of confidence I needed. What are you up to now? Did you come together?" I asked, looking between the two.

"No, we just happened to be walking in around the same time," Loren answered.

"She wishes," Wells joked, causing Loren to roll her eyes playfully. "I know the perfect way to celebrate, though!"

"How's that?"

"By watching Kitten get her first tattoo."

Twenty Seven

LOREN

They both looked at me, Wells with a smirk at sharing the information, and Monroe with surprise and heat. I wanted to hide from their gazes, my self-doubt nature kicking in, but reminded myself there wasn't anything wrong with getting a tattoo. Well, Jaqueline might disagree with me, but I didn't feel that way or care what she thought anyway. Tilting my chin up, I leveled Wells with my determination and then looked over to Monroe with a smile.

"That's correct. I lost a bet, but I'm actually excited about it. Feels a bit… rebellious."

"It's hot, Lo."

"Oh? I didn't expect you to respond that way," I admitted, blushing. "I thought you were going to tell me it was dumb."

"Not at all. In fact, I think we should all get one!"

"What? You're not serious?"

"Absolutely. Sounds like an excellent way to cele-brate. You think he has time to squeeze us in before I have to pick Levi up from school?"

"Um," I bit my lip, unsure how to do this. "I can

check. I wasn't supposed to go until this afternoon."

"Well, check. I'm going to say hello to a friend in the clerk's office real quick, but let me know. I'm interested." He pointed at me as he walked off, leaving Wells and me.

"You planned this, didn't you?"

"I have no idea what you're referring to."

Yet, the light in his eyes told me otherwise. I didn't hate the idea of them joining. It was nice being around Wells now and getting to know him without wanting to punch him. Granted, there were still moments I wanted to punch him, but there were far more where I didn't, and that was a nice change.

"I'm glad the custody case worked out in Monroe's favor. I was so worried for him," I admitted.

"Well, based on what I know of Brittni, I hope she gets what's coming to her. She's been a bitch since I met her, and she used Monroe to get the life she wanted. She never loved him, only what he could provide for her. Once that wasn't enough, she leveled up. Though, from the looks of it, she won't be married to him much longer either."

"You take joy in her suffering, don't you?"

"Why shouldn't I? She's been against our friendship from day one and then tried to use his sexual orientation as a reason for him not being a good father. She purposefully picked the previous judge who had a personal connection to me, and not in a good way. She wanted to make sure Monroe didn't get any leniency. She's a conniving twat, and the less she's in Levi and Monroe's life, the better. I thought someone like *you* would agree with this?"

"Someone like me?" I had a feeling what he meant, but the way he said it had me feeling caustic, my hackles rising.

"Who works with kids whose parents have divorced. I'm assuming you do anyway."

"Oh. I thought you meant something different. Yes, I do work with families with strained relationships. It's difficult on the child when there is tension between parents."

Wells walked toward me, and I backed against the wall and found him towering over me. "What did you think I meant, Kitten?" He purred it and licked his lips as he watched me. His arm was braced over me against the wall, and he leaned down to speak to me. It was intimate, and I dare say it had my panties becoming slick as I stared into his eyes.

"Um," I mumbled, finding it hard to pick the words I needed. Licking my own lips, I tried to draw saliva into my mouth. This close, I'd forgotten the question he'd asked to begin with.

"I asked what you'd thought I meant, Kitten. You seem to be having a hard time remembering."

"Oh," I blushed. "I thought you were saying I'd know because she's a pompous rich girl like me."

He grabbed my chin, catching me off guard. I sucked in a breath, the fear rushing in me at first until I realized he wasn't gripping it hard. No, Wells' hold was gentle, more of a domineering grip than an aggressive move. His eyes didn't miss my flinch, and he lowered his hand, rubbing soothing circles into my flesh.

"Don't for one second think you have anything in

common with that cow. You're in a completely different league than Britt Bitch will ever be. Do you understand?" His tone had gentled, but the ferocity was still there.

"I think so. Or at least I'm starting to."

"Good, Kitten," he purred, and damn if my panties didn't disintegrate right then and there. I whimpered, and he smirked. I think if Monroe hadn't walked over right then, I would've been dangerously close to giving in to Wells and kissing him senselessly against the wall.

"I'd ask if I was interrupting something, but I think I'd like to join more than interrupt."

Laughing, I turned and took in his heated gaze. "What am I getting myself into?" I mumbled, pulling away from Wells. "I didn't have time to ask Nicco yet. Wells kind of dominated my time, but let me call him right now, and I'll see if Nat's available. I haven't talked to her in a few days."

Stepping away, I took a deep breath, using the call as an excuse to clear my head. Pulling out my phone, I called Nicco first. He answered on the first ring, a blush rising to my cheeks at his sleepy husky voice.

"Beautiful, I hope this isn't a call to cancel this afternoon? I've been looking forward to it all week."

"Good morning, stud," I sang, stopping his rant. His chuckle at the nickname filled my ear, and I found myself grinning wide.

"Good morning, Beautiful. Sorry, I'm just really looking forward to spending time with you."

"Now I feel bad asking," I hedged, biting my lip.

"If you're not canceling, then please, ask."

"Well, I'm at the courthouse with Monroe, and he won the custody case."

"Oh, that's incredible."

"Yeah, it really is. I'm so happy for him. He really is a good father."

"So, what does this have to do with today?"

"I bumped into Wells on my way in, and he had to cancel last night for something, and I told him I couldn't work out today because I had my appointment with you."

"Mmhmm."

"So, when Monroe said he wanted to do something to celebrate, Wells let it be known I was getting a tattoo today."

"Ah, I think I see where this is going."

"Well, if you're able, can you fit two more in? We could come over right now."

"Hmm. On the one hand, I don't get individual time with you, but on the other hand, I get to see you sooner and perhaps longer. It's really an easy answer, Beautiful."

"Oh?"

He chuckled, the sound doing amazing things to my body. I was starting to learn I had a thing for voices. My session in the sensation room had been an enlightening factor.

"Yes, Beautiful. If I get to be with you, I'm good. I tell you what, though, grab me some coffee and some of those awesome donuts at that place you were talking about, and I'll meet you all there."

"Thanks, *stud*," I giggled. "You're the absolute best."

"I like when you get all lovey-dovey, Loren. It makes

me tingle inside."

"Well, if it lasts longer than four hours, you should consult a doctor."

The laugh that bubbled out of Nicco had me feeling light, grinning from ear to ear.

"I'll keep that in mind. I'll see you soon, babe."

"Bye, Nicco."

Hanging up, I turned, smiling, and found them watching me.

"That sounded like a fun conversation. Did he say yes?"

Nodding, I tucked my hair back. "Yes, we just gotta pick up donuts and coffee. Let me check with Nat real quick, now."

I decided to call, finding it easier and easier with each person I let into my circle. She also answered quickly, and I wondered if I'd just been calling the wrong people all my life.

"Girl! I've missed you. I haven't heard from you since last week. How did everything at the club go?"

"Oh, wow. Has it been a whole week? Shit, I'm a horrible friend. A lot has happened since then."

"Now, this sounds good. You free? Want to grab coffee?"

"Sort of. I was calling to see if you could pick two of the guys and me up and take us to Nicco's. We need to stop and get coffee and donuts first. I'm getting my tattoo today."

"Okay, okay. A lot *has* happened. Two guys? Nicco's? Any chance we can dump them so I can get the scoop?"

"Ha! I'm sure we can be creative."

"Send me the address. I'll be there soon, and you can fill me all in."

"Sounds good. Thanks, Nat. You're the best. We definitely need to schedule another girls' night, though. Whether movies in or out, I don't want to lose the friendship we've made. You're important to me. You, Cami, and Stacy."

"No worries, girl. We're here for you. We're not going to get mad at you just because you're getting some dick now. Fuck that shit. Power to the vagina and all that."

"Nat, I seriously don't know where half the stuff you say even comes from."

"Me either!"

"Okay, I'm hopping in the beast mobile. Send me the deets. Laters."

She hung up before I could respond, and I quickly sent her the address to put it in her GPS and make her way here. I'd walked a bit away from the guys, so I gestured to follow me downstairs. The air was cool outside, and I breathed it deeply. The sky was clear today, and it looked like it would be a nice one.

Both men came to stand on my sides, and I had a dirty thought emerge, my cheeks heating. "I um, spoke with Nat, and she's on her way. So, I guess we're all getting tattoos."

They both smiled, murmuring while we waited about what they wanted and where. It was turning into an exciting day full of spontaneity and impulse decisions. But I didn't hate it. I quite liked it, actually. A lot.

NAT and I stepped into the donut shop a few minutes later, the smell of yeast and sugar hitting us as we entered. Wells and Monroe had gone into the coffee shop next door, allowing me some time to catch up with her. The ride had been pleasant, but I hadn't missed the side-eye she kept giving me the whole way here. It had become a game at this point, seeing who'd cave first.

"So?" she nudged, finally giving in to asking.

I kept walking, a slight smile on my face as we got in line. I didn't want to give everything away. "Whatever do you mean?"

"Don't play coy with me, girl. Not only is that Mr. Hot Neighbor and Mr. Complicated, both whom I'm certain you want to fuck. There's the mystery man from last Friday you went home with." She crossed her arms, not caring the couple in front of us had turned to look at her loud proclamation.

Clearing my throat, I prayed for my face to stop flaming at her words. "Okay, well, when you put it that way, I've kind of been a huge slut this past week."

"Girl. Don't. No slut-shaming here. It's only problematic if you didn't want to do it. Did you enjoy it?"

"Yeah," I admitted, "it was amazing, actually."

"Then no shame. You should be shouting how good you got the D."

"Okay, good point," I agreed, laughing. "Sometimes... I still feel I'm going to be judged."

"Yeah, well, you left those haughty bitches on the curb. Clear your mind of all the judgment, and share the deets with your main peeps."

Laughing, I shook my head. "Girl, you're one of a

kind. I think Lily has been teaching you too many slang words, though. But seriously, why couldn't I have met you years ago?"

"You weren't ready for me yet." Nat winked, her personality shining through. "We're here now, and that's all that matters." She linked her arm in mine, and I felt genuine adoration for this woman.

"Very true. You know I adore you, right?"

"Of course you do, because I'm awesome." She tossed her hair over her shoulder in a dramatic fashion, making me laugh again. I needed to hang out with her more. She was good for the soul.

"So…" Raising her eyebrows, I gave into the demanding woman next to me.

"Okay, okay," I joked. "Well, Friday, I went home with Saxon after we, you know," I whispered, "in the sensation room. Then there was the wedding on Saturday, where he and Nicco crashed. Oh, wait." I stopped remembering more. "Shit, so much has happened. I went home with Sax, and then when I returned to my condo, Nicco was waiting for me in the lobby."

"Whoa!"

"I know! It's been a bit of an emotional roller coaster."

"Sounds more like an orgasmic one to me! That's a ride I'd ride all day long!" Laughing, the couple in front of us turned and looked, turning their noses up at us. Natalie stuck her tongue out at them, and they turned around quickly.

"Anyway, does that mean you've forgiven Nicco?"

"I'm on my way there. I told him I needed to take things slow and get to know one another more before we jumped into the physical side of things. He does that part so well. I'll forget my head if I sleep with him."

"So the wedding?"

Nodding, I looked at the donuts available as we inched by the display case. This place really was crazy busy. "Apparently, Monroe had told him I was going to the wedding that evening alone, so he crashed it. Well, I guess technically he was invited. He called and surprised my cousin with an upgrade."

"That's generous. I think he really likes you, for whatever my opinion is worth."

"I think so too. It's just hard to believe he won't hurt me again."

"That's fair. So, how did the other two come into play?"

"Well, I had sex with Sax at the wedding, and then Wells invited me over to train on Sunday, and I was surprised it was at Atticus' house. Jude got to hang with Imogen, so that was nice. Honestly, it happened so fast."

"Wow, really? I'm so happy for my man Jude getting his girl back."

Nodding, I chuckled. "Yeah, he's been over the moon." Blowing out a breath, I recounted all the things I'd just said in my head. "Geez, there's been so much in a short period of time. It's all kind of a blur."

"What about the dynamic duo in the car?"

"Oh, well, Monroe and I have been talking, and then we've had dinner a few times. He was still focusing on his case, but that was resolved today. So that's what led us to the tattoo."

"Don't think I didn't notice you failed to mention Mr.

Sexy." Raising her eyebrow exaggeratedly, I ignored her as we finally made it to the register. Ordering an assortment of donuts with a few I wanted, we stepped to the side after I paid and waited for them to be boxed up.

"So the tattoo?"

"Oh, yeah, that was from my first date with Nicco, we made a bet, and apparently I lost, though that's subjective. But now, I have to get a tattoo."

"Girl! If I didn't have to take Lily to an appointment later, I would so come and watch this." She practically bounced up and down in excitement.

"I don't understand what everybody is so excited about. It's watching me get poked with needles. How is that exciting?"

She rolled her eyes like I exhausted her with my naïveté but swatted me good-naturedly. "Because, Lor, it's the total opposite of you. So you already know it's going to be fabulous, and something about seeing you break free from the shackles of what is proper and whatnot is addictively fun."

"I guess I can see how that would be something people would want to see. Like when someone discovers something for the first time, and you just know it's going to be awesome. Getting to live through their first-time experience vicariously reminds you of your own."

"Of course you go and make it all psychological and smarty pants, but, yeah, I suppose it's exactly that."

Laughing, I cringed a little. "Sorry, habit. I'm nervous, and I go into therapist Loren without realizing it. I've been trying to play it tough, and I mean, I am excited. I trust Nicco, but, you know, it's… *permanent*."

"Nothing's ever permanent anymore. There's laser removal." She lifted an eyebrow at me, and I had to give it to her; she had a point.

"Okay, true. I feel a little bit better now. Your turn, by the way. You don't escape the dick confessional by making me only talk about myself. How did your night go with Mr. Deep Sexy voice? Byron, wasn't it?"

"Oh, Lor, I rode that dick all night long and the next day. It was so good. I couldn't walk for a day," Nat beamed, fanning herself. "If my mom hadn't been harassing me to come and get Lily, I would've ground-hogged that cock. I wouldn't have come out until next winter."

Laughing, I almost dropped the donuts the man handed to me as she said that. "Nat, I swear, you say the craziest stuff, but I love it. I never know what to expect. What about the other girls?" I asked as we started to make our way out the door.

"Stacy met someone, and Cami had her fun as usual. They're good."

"I gotta hear about Stacy! I should give her a call. As a matter of fact, we should all get together this weekend. When are you free?" I always asked Nat first because I knew she had the most challenging time finding sitters she trusted for her daughter. Cami was pretty flexible with her work schedule, and Stacy, it just depended as well.

"Ooh, let's do brunch! I'll find a sitter. If I take one of those donuts, my mom might even offer to watch her overnight!"

"Go for it. Donut for a good cause! Text the girls then,

and let's meet up somewhere."

"Deal," she agreed, pulling out her phone with her other hand. I watched as she took a giant bite out of the donut.

"I thought that was for your mother?"

"Nah, I decided I needed it more. She'll watch her no matter what."

"You could've just asked for a donut, bish!"

"It's more fun taking it."

"Oh, is that your sage wisdom for today?"

"Yep!"

We exited the place, and I had a massive smile on my face. I spotted Monroe and Wells leaning against her SUV as we made our way over.

"I know they're yours, but man, what would it take to let me be in the middle of that hottie sandwich?"

"More than a donut," I swooned, chuckling. They really did paint a tempting picture.

The guys smiled at us, looking at us curiously as we walked up laughing. My face was beet red, but it had been fun, and I didn't even care that the couple in front of me had turned and said, "I'll pray for you," before walking out. People needed to mind their own business.

"I'm not sure I want to ask what's so funny," Monroe said as we got into the car.

"Life," Nat replied, giving me a wink.

"For some reason, I don't believe you," Wells replied, giving me a smug smile, his eyes narrowing at my red cheeks. Miming, I zipped my lips, refusing to say anything to those two. I hadn't missed the fact I hadn't denied them being my guys or that I wanted to be between them. Seemed I was beginning to warm up to the idea and accept it.

We pulled up to the shop a few minutes later, and I steeled myself for what awaited me inside. Giving Nat a quick hug, the three of us got out and headed into Ignite Ink. Cassandra was behind the desk as usual, and I began to wonder if she ever got a day off.

"Hello, Darlin'. What do you have here today?"

I knew she didn't mean the donuts, so I introduced her to the two pieces of eye candy behind me. They were polite and flirted with the older lady, endearing themselves to me a little more. Even Mr. Surly had a smile for Cassandra.

"I bought some donuts for everyone. Want to grab one before Nicco tries to eat them all?"

"I knew you were my favorite!" She beamed, taking a napkin and pulling out a glazed chocolate donut.

Nicco walked around the corner just as she took it. He grinned before he started acting affronted by Cassie. I couldn't help but love their flirty dynamic. "Hey, I thought those were for me? Cassie, are you stealing my girl and my donuts? I thought we were friends?"

"She's prettier than you, boss. Plus, I think you might have competition with Thing 1 and Thing 2."

The two behind me sputtered at her reference, and when I peeked at them behind me, I noticed how red their faces were. Nicco took the donuts from me, acting like he would hoard them all, and had us follow him back to his private studio. I hadn't realized he had his own, so I looked around the room in awe as he spoke with Monroe and Wells.

"Do you guys have any ideas on what you want?"

"We think so, but it wouldn't hurt to look at your portfolio."

"Absolutely. Let me know if you have any questions, and I'll tell you what I can and can't do."

"Sounds good. Here, I think this coffee is yours."

"Oh, thanks, man."

"No problem. Thanks for letting us crash. I'm sure you wanted to spend time alone with Lo, but something about watching her get a tattoo sounded like the perfect way to celebrate."

"Oh, yeah. Congrats on winning custody."

"It feels weird to hear it like that, but I guess that's accurate. And thanks. I'm just glad to have my son back."

"Well, the fact you think about it that way already tells me you're a good father."

I couldn't help but smile at their conversation as I looked at some of the designs on the wall. Wells walked up behind me, his body close to mine. "He's talented. You feeling okay about everything, Kitten?"

"Mmhmm."

"If you start to panic, just think about kicking me in the junk. Seems to work wonders for you."

Laughing, I turned around, facing him. "You're right. It does." We stood staring at one another, the hallway incident filtering back to me. Nicco walked over, grabbing me, breaking the rising sexual tension.

"Okay, Beautiful, you ready?"

Nodding, I laid back in the chair. "Yup."

Here goes nothing.

Twenty Eight

NICCO

Loren lying on my table waiting for me to ink her was close to the most erotically beautiful image I'd ever seen. The first had been watching her fall apart in ecstasy in a crowded room as I plunged my fingers in her under the table. Ideas of bringing her to that point again swirled in my head, and I had to shift my erection before I sat down on my stool. I'd been dreaming of inking Loren since I'd thought of the idea. Taking her hand, I linked our fingers together, excited the moment was here.

"Alright, Beautiful. I'm working on an intricate design for you," I said, watching her breath hitch at the idea, and I knew my assumption had been correct. "But," I winked, "for your first tattoo, I thought it was only fair to do something small. I wanted it to have meaning for you, even if it was a bet. I'm not going to tattoo 'loser' or anything on you. My hope is, you'll be like most people, and once they get one, they love it and become an ink junkie." She relaxed at my words, her face bright now with anticipation.

"I really hope you don't hate the experience, but if

you do, then hopefully it won't be something you regret. Though my hope is you'll like it, and the next one will be your decision to get. I'll be ready with my design when you are. So, today's tattoo won't take very long. Do you want to know beforehand and perhaps add some suggestions or wait until I'm done?" I arched my eyebrow in question, waiting for her response. Loren looked me in the eyes, assessing me thoroughly, but it only took a few seconds before she decided.

"I trust you."

Those three words had never meant more to me, and my heart soared. The realization I could have the dream I've wanted, which now encompassed her, hit me squarely in the chest. Loren had changed me, giving me something to look forward to, a person to fight for.

And I'd almost lost it.

This was my chance, and I would do everything in my power to not screw it up again. Smiling, I squeezed her hand.

"Okay. Did you pick an area?" She bit her lip, but then pointed to her wrist, a question in her gaze.

Nodding, I reassured her it would be perfect. "Well, let's get started." Cleaning the area, I sketched the design on her carefully, wanting everything to be perfect. Once I had it ready, I prepped my gun and looked up. She'd been watching me, not what I was doing, but *me*. A rush of endorphins filled me, and I smiled happily at the beautiful woman I was falling in love with.

"Alright, Beautiful. It might sting a little. Do you want to listen to music? Talk to those two knuckleheads?

Or I don't know, watch a movie? Everybody has a different process, so do what feels good to you."

Loren's breath hitched, and she began to panic a little. Her skin grew clammy to the touch, and I wondered if I'd pushed her too far. Opening my mouth, I was about to offer her an out when Monroe stepped in.

"Hey, Lo, tell me about how you bested Wells with the dog you've been working with." His brows crinkled in delight while Wells scowled at him. It didn't have his typical vehemence, though, so I knew it was all for show to get her to relax. I motioned to Monroe in thanks for distracting her. I wasn't sure if Loren would've been able to distract herself on her own, too much in her thoughts.

Brushing my thumb over her pulse point, I waited for it to calm before I began. Turning on the gun, I let her get acquainted with the sound first and slowly brought it to her wrist. Loren tensed at the first press of the needle, jumping a little, but I'd been prepared, so I held it until she became used to it. The guys kept her distracted, asking her things, and I found myself actually thankful they were here. As much as my fantasy was to ink her up and have my way with her, it wouldn't have been today.

Focusing on my work, I zoned out, concentrating on the ink. When it was finished, I turned off the gun and wiped it clean, admiring the way my work looked on her creamy skin. It was sexy as hell, and the erection I hadn't managed to get rid of yet, became even more uncomfortable and pushed against the zipper. Rubbing my thumb over the ink, I found myself nervous as I waited for Loren to see it. What if she hated it? Had I overstepped?

Clearing my throat, I took a deep breath. "Hey, Beautiful."

She turned, her face a brilliant smile and her eyes alight with happiness, and I sat and stared for a second. I'd told her I'd deal with figuring out how things worked with her dating other guys, but inside I'd been jealous, set on making her see I was the one for her. Then Sax had entered, and I knew I couldn't win against him, and despite Atticus' denial, it was clear he found her fascinating. I'd ignored the reality, only wanting to get her back in my life first.

But here I was with two men I didn't know well, and for the first time, it didn't seem like such a crazy thing. If I got the benefits of them making her happy, how could that be bad? Loren wasn't just any girl. I'd already discovered that when I had to be without her for nine excruciating weeks. I didn't think she would tell me she wanted to be with me if she didn't have feelings for me. Nor did it seem like she would eventually like one of us more than the other. Even though she was new to dating, experiencing sex, and all it had to offer, she excelled at it.

Perhaps it had to do with her natural ability to care for people and to have multiple people she helped on a regular basis. I didn't understand how her job worked, but I knew it was more than teaching skills to others and listening. There was a whole emotional aspect that you either had or didn't. I was starting to believe this part of her that could care about multiple people at once could also potentially love more than one person at a time. When I really thought about it, I hadn't felt left out or excluded in the few times she'd been with me and other men present.

I was jealous. I envied the time she spent with them, but I hadn't felt discarded. Even when Loren was in the arms of another man, I'd still felt seen by her. That was something to consider.

"It's done already? Wow, that wasn't too bad at all."

Loren's voice was soft, and I nodded at her question, butterflies filling me. I watched her face as she looked down at what I'd drawn. She gasped, a tear sliding down her face as she looked up, and it was the moment I knew I'd never want any other woman. She'd just enraptured me forever with one beautiful look.

"Nicco, it's breathtaking. I don't even know what to say."

I looked briefly over at the other two. They looked curiously at the tattoo but were giving us a little bit of privacy. Reaching up, I wiped her tears with my thumb, saving them. Whispering, I relayed the meaning, not sure how much she'd shared with the others.

"It has a few meanings. The infinity symbol represents your never-ending hope. The birds are meant to symbolize a few things. This big one is you, showing your freedom as you fly your own path. This one… I'd like it to represent me, but maybe it's more about the people you'll meet along the way that are helping you spread your wings and try new experiences." The last one, I touched reverently, looking down at it before I looked up. She lowered her eyes, and I knew she understood. "This little one, it represents loss, but it's not lost or forgotten. It's part of your future as you soar toward it, never to be forgotten. Mostly, I wanted something simplistic and meaningful to represent you taking flight, no longer living on the sidelines."

She dipped her head, and I wiped another tear with my other hand. "Your life might be different than you imagined, changed from what you thought it would look like, but it doesn't mean it can't be better. Beautiful, you have the whole world to explore, and I hope to be part of it."

I hadn't planned on kissing her, but as I stared into her eyes, sharing this moment, it felt like the right time finally. So I pressed my lips to hers, not caring there were two other men in the room. In fact, until I heard one of them move, I'd forgotten, lost in the feel of Loren's lips beneath mine.

It was a simple kiss, just a press of our lips together. But it sealed my heart on hers, as I pledged to never hurt her again, vowing to do everything in my power to always be what she needed... at least from me. Ultimately, it was a kiss placing my heart in her hands now. Before, I hadn't been careful enough with hers, and now, I had to trust she wouldn't crush mine. I might not be the only one, but I accepted I would be okay as long as I *was* one.

Pulling back, I smoothed her hair back, staring into her eyes. "You have me if you'll accept me, however, you need. Even if I'm not the only one."

Loren peered back, and I watched as this beautiful woman transformed in front of me, almost like she'd just gotten back a piece of her own heart, strengthening the core of who she was. When she smiled, I was glad I was sitting down, or I might've fainted from the pure beauty of it.

"I want you there, Nicco. I do need you, more than you can possibly know." I kissed her nose, placing our foreheads together for a moment. "Besides, you *are* my tour guide after all."

Smiling, I pulled back, a chuckle escaping, and I looked over, finally acknowledging the others in the room. "Who's next?"

"I think I'm reconsidering," Wells jibed. "Do you give that treatment to *all* of your clients?"

"Nah, you have nothing to worry about, Crash. I only do it for the really pretty ones. Now, Monroe," I winked, "he could be a candidate." I'd decided to give Wells a reminder I wasn't some young chap, but deadly when I needed to be by using his fighting name, asserting my dominance, but then I saw Loren tense a little, and I knew I needed to break the ice between all of us. I could be that for her. Thankfully, my comment had the other two men pausing before bursting into laughter, Loren's giggle joining in.

"Ha, looks like you have competition, Wells. Better get in line," Monroe teased back, and I found myself liking these two.

They seemed like the opposites of me at first glance. And despite Crash being someone in my world and a prime candidate to join Sax and Atticus in their resting asshole face competition, he didn't have the dark vibe that hung around us in the underground. I'd gotten to know him over the past few months with training, and I'd guess we were friends. He was rough around the edges, but I'd found he had a squishy center, the dogs being the clearest sign of this. He'd definitely brightened as well over the past few weeks with Loren back in his life, and I wondered who he'd be the more he shed his damaged, bad boy layer, that I was beginning to accept was a cover-up.

Monroe seemed squeaky clean, but every now and then, I'd catch a hint of something and knew he wasn't one to discount. His devotion to his son and commitment to being a good dad told me wonders about him. He seemed like someone I wanted in my corner at the end of the day, and I found myself excited to make a friend outside of all the dark, scary world the mafia tended to be.

"You know, Beautiful, you seemed to have collected a rather interesting bunch of men. I'd dare say even a few bad boys."

"Nah, you all might look like the bad guy, but you all have good hearts. I know. It's my superpower."

Laughing, I shook my head as I finished cleaning up and preparing for the next one.

"Oh, does that mean you've finally quit denying your attraction toward me, Kitten?"

"Pfft, never. I'm just nice to you, for Fort's sake."

"Lies, Kitten. I'll get you to cave."

Their dynamics were fun, and I'd dare say, a little hot. I never thought I'd be into sharing, but here I was, finding myself aroused by her flirting with another guy.

"Hop to it, Crash. I'm looking forward to this." I patted the chair Loren had climbed out of, and he sauntered over, his 'I hate the world' attitude on display. "So, what are you doing?"

Over the next few hours, I worked on Wells and Monroe, giving them tattoos. We'd eaten the donuts, listened to music, and were talking about ordering lunch since it was past noon. As they discussed options, I focused on the "always" tattoo Monroe had wanted, the 'A' being the deathly hallows. It was a cool tattoo, and when he told me the reason behind it, I liked the idea even more. It was a perfect way for him to celebrate getting custody of his son by using the word they said to one another.

"Done. What do you think?"

"It's awesome, thanks, man." I cleaned it one last time and then wrapped it, going over the instructions with him for cleaning. When I was finished, I cleaned up the entire room, sanitizing everything, the motions a habit at this point. When I finished, I hoped they'd decided on some food because I was starving.

"Any food decisions?" I asked, turning, wiping my hands with the paper towels.

"Yeah, we were thinking—"

"Hello," Wells answered on his phone, holding up a finger to wait a second. "Really? Oh, that's good news. Thank you so much, Tom. I'll look for it in my inbox here in a minute." I looked at them as Wells talked, not understanding. Loren and Monroe looked as lost as me, so when he chuckled, I looked back to him, picking up the tail end of his conversation.

"Oh, he's still as ornery as ever, but I've found a secret weapon. The one you helped, actually. Fort's taking a liking to her, so it's going a little better, but I do mean only a little. Ha, okay, man. Tell Jannie I said hi. Talk to you later."

He hung up and looked at Loren, a massive smile on his face. "What do you say we grab lunch on our way to claim your dog, Kitten?"

"Barkley?" Loren gasped, tears already in her eyes.

"Tom got the papers for me. She's officially registered with the American Kennel Club now, and along with her vet records showing you were the one who took her and listed you as the owner, you can legally claim Barkley. All Brian has is a receipt showing he purchased her. Get this though, Tom found from the seller that it was listed as 'a gift for my wife, Loren.' Barkley is yours, Kitten, and there's nothing he can say or do anymore. I promise."

Loren leapt up, wrapping her arms around him in gratitude. A small jolt of jealousy surged, but it went away when I saw how happy she was, confirming I could do this. I could be with Loren. Now, I just had to find a way to keep her safe. I wouldn't lose Loren, even if I had to darken my soul in the process.

TWENTY NINE

Adrenaline rushed through me as I walked up to the front door of the house Atticus had sent us to. I'd texted to ask for the address, letting him know we had the proper paperwork and I would be going to retrieve Barkley today. His message had been short, clipped even, and I wondered if I'd upset him the other day. A smug smile pulled up at the corners, knowing I'd gotten under the skin of the unflappable man.

"Excited, Lo?"

I turned my head, not understanding his question, and a little weirded out he thought I'd be thrilled about getting to Atticus. When Monroe gestured toward the two-story brick house before us, my cheeks heated in realization. Focus, Loren! This was important.

"Oh, yes," I confirmed. Taking a deep breath, I knocked on the door and waited. When no one came, I rang the doorbell. A frenzy of barking erupted, one sounding very familiar. I was practically bouncing on my feet as I waited for someone to open the door. Monroe had walked up with me, Wells and Nicco staying back unless we needed them. Atticus had sent over a car to take us, a dog crate in the back as well.

His thoughtfulness was appreciated, only adding to the mystery the man was becoming, and an action I could understand versus his words.

Pressing the doorbell again, I was about to become that annoying person who held it down until someone came, when a voice yelled from within.

"Coming! You can stop with the doorbell already. Fucking hell. Can't get any sleep in this place."

A disheveled woman opened the door, and I vaguely remembered her from the art show Jude had been in a few months back. I'd been in such a panicked state, I hadn't really taken in my surroundings, and yet a hint of familiarity peeked around the edges of my subconscious. She saw me first, looking annoyed at my presence but not placing me either. However, when she spotted Monroe, she straightened and simultaneously began to primp and scowl at the man.

"What are you doing here?" she directed at Monroe, but he said nothing, allowing me to have this.

"I'm here to retrieve what belongs to me."

"Excuse me?'

"I'm here for Barkley. I believe my ex-husband gave him to you."

"Listen, lady. I don't know who you are or what you think you're doing here, but I don't have your dog."

"If you don't know who I am, then how did you know Barkley was a dog? I could be picking up my child for all you knew since you so eloquently stated you didn't know who I was?"

She sputtered, not able to formulate an answer to cover her lie, and a feeling of confidence rose in me. Channeling my inner Elle Woods, I thrust the paper we'd printed at her.

"This certificate states *I'm* the rightful owner of Barkley, who I know is here. Not only do I have evidence indicating the fact, but I can hear her. So you can either hand her over to me now, or I can call the police. Which is it going to be?"

"You can't prove anything, and the police won't come for a dog." She narrowed her eyes at me, crossing her arms.

Raising my eyebrow, I felt vindicated getting to use it on her. "Really? That's what you're going with. You see, Christine, it is Christine, correct?" I asked but didn't wait for her to reply before continuing. "Dognapping is considered a step below kidnapping, and last time I checked, kidnapping was a felony. So you're looking at, what?" I turned to Monroe, "Three to five years?"

"At least," he agreed before casually placing his hands in his pockets and being the strong, quiet presence I needed. Christine swallowed, realizing what she was up against.

"But sure, call the cops. I'd love to tell them how my ex lied to me about my dog dying and then hid her out here at his new fiancee's house. I'm sure there are some other charges we could file as well, like aiding and abetting. So, please, go ahead. You'd be saving me the call."

Her face went white before she swallowed, looking nervously between us. "Oh! Barkley, you say? I thought you said Parkley. Just a moment, and I'll grab her."

She went to shut the door, but Monroe stopped it. "I'd prefer if you left it open, or perhaps we could come in while we wait? I'd love to see my niece if she's around?"

"Oh, she's at school, but I'll leave the door open, habit." She quickly let go of the door, scampering off to hopefully gather Barkley and send us on our way. The adrenaline I'd used to stand up to her was fading, and I sagged against Monroe. His arm wrapped around me, pulling me close, and I exhaled as the relief hit me. His hand rested casually on my hip, and I found myself feeling supported by just that touch. It only confirmed how vital touch was, something I'd never been given freely.

I could no longer ignore the truth. Every encounter, every piece of affection before these men had served a purpose and never had been an act of comfort. With Brian, it was about meeting his needs, and my mother, always about appearances. My father had been the only one who would regularly offer hugs, but even thinking of them, I'd never felt this at ease. I wanted to believe it was because I didn't have the same type of relationship with him as I was building with Monroe, but it was more than that. Intimacy wasn't always sexual, and it was something I was beginning to crave in all my relationships.

I heard nails tapping on the floor drawing closer, and I straightened up. Monroe kept me pulled to him, though, his hand remaining where it was. When she came into sight a moment later, I practically jumped up and down. My feet started to move forward to go to her, but Monroe held me anchored to him, a slight shake of his head not to move. Planting my feet, I waited as patiently as possible for Christine to bring her.

Kneeling down, I greeted my dog, who had gone ballistic, licking me all over. I pulled her close, wrapping my arms around her and burying my head in her fur. The pain I'd felt at losing her lifted, and I realized how much I'd been suffering with her out of my life. I'd been so low before I hadn't noticed, and the only reason I hadn't fought him in the first place. Apathy had become my state of being and a dangerous place to be.

Opening myself up to feelings meant all the good and bad ones, and I wondered whether it was because I'd never truly felt emotions as deep before or if I'd been so numb that all emotions now felt more powerful in general. It was hard to tell when the before was jaded, littered with lies and betrayals.

"Thank you for taking care of her."

My acknowledgment stunned the woman, and she shifted uneasily, handing some items to Monroe. "Yeah, sure. No problem."

"We'll be out of your hair now. If Brian has any questions, you can tell him to speak with my lawyer." She blinked, a look of shock on her face. We'd taken two steps when she stopped me.

"We're not really engaged. Turns out, it was only a ploy to make you jealous."

I pivoted, assessing the woman. My movement had her stepping forward and gripping my hand. Her face had changed, and I saw the same fear I'd seen so many times in my own eyes. Handing the leash to Monroe, I motioned for him to give me a minute. Once he was clear of the house, she opened up like a floodgate.

"I thought he actually cared about me, that he was the answer to all my problems. Paisley's dad left me a few years ago, taking all of our money with him. I was left with the house, but I'm barely able to keep it up. He ruined my credit, and it's near impossible for me to get a job and take care of my daughter. I met Brian at a function, and I thought, here's a good man, one who will be the father Paisley needs. It was like a fairytale at first, and I thought my life was finally going to change. But even before we ran into you at the fair, I'd started to grow suspicious. He talked about you non-stop, complaining and blaming you for all of his problems. I..." She stopped, wiping her eyes, her lip trembling as she attempted to gather herself.

"I ignored it because things were better. I wasn't having to worry about paying my bills or where the next meal would come from. But then..." she looked at me, and a piece of me I'd buried recognized something in her.

"He changed?" Hesitantly, she confirmed with a minute dip of her head, and I found myself reaching back to grab her hands in support this time.

"It was small things at first. A comment here or there that would make me stop and wonder if he had really just said it. Then they became more frequent, and I wondered where the man I met was. When he... when he smacked me one night for not having dinner ready when he got home, that was when I knew he wasn't the answer, but the *nightmare*."

"Can't you break up or tell him to go, especially if it's not real?"

"I tried. But that's when he proposed, or so I thought. When I heard him talking about it, I'd been hurt, but mostly, I thought it was my way out. So I didn't confront him. I gave him back the ring and said I didn't feel I was ready. It was an excuse, but I didn't want to set him off. He apologized and lavished gifts and flowers on me, and things got better, but inside I feared for the day he'd drop the act. The day before we ran into you, it had been awful, and I think that was why I was so hateful toward you. If I couldn't leave him, then I had to blame someone else."

I nodded, her reasoning making sense. She sucked in a breath, steadying herself, and I wondered what the next part was that had her so shaken up.

"After the incident at your parents' house and the comments your mother made, I told him I was done. I didn't want to be engaged anymore, and no amount of apologies would change it. He went crazy. He destroyed furniture and called me a bunch of names. Telling me I was a cheap alternative to the real thing and I would never measure up, so he'd used me for the only thing I was good for and that he would never actually marry me, that it had all been pretending to make you jealous."

Sucking in a breath, I held her arms, attempting to give her strength. Tears rolled down her face, and I wiped one away. Christine's lip wobbled, but she didn't stop, and I respected her for that. She was stronger than she realized.

"I knew it hadn't been real, but hearing him say those words… He tried to rape me that night, but I managed to escape and lock myself in the bathroom. By morning, he'd sobered up and had cleaned all the broken pieces. He acted like none of it had happened. I'm just glad Paisley wasn't here for any of it. I told him to get out at that point, and he laughed in my face. He said… he said," she gulped, holding my eyes. "He said he had a plan for me and until he got what he really wanted, I was to shut up and be the good slut I was, and he'd continue to pay my bills. After that night, I was too scared to try to leave again. So I did what he said. A month ago, he quit coming over, and I felt relieved. I hoped it meant he was done with me. Then he showed up a few weeks ago with Barkley and told me to keep her hidden. She was such a sweet dog. I didn't mind. I didn't know she was yours, though, I swear."

Believing her, I accepted her reasoning and pulled her into a hug. Brian could be scary when he didn't get his way, using aggression to control others. He hadn't had to use it on me very often, but I'd seen it emerge at times. There was a broken lamp here, a shattered picture frame there, and one time when he'd grabbed me by the wrist. Looking at it now, it seemed like it had only been a ticking time bomb before he'd escalated to this level with me. In a way, I was suddenly grateful he'd asked for a divorce.

It felt shitty of me to think that when the woman he'd escalated with was shaking in my arms.

"I'm sorry you've had to go through this. Do you need help?"

She looked at me oddly, confused as to why I would be offering help. "Why would you help me? I've been nothing but hateful."

"You have, but it doesn't mean I don't see a woman who needs assistance. A woman who has found herself in a difficult situation where she feels there's no way out. I don't think we're going to become best friends or anything, but I'm not going to deny you help, just because you called me a bitch."

"You really are kind. I'm glad Monroe is with someone like you. My sister, she's not the nicest, and I know what she's been planning. I even wondered if she was sleeping with Brian, the way they both acted."

"Possibly. Though she was taken to jail this morning for contempt, so I don't know how much trouble she'll be for you at the moment."

"Wait, what?" I couldn't help the smile that spread across my face.

"Yeah, there was a court hearing for custody, and Monroe won. There were a bunch of other charges filed against your sister. When she didn't comply, she was taken away for contempt."

"Shit. Okay. This might be the perfect time for me to escape. But there's something you should know."

Nodding, I waited for her to tell me. She looked worried again, biting her lip, and I squeezed her hand to reassure her.

"I overheard another conversation between Brian and your mother. I'm not sure what it all means, but one of them is in trouble financially. I don't know all the details, but it sounded like you were their way out of whatever they were involved in. Something to do with a trust that was coming to term. But to be granted access, they had to have you. They need you for something, Loren, and I don't think they'll stop until they get it. Barkley was just one way they wanted to control you. They have something else you want as well."

Dread pooled in my stomach, and I asked the question I didn't really know if I wanted the answer to. "Do you know what?"

She looked me over but eventually shook her head. "No, but I can find out. If you can help me get a plan together to leave, then I'll get you the info."

"Done. Though, Christine. I would help you without you having to do something for me."

She smiled softly, tears coming to her eyes again. "I know. But I need to start standing on my own feet, and that means not owing people things. This way, I feel like maybe I'm helping you too, and that's a nice feeling." I nodded, understanding what she meant.

"You know, I never thought you would be the one to help me see a way out or that I could even leave, but you have. I kind of became a stalker in regards to you, eating up any morsel of information I could find."

"Um, okay." I shifted uneasily, wondering if Single White Female was about to be uncovered here.

"Sorry, I know that sounds weird. I just meant you gave me a person to look up to. If you could get out and restart your life after the things I heard from Brian and your mother, then I could too. You gave me hope."

Empowerment from helping her just by being myself and finding my own way to healing surged through me. Fuck, that felt nice. To know someone had been watching the steps I took, the battles I faced, and saw the progress I made, felt really validating. Even more in some ways than therapy because it wasn't just the words I said, but the choices I made in my own life. *Me.*

"While I don't know if some of the things I've done are worth repeating, I'm glad I could be that for you. Here, give me your phone, and I'll give you my number. Call me if you need anything or if things don't go as planned and you need to leave quickly. I'll help you go wherever you want and with whatever you need, like money or supplies. Monroe will too. He's a good guy, and I know he cares about Paisley."

"Thank you, Loren. You really are too good for him. And even though I hated you because you were so perfect, I'm glad I got to see the real you."

"Me too. But I'm not perfect. Nowhere close."

I hugged her again before putting my number in her phone. Walking back to the car, I spotted the guys. Monroe leaned against the door, watching me, while Nicco was a few feet away talking on the phone. Wells had Barkley in the back, talking to her with the trunk raised, and I grinned at the sight of him with my dog. He was winning me over bit by bit, and I knew I'd fall into his trap soon. It just felt nice to make him work for it for a while. When Monroe saw me coming, he walked forward, taking my hands.

"Everything okay? What did she say? Do I need to go and threaten her with lawsuits or something?"

Shaking my head, I think I said the only thing that could've surprised him.

"No, we're going to help her, Monroe. We're going to help Christine and Paisley escape."

THIRTY

T he conversation I had with Christine lingered in the back of my mind all through the evening and the next day. It felt strange, feeling empathy for the woman, but I did. We weren't as different as I first imagined, except now, she was the one trapped with no way out. I'd escaped him, at least. I knew how imprisoned she had to feel, and I hoped she would take me up on my offer to help.

When I'd relayed everything to Monroe, he'd softened, and perhaps even respected her a little now. She'd always been in Brittni's shadow and hadn't made the best choices in life as she tried to keep up, making a name for herself. I'd assumed they were from the same circles I was growing up, but Wells was all too happy to let me know they'd come from the poor side of town and liked to pretend they were better now. The part that had irritated Monroe the most, though, was that she might've been targeted, a ploy to use against him.

I still didn't buy that level of deceit because it felt too far-fetched. How could my mother have known my neighbor would be Monroe? I still think it was a coincidence due to the elite circles being small. She might've been targeted, but not in the way he assumed. I think Christine was being used to cover their tracks and take the fall if anything happened. She was the one who had Barkley, after all. Plus, the fact he'd been paying her bills, it all smelled like a setup. I didn't have the heart to tell her she was chosen because she would be an easy suspect in whatever scheme he'd cooked up. She'd just started regaining her confidence. I didn't want to take it away.

So I lied to myself, saying it was for her own good. But really, it was for mine. I didn't want her to crumble before she discovered the information I needed. I could finally uncover what my mother was up to. I didn't like thinking of myself as selfish, though, so I shoved it away, covering it with the knowledge I was doing a good deed. It was dangerous how well I could twist a lie into truth if it benefited me.

Maybe I wasn't any better than my mother after all?

Thinking about it wasn't productive, though, so I shoved it down, cringing at the discomfort of having to lie to myself, placing the mask back on. Only this time, it shielded me from me.

We'd dropped Monroe off so he could pick up Levi, and Wells took Barkley until I could get it worked out with my condo. It had to be approved by the co-op before I could bring her there. So in the meantime, she got to play with all of his furry children as I'd started calling them, much to his dismay. It was fun to see him wince, but he didn't deny it, so I think he secretly liked it.

Nicco and I hung out for a while after everything, and it was nice to have a night in with him with no expectations. We cuddled on the couch, and the kiss he gave me when he left had me pulling out my vibrator later.

Today, I had a full day ahead of me, and the thought didn't exhaust me as it once had. In fact, I looked forward to all the things I had planned. Jude needed to be dropped at Ignite to work on a project with Mitzi. She had agreed to allow him to do his internship there, making Jude ecstatic to give back to the center. Afterward, he was going to hang with Nicco until I could pick him up. Wells didn't want to bring two dogs into the city, so I was making the trip out to his house to see Barkley and Fort. Then we would train there.

Around lunchtime, I'd pick up Jude, and we would head over to the Master's place. I wanted to touch base with Immy again, and Sax had asked to spend some time with me. Jude had wanted to see Immy as well, so it worked out. Sax said he'd put him to work while I spoke with Imogen, then we'd switch. It felt like I was organizing playdates, and I chose to keep it that innocent in my mind. Yep, denial was bliss sometimes.

Then that evening, it was a movie and game night celebration with Levi and Monroe. Last night was their time to reconnect. I felt it was vital for them to have that unsupervised. Plus, Monroe had to break the news about Brittni. But tonight, Monroe wanted to celebrate, and I was looking forward to it. I'd missed Levi as well. I held a bright spot for the kid and his love of cookies.

If I really thought about it, I had three dates planned

today, but who was counting? I wasn't going to complain.

"You ready to go, Juju?" I asked, laughing.

Jude looked up from packing his bag, giving me the most teenager look he'd ever given, as he looked up at me through his eyelashes. It clearly said he was disappointed in me. "No."

"Ahh, come on, Juju. It's so cute."

"No."

"Fine," I pouted. "You ready?"

"Yeah."

We headed out to the garage, taking my car since I had a million places to be today. I didn't want to use Natalie even though I knew she wouldn't mind. I didn't want to be shackled to a time limit other than the ones I had. I tried to use Nat as much as possible because I knew she needed the income, and it was a fun way to see my friend, but I was also mindful not to overuse her, not wanting her to think the friendship was only about that. She had indeed become one of the best girlfriends I'd ever had, and I couldn't imagine not having her in my life.

Unlocking the car, the beeping sounded as we approached, but before I made it to my door, I jumped back, almost knocking into Jude at the sudden movement. A man had stepped out from the shadows, scaring me as he approached.

I grabbed my necklace, ready to pull the ring of the necklace Sax had given me to release the blade when I realized who it was. I didn't let go, though. The danger was still present.

"Brian. What are you doing here?"

I tried to keep my voice firm, but my body had viscerally reacted to him despite my need to stay confident. I felt Jude at my back, touching my elbow, offering me his support. It helped to steady me as I took in a few breaths when Brian stalked closer.

He was pissed, the anger clear as day on his face, and I stiffened. God, I hated how scared he made me feel, how small. The panic was climbing up my throat, attempting to override my need to be strong. I debated what to do, if I should send Jude away to get help, or if keeping him here meant Brian wouldn't cross any lines. But I'd been frozen for too long, and he was practically on us already.

"Promise me if things go sideways, you'll run and get help. Call Sax or Monroe. But don't try to step in. Help is the better option," I whispered over my shoulder to Jude.

"I don't know if I can promise you that, Lor."

"Please," I begged. "I don't think it will, but if it does, I want to know you'll be safe and are getting help."

"*Fine.* I promise."

No sooner had he said the words than Brian made it to us. The first thing I noticed was his smell. He reeked, the sourness was pungent as it seeped from his pores. Brian was clearly drunk at 8 am. The second was the disorderly way he was dressed, most likely still in the clothes from the day before. And the third was the black eye he sported. I really hoped whoever had hit him made it hurt. Worry that it could've been Christine and something might've happened to her spiked, but I blocked it out, needing to focus on the here and now.

"Brian. What are you doing here?" He still didn't answer, only sneering at me. He leaned down, bringing his face closer to me, and I immediately took a step back, trying to get out of his range. I was just about to send Jude away to get help when Brian spoke.

"You think you're so clever. Getting things over on me, huh? Newsflash, Loren! You're nothing but a whore, spreading her legs for the wrong people. They aren't who you think they are. Both of you will get what's coming to you. Just you wait. I tried playing nice, but you had to screw around with what I had going. So now, I'm going to screw around with your life!"

"Brian, you're not making sense. I haven't done anything to you."

"You've done everything!" he roared, his rage on the surface. His face was so red, it was purple, his fists tight as I watched him open and close them. His chest moved up and down with his breathing, and there was a thin film of sweat on his brow. I catalogued everything, taking in the danger and assessing the risks, a game I'd gotten really good at during our marriage. How had I thought it was normal?

He staggered toward us again, and I took another step back, my hands raised out in front of me. Jude held onto my bicep, moving with me. Feeling him there, it was the courage I needed.

"Brian, if I've done something, then let's talk about it when you're sober and much calmer. This isn't the best idea. You're clearly upset, and I don't—"

"You don't, what?" he scoffed. "You're so blind to the truth. You walk around with your rose-colored glasses, seeing the best in people. Well, guess what, Loren? Everyone uses you. *Everyone.* They see you as an easy target, and they attack. You were always so blind to the things I did in our marriage, convincing yourself everything was perfect."

He rolled his eyes, his body wavering as he became worked up. I tried to block out his hatred, reminding myself of what the truth was. Still, each blow was a strike against my vulnerability, and I soon found myself bleeding out emotionally as he wrecked my carefully structured walls.

"I was *never* faithful to you. Not at any point when we were dating. You were such a bore, but apparently, I only needed to treat you like a slut, and you would've opened your legs more. I can't believe I trusted your mother to deliver on her promises and pay me the money I was owed, but she's a lying bitch too. Now I'm *ruined*, and it's all because of you, you heinous bitch. I hope you rot in Hell."

Brian spat the last part, the spit hitting me in the face, and it was the jolt out of the frozen panic I needed. Wiping it from my face, I didn't hesitate as I grabbed his shoulders and kneed him in the groin. Then, I used the palm of my hand to strike him in the chin. He staggered back a step, moaning as he attempted to recover from the force, holding his hands over his sad dick. Without even having to think, I lifted my leg, kicking him in the temple, sending him backward and falling completely to his back. I stood there for a second, amazed at what my body had done, and realized the importance of muscle memory.

Brian laid there moaning on the ground, and I'd had it. I was done feeling scared by him. Walking up to him, I managed to stop myself from stepping on his fingers, barely, but I did. The logical part of my brain knew I couldn't push past the self-defense line and stagger over into assault. All the years of pent-up aggression and complacency came spilling out of me, though, and I let him have it with my words. I doubt he even heard me over his own groans of pain, but it felt nice to get it all out.

"*You're* the asshole, Brian, not me. I don't know what you and my mother are up to, but I'll find out. Stay away from me, or next time I'll get a restraining order. I'm done with your manipulating, narcissistic, mansplaining bullshit. You can take your gaslighting ass and stay the fuck away from me." I started to walk away, happy with my delivery when he had to have the last word.

"You're such a stupid bitch. You'll pay for this."

Turning, I lasered him with my glare. "No, Brian. I won't. Because this garage has surveillance cameras, and all I did was defend myself from my drunk, aggressive ex-husband. If you did anything to Christine, it will add to your charges and evidence of guilt. And you're wrong, you know," I cooed, crouching down closer to his face. "I spread my legs for them because they're *phenomenal* at sex, and it turns out *size* does matter. So... sorry about your tiny dick, you suck as a human and at sex." Patting his cheek, I stood, brushing off my hands as I walked away, needing his filth off me.

When I looked up, I realized I had an audience. Standing where Jude and I had been was not only my foster son but Monroe and George. The three of them all held looks of shock on their faces, but when they saw me, they started to applaud. My cheeks heated, but it felt nice, and I found myself doing a silly little bow toward them. George walked over, patting my shoulder.

"I'll take care of this rodent for you, Miss." He winked, walking over to the still moaning piece of trash. When Brian saw him, he started to cry foul and ask for me to be arrested. George shook his head and pulled out some zip ties, locking his wrists together. Monroe reached out a hand and pulled me into him, and I felt my body stop shaking. I'd been confident, but it had still taken a toll on me. As usual, Monroe's hugs were a warm balm to my outer edges, and I found myself settling into his embrace.

"How did you know?" I finally asked.

"Jude. He texted me to bring security to the garage, STAT. I ran out so fast, I could barely get the sentence out to tell Levi to lock the door before I was taking the stairs two at a time. But when George and I got here, you already had it handled."

He pulled back, cupping my face as he did, pushing the hair out of the way. "I've never been so relieved and turned on at the same time," he whispered, thrusting his erection into me. Biting my lip, I barely managed to contain the moan that wanted to spill from my lips and escape. Lifting up, I kissed him quickly before pulling away.

"*Later.*"

"I'm holding you to it."

Nodding, I turned to see what was becoming of Brian

while keeping one arm around Monroe's waist. I briefly wondered if I would need to make a statement as I watched George haul the protesting asshat up. Reaching my hand out, I pulled Jude into our little huddle, wrapping my arm around him. Laying my head on his shoulder.

"Thanks, JuJu." He groaned but didn't move away, causing me to smile. "You're a smart kid," I offered. He'd been cognizant enough to keep his promise by getting help and staying with me. Seemed I needed to get on board with the whole phone thing finally. He blushed at my compliment but turned to me, a determined look on his face.

"I didn't want to break a promise, but there was no way I was leaving you, Lor. Misfit Penguins, remember?"

Nodding, I pulled him closer. Seriously, this kid had my heart. There was no letting him go now. George walked toward the elevator, Brian continued to rant and rave, but no one was listening for once. I relaxed once they were gone from sight.

"Shoot. Do you think I need to give a statement or something? I meant to ask George."

"Go ahead. I'll tell them you'll stop by tomorrow to leave one. They have the video footage anyway, so enough to lock him up until Monday morning. Look at us babe, getting our ex's jailed a day apart. It must be 'Locked up' weekend. Maybe it was a 2-for-1 sale?"

Laughing, I pushed him for his bad joke. When I got to the car, I remembered Brian had been lurking there, so

I called out to Monroe once again. "Um, you think you could help me make sure it wasn't tampered with. He was around it when we got here. How he knew I'd be taking it today, now that's a mystery." I chewed that bit of information over in my mind as Monroe shuffled his feet.

"Um, sure."

Together, we all pretended like we knew what to spot as we kicked the tires, peered under the hood, and then crawled under the car. Nothing looked amiss, and since the car hadn't been moved in a while, there was a good layer of dirt that hadn't been disturbed either. Odds were, it wasn't messed with, considering Brian didn't know how to do anything and had been drunk. Once we were done with our inspection, Jude and I hopped in, and we continued on with our day, hoping the rest wasn't as exciting.

SIX HOURS LATER, I walked back into my apartment after a whirlwind day, in desperate need of a shower. Training had gone well this morning, and when I relayed my takedown of Brian, Wells had been impressed, but made me go over other moves to make sure I didn't just get lucky next time.

The dogs were getting along well, and I loved how Fort and Barkley seemed to have bonded. My two babies instinctively knew they belonged together. I hadn't told Wells yet, but I wanted to contact the farm and see if I could get Fort when he was finished. I'd grown too attached to him to let him go at this point. I didn't know how Wells did it.

Imogen and I had a good conversation as well, and she'd open up a little more about her capture. She hadn't said it yet, but I had a bad feeling she'd been raped, and I knew it was going to be a hard thing for her to tell when she got to that place. Sax had made me a picnic lunch, and we sat outside in the backyard under the trees. He even pulled out a guitar and played a song for me. It was such a different side to him. I didn't know how to take it. And for once, we spent the whole time with all of our clothes on. I was dangerously close to falling for the dirty talking brute. I was beginning to think I didn't care about the consequences and wanted to jump all in headfirst.

Atticus had tried to talk to me again. I'd thanked him for his help in both of the situations I'd asked and had given him the information I'd recovered from Christine about a possible trust. But, unless it was something about Immy, I didn't have any further reason to talk to him at the moment.

The small voice inside who liked to people-please whispered I was too hard on him, too unforgiving. The woman who'd sat through his ridiculous dinner table conversation knew otherwise. I knew he saw me as a threat, but it didn't mean I was someone he could control. I was learning I liked standing up to Atticus, and that might've been his biggest mistake of all—giving me an outlet for my rebellious nature to emerge.

"I'm going to shower. Can you preheat the oven and put the cookies in when it beeps? The directions are on the box."

"Yeah, sure."

"Thanks, JuJu."

"You're not going to stop, are you?" he asked, looking annoyed, but I could tell he secretly liked it.

"I will if you hate it."

He paused in his doorway, thinking. "I guess as long as it's just us, I don't mind. Just, you know, not around people my age."

"That wouldn't be anyone in particular now, would it?"

"I don't know what you're talking about." His face blushed, and I grinned wider.

"Uh-huh. Sure. Good talk. Don't forget about the contraceptive one we had!" I yelled as he shut his door, and I heard him moaning in distress.

"I take it back. Nope, you can't call me that."

"Too late, Juju!"

Laughing, I ran to my room and took the world's fastest shower before putting on my comfy pj's and blow-drying my hair. When I came out, Jude was taking the cookies out of the oven, and someone knocked on our door.

"Perfect timing, I'll grab it."

Pulling it open, I found Levi and Monroe grinning at me. "Levi! I've missed you, bud." Squatting down, I opened my arms, becoming more familiar with hugging people but wanting to offer him the chance to say no. He rushed forward, hugging me tight, though, and I melted. "Missed you too, Lor."

I secretly loved all the little nicknames the guys and people in my life were giving me. I'd never had one before outside of sweetheart, and now that one made me cringe.

"Guess what we made, just for you?" I asked, pulling back. He sniffed his nose, his eyes going wide.

"Are those cookies?"

"Not just any cookies, but the kind they served at the art show."

"No way!" He took off running, his batman pj's swishing by me as I stood, and I could hear him calling out to Jude as he made it to the cookies.

"You doing okay after everything this morning?"

"Yeah. I was shaken up at first, almost fell back into the place I'd been with him, but when he spat on me, it was like the slap I needed to retake my control. Plus, I got to play with the dogs and punch Wells. That's always a good way to spend my day."

"I'm starting to think you have an obsession with punching him."

I shrugged. "He was so surly in the beginning, he's kind of owed it. Now, it's more like foreplay."

"So, there is something between you two then?"

"I think so. I'm trying not to think about naming it all and just letting things play out how they do. I worried a lot about having to choose, but realized I'm not keeping anything a secret and no one has asked me to be exclusive. So, I'm spending time with the people I like and letting things evolve as they do."

"That's very mature and go-with-the-flow of you."

"I'm trying, okay." I laughed, pushing his shoulder. "What about you? Have you guys talked more?"

"Yeah, we have. And I'm trying too. Now that I'm not

so worried about the custody, I think I could entertain it. I want him in my life. It's just figuring out what that looks like. I want us three to talk about it when you're ready to take that step."

"What if I'm ready to take that step with you?"

"Then I'd suggest a sleepover," he winked, pulling me into his arms.

"I like the sounds of these plans."

Smiling wide at each other, the moment was broken when the boys came into the living room, carrying a plate of cookies and talking a mile a minute. We settled down to watch movies, ordered some pizzas, and I enjoyed the relaxed evening. Monroe updated me on his conversation with Christine, and she was fine for now. It eased some of my worry in that department.

The whole evening, I couldn't help but think how nice it felt being part of a family, one that I'd made myself of people I could be the real me with. Mostly, I tried to ignore the plaguing insults Brian had thrown and focus on the now, and what I was learning to be true.

Eating cookies, laughing, and snuggling were how I planned to conquer the lies tonight.

THIRTY ONE

LOREN

The past hour had been an excruciating exercise in self-control. Monroe and I were curled up on the lounge part of the couch, our legs entangled with one another as we watched the movie. Levi had snuggled close for a while but then had joined Jude on the floor in a bed made of pillows. They both snored softly now, curled up with blankets. If Monroe hadn't slowly been torturing me for the past hour with his gentle touches on my skin, I probably would've been content just to watch them sleep.

Yet, as the credits played, I quietly stood and took Monroe's hand. He chuckled, knowing good and well what he'd been doing to me. Shaking my head, I motioned for him to be quiet as I led him down the hall. I grabbed my phone this time, patting myself on the back for remembering, and made sure to lock the door to my room behind me. The moment the lock snicked closed, Monroe had me in his arms, kissing me against the wall.

"Fuck, Lo. I've wanted to do that for the past hour."

"I know, jerk. Your fingers have been teasing me." I smacked his chest but smiled, letting him know I wasn't actually mad. "How about you take me to that bed and fuck me like we both want?"

"That sounds like an epic idea."

Bending low, he scooped me up bridal style before I could protest, a slight squeal leaving me as he did. He delivered a smug look as he walked us over before gently laying me down. "I might not look as burly as Wells or Sax, Lo, but I can pick up my woman."

"Your woman?" Monroe grinned, searing me with a look that had me squirming with his intentions.

"Yes, Loren. You're my woman. Time I show you just what that means."

Monroe's lips met mine, pressing hard into my own as our tongues battled it out in a passion-filled kiss that left me panting when he pulled away. I bucked up, needing contact as he started to drop kisses down my neck, and blew on my skin. I moaned as he nibbled his way down to my collarbone. His hands pushed up my shirt, palming my breasts as his thumbs rubbed over my nipples. The peaks were stiff as he played with them, and I ran my own fingers through his mop of curls, pulling him to me more.

We kissed as only Monroe seemed capable of doing, like we had all the time in the world. He never seemed rushed and took his time, slowly enjoying my body as he uncovered it piece by piece, leaving me a writhing and panting mess in the process. Moaning, I couldn't take it any longer, and I bucked up, yanking him down to me.

"Monroe, if you know what's good for you, you'll—"

Except I didn't get to finish my sentence, a long moan escaped me instead as Monroe plunged two fingers into my aching cunt, dripping with need. Throwing my head back, I gave in to the pleasure and the friction I'd been needing. His edging and teasing for the past few hours had me quickly tumbling into an orgasm when he rubbed my clit with his thumb, pinching my nipple with his free hand.

"Oh, fuck."

Once I'd orgasmed, it was like a switch flipped, and he yanked my clothes off me quicker than I could count before slamming into me, a deep moan of his own ricocheting around the room. Almost as if to show me he could toss me around too, his arm banded behind my back, and he lifted us to a sitting position. It was intimate being this close, and I wrapped around him, pressing my breasts against his chest.

"Fucking hell, Lo. Is this what sex is supposed to feel like?"

I smoothed his hair down, cupping his cheek as we slowly rocked into one another, content to lock eyes for the moment.

"I didn't know either, not until, well, Nicco. I felt like I'd been lied to my whole life," I admitted, chuckling. He kissed my lips softly once, then again, reassuring me.

"I like that you talk to me about them. I thought it would be weird, but it's not. I like the fact that we can be bare assed together, my cock deep inside of you, and still carry on a conversation. It makes me feel like no matter what it is, we can share it with each other. I don't know," he admitted, smiling, "it's just nice and comforting."

Tightening my walls, I watched as he hissed a breath, his eyes closing briefly before opening. Monroe's pupils were blown, and I rocked up as I tangled my fingers in his hair again. I didn't know how we could possibly be any closer at that moment. It felt as if we were sharing the same air and heartbeat.

"You are pure comfort, Monroe, and I love that I can be open with you too. I never have to censor myself, and you give me the space and opportunity to talk things out without backlash. You're one of the most amazing men I've ever met."

"I don't think I could ever stop being in your life now. Not after this…" he kissed me deeply, stopping his own sentence, every ounce of passion in his entire body transferred through his lips as they pressed into mine. Monroe's hands threaded through my hair, the soft caresses, bringing me closer to him. His hands dipped as he thrust up in me, grabbing my ass as he did. My skin felt like it was on fire, his tongue devouring mine, and I lost my head.

I'd had hot kisses before, I'd even had sweet kisses, and I'd definitely had passionate kisses, but this… this kiss was a body-melting, toe-curling, your essence leaving you and joining the other person type of kiss.

If Monroe's arms weren't wrapped around me, I wondered if I would've full-on swooned from it.

As it was, I sighed when he pulled away, blinking my eyes open slowly to stare at the man who made me feel so cherished. He gently began to lower us to the bed, his arms cupping my head as he placed it on the soft surface. Monroe began his slow and tortured pace again, and outside the one second where he'd seemed to have snapped, plunging into me, this seemed to be his preferred method. It drove me crazy with need, and I was soon panting into his neck, grabbing his ass cheeks to move faster.

"Ssh, Lo. Just enjoy it and let your body feel everything."

His slow thrusts in and out felt nice, and I tried to let go of my desire to reach orgasm immediately and relax into it. It was offering him control in a different way, allowing him to direct my pleasure. I realized how much trust I placed in his hands, something I hadn't fully done with a man since Brian. Gazing into his eyes, though, I knew I could.

Since I'd spoken with him in the elevator, there hadn't been a day gone by that he hadn't shown me his true self. Monroe was loving, protective, and steady. He valued family, honesty, and staying true to your word. I'd been gutted when he'd said he had to step back from us, needing to focus on Levi, but I'd misinterpreted the situation. I was so used to being hurt, tossed aside, and discarded, I'd assumed he was as well. Coming on the heels of Nicco and Sax disappearing, it had cut me deep, right to the center of who I was.

My baggage wasn't his, though, and when I looked at it now, with a different perspective, I couldn't help but admire him for doing the hard thing. There was no doubt in my mind that what he said was true. He *wouldn't* leave me. Not willingly, at least. And that had value.

So I relaxed into his arms, giving over my last shred of hesitancy at trusting him, and placed my heart in his hands this time. Staring into his eyes, I saw the moment he noticed the shift as well. The moment I relinquished every ounce of the mask I hid behind, revealing my naked truth to him.

The fear in me wanted to rise up and cover myself in a protective film to shield me from potential harm. But I pushed it back, wanting to brave this moment and share everything with him. There was no more hiding from Monroe, not when he'd so effortlessly pushed over all my barriers, proving he'd be there. It was my turn to show up for him. I'd been making small steps, and now I needed to leap.

"Wow. You're breathtaking, Loren. Thank you."

His palm caressed my cheek, his thumb running under my eye, as it fluttered closed at the contact. It was caring, and I daresay, *adoring*. I felt Monroe lift one of my legs, hooking it into his elbow as he rocked into me. I opened my eyes again, staring intensely into his as he pushed forward with a little more force but still at that slow back and forth.

His pale green eyes felt alive, and I pulled his lips down to mine, wanting every inch to touch. It didn't take much longer, and as we stared into one another's eyes, I felt us fall over that edge, weaving our hearts together as we both gasped out in ecstasy.

"That was the most beautiful love-making I've ever experienced." His tone held reverence, and I couldn't deny he was right. It had been *love-making*; even if we weren't saying the words out loud, our hearts had said them for us through our bodies.

Monroe continued to cherish me as he pulled out and walked into the bathroom. He returned a few minutes later with a warm washcloth and proceeded to pamper me. By the time he'd finished, I felt as if my muscles were jelly, and I'd become boneless. I heard the door unlock as he left the room, but I was too blissed out to move. A few minutes later, he came back, crawling in behind me as he wrapped me up in his arms again, spooning me.

"I checked on the boys, and they're still asleep."

"Oh, good."

"Thank you for waiting for me. I think I was meant to meet you when I did, to show me I could have good things in my life. You're my good thing, Lo."

"I could say the same about you."

"Well, I said it first, so tough cookie."

Giggling, I rolled over so I could face him. "Since we're thanking each other, I'd like to say thanks for being patient with me. I know I haven't made it easy at times."

"You're easy to wait for. Especially when I get here, and you show me the real beauty you've been hiding. I feel like I'm the lucky one."

"Well, we can both be lucky then."

"I'll agree to that."

"You're such a lawyer sometimes. It's cute."

"Oh, you think I'm cute?"

He rolled me onto my back and began to tickle me as he simultaneously left kisses. Laughing, I curled up into a ball, attempting to swat him off me. "I surrender. I don't know what from, but I do."

"You surrender to calling me sexy, or hot, or manly."

"Fine! Fine! You're very manly, Monroe. Oh, so manly!" Giggles poured out of me, and I couldn't remember ever feeling this light, this happy… *this free.*

When he stopped, he gave my lips a quick peck before wrapping us up together in a hug. "You give the best hugs."

He snuggled closer, rubbing his nose along my neck, breathing me in. "Is that so?"

"Mmhmm."

"Would it ruin it then if I tell you it's so I can feel your body pressed against mine?"

"A little!"

"Well, then it's definitely not that."

"I'd say you're cute again, but I can't survive another tickle fight."

"What am I then?"

"Hmm, you're like a warm hug."

"A warm hug? So, I'm basically Olaf?"

"What's wrong with being Olaf? He's a great character. But you're wrong. He said he liked warm hugs, not that he was one."

"Oh, my apologies. I didn't mean to disrespect a fake snowman."

"You better watch your mouth, sir! Disney movies are to be protected at all costs!"

"Welp, I finally found it."

"Found what?"

"Your one flaw."

Smacking his chest, I shook my head. "How is that a flaw?"

"Because Disney isn't real life. I much prefer the Grimm Fairy Tales."

"It's not meant to be real life. That's the whole point!"

"Well, I'll compare you to a fake snowman and see if that makes you feel good."

"Fine. You're like a warm hug…" I paused, thinking when the idea came to me. "You're a warm hug for my vagina." I grinned wide, proud of myself for that retort.

Monroe stared at me for a split second, my words hanging in the air as he comprehended them. Laughing out loud, the sound was full of happiness, and I joined him.

"Oh, Lo, I take it back. You are perfect."

"Nah. But I like that you think I am, flaws and all."

"Your flaws are what make you, you. Of course, I love them."

Smiling, I fell asleep in his arms, contentment filling me as his words imprinted themselves on my heart.

Rushing into the restaurant, I slowed when I saw the girls sitting around a table. I smoothed my clothes down, a broad grin on my face as I approached. It might have taken me thirty-two years to find genuine friendships, but it had been worth it. These women had shown me more kindness, acceptance, and understanding than all of the ladies I'd gone to school with or been in similar circles as. When they spotted me, an enthusiastic 'welcome' rang out from them, and they all stood to hug me.

Hugs—they were quickly becoming my favorite thing.

"Loren!"

"Hey, guys! Sorry, I'm a little late."

"Girl, it's fine. Besides, you're usually fifteen minutes early for everything. I think you've banked a few minutes to run late with," Nat teased.

"Yeah, I mean, hopefully, you come bearing a fun story?" Cami eagerly asked.

Laughing, I didn't know if it was possible for my smile to grow wider. I waited until the server took my drink order, returning quickly with some coffee. Stirring in some creamer, I picked it up, a coy smile on my face as I took a sip. Looking over the rim, my cheeks heated as I shrugged one shoulder. "Maybe."

"Oh! There *is* a story!" Cami exclaimed, smacking the table in her exuberance, the silverware clattering as she did.

Ducking, I hid my face behind my hair as I set my coffee down. Nat didn't let me off the hook either, quick to goad me with the other two.

"Oh, there's a story. I'd say a couple, actually."

"Hey!" I teased, sticking my tongue out at her. Sighing, I couldn't even pretend to be mad because I was so happy. I didn't think I'd ever felt this blissful before. It was a sad thought, but I pushed it away, focusing on the fact I was, not that I hadn't been before. The before didn't matter now.

"Where should I start?"

"At the beginning, duh! Give us all the juicy details," Stacy enthused.

So while we drank our coffee and waited for our food, I filled them all in on my night with Sax, going over to Atticus' house, getting a tattoo, getting Barkley back, and kicking Brian in the junk.

"What! Why couldn't I have been there for that? Please tell me there's footage of this?" Cami begged, slapping the table again. A couple of other people looked over, eyeing her, a few turning their noses up at her outfit.

She was dressed as seductively gorgeous as usual in a low-cut top, her red hair curled around her. She always managed to draw the looks from others, whether from lust or annoyance. Cami was all personality, and while I found I loved it, I saw the looks others shot her loud 'take no prisoners' attitude. If I'd still been in the clutches of Jacqueline, I would've been eyeing her as well. Mostly because I'd be jealous she could be so free to be herself.

"Actually," I chuckled, "I didn't know this until last night, but apparently, Jude recorded it."

"Oh man, I'm so texting him to send it to me." Shaking my head, I smiled at the server when our food was delivered. Before I could even take a bite of the delicious-looking omelet, Cami was squealing in glee across the table.

"Epic, Lor! Oh my God, that is the best thing I've seen."

"He sent it to you?"

She grinned wide, passing her phone to the other two to watch. They all huddled around the phone, watching it. It was weird being applauded for something I usually wouldn't feel proud of. The high-class snob in me wanted to berate me for using violence and lowering myself to such basic responses. But that highbrow person, she wasn't me—not anymore. Plus, she'd never been free, and now that I was, I couldn't imagine ever being trapped again by the shackles of the elitist society.

Loss of freedom was too high a cost to ever belong to that world again.

"Seriously, that's hot, Lor. You seriously have me considering physical activity. Do you think Wells would train me?"

"And me!" Stacy piped in, and the small amount of fear I'd catch at times flicked in her eyes, and I knew more than anything she needed to feel in control of her body and safe.

"I can definitely ask. He's trying to get in my good graces, so he might be willing. He's a bit of an asshole, though, so be prepared for him to be surly toward you."

"I can work with that," Stacy confirmed, a look of hope on her face. If Wells said no, I'd find someone else, it seemed important all of a sudden.

"You've had a very fulfilling week."

"Oh, I also slept with Monroe last night," I stated right before taking a bite, smiling smugly at them. Their shocked expressions had me grinning wider as I took another bite, but this one I almost choked on when I heard *her* voice behind me.

"Loren, it seems you continue to embarrass me with your lewd behavior, and now you're bragging about physical violence against your husband? You've sunk so low, dear. I don't know what I've ever done to deserve this treatment."

Coughing, I grabbed the water in front of me as I tried to dislodge the egg that was wedged there. The cool glass also gave me something to focus on as I attempted to get my breathing under control. Setting it down, I looked up at the girls, their faces a mixture of disgust, shock, and anger as they looked at the woman behind me.

Carefully, I placed the napkin from my lap on the table, turning on my chair to stand from the table. I realized my mistake as soon as I stood. In my haste to get to the table, I hadn't taken in my entire surroundings. My inner critic shouted at me, reminding me if I hadn't had round two with Monroe this morning, I would've been on time. I could've preempted this attack. I could've chosen somewhere else to sit or even kept my bragging to myself. The usual cowering I did in her presence wanted to emerge, giving in to the shame she cast on me for not living up to her expectations.

Pushing my shoulders back, I used my height to my advantage and stood looking down on my mother. Those inner insecurities had surfaced for a moment. But it was only a moment. The love and acceptance I'd found last night shined bright, casting those demons away. There was nothing wrong with my choices. Nothing wrong with me sharing it with my friends. And there was absolutely nothing wrong with me standing up for myself and wanting to be loved.

"Mother, how nice to see you here. This isn't your typical Sunday place. Did something happen at the club? Hope you haven't offended anyone with your trite behavior."

Jacqueline's face scrunched up, and I knew I'd unknowingly hit a nerve. Interesting. I filed that away to look at more later.

"Your father and I decided to try something new. That's all."

I peeked around her, spotting my father sitting at the table. He looked worn down and embarrassed by my mother for once.

"Hi Dad," I greeted, offering him a smile.

"Loren, it's nice to see you. I've missed catching up. How is… Jude?" He finished, despite my mother giving him a disapproving look. His eyes had cast over to her, but I saw him defy her, asking anyway. It gave me hope he wasn't as despicable as Jaqueline was. Kenneth still had a lot to make up for, but perhaps he wasn't unredeemable. I held onto that morsel of hope for my dad.

"Jude's great. He's doing an internship with Mitzi and doing well at school."

"That's good, real good. I'll have to check with Mitzi and see if she needs any more volunteers. I could use a new outreach, get me out of the house more."

I didn't miss the way his eyes flicked to my mother again or the challenge in his voice at getting out. Something was going on here, and I needed to get to the bottom of it once and for all.

Jacqueline was not happy to be dismissed, stomping her foot down like a toddler.

"Yes, Mother? Do you have something productive to add?"

"Productive? How about you answer my questions?" she screeched, pulling in more onlookers.

"I have nothing to say to you. Now, I'm going to return to my friends and tell them all about the amazing sex I had with one of my boyfriends. Enjoy your meal."

I spun on my heels, sitting back down delicately. I placed my napkin back in my lap, crossing my legs gracefully. My shoulders stayed back, and when I raised my head to the girls, their faces had changed to looks of respect and glee. I grinned back at them, happy to have them with me. Cami winked, and I just knew whatever came out of her mouth would be a doozy, but I couldn't wait, knowing she did it to help me stick it to my mother.

"Have you had any of them together yet, Lor? Are there threesomes in your future?"

Sputtering in laughter, I couldn't help but chuckle at her. Lifting my coffee, I tipped it at her. "One can only hope."

We all heard the huff of annoyance and outrage behind us, but we ignored it, returning to our meals and conversation. My hands shook a little, but as I relaxed back in my seat, listening to them share about their weeks, it began to slow. Nat reached over, squeezing my leg under the table, offering me support. I nodded to her as Cami talked loudly about her last threesome, and I laughed, knowing it was killing my mother.

While it was embarrassing having my parents hear about my sex life, I wasn't ashamed of it. It had been scary standing up to my mother, her years of gaslighting and emotional abuse leaving a scar on my soul. But I chose myself and would keep choosing myself, proving I was strong to me and others.

I had a feeling I would need it for what lay ahead. Because I hadn't missed the change in routine or the way my father looked relieved to get out of the house. Whatever my mother was hiding, it would hit the fan soon, and I didn't want to be in front of it when it did.

I felt a slight squeeze of my shoulder a few minutes later, and I knew it had been my father. It was another win in his column of pulling away from the toxicity that was Jacqueline Hanover.

THIRTY TWO

WELLS

Panting, I swung an uppercut at the mitts Nicco held, tapping them as I bounced on my feet. We'd been training for the past few hours, and I was feeling better than I ever had. When I successfully landed a kick, he dropped his hands, giving me a wide grin. I still didn't like the kid, but I respected him. It was progress.

"You're on fire, Crash. There's no way you won't win this week. Are you feeling ready? It's your first fight back since you were—"

"Beaten to a pulp by Delgado? Yeah. I'm ready." I wiped my brow, the hard edge of the tape scratching against my skin in the process.

"You're definitely going to be a contender for the new venue when it opens. Even at your age, I think you have a shot at making a name for yourself if that's what you want."

"What I want?" I scoffed. "How about you lay off my age? I'm 35. I'm not ancient."

"I'll drop it, *old man,* when you stop calling me kid." He gave me a pointed look, his smile smug as I shook my head.

"Fine." Smirking at his win, he walked over and helped me with removing the tape and then checked on the tattoo he'd given me.

"I should've thought of where you wanted this before I did it with your fight coming up," he groused, lifting the tape we'd placed on it while I worked out. When he peeled the layer away, his fingers brushed against the ink, and I stifled a groan. It was sore, but I didn't want him to know that. The guy was too cocky for his own good.

"What made you choose an arrow?"

Shrugging, I turned my back as I grabbed a towel and water. I didn't want to tell him the real reason.

"Come on, man. I'm the artist. I should be given the reason, at least. I promise not to tell if it's embarrassing or something."

Sighing, I turned and observed him. Nicco's face was relaxed, his eyes honest, and I saw the true man standing there for once. Not the joker, not the party guy, not even the mafia 2nd in command, whatever that was… I just saw *him*. Crossing my arms, I stared him down, wanting to know if he'd push back. When he didn't, I caved. If he could be honest with me, I could do the same with him. I ignored the fact that I also wanted to share it with someone.

"I'm sure you know what arrow tattoos represent," I barked, not exactly hitting the sharing portion I'd gone for.

"I know any tattoo can have various reasons and depend on the person. So try again."

"You're annoying." I rolled my eyes, but reminded

myself I'd wanted to share.

"Perhaps," he shrugged. "But it's part of my charm. Now, spill, or I'll just assume it's because you don't know your right or left, and the arrow symbolizes, this way is up, stupid."

"You're beyond annoying. You're moronic."

"Stupid it is." He spun on his heels, heading out of the gym, and I dropped my head back, looking up at the ceiling as I counted.

"Fine. It has two meanings," I sighed. Leveling my head, I found him turned, a smirk on his face again as he waited. "The first one, the broken one, represents me letting go of the past that has burdened me, and breaking myself free of that path. The second one represents the course I'm setting for myself and the freedom I have."

"Cool."

He spun, walking away, and I rolled my eyes. "That's all you have to say? *Cool*?"

"No, but it was fun to watch you get all annoyed by it." He came back into the room, stopping only a few feet from me this time. "You picked a badass tat. I'm impressed with the thought that went into them. You seem more of a spur of the moment type of person, not one that thinks through shit."

"Ah, well, you'd be wrong. I'm the 'overthink it to the tenth degree, can't figure out a solution, so I just fake it until the last minute and hope it works out' type. Which it never does, by the way."

"That explains a lot about you, actually."

"How so?" I asked, crossing my arms in the other

direction. I didn't want to admit how curious I was of his answer.

"I'm guessing your life wasn't easy growing up, creating that unstable backdrop for you. There's also this attitude of wanting to prove yourself to the extent you will often put yourself in situations, even if it's unsafe. For example, trying to fight with broken ribs. You're stubborn and don't trust a lot of people, throwing up that guarded front to protect yourself, which led me to the troubled childhood."

"You make me sound like a neurotic asshole," I huffed, not wanting to admit how he so easily voiced all of my fears.

"I wasn't finished, but you are an asshole. You can't deny that."

"Fine. But I like *surly* better."

"I'm sure you do since a beautiful woman calls you that."

Narrowing my eyes at him, I waited to see if he had anything else to offer.

"What I was going to finish my spiel with," he paused, giving me a pointed look, "is that you're also compassionate and have the capacity to care deeply for those who make it past your barrier. Dogs are easier to trust because they give you their love unconditionally and won't ever betray you. You've trusted the wrong people in the past, and it's screwed you over."

"What are you, like, a psych major or something? Been taking lessons from Loren on how to deconstruct a person?"

"No," he replied, grinning before shaking his head.

"I'm just observant, a habit of this life. I'm actually going to school to be an art teacher."

That had me raising my eyebrows. "You can do that? Be a teacher while in the... family?"

"I used to think I could. I don't know anymore."

"That sucks. I guess someone does have it worse than me. I can still try to be something I want."

He nodded, a sad smile on his face. "Fair. Though I didn't tell you any of this to weaken you or gain an advantage." Nicco walked a little closer, leaving barely an inch between us. "I *told* you because I think we have a lot of similarities. We just chose to showcase them in different ways, but I'm not new to stubbornness or doing something for the wrong reasons. I know you teamed up with us to keep Loren safe and get yourself out from under your debt. I don't begrudge you for that. It was smart. I just don't think you have to work so hard to hate us. Despite being the criminal underground, I like to think of us as the good guys. We could be a family for you, or at least, I could be a friend. This doesn't have to be only about winning a fight. We also both care about the same girl. You can deny that too, but I can tell. This doesn't have to be only a transactional thing here. That's all I wanted to say."

He whispered the last part, his eyes searing into me, and I found myself wanting to believe him, my usual ire not bubbling up to the surface. Slowly, I agreed. "Okay, I'll give you a chance to prove you're not a heartless bastard. But I don't forgive easily, so if you mess it up, *that's* on you."

"There's that rough exterior already, assuming I'm

going to screw you over. *Trust*, Wells." He slapped me on my shoulder, spinning on his feet as he left, and I was left wondering what the hell had just occurred and why I felt so weird about it. I didn't miss how he'd used my name that time either.

THROWING THE FOAM FOOTBALL, I watched as Barkley and Fort chased after it, both wanting to catch it. Barkley managed to snatch it out of the air first, her sheer size and breed being an advantage over Fort. She ran to bring it back, her doggy smiles excited at winning the ball. I watched as Fort sulked back, not happy to lose, and a sudden realization smacked me in the chest. Fort was me in dog form. I watched in amazement as Barkley stopped when her new friend wasn't with her. She turned, saw Fort laying on the ground with his head on his paws, and walked over to him, offering him the football.

It was a simple thing, watching these dogs bond and care for one another, but it struck me to my core. When Barkley nudged him, he lifted his head but still didn't budge. When she yipped, nosing the toy, Fort moved forward a little more. Finally, Barkley yipped at him again, bouncing on her paws in a playful pose. When he got up, playing this time, she chased around him, encouraging him to keep running. That damn dog had been more successful at getting him to do what he needed than I had. It only solidified my impression that Monroe was like Barkley, and even Loren on occasion.

Thinking about the two dogs that way, I knew they

needed to be paired. I'd already wanted to give Fort to Loren, and this only confirmed the decision for me. Whistling, I motioned for them to come inside. They'd long discarded the football, choosing to roll around in the grass instead as they chased one another. A car drove up the drive when I rounded the house, and I stiffened. It was unfamiliar, and I hadn't been expecting anyone. I ducked back to see who it was, and I motioned for the dogs to sit. I relaxed when Loren got out. Stepping out from my hiding spot, I met her as she made her way to the door. The dogs were hot on my heels once they'd seen who it was as well.

"Hey, guys. Have you both been good?" she asked, bending down to pet them as they licked and jumped on her for affection.

"Kitten, did we have an appointment I'm not remembering?" I smirked, attempting to dampen the sarcastic tone. Defensiveness, as Nicco had stated, was my go-to response, and I was trying to change it, but it was a slow process. Thankfully, she smiled at me when she looked up from the fluffy mongrels.

"Nope. But I wanted to see you."

"Me? Or the *dogs*?" Her reason had taken me by surprise, so when she stood and walked over, I stiffened.

"You, Mr. Surly."

"Okay, do I owe you money or something?"

Loren rolled her eyes, swatting me. "No. I could want to spend time with you, just to spend time with you, Wells."

I raised my eyebrows at her answer. "We both know I'm not the 'spend time with' type of guy."

"Maybe not now, but I think you could be."

"Listen, Kitten," I sighed. "I had a long morning training. There's a fight coming up, and I need to mentally prepare for it. I don't have the energy to play mind games today."

"Ah, so Nicco whipped you into shape this morning, and that's why you're so grouchy," she mused.

Hanging my head, I counted to ten. I didn't want to admit it had nothing to do with training and everything to do with all the confusing as fuck feelings I was having. When I felt her hand on my cheek, I jumped, not having expected her to be there.

"Hey, seriously, are you okay? Do you want to talk or something?"

Looking into her eyes, I saw sincere kindness, and all I wanted to do was take her up against the wall and fuck her. I couldn't do the feeling shit, wanting to immediately replace it with the physical. The reality that I would screw this up eventually hit me, and I stepped back. Hurt flickered across her face, and it gutted me even more.

"I'm not good for you, Kitten. I thought I could be the man you needed, but I was wrong." I stepped back more, the pain on her face now a knife to my gut. "You have enough men already clambering to be with you as it is. You *don't* need me."

She stared blankly, wiping a tear from her face. Loren turned to go but stopped, spinning around quickly, her hair whipped out around her. The change had been so abrupt, it froze me to my spot. She yanked on my shirt, forcibly pulling my face to hers. The hurt had morphed into anger, and I worried for a second she'd knee me in the balls again. I deserved it, though, so I did nothing to block her.

Instead, she kissed me.

Loren's lips were soft, but her mouth demanded that I submit to her. I resisted for a second, long enough to appease my barriers, and then I succumbed to everything that was my kitten. Lifting her up, she wrapped her legs around my waist as we devoured one another. My hands gripped the globes of her ass, my cock straining against my pants to be free as I ground into her.

She pulled away, and I moaned out in distress, missing her lips on mine already. It was as good as I remembered, her perfect body against mine, her hot lips devouring my tortured soul, that decadent feeling of ecstasy.

When she didn't place them back on mine, my eyes fluttered open to peer at her. Her hands gripped my face firmly, and I knew whatever she said, I would either hate or love. There was no in-between when it came to Loren.

"I'm not going to let you do that. I'm not going to let you push me away because you're scared. I've been scared my whole life, and it got me nowhere. So, no. You're not allowed to push me away, not after all the work you've done to earn my trust. Believe in yourself, Wells. I do."

My eyes fluttered closed at her words, her thumbs smoothing under my eyes softly. It was intimate and gentle, and it completely melted me. Nodding, I placed my forehead on hers, my breathing labored as I attempted to reign in all the fucked up feelings I had.

Eventually, I opened my eyes and pulled back to find her watching me.

"I'm sorry. You're right. I'm a screwup, Kitten. It's my nature to push people away. I just don't want to hurt you. You're the best thing in my life, you and Monroe, and I so want to be worthy of you both."

"Don't you get it, Wells? You are. Your worth isn't determined by the number of asshole things you say or whether or not you screw up. It's based on who you are as a person. And underneath that battered armor you wear, there's a loving, good person. Someone who fights for the light parts of themselves within, to win against the dark sections of your past. You don't have to be defined by it any more than I do mine. Don't give up on yourself. I'm not."

"You know, you're not bad at that whole therapy thing."

She smirked, her lips tilting up slightly. "Oh, Surly, this wasn't even close to the emotional ringer I'd put you through for therapy."

I laughed, caught off guard by her taunt. "That has to be the nerdiest and healthiest threat someone has ever given me."

Guffawing, I found myself glad she hadn't run away when I'd been stupid enough to push her. "Fuck. I'm sorry, Kitten. I got scared."

"It's okay. It is scary. That's why the buddy system is so important."

"The buddy system, huh?"

"Yes. It's a highly recommended technique."

"I think I'm going to need more information on this system."

"Good thing I'm an excellent teacher then," she said, smiling.

"I have no doubt, Kitten."

"Um, Wells?"

"Yes, Kitten?"

"You can put me down now."

"Never."

Kissing her again, I didn't put her down for another ten minutes as I thoroughly devoured her mouth, making sure she knew I wasn't backing down from my promise this time. Eventually, I placed her feet on the ground, and we went inside. Loren helped me feed the dogs as she gave them all some love.

"Are you going to tell me now?"

"Tell you what?"

"The real reason you came here." I leaned back against the counter, my arms crossed as I waited for her to spill. Her cheeks heated, and I knew I'd been right.

"Fine. I did have something to ask you, but I could've done that over the phone. I wanted to see you, so the ask thing was really an excuse, not the other way around."

Grabbing her hips, I pulled her into me. "I'm glad you did. What do you want to ask, Kitten?"

"At brunch, I was telling the girls how I defended myself against Brian, and well, they were curious if you'd be open to teaching them a few things as well." Loren looked up at me, her dark eyes big and open as she asked, and I realized it wasn't just her wanting me to do something for her friends. This ask was because she believed I could help these women, give them something back. It was at that moment I started to understand the difference Nicco had talked about. How a family could help you out of the goodness of their heart because they cared about you, not because they owed you or wanted something in return, or worse, were only using you.

Kitten believed in my ability and wanted my help because she trusted me. The realization, along with her words earlier, planted itself in me, and I found myself nodding before I even thought it all the way through. "Of course, Kitten."

She hugged me, her arms tight around my waist, and I held her for a few seconds, content to have her in my arms. My lower half had other ideas, but I squashed them, focusing on the relational side of things first this time.

Loren stayed for a few more hours, and we ended up making dinner together and watching a movie. When she went to leave, I kissed her against the SUV like a teenager, making out for a long while. When I pulled back, I smoothed her hair behind her ears, relishing in the fact her lips were puffy because of me.

"Who's car is this, anyway? I didn't recognize it earlier."

"Oh, it's a rental. When I came out to my car this afternoon, there was a flat, and the spare was flat too, so I'm having it worked on. In the meantime, I rented this. It's pretty nice."

"Do you need help with the spare? I can change it for you."

She grinned, her cheeks rosy. "No, it's fine. But thank you, that's sweet."

"That's me, *sweet.*"

"I think you can be when you want." She kissed my nose and went to get in the car.

"Hey, Kitten?"

"Yeah," she stopped, looking back. "Would you..." I stopped, swallowing to gather the courage. "Would you want to be my date for the fight? Or my support person or something?"

"I'd love to."

She got in after that, shutting the door, and turned the car around. I watched her the whole time, not wanting to miss a thing. The fact I'd been stupid enough earlier to think I could let her go, blew my mind. As the dust from the gravel settled, I finally made my way inside. Fort and Barkley both laid by the door, sad expressions on their faces at her departure, and for once, I agreed.

THIRTY THREE

Sax and I sat across the street while we watched Marcus meet with Darren. I couldn't decide if Delgado had become this cocky, meeting with his spy out in public so openly, or if he knew we were watching and either didn't care or wanted us to know. None of the options were good, and I swallowed as I realized how unprepared I was for this war.

I would lose them all.

The ice that gripped my veins more and more as I faced the reality of not being enough slid through me, freezing me to the spot. Clenching my fists, I tried to shake it free, to have it let go of its grip on me. I couldn't be weak. My father was an asshole, but he'd trained me better than this. So, what was I missing?

"Something stinks," Sax commented, peering at the two being all chummy outside the new club Darren was opening. I nodded, worried if I opened my mouth, I'd give away my fear too easily.

We'd found the old supermarket easily after Simeon's confession. Then a couple of reports came in about Delgado's men poking around in the speakeasy. Our sources had uncovered Darren was set to open within a week with a spectacular opener. He'd rushed through all of his permits to beat our opening. I had someone in the city permit office going over his applications to find any loophole I could use to shut him down.

The things I'd set in motion had panned out as I expected, but I still felt behind Darren. I didn't know what his endgame was. Did he just want to control all of Chicago? Was it only about power and money? Was Darren only trying to one up the Mascros?

Sax's phone buzzed, and he checked it, a smile appearing on his face. Bitterness seared away the ice inside me as I watched him type back out of the corner of my eye. I'd gotten myself so twisted with Mrs. Carter I didn't know which way was up anymore. To no avail of my own, she hadn't left, and the others appeared insistent on her being in their lives no matter how much I attempted to thwart them. When I'd finally accepted that she wasn't going away, it had been too late for me.

The look on her face as she dismissed me last week had left a gaping hole where my heart had been. Sax apparently agreed, looking over to me once he'd put his phone away. "It's not like you to give up so easily, Mas."

"I tried. She doesn't see me that way and has plenty with you four. What is there left for me to do? It's done. I'll still protect her, but she's your problem."

"Your insistence that she's the problem *is* the problem. You need to get out of your head and boss up. Are you not the Don? The Mafioso boss? The *Suit*?" He raised his eyebrow at me, a look of clear annoyance that I was playing it so safe.

"So you're saying I should quit playing nice and demand her to let me fuck her?"

Sighing, Sax hung his head and took a few breaths before he leveled me with his gaze. "No, *Atticus*. I'm saying quit pussyfooting around your feelings and own them. Tell her you're sorry, and do something about it. Make fucking amends."

"You don't think I haven't tried that?" I yelled.

"I think you did just enough to say you did, but you didn't put any real effort behind it. Spitfire… She's not a Michelle. She can't be bought with money or flashy things. Those things don't impress her. She grew up around wealth and can support herself. She doesn't need *you* to save her."

"Then what use am I?"

It came out softly, and I turned my head to the window, not wanting to show the fear that I had no purpose other than to be in charge. Sax placed his hand on my arm, the gesture surprising me. The realest expression I'd ever seen on his face stared back when I turned.

"You're so much more than your father ever gave you credit for. You're Atticus—my best friend, Ims' brother. You're the boss, but you're also compassionate. You carry so much on your shoulders, wanting to shield that burden from everyone else. You're smart, business savvy, and since you took over, the family has never been better, and you did that in only nine months. People are happier and no longer scared for their lives. You've made the Mascro line into the family you wanted, the one we dreamed of. You've successfully opened three businesses, one you rebranded, and are on your way to having the premier sporting event venue. You're making the family clean and giving people a future, a real future."

He stopped, his nostrils flaring as he gritted out the last part. "Don't for one second think you have nothing to offer. It's time you let Jaz, and the guilt that you couldn't save her, go. Neither of us could in the end. More importantly… Loren *isn't* Jaz. You might not need to save her as much as you think. Drop the bullshit and do whatever it takes. That's the man I know as my best friend. The one who was willing to take out his father to save his sister. The one that is willing to sacrifice his own happiness for his best friend. But you don't need to. Not this time."

At the end of his words, he yanked open the car door, striding across the lot as he made his way to the car Marcus was heading to. I hadn't even realized they were done, but Sax, in his observant nature, had not only handed my ass to me, but kept his eyes on our target. I watched as he incapacitated Marcus in one move and then threw him over his shoulder. I jerked out of my stupor and lurched the car forward to meet him.

Getting out, I helped Sax restrain the traitor and cover his head in the back. We both were back in the car, pulling out in under thirty seconds. This wasn't something we'd had to do in a while, but with the possible breach, I didn't want to leave it to anyone else. Decked in all black and in a borrowed vehicle, we made our way to the warehouse on the other side of town for a family meeting.

I'd called an unscheduled gathering to address the dissension I'd heard lately since Uncle Seth had 'disappeared'. I needed to rally them together, squelch the grumblings, and remind them who I was. *The boss.* In an attempt to get ahead of Darren, I'd also reached out to Ethan Rawle. It was time to form an alliance despite my hesitation on the matter. Perhaps, it would even give me a better look at what their organization was up to and how far down they'd fallen in their business endeavours.

Sax's words wormed their way through my head as I drove, focused on the feel of the steering wheel as I careened through the streets. It wasn't my Bugatti, but the Camaro still handled well. It wasn't as flashy either, fitting into the side of town we'd been on.

Sax didn't say anything else the rest of the way. I wanted to believe it was because of the man in the back, but I wasn't one hundred percent certain of the fact. Sax had a tendency to say his piece and then let you stew with it. He wouldn't say anything else about it unless I brought it up. Swallowing my pride, I took a step forward.

"Thank you. I'm… struggling more than I'd like in my father's absence. His shadow was large, and I wonder if I'll ever escape it," I whispered.

Sax turned, his face flat in work mode, assessing me. "There's more than one way to escape the shadows, Mas. Sometimes, it's as simple as turning on the light."

I drove, stunned at his meaning. It was poetic, and I wondered if I'd underestimated my best friend my whole life.

"Did you make that up?"

A deep bass guffaw tumbled out of the man, and he turned, shaking his head as he smiled. "No, Immy made me watch those movies with her. The bearded guy said it, and I thought it sounded nice," he said, shrugging.

"Admit, you only remember it because the man had a beard," I jested.

"Beards instantly make you wiser," he smirked, stroking his own beard.

"I thought beards made you older? Or was it lazy?"

"You're just jealous because you can't grow one, Mr. Patchy face."

Laughing, I didn't acknowledge his statement or the partial truth of it. I'd tried once, and it *had* been patchy, but it also didn't go well with my clean look. I found it more intimidating to scowl down at others when they could see my whole face.

"What movie is this? If you liked it, maybe it's worth a watch. I realized the other day I'm severely lacking in pop culture references." My conversation with Mrs. Carter reminded me I didn't take time for frivolous things. I'd never cared before, but her shock had made me wonder what I was missing.

His face tinted red a little and I wondered what movie he would be embarrassed by. "You didn't… watch something inappropriate with my little sister, did you?" I choked.

"Don't be a fucking sicko, Mas. Besides, Ims is like a sister to me." His whole body convulsed in revulsion, and my heart rate slowed back to normal.

"Sorry! You just seemed embarrassed. It was the only thing I could think you wouldn't want to tell me."

I pulled between two buildings in an alley, and Sax immediately exited the car, avoiding the question. Sighing, I turned off the engine and wiped down the areas we'd touched. We'd both worn gloves, but it was always a precaution. Pulling the black sock cap off when I exited, I shoved it in my pocket. The fucking thing had heated my head, and my hair stuck out in all angles. I smoothed it down using the tinted window as a mirror the best I could. The trunk slammed, and I watched as Sax walked over, the deadweight still out on his shoulder.

"How hard did you hit him? Is he still breathing?"

He shrugged, the body moving up as he did. Sax started toward the building a few blocks over as we left the car behind. One of our 'friends of the family' would retrieve it later. I trusted Pops to only send a trustworthy person to retrieve the car and return it, but it didn't mean I was stupid. Leaving prints on something was the sure-fire way to find the feds at our door. So while it would probably be disassembled and sold, we didn't need our DNA anywhere in the car to be used against us. Paranoid? Maybe, but if you weren't suspicious in the mafia, you were dead.

I spotted Lucca and Joel waiting at the end for us, so I stopped, needing to know before we became our mafia roles.

"Seriously, I promise not to laugh. What movie was it?"

He exhaled heavily, stopping in his tracks. Sax looked over his shoulder at me and finally gave in. "Harry Potter, okay. She bugged me enough at the estate I gave in, feeling bad for keeping her away from everyone. We had a whole marathon the weekend you went to deal with the permits in the city. *Now*, can we go? This asshole is heavy from all the bullshit he spews."

Blinking, a broad smile crossed my lips. "She conned you too?" I laughed. Picking up my pace, I came level with him. "I think she's successfully managed to get four people now."

Sax snorted, shaking his head at the realization. "I should've figured. Beau and Topher kept giving me knowing looks."

"I'm having a hard time placing the bearded guy, though?" I mused, thinking of all the characters. It had been a few years since I'd sat down with her, but it wasn't like I watched a lot of movies for them to fade away.

"You know, the one in charge."

I stopped in my tracks, a laugh spilling out before I could catch it. "Do you mean *Dumbledore*?"

Sax kept walking, and I jogged to catch up. "You do, don't you?" I chuckled. "I bet you're a Hufflepuff too," I teased, wanting to bait him.

"Fucker, I'm a Gryffindor. Check your Slytherin ass at the door."

"Ha! You admit to taking the test then."

Sax paused, shaking his head before giving me another look. "If you breathe one word of this..."

"You'll what? Use your wand on me?" I smirked, crossing my arms. The lunacy of this conversation before we went into the meeting wasn't lost on me, but I found myself needing it.

"No, I'll tell Immy you were the one who outbid her on the signed first edition of Order of the Phoenix."

Shocked, my mouth dropped open as I ran to catch him. "What? How do you know that? You *can't* tell her, she'd kill me." I yanked his arm, needing to know. Sax raised his eyebrow, refusing to answer.

"Fine, what do you want?"

"For you to admit you like Loren and that you'll actually try until she gives you a chance to show her you're not an asshole all the time."

"I thought you were leaving it up to me."

"I changed my mind."

Dropping my head, I looked up to the sky as I debated. Focusing back on Sax, I sighed. "Fine."

"I'm user DumbledoresBeardBro."

Stunned again, I had to catch up as he took off. "I don't think that means what you think it means," I said, laughing.

"Whatever, DracoWasRobbed."

His flippant comment threw me, and I found myself laughing as we approached the two men. They gave me odd looks, and I sobered quickly, pulling the boss mask on.

"Is there a problem, Joel?"

"No, boss."

Lucca and him gave me the recap of the family members who'd arrived so far as we walked toward the door. Despite having to become the cold Atticus again, it didn't feel as suffocating this time. Perhaps it was what Sax said or our insane conversation. But more than likely, it was the statement about the light and how I suddenly understood.

Loren was the light.

And maybe I didn't have to hide as much as I thought. I guess it was time to shed some light myself. It was time to step out from the shadows of Masters and place my trust in her.

It was time for Mrs. Carter to learn just who the Mascros were, and I had an idea of how to do it. If I was going to share our true identity, it would need to be with flair. Because Sax was right, I was changing what it meant to be a Mascro, and I needed to show her both sides.

THE FAMILY MEMBERS present were growing restless as they discussed their concerns. My neck was killing me from holding up all the bullshit, and my temples throbbed to the rhythm of a million steel drums. My shoulders were so tight, I didn't know if even the world's greatest masseuse could get the knots out. There was no relaxing for me, not anytime soon.

"Chadwick, I hear your concern, but there's nothing to be done. We're moving into more legal revenues of income. By doing that, I'm stepping out of other areas. It won't affect your bottom line unless you've been stealing from the family. So, what's your real concern? Are you upset because you can't skim off the top, or are you really going to miss hawking stolen and fake goods?"

Lasering him with my cold stare, I waited to see if

he'd give himself away or bow down as I observed every detail. His jaw clenched, his nostrils flared, and his fist was clenched tight, twitching as if he wanted to reach for something. A few others shifted away from him, either to not be lumped in with him by association or to get out of the blood splatter range.

"Of course, *boss*. What the Suit says goes."

Lifting my lips, I gave him a deadly grin. "You'd be wise not to forget that. Your family and soldiers all have new positions equal to what they were doing on the docks. We're relinquishing our area of the business over to the Rawle's in exchange for their allied forces against Delgado. We'll continue to receive shipping rights through them as they will now control the majority of the docks." I paused, narrowing my eyes to send my message through. "If anything, this is taking things off your plate. You should be *grateful*."

Chadwick assented, but I didn't miss how his eyes shifted to one person in particular or how he didn't seem pleased by the news. Zeroing in on Joel, I waited him out as I leveled him with a cold stare. When his head dropped, I shifted my eyes to Hugo, his guard, to hold him back. It seemed Joel had been keeping secrets after all.

"Upswing opens in a few weeks. This is the new direction for our family. We're not weakening ourselves as some of you have suggested, quite the opposite, in fact. In honor of Upswing opening, there will be a party for the entire family at the estate. You're all invited along with your family members. It will be a night of celebration and a reminder of who we are."

Clearing my throat, I started our family motto to end the meeting. "We are family foremost, bonded by blood second, and one house above all. *We are Mascros.*" The gathered men of honor chorused my words, and for once, I didn't want to throw up at the thought of what it meant to be a Mascro.

At the end of the chant, they all dispersed and left. I watched Hugo lead Joel over to the smaller conference room. He protested at first, but when he looked back and saw me watching, he swallowed, nodding. It would be easier for him if he went along. Things at this base of operations weren't as complex as the estate house, but it was closer and easier for everyone to gather.

When we didn't have top-secret information to go over, we tended to meet here for convenience's sake. It appeared to be a rundown sports store on the outside, but the inside had been transformed into rooms for members to use while here, meeting areas, and common spaces to build camaraderie. Nothing of value was left here to indicate anything other than what was presented, but it was a large space to gather. And tonight, it would also be where the fate of our future was decided.

While Joel stewed in a separate interrogation room from Marcus, I walked out with Sax to finalize things with Ethan. We found the older man looking at the photos on the wall when we entered the makeshift library/office area. He didn't turn at our entrance but kept looking at the pictures. I glanced at Sax, who shook his head. He didn't know why that photo would be curious either. Clearing my throat, I waited for him to acknowledge us.

"Hello, son." He finally greeted me, but kept his back turned. It didn't send a good vibe through me. His disrespect was obvious and what he thought of me as head of the family.

"*Ethan.* Is there a reason you're choosing to disrespect me on my own turf?"

He turned slowly, a sly smile on his face. "No disrespect meant, Attie. It's truly good to see you, son. What, has it been twenty years since I last saw you two?" He asked, looking back and forth between Sax and me. I didn't miss the way he used a nickname, or referred to me as 'son'.

"Potentially. I last remember the Chicago families getting together the summer after I graduated from the University of Chicago. That would've been closer to fifteen years ago. Before..." I started and then stopped.

"Before the great fallout, I believe you were going to say."

I nodded, not wanting to bring up the last time the city had almost fallen into war. All the families had splintered then, the main three, Mascro, Delgado, and Rawle, remaining the most powerful. But the Rawles had suffered the most—Ethan's family included. A lot of lives were lost before a truce and peace were found.

"My boys have already begun to clear out the facilities. We thank you for your offer, and are set to take over the port at the end of the month. I've sent the final papers over to your lawyers. You've kept up your end of the deal, young man, so what do you need from us?"

He clasped his hands in front of him, and I decided to observe him this time. Grey peppered his temple, but his mustache remained full. He was dressed more casually than I'd seen him before. He had on black slacks, but only a button-down with no tie, and the top open. His shoes, while nice, were older, years of wear on them. Perhaps, things had been harder for the Rawles than they had let on. I filed the information away.

"I'm stacking my deck momentarily. When I need you, I'll let you know. I wanted to ensure I had a jack up my sleeve when the time came."

"Understood. The Rawles will stand with you. I'll see myself out."

He clapped my shoulder as he passed but stopped in the doorway, glancing back briefly. "Your mother, she was gorgeous. I never saw two brothers fight over a girl more than Dayton and Benny. I think Seth would've thrown his hat in the ring as well if he wasn't already promised to the Lucero girl. Your father, he didn't love Shayna like Benny had, though. For Dayton, it was about winning. Don't ever forget that about your father."

"Good thing he's dead," I retorted, the comment causing my irritation to rise.

He dipped his head in acknowledgment and left as quietly as he'd come. I looked to Sax, and he studied where he'd left, before walking over to look at the picture. I followed but still didn't understand what was so interesting about it.

It was from before I was born, taken on the North shores of Chicago, the water in the background. My mother sat in the middle of two of the brothers. My father's hand was placed firmly on her thigh, his eyes holding confidence as he stared at whoever took the picture. Benny sat next to her, their legs touching, but nothing else. His eyes were looking at her, though, from the side. My mother's smile was forced, her eyes holding some fear as I peered closer. Looking more thoroughly, I pointed to something in the background.

"Wait… is that Ethan in the background?"

"It looks like Austin here too. Were the former three Don's friends at one point?" Sax asked, looking at me in shock.

"I don't think they were friends. I think they were all there for my mother."

The other two men stood off in the background, but it was clear who they stared at as well. I hadn't thought about her in years. For most of my life, she'd been gone, so it wasn't as if I missed someone I barely knew. But maybe I needed to look more into my mother's history. Just who was Shayna Costa?

THE WEEK PASSED, and I hadn't found anything suspicious about my mother's family that I hadn't already known. She was a descendent from a family in Italy with ties to automobile manufacturers. I supposed that might be where my love of cars stemmed from. I racked my brain, trying to remember the story my father had told me about her. She died when I was young, from a heart condition. Which in the criminal underground could mean a variety of things.

Nothing stood out in the records or the bits of information I could gather from my father's papers. Nothing as to why there would be future crime lords gathered together. It had me thinking of Benny too. He'd been reported dead during a crime fight when I was younger. I only remembered because a few years later, Nicco had come to live with us when his mother died too.

Shutting the photo album, I shoved it in the side drawer, locking it. If there were family secrets inside, I didn't want anyone else finding them first. The phone ringing had me shoving the key into my pocket and quickly answering when I saw who it was.

"Mrs. Hildebrand, thank you for calling me back."

"Of course, Mr. Mascro. How can I help you? You mentioned something about making a donation?"

"Yes, and I actually wondered if you'd be interested in a benefit dinner for the center, hosted by our family?"

"Oh, wow! That's so generous of you, Mr. Mascro. We'd love to be the recipients of such a gift. Will Mr. Collins be involved?"

"Yes, I'll clear it with him and be in touch. My assistant will take care of all the details. I want to make it something that Mr. Jude Franklin would like."

"Well, Jude is very fond of photography. He's also interested in music, hockey and has a knack for technology. How do you know Mr. Franklin, if I may ask?"

"He's friends with my sister, and I'd like to do something for him and Mrs. Carter."

"Ah, I see now."

"Whatever, do you mean, Mrs. Hildebrand?"

"I think Loren will be happy with this."

I choked, not expecting her to call me out so blatantly. Before I could respond, she was already prattling off ideas and letting me know she'd be in touch with my assistant. She hung up, and I sat there stunned, not sure what had just happened. Sax walked in, looking at me oddly at the look on my face.

"Everything okay, Mas?"

"I think I was just bamboozled by an old lady."

Sax had been tossing peanuts into his mouth, and at my phrase, spat them out all over the floor. Now, he was coughing, a shocked look on his face as he attempted to regain his breath. I sat back smugly, feeling much better now at his distress.

"I feel like I should ask what this is about, but I'm scared to," Loren's voice said, filtering through the office. I sat up, nerves exploding in me now that I knew I wanted to be with her. *Fuck.* How did I do this? I'd never cared before.

Sax waved her off, laughing now at the whole thing. Loren looked between the two of us, not sure what to do. She cleared her throat and walked further in, addressing me as cold and polite as she had since that day in the car.

"You wanted to see me, Mr. Masters?"

"Yes, please have a seat."

Sax gave me a curious look and then motioned if I wanted him to stay or leave. I shook my head slightly, needing him here, even if only for moral support. It had been a few days since our family meeting and my commitment to him to try harder. Mrs. Hildebrand calling was the last piece I had needed to cement phase one.

"Did you find anything out on the trust?"

"No, not yet. I asked you here because I've decided to

host a benefit for Ignite Youth Center. I've just gotten off the phone with Mrs. Hildebrand, finalizing the details."

Her eyes widened with surprise, and I took joy from shocking her. "Wow, that's very generous of you. I know Jude will be happy to hear about it."

"I was wondering if you'd be my date to the event?"

"Oh? Um, *me*?" she asked, biting her lip, looking at Sax briefly.

"Say yes, Spitfire. This is Mas' way of saying he's an ass but is trying."

I gritted my teeth but didn't dismiss what he said, only nodding when she looked at me. "Well, okay, yes, I accept."

"Wonderful. I'll send over the details. I know Immy would cherish some help in picking out a dress, and in appreciation of this, I would be honored to purchase yours. Before you deny it, just consider it. You could make it a whole day and get ready together. She hasn't had much of that."

She snapped her mouth shut, the refusal on her lips evaporating at my mention of Immy, and only nodded before getting up to exit the room. Her hand brushed over Sax's in a gentle gesture, and I saw the bearded mountain practically swoon at the touch. He looked at me, and when I didn't move for him to stay, he followed her out.

Relaxing back in my chair, I took a deep breath. The fight was tomorrow night, the first of the small ones leading up to the opening of Uprising. Wells was on the ticket, and it was set to be a big night. I hadn't had space to breathe all week, from the family meeting and dealing with Joel and Marcus, to making amends, and researching my mother's family history, it had all sped by quickly. Resting my head back on the headrest, I closed my eyes, needing a few seconds.

The knock jolted me, and I sat upright, kicking my desk in the process. The knock sounded again, and I smoothed my hands over before calling them in.

"Enter."

Topher entered with a package in his hand, his face a little green. "Um, boss. I think you need to see this. We were checking the mail when we came across it. There's no return address, just a note, and the um… contents."

I gestured, motioning for him to bring the box closer. He sat it down, handing me some latex gloves. Putting them on, I grabbed a letter opener from my desk and lifted the lid. Inside sat a finger. It was bruised and appeared to have been severed from the person for a few days based on the coloring. Dropping the top, I put my hand out for the note.

Opening it, I wasn't surprised who it was from, only that it meant he was tired of waiting.

Little Mascro,

I've enclosed a gift. It's just a sample of what awaits your family. This pretty redhead, she's a fighter. It was so fun watching her bleed. It's time for you to pay up, hold up your father's end of the deal. Otherwise, I'll start taking more members of your family, beginning with the women. I'll make an exception for the pretty therapist. I wonder if I could get her and Immy for a 2-for-1 deal? If you don't want to find out, then you'd be wise to follow through.

As they say, time's up.

I have a cargo ship arriving tomorrow night at your docks. I need your guys to clear it, make sure it passes inspection without any red flags, and deliver it to my warehouse.

Do not open it. Do not try to double-cross me. Do not set me up.

If you fail to meet these terms, then not only will the pretty redhead continue to lose body parts, but for each minute you're late, I'll break a bone in your fighter tomorrow night. You're not the only venue in town anymore, Little Mascro, and I think you'll find I have some fighters who will decimate yours.

You can't get out of this. I have you stretched in too many places. Your only hope is to do as I ask and pray I let your pretty cousin live. Maybe I should keep her as the interest owed?

I'll see how generous I'm feeling.

Tick tock, Mascro. Which door are you going to choose? Time to get your hands dirty.

-D

Thirty Four

Each week I continued to have a session with Dayton, I questioned my sanity. Apparently, I needed to be firmer with him because the gentle comments of attempting to find him a new therapist had gone unnoticed. He'd make excuses and mediocre attempts to give me what he expected I wanted. Yet, it was all nonsense, circular, and inevitably useless for both of us. And I was done.

I concentrated on keeping my face relaxed despite the strong desire to roll my eyes at his current tirade. He'd even taken to lying on my couch, his feet propped up on the end as if that made a difference. It was such an elaborate show; it annoyed me beyond belief.

"My brother, now he's someone who tried to steal my life from me. It wasn't enough that he didn't win the girl when Shayna flat out chose me, but he had to keep hanging on to her skirt tails. He was a beggar, happy for any morsel she'd give him. Of course, she was kind to him, but I knew how much she despised his constant attention. It was pointless. I didn't care that we'd had an agreement to share between my friends, creating a united front for the city. In the end, there could only be one winner, and clearly, it would be me."

"It sounds like you enjoy winning, being first?"

"Is that even a question? Of course, I do. That's how you show everyone you're the best and smartest. What's the point if people aren't envious of it?"

"You put a lot of value on what others think. Did you have feelings and want to be with this girl, Shayna?"

"Of course, I did. Don't ask stupid questions. She was beautiful, the most attractive girl here at that time. She'd caught the eye of my two friends and brother. Of course, Seth was already promised to someone, but he wouldn't have won in the end. Despite being the oldest, he didn't have the stomach for things like I had. Our father saw that and began grooming me to take his place, only using Seth as leverage to make us stronger. We were only middle of the pack back then, but with each move my father made, the more power we accumulated."

"Was power the only thing that mattered? What about how your brother felt, or even your friends? It sounds like you took something your brother cared about, and you only wanted to win."

He dropped his legs to the floor, sitting up as he placed his elbows on his knees, searing me with a cold look. Fear rushed through me for the first time in his presence, and I found myself itching to grab the door. It was stupid of me to keep him on the schedule this late when no one else was in the office. He'd canceled earlier in the week and apparently had sounded desperate to Doris to be seen. She'd added him to my schedule before I could protest.

Yet, the entire time he'd been in session, all he'd done was complain about his son ruining his family name. First, because he couldn't handle it—which apparently was a huge deal for him—second because he let sentimental relationships get in the way of making the hard choices, and third because now his son was too caught up in a woman to see what was right under his nose.

It was the third bullet point where he'd then trailed off to talk about how he'd handled a woman coming between him and his friends long ago. At this point, I was so bored and tired of hearing how great he was, I started to feel sorry for his son. This man was clearly a narcissist, and anyone trying to live up to his standards was doomed to fail.

But now, the shift in the energy as a whole made me tense as he pierced me with his gaze. I saw a flash of hatred and disgust as he looked at me, but it was quickly replaced with compliancy as he altered his entire stance in a split second. His shoulders slouched, his posture turned inward, and I watched as he began to fidget.

It was all fake, an illusion of what he wanted to show me. I'd given up at this point in figuring out the purpose because I was certain there wasn't one. He was sent to torture me, plain and simple.

"Power had been the only thing my father saw as worthy, so I guess you're right. I got caught up in it, taking what I wanted or thought would serve me the best. It wasn't enough though, I still needed more to lord over him than power, so I took everything else he had."

"How did your brother respond to you taking his things?"

"He fought back at times, and at others, he bowed to me, knowing I'd won. It was the last thing I took though that I enjoyed the most."

"That sounds significant. What was different about that time?"

He smiled, that cold sinister one, that made my skin crawl as he peered back at me. "I told him I knew he'd been sleeping with my wife for years, so I planned a trip for them both to take."

"You planned a trip for them?"

"Yes, it was rather extensive planning, and I felt proud of myself for all the thoughtful details I put into it for them," he boasted, the smugness rubbing me wrong.

"That doesn't sound like the behavior you reported in your relationship with your brother, to let him win in the end."

"You're very clever, Mrs. Carter," he pointed, shaking his finger manically. "Well, you see, before he left, I told him it was okay that he was sleeping with my wife because I'd been raping," he stopped as my stomach dropped out of me before he corrected himself. I didn't buy it though. "Apologies, that's not the proper word. I'd been role-playing with his slut of a girlfriend, some escort, for years, where I pretended to rape her for fun. She was into that sort of thing, you know," he winked, making me want to bleach my eyes out. "In fact, he wasn't even the father of his son. *I was.*"

"So let me make sure I understand this—" I started, but was cut off.

"You understand it perfectly, Mrs. Carter. Don't play dumb."

"Dayton, while I'm open to however you wish to express yourself, I do have boundaries, and one of them is respectful language toward me. Please do not speak to me in that way again."

He clapped, standing, "Very good, Mrs. Carter. I was beginning to wonder if you had it in you." He walked toward me, towering over me with his height. Swallowing, I licked my dry lips as I attempted to gather my thoughts and how I could get myself out of this situation in one piece.

"Um, you planned a trip but told your brother you'd been sleeping with his girlfriend and had gotten her pregnant, but she was under the assumption it was your brothers?"

"Exactly. So his son, who he hoped to raise to overtake me one day, was, in fact, mine. It was the last crushing blow to him as I sent him and my wife off to their forever vacation."

He practically loomed over me at this point, and I leaned back in the chair as much as possible, not able to get up due to his position. I'd never been more scared in my life, and I knew I could never see him again, not after this. The power dynamics were off, and I couldn't challenge him if I was afraid of him. His cologne was thick, suffocating me as he stared down at me. His face was blank again, no hint of anger anywhere, and it was scarier than all the anger he'd ever shown.

"Thank you for this session today, Mrs. Carter. You've been wonderful. I feel so much better since coming to see you. In fact, I think I'm cured. I'd like to terminate my therapy. I won't be returning."

He said it all with a blunt look, his voice flat with little to no emotion behind any of the words he spoke. It could've been something he rehearsed, for the amount of inflection given.

Swallowing, I nodded, not having it in me to say anything else. He smiled at that, leaning back out of my space as he moved toward the door. I gulped, the air rushing in as I realized I'd been holding it. The air was permeated with his cologne now, the smell was one I wouldn't forget for a while, so distinct in its sandalwood and dark notes.

He paused at my door, barely looking over his shoulder as he gave me his last parting words. "Do you think I should give my son another chance, or is he a lost cause?"

I struggled, not knowing what to say. I didn't believe he was owed a chance based on the bullshit he'd spat in here, but it wasn't my place to judge or decide that for him or his son. So, in a very robotic voice, I replied.

"Second chances are always worth it, even if only for your own conscience."

"Very well. You've been ever so helpful, Mrs. Carter. I do wish you the best of luck for the things to come."

He strolled off, practically whistling as he went, and I sat there stunned for a solid five minutes before the vibration of my phone jolted me out of the trance I'd fallen into. My head was all over the place, so I closed my computer and grabbed my bag, leaving my notes to do tomorrow. I needed to make sure to let them know not to schedule him again if he changed his mind about returning. There was no way I could handle anything else to do with Dayton Mascro. I made a note to file a report as well, not convinced he hadn't raped someone.

I found Imogen and her chaperone standing in the lobby, and I quickly turned off the lights and locked the office door. She had paused, an odd look on her face. She didn't even see or hear me as I spoke to her, lost in her own thoughts. Placing my hand carefully on her arm, she gasped, blinking as she took in her surroundings.

"Loren, hi, sorry, I... I don't know what just happened. I walked in, and then the next thing I know, you're standing here. I think I blacked out. It felt like I was... back there for a second," she whispered.

Concerned, I looked to the guard. "How long have you been in the lobby?"

"About five minutes, ma'am. When we entered, she stopped in the middle of the floor. I just assumed she didn't want to sit down. Her back was to me, so I don't know what her face or anything looked like. That's my fault, ma'am."

Shaking my head, I didn't want him to feel bad. He wasn't to blame. I glanced around the room, taking in the things that might be different. There was a new musical track playing. But everything else seemed the same.

"Is it the music? Did that pull your focus?"

Imogen tilted her head, listening, before returning to me, shaking her head. "No, that wasn't it. I honestly don't know. I'm okay now, though. It seems to have passed."

"Okay, but if you remember anything, you let me know, okay."

She agreed, biting her lip, and I linked our arms

together as we made our way out of the office. I locked the last door, and we continued on our way, going the same way I had with Atticus. When we climbed into the SUV, her expression was more relaxed, and she easily fell into excited chatter, pushing away my fears.

"This is going to be so much fun. I can't wait to try on dresses. I haven't had anyone to do this with in a while or anywhere to go. Before… you know, my mom would take me, but she hadn't wanted to leave the house in the last couple of years. I worry I missed something, that maybe he was hurting her, and that was why she turned inward."

"It's hard to know, sweetie. You'll make yourself crazy if you try to figure out all the things you could've done differently or noticed. Just focus on what you can learn from the experiences instead of what you could've done differently. And yes, they are different."

"Yeah, you're right. I do get stuck in that loop at times if I'm not careful."

"It's understandable, but no one blames you, remember that. You okay to go still?"

"Of course."

For the rest of the ride, we discussed the different types of dresses and what she was hoping to find. I realized she'd never really been to any school dances, and I was even more excited to share this with her. It still felt odd having Atticus buy me a dress, but the gesture was nice. He was starting to win me over more with his efforts, especially the benefit. I didn't trust him fully yet, but I was warming up to the idea of him being in my life. At least as Immy's brother and Sax's friend. Or was it more his Boss? Either way, he was going to be in my life for the foreseeable future, so I might as well attempt to get along with him.

When we pulled up to a store, I was in a bit of shock as we got out. It was a high-class boutique that was appointment only. I'd seen the store advertised and passed by it several times, but I'd never stepped foot into it. Imogen looked at me, a funny smile on her face when she noticed my glee.

"We have the whole store. Attie called ahead with our sizes and what it was for, so they've picked some things out for us ahead of time. There's still one more surprise inside. Come on."

She pulled on my hand, my stunned body moving easily with her efforts. When we walked into the gleaming storefront, I found two smiling faces waiting for us. Nat and Stacy stood in the front of the shop, champagne glasses in their hands and broad smiles on their faces. I hugged them both, and we all slightly jumped up and down in exuberance as we greeted each other, giggling at the fact we were in this store. It had been out of my price range, so I could only assume it was out of theirs as well. I was delighted Stacy was here, her eye for style a must-have with something this extravagant.

"I'm so glad you're here!"

"Me too. I've dreamed of this place for years, never thought I'd step foot into it," Stacy gushed.

"I have to say, when Atticus called and told me to get the girls together, I was impressed. I think he likes you," Nat whispered.

I rolled my eyes, not ready to entertain that fantasy. "Cami not able to make it then?"

"No, I couldn't get a hold of her. I'll have to stop by her place later if I don't hear from her and make sure she's not sick or something. She's going to be so jealous she missed this! Come on, let's try on some dresses."

"Wait, you're trying them on too?"

"Uh, yeah. How else will we know they fit?"

I looked at her, not blinking for a second. "You're going to the benefit too?"

"Yep."

"Okay, well played, Atticus, this is definitely a bunch of bonuses in the forgiving you column."

"Girl, you know you want to add that dick to your train." Nat gave me a pointed look, but I shushed her, looking for Imogen, hoping she didn't hear Natalie. I think that conversation would be more uncomfortable than the one I'd had with Jude.

"Keep it down. Geez, you're like a freaking puppy. I can't take you anywhere."

"Oh, but if I was a puppy, I'd be one of those cute little ones, and you could take me with you because I'd fit in your purse." She lifted her hands up like paws, sticking her tongue out as she panted like a dog. I couldn't help it. I laughed, Nat's personality being too fun to get mad at her for.

"Yeah, you so would."

Linking arms, I grabbed Imogen with my other, and we finally made it into the dressing room, where a room full of colorful dresses awaited.

A FEW HOURS LATER, I felt like a princess after trying on so many extravagant gowns, shoes, and accessories. Nothing in the store had price tags either, which made me nervous since I had no idea how much everything was totaling up to. Imogen and I had picked our dresses, shoes, and jewelry, and we were waiting now while the other two finalized their choices.

Stacy had helped us, shooing the other attendants away and only having them bring her things. They'd given her the stink eye for a bit, but when they saw her style, they let her do her thing. She was now trying on her own dresses since she hadn't been able to, and Nat hadn't made up her mind yet, more indecisive than I'd ever thought she'd be.

So Imogen and I lounged back on the chaises, content to lean against one another in silence. When she sat up a few minutes later, I turned and looked at her. She'd become more withdrawn the past half hour, and I wasn't sure what had happened. She was biting her lip now, her eyes darting all over the place.

"Are you okay, sweetie?"

"Yeah, I think I know what happened earlier."

"Okay, do you want to talk about it?"

"Yeah, I think it will help. When I came into the lobby, the smell triggered me, and I was back in that room. I… " she swallowed, her words wobbly as she looked up to meet my eyes. "I hadn't smelled that fragrance since my father, and the last time I saw him was when he came to tell me goodbye. He said,… it was my time to prove I was worth it, to show him I had what it takes. My mother had been useless in the end, and he apologized for making me watch it but felt it was necessary to shape me into the woman he wanted me to be."

Imogen took a big deep breath, a tear sliding down her face as she stopped to collect herself. Reaching out, I grabbed her hand, squeezing it. I didn't say anything knowing any questions right now would disturb her story retelling. Offering her support, I reminded her she was brave and strong. She squeezed back before starting again, more steady this time.

"I guess this was after the first night. I can't remember the time exactly. But he sat on the bed, and I recall being able to smell him so strongly in that room because everything else smelled like vomit and moldy cheese. I used to love his smell, but in that dank room, it was like my love for my dad taunted me, reminding me what I would never have again—safety."

Imogen wiped her eyes, and I waited to see if she was done. When she started again, I held on for dear life, knowing this next part would be the hardest.

"He left, and my husband-to-be walked in. He was handsome but slimy, and there was nothing but coldness in his eyes. I'd seen that look before on mens' faces and knew nothing good for me was coming. But he told me I wasn't ready for him yet. He boasted how he didn't fuck children," she spat, the anger rising in her voice. "But didn't want me to be inexperienced either, so he was going to use me as a reward for his men."

Imogen's voice broke off at the end, her lip trembling as she recalled the horrors. I pulled her into my arms, soothing her back. I looked up and found Nat frozen, horror on her face at overhearing what Imogen said. When she saw me, I indicated for her to give us a minute, knowing Immy wouldn't want the others to know. Nat assented, wiping a tear from her face as she backed out, stopping anyone else from entering as well.

"I tried to block it out, the things they did to me, but sometimes when I least expect it, they flash through my memory. I just want them to stop." She pulled back, her face a watery mess. "Can you help me, Loren? Please?"

"Of course, sweet girl, of course." I pulled her back to me, my own tears falling into her hair as I rocked her, wanting to soothe her however I could. This precious girl had been through too much, and she didn't deserve any of the horrors she'd faced. I'd do everything in my power to help her retake her body, mind, and future.

THIRTY FIVE

LOREN

Kneeling down in front of the concrete block, I brushed the leaves and debris off the surface that had collected there before placing the single purple rose. I hadn't been able to bring myself to look at the head-stone yet, the reality of it, too hard to do without preparation. The fact I was here at all still amazed me. I hadn't been able to step foot here since the funeral. Since the day I had to bury my baby.

Taking a deep breath, I kept my eyes closed as I lifted my face to the sun, needing to feel its warmth first, to remind me I was still alive despite the chill that had settled into my bones. Sucking in another breath, I fought against the urge to turn and go, to leave and try again another day. I owed it to myself and my child to do this. It was time. Slowly, I opened my eyes and focused on the gravestone in front of me.

Violet Anne Carter

A sob bubbled up, escaping as I ran my finger over the name engraved into the stone. Brian had thrown a fit over the cost, stating it was unnecessary, but even in my weakened state, I'd insisted. That had been when I still thought we were a team, grieving together. I guess I should've seen it for what it was at the time, but I'd been blind to my own grief and suffering through the trauma my body had experienced itself.

As much as I was beginning to enjoy my life now, happy to be free of Brian, I wish this sweet baby hadn't had to perish in the process. The tears fell down my face, and I let them. The grief needed an outlet for once.

Most days, I tried not to think about everything that occurred three years ago, pushing it aside in order to make it through the day. My life had been sad enough. I didn't need to reminisce about the child I'd lost, as well. The child I'd only got to hold in my arms for mere moments.

Crying today felt different than the tears in the past, though. Today, it felt more final, cathartic even. Maybe it was the fact my life had finally begun to move forward, or I no longer clung to the false belief it would magically revert back to a time when I'd been happy.

The truth was, I hadn't been happy. Not really.

I stayed in my spot, sat back on my haunches as I stared at the name on the tombstone for so long, I lost feeling in my legs. I'd entered some meditative state as I focused on the name, and I let go of all of the dreams and hopes I once had attached to this sweet baby. Nicco's tattoo might be symbolic, but at that moment, I truly felt them fly away from me, leaving my body to join the one they belonged to. The weight they'd always been, the one I'd grown so accustomed to, it felt odd now with it gone.

Drying my eyes, I stood, kicking my legs out as I

tried to get feeling back in them. The tingles shot up, and I found myself dancing a little to disperse the sensations. Of course, it was in this state that he found me. His voice sent a chill down my spine.

"Looking gorgeous as usual, even surrounded by death, or maybe even more so because you are."

My head snapped up, meeting his gaze, and I swallowed at the fear that coursed through me. The dangerous man who knew far too much about me stood only a few feet away. His dark hair was styled, his face clean-shaven, and he was dressed well today. Black slacks, shiny dress shoes, and a grey button-down shirt adorned his body. The sleeves were rolled up, showcasing some tattoos. I couldn't remember if I'd seen his arms before, but I found myself staring at them.

When I realized he'd been quiet, I looked up, meeting his curious eyes. Amusement danced along his features as he watched me. Holding his gaze, I crossed my arms and balanced my weight on the balls of my feet to prepare myself to run if necessary.

"I think at this point, after three meetings, I should know your name. You seem to know a lot about me, after all."

My heart raced, and I was a trembling mess inside. I hadn't been prepared to face down someone so quickly after processing the emotional turmoil, but I faked it the best I could, steeling myself with a hard exterior.

He grinned wide, his hands in his pockets now, with what I could only assume was an attempt to disarm me with his casualness.

"I'd thought you'd never ask, gorgeous. I'm Darren Delgado."

"Okay, Darren. How about now, you tell me why you keep seeking me out?"

"Feisty," he chuckled, taking a small step forward. "I like that about you. My sister was feisty too." His eyes went dark when he spoke about his sister, and he took another step forward, and I found myself moving backward with each one he took.

"You still didn't answer my question, Darren."

"You're right."

My hands brushed against tombstones as I moved past them, and I suddenly felt like a mouse caught in a trap. But I kept moving, too scared of what it might mean if I didn't. There was no way I wanted his hands on me, and I doubt I'd get the element of surprise on him this time. The realization that two guys had been with him before had me searching for them too late.

A gloved hand clamped down on my mouth a second before my body bumped into someone. Darren smiled wider, continuing his slow approach toward me.

Breaths rolled in and out of me at a quick pace as the foul-smelling material blocked my airway. Things started to go fuzzy, my panic increasing when it was wrenched away. Dropping to the ground, I sucked in the clean oxygen, coughing, and hoped it would clear whatever had been on his glove from my system. I heard grunts and movement, but I was too disoriented to focus on anything around me outside of breathing.

When a hand touched my shoulder a moment later, I jumped, raising my fists in protection. The necklace caught my eye as it swung up with my momentum, and I put my finger into the ring, ready to pull it, as I focused on the man in front of me. He seemed familiar, though, so I waited, leveling him with my gaze.

"Don't touch me, or I'll have my boyfriend here before you can even blink."

The man was crouched down in front of me, but he gave me some space as he placed his hands in a placating gesture in front of him.

"Are you okay, miss? I'm Beau. We sort of met a few months ago when you were with Nicco?"

I blinked at his question and looked around. The other man was gone, so I hoped it meant this one had scared him off. The mention of Nicco had me relaxing as well, and the familiar face locked into place. I swallowed, nodding.

"Yes, I'm fine. You were at the fight, right?"

He dipped his head, smiling. "Yes, ma'am. I've called Sax, and he's on his way."

"Sax, okay, yeah." I was distracted again, trying to put the pieces together. "Thank you, by the way. I... yeah, just thanks."

He nodded, standing this time and offering me a hand. I took it, not sure I could stand on my own after the chemical anyway.

"You're welcome. I know it's not my place to say this, so please excuse my overstepping, but I wanted to thank you for the difference you've made in not only Miss Imogen but Saxon and Nicco have been happier since you entered their lives. Even the boss seems to be improving, but don't tell him I said that," he chuckled, conspiratorially.

I found myself smiling with him, his presence feeling safe despite being one scary dude. He had to be as tall as Sax but was more nondescript, blending into the background. His eyes were kind, though, even if shielded. "Your secret is safe with me," I answered, smiling up at him.

"Keeping secrets, Spitfire?" Sax's voice rang out, causing me to jump toward Beau, his arm coming around me in a protective gesture.

Sax's jaw ticked, and I watched as his fists clenched when his eyes narrowed in on Beau's hand on my arm. Beau noticed as well, dropping my arm and stepping away. Bowing his head toward me, he fell back into the silent man, nodding to Sax as he passed.

Once he was gone, my bearded neanderthal relaxed and immediately advanced on me. "Spitfire, are you okay? Why didn't you use the knife? Did he hurt you?"

Placing my hands on his chest, I looked up into his eyes, the concern and worry evident, easing my own fear. "I'm okay. He um… just talked. Told me his name, and when I realized there were two men with him last time, that was when they grabbed me, putting a hand over my face. His glove smelled like chemicals, and things went fuzzy. I guess that was when Beau stepped in. I remembered my necklace then and went to pull it, but he reminded me I knew him. I'm sorry."

"Why are you sorry, Spitfire?" his brow raised in confusion.

"I don't know. I guess I feel like I need to apologize

for making trouble. I don't know why this Darren guy keeps following me."

Guilt flashed over his face, and it was then I realized he knew. All the pieces I'd been avoiding putting together for fear of what it would mean and the choice I'd have to make slammed into me. The real one, not the one where I thought I'd have to choose between all the men I was falling for, but the one where I had to decide between right or wrong.

Because I knew deep down their world was dangerous. I might not have realized it at first, but with each encounter, my brain collected the evidence, storing it away until I was ready to face the facts. Yet, now that I was here, it didn't seem so black and white anymore. Who were the good guys, and who were the bad guys? I used to think it was clear, but life sucker punched me and turned everything I knew upside down. The good guy was no longer good; the lies he'd spilled in the name of truth were a mark against my stomach.

So maybe it wasn't about good or bad anymore.

Maybe it was about the truth and the lies, and yet that felt dangerous as well. Was it better to tell a lie for a good reason than the truth for the wrong?

I'd experienced both, and I was beginning to think not all lies were created equal.

This choice would be dangerous, but, had I not felt more loved, more cherished, and safe in the times I'd been with them than I ever had with Brian? Had I not sought out the danger in the first place?

Maybe the dangerous part was ignoring who I was

and what I needed. Perhaps that was my dark confession.

I wasn't as good as I once believed either.

Their darkness called to my lightness and their pain to my own. The danger in the shadows lurked, but I found myself dancing with it instead of shrinking away in fear. The truth was, I'd been lying to myself the whole time, wrapping it up in good deeds and justification.

In reality, it had felt good to punish Brian. So maybe I was no different than these men who, while they hadn't straight out told me who they were, they hadn't lied about it either.

The truth was… deep down, I'd known all along. The brave thing would be acknowledging that and finally dropping the mask on who I was, on the woman I pretended to be, and embracing all the parts of me—good and bad.

Looking up into his eyes, the last visage of the mask that had clung to me fell away as I accepted my truth and theirs as a whispered confession left my tongue.

"Sax, are you in the mafia?"

Epilogue

Jude

Mitzi had kept me late going over photo ideas for the benefit, and I was still in shock it was being held in my honor. I'd never had anyone care before, much less throw something to raise money for a place I attended. I was nervous about wearing an actual penguin suit this time, but Monroe said he'd take me. At least I had someone to do those kinds of things with now. A few 'someones' if I really thought about it.

I didn't try to understand Lor's dating relationships, but I didn't disapprove of it either. She got to spend time with people she liked and who were good to her. If they all agreed, who was I to tell them no? I'd spent enough time in homes with traditional families to know it wasn't all it was cracked up to be. If Lor and I could make a family, and it included a bunch of other people who thought she was awesome, I was all for it.

I was especially fond of Monroe and Nicco, mostly because Sax and Atticus scared me, and Wells always seemed like he'd rather eat tar than have to talk to me. He wasn't rude, just not very chummy either. We'd bonded at least over the dogs, so I hadn't entirely written him out as my favorite daddy yet. Chuckling at the joke, I didn't notice him waiting for me as I hopped down the stairs.

"Jude."

Snapping my head up, I came face to face with someone I thought was a ghost. Someone I hadn't seen in months. Someone who'd abandoned me.

"What are *you* doing here?"

"I need your help."

"There's nothing I can do for you."

"You're wrong. You can help… save me."

"Save you? The last time I saw you, I was arrested. I want nothing to do with you, big brother."

"I'm sorry about that. Just come with me and meet my boss, and he'll explain everything. It's an easy job, I promise. Then we can be a family again."

"No. I already have a family, and it isn't with you, Cameron."

Spinning on my heels, I stomped away, only stopping when he spoke again.

"If you don't, they'll kill me."

I swallowed, debating. The last time I'd seen him, he'd been dealing drugs, and I wanted nothing to do with that. I didn't want his death on my hands either, though. Slowly, I took him in again. I couldn't tell from this distance if he was using, but he looked cleaner than last time, and there wasn't any manic energy about him, but I still didn't trust him.

"Fine. But not tonight. Give me your phone and send me a time and place. If I can make it, I will."

"Look at you, little bro, you got yourself a sugar

momma, and now you're all cocky and shit, making demands of me."

"Fine. Good luck with your life. I'll look for your death in the obituaries along with dad's."

I spun again, feeling relieved. I'd done my part. It wasn't my fault if he was stubborn. He yanked me back, catching me by surprise.

"Fine. Here."

Rolling my eyes, I typed in a number quickly, handing it back, before walking away. I just prayed my gamble had paid off. Quickly, I pulled out my phone and sent a text to the number I'd just used on Cameron's phone.

ME: I need your help.

CAMI

WATER DRIPPED FROM SOMEWHERE, the sound a constant pinging in my ears. My head was hanging down, my hair a greasy mess of red strands. I didn't know how long I'd been here, and it had all become a blur at this point. My hand throbbed, the place my finger had been a reminder of the violence I'd endured already.

I'd been so stupid. I thought I could change him, that I'd be the one to fix him. In reality, I was just another dumb woman who thought their vagina was the golden ticket to getting men to do what they wanted. With my psychology degree looming, I thought I'd been up for the task, though.

Fucking joke was on me. I'd be lucky to graduate now.

The door squeaked open, the screech of the metal against the floor crying out into the room. I didn't know where I was, but I knew I wasn't getting out of here. It was too isolated and secure for any chance of survival. If only I'd started those self-defense classes sooner, maybe then I wouldn't be in this situation.

Except that was a lie too.

My head was yanked back, a groan leaving my dry and scratchy throat as I cried out from the movement. It took a minute for my eyes to focus, but once they did, it was the same view I'd seen since I woke up and found myself in this place.

"Hello, pet. Did you miss me?"

He smashed his lips to mine in a bruising kiss, and sadly I used it as a way to take some of his saliva, needing the wetness for myself. He bit my tongue in response, and I retreated, falling back into the good little soldier he wanted me to be.

I wanted to give in to the escape he kept offering me, but I couldn't betray my friends that way. It was only the hope that the longer he kept me here and alive, they had another day to live.

It wasn't their fault I'd fallen in love with a monster.

When he pulled back, he smoothed my hair down in a soft caress, and I had to focus on remembering the pain and not fall into his trap again.

Nevertheless, he'd told me the truth from the start. It was myself I'd lied to.

"Answer me, pet!"

"Yes, Darren. I missed you."

The words were barely audible, my throat as dry as the Sahara at this point, but as I whispered the words he wanted to hear, I vowed to myself to survive this and make him pay.

There was nothing more dangerous than a smart woman, after all. My mama had taught me that.

To be continued in Dangerous Vows

LETTER FROM THE AUTHOR

Did you know that while writing this book I realized I was going to need four books? Mostly because as you read, Atticus decided to be a resistant asshole. So, in adding a book, it changed where this one ended. I thought I knew what I wanted it to be, but then the moment in the cemetery happened, and Loren had that realization about herself and good and bad, and she finally asked the question! And that was when I knew it was the ending for this book. So, I had to go back and write the chapter before it with Immy, and creepo Dayton. Body shudder, am I right?

So, that's how the ending came about!

I hope you felt Loren's growth in this book as she began to discover things for herself and find her own worth. Jude and her, misfit penguins for life! Their scenes are some of my favorites. I just want to wrap Jude and Immy up in a blanket and make them hot chocolate or something.

Lots happened in this book, at least I felt it did. The

guys had to come to terms with things, and Loren had to find her footing. You know what that means, right? Book three is going to start off running! So, hold on to your hats! It's going to charge ahead at full steam.

I've set it out for end of March, but I expect it will be February, so stay tuned!

ACKNOWLEDGMENTS

There are several people I have to thank when it comes to this book. First is the woman who has become part of my brain and soul over the past year. Each book, I wonder how I can kidnap you and carry you around in my pocket. Emma, you're never allowed to leave me. Understood? Good, I'm glad we got that cleared up.

Kayla, you've become a dear friend and offer great feedback. Thank you for loving my characters, putting up with all my crazy, and telling me it's never too much Harry Potter references.

Cat, Tori, and Marla, thank you for being awesome and catchy all those sneaky things that slip through. Cat, a double thanks for the lawyer assist and making sure I had it all together.

To my lovely Beta Diva's—Amber, Megan, Jenni, Michelle, Shawna and Lindsay, I appreciate you all so much! The thirsty comments give me life, and the joy and exuberance you show for my characters is the absolute best! Seriously, thank you for boosting my morale, and reminding me why these characters and stories matter.

Thank you to Shayna for lending me her name for Atticus' mom. When you won a contest to be named a character, you probably weren't expecting that one? Hope Shayna Costa does your name proud.

To all my ARC readers, I love seeing all the edits and reviews. Your passion for the story is everything. Thank you for being part of my journey.

To you, the reader, thank you for continuing to trust in me as an author, and reading my words. I hope to always write characters you can connect with.

To my husband Rob, it's been an incredible year, eight books, and a whole lot learning how to do this new journey. Thank you for supporting me and being proud of my accomplishments.

And lastly, Happy Birthday peanut. Thanks for lending me this day and being the heart of this book.

ALSO BY KRIS BUTLER

Dark Confessions

Dangerous Truths

Dangerous Lies

Dangerous Vows

Dangerous Love

The Council Series-Completed Winter Sports Series

Damaged Dreams

Shattered Secrets

Fractured Futures

BOSH Bells & Epic Fails-

The Order (Council Spinoff)

Stiletto Sins

Lipstick Lies

Sinners Fairytales (standalone)

Pride

Tattooed Hearts Duet-Completed Romantic Suspense

Riddled Deceit

Smudged Lines

Vacation Rom-Com

Vibing

Kris Butler writes under a pen name to have some separation from her everyday life. Never expecting to write a book, she was surprised when an author friend encouraged her to give it a try and how much she enjoyed it. Having an extensive background in mental health, Kris hopes to normalize mental health issues and the importance of talking about them with her characters and books. Kris is a southern girl at heart but lives with her husband and adorable furbaby somewhere in the Midwest. Kris is an avid fan of Reverse Harem and hopes to add a quirky and new perspective to the emerging genre. If you enjoyed her book, please consider leaving a review. You can contact her the following ways and follow Kris's journey as a new author on social media.